Our Lady

of the

Lowriders

A Novel

Doug Lambeth

Sashee Press
Pullman, Washington

Published by:

Sashee Press

Pullman, WA

ISBN 978-0-9728-2181-0

This book is a work of fiction. Names, characters, places and incidents are products of the author's imagination or are used fictitiously. Any resemblance to actual events or locales or persons, living or dead, is entirely coincidental.

Ard1651@hotmail.com

Additional copies are available at: www.lulu.com

Our Lady of the Lowriders

Part One

Our Lady of Perpetual Sorrows Grammar School
1961-1968

Chapter One

Sister Mary Annunciata wants to kill me.

I can tell. Everything about her says, "Kill Roger": those black, mean eyes, the angry red cheeks, the smile that isn't really a smile. A gold crucifix necklace slides across her cardboard chest cover as she moves. Jesus on a swing. More shiny white cardboard frames her face. Maybe someday I'll understand the reason for all the cardboard coverage, but right now it doesn't matter. I'm just a terrified little kid.

Because Sister Mary Annunciata wants to kill me.

"Well, Roger?" she demands.

The beady eyes eat a hole in me. My Cheerios churn. I'm going to throw up. I know it. All because I can't remember what the ninth commandment is. I always get the covets confused.

"Answer me, Roger!"

"I don't know."

Now she heads for me, cardboard flapping, black habit flying, thick-soled black shoes *clack-clacking* on the yellowed floor. I'm definitely going to throw up. My classmates turn and watch me and wait. Some, like Jesse Montoya, smile. Others look terrified. They know it could just as easily be them. I close my eyes. Maybe it's just a bad dream. Maybe Sister Mary Annunciata won't try to kill me. Maybe it's all a mistake. Maybe I'll wake up and the horrible, rosy-cheeked monster will turn into smoke, safely put away for another nightmare, maybe....

"Roger!"

I open my eyes. She towers over me, a wheezing, giant black-and-white beetle. I look up at the hair in her nose. Oh, my stomach. The Cheerios have definitely turned on me. Little tears wet the corners of my eyes. I pray silently to Jesus: Please don't let Sister Mary Annunciata kill me.

"You're to stand when I ask you a question, Roger. And if you don't know the answer you are to say 'I don't know the answer to the question, Sister Mary Annunciata.' You are not to simply shake your head and say 'I don't know.'"

I scramble to my feet. My eyes are level with the bottom of her chest cardboard. Up close she's even scarier. Her breath smells like Vapo Rub mixed with pee. The classroom is quiet. I don't know what to do next. And I hope she doesn't, either. But then the cruel monster inside her rises up in holy Catholic glory.

"Hold out your hand."

I hesitate. She growls, grabs my hand and flips it palm up, pulls a metal-edged ruler from under her habit and whacks me.

I don't know which is worse: The stinging pain, or the humiliation of being helpless. What gives her the right to do this to me? Who said it was okay for her to treat me like garbage? It's my first brush with mindless power. I can't understand it. It's no fair.

She smiles with mean satisfaction as a red stripe rises on my palm. She inspects it and her smile grows. No doubt about it, she's proved she's the boss. Smacked a kid into obedience.

"Sit down, Roger."

I sit and sniff back tears. She sweeps away and orders Jesse Montoya to tell her what the ninth commandment is. His smile vanishes because he neither knows nor cares about the ninth commandment, but at least he remembers the proper way to answer and doesn't get smacked.

I spend the rest of the day glaring at Sister Mary Annunciata when she's not looking. She's teaching me about meanness, the "there's nothing you can do about it" rules that the Catholic Church is beating into me.

I hate Sister Mary Annunciata.

Mom knows something's up. Kids can't hide hurt very well. That talent comes later.

"What's wrong, honey?"

I watch *Felix the Cat* through watery eyes. I don't answer. What can I tell her? She's always been nice to me, but how could she possibly understand? I stare at Felix and Poindexter.

"Honey? Roger?"

She comes over to the TV and sits down next to me. I start to cry.

"Sister Mary Annunciata...."

"What about Sister Mary Annunciata?"

"She hit me." I rub my wet nose. There, I told her. I feel a little better.

"Why did she hit you?" Mom sounds mad, like maybe she's going to go over and hit Sister Mary Annunciata across her palm with a ruler.

"'Cause I didn't know what the ninth commandment was. And 'cause I didn't answer the right way."

Silence. She looks over at Felix and Poindexter. The Professor shouts at Poindexter about something. I start to feel much better. Mom's my friend.

"Sister Mary Annunciata must've had a very good reason to discipline you. Maybe next time you should remember what she tells you. And learn the commandments. Jesus wants you to know them."

That's it? *Jesus wants you to know them?* Mom doesn't love me anymore. I feel more alone than I've ever felt. How can she desert me like this, how can she tell me I was wrong? A crazy cardboard-covered monster attacks me for no reason and it's my fault? I decide right now that I'm on my own. I can't depend on anybody, even Mom. I nod. Sniffle. There's no use talking about it anymore. I look back at the TV.

"Remember to obey Sister Mary Annunciata, Roger. At school she's just like your dad or me. Or better yet, she's just like Jesus. Do you understand? It's as if Jesus is back on earth and He's in the form of Sister Mary Annunciata. If Jesus told you to do something a certain way, you'd do it, wouldn't you? You have to listen to her. And don't talk back. It's like talking back to Jesus."

I nod miserably. She gives me a friendly shoulder squeeze and leaves.

Jesus wouldn't—*couldn't*—be that mean.

In first grade I'm learning very quickly that some people are just plain bad. Like Jesse Montoya.

He's bigger than the rest of us, and sometimes he's a bully. He has brothers and sisters and cousins scattered through every grade of school, and I've heard the nuns make jokes about all the Montoyas at Our Lady of Perpetual Sorrows.

For some reason Jesse Montoya has made my life miserable ever since school started. There's something about me he doesn't like. I don't know what it is, I've always tried to be nice to him and stay out of his way, but something about me makes him mad. He says mean things. He teases me. He pushes me around. Sometimes I hate him almost as much as I hate Sister Mary Annunciata.

Everything's under control until I say to my friend Phillip that Jesse Montoya is ugly. Jesse overhears me, and he's mad. He wants to hurt me.

Bad.

"*Pendejo* Roger! Retard! Take back what you said about me!" He shoves me to the ground.

"I am not a retard," I sputter, getting back up. "*You're* a retard!" I don't know what the Spanish word was he called me, but I know it's not nice. I hope he doesn't hear the squeak in my high little voice and notice the way I'm shaking.

He glares at me. A crowd gathers. Even some big third graders wander over for a look. As I watch him watch me I need to decide, do I fight or run away? Do I tell Jesse Montoya to his face to leave me alone, do I tell him I hate him? He's made things hard for me for a long time. But is it really smart to tell him what I think? I think so. Something inside makes me feel that the world and Jesse Montoya need to know what I think and I shout, "You're ugly and mean and I hate you!"

There. The recess world of Our Lady of Perpetual Sorrows Grammar School knows what Roger Donnelly thinks about Jesse Montoya, and I'm proud they do.

Then Jesse Montoya slugs me in the stomach.

I fold in half like a piece of the lined yellow paper we write on. It feels like he punched a hole in me and let all the air out. I gasp for breath and look up through blurry eyes and see Jesse Montoya laughing. And so is everyone else. Even the big third graders are making fun of me as they drift away. I can't let it happen. I was just telling everybody what I thought, which also happened to be the truth. It's not right that I'm being punished and laughed at.

I swallow a huge gulp of air and lunge at Jesse, I pull him to the ground, and we wrestle and slug. Jesse Montoya's not laughing anymore. And the big third graders are wandering back for a second look.

We roll across the loose bits of gravel on the paved playground, and pieces grind into my skin, but I don't care because all I want to do is get my pride back from Jesse Montoya and I'll kill him if that's what it takes and I punch and claw and bite and then I'm somewhere else. A hot white flash hits my head, I can feel and taste and see and smell it and I don't know where I am but the feeling, it's power and anger, I can do anything to anybody anytime and then the white flash vanishes and I'm back on the gravelly playground at Our Lady of Perpetual Sorrows Grammar School and I taste blood.

Jesse Montoya's crying now, and the big third graders are impressed. It's even gotten quiet. Nobody's laughing at me anymore.

I hit and claw and bite him but it's not fun. I see blood on him and taste and feel blood on me; I want the white flash to come back so that I'll feel the power of pounding on a bully like Jesse Montoya, but it doesn't come back and then somebody big pulls me off and tosses me to the ground. I skid and more loose gravel rips my skin; I look up at the bright blinding sun to see who it is.

Sister Mary Annunciata. The sun behind her haloes her black-and-white cardboard head like the saints in the windows at church. It's so bright I can't see her face, only the outline. And I decide to do something stupid. As long as I've taken care of one problem, why not take care of the other? I'm already bloody, I've already got gravel burns and burrowers under my skin, why not finish Sister Mary Annunciata off while I'm at it?

I lunge at her. Pound her. My puny little fist beats against her cardboard chest and one hand gets tangled up in her giant rosary. I pound and yell but I don't think it's going to work on Sister Mary Annunciata the way it worked on Jesse Montoya. If the white flash comes back maybe, but I don't feel it coming. And then I realize I'm up against a greater force. Jesse Montoya is just a kid like me. Sister Mary Annunciata is Jesus! And nobody can take on Jesus and win.

I stop hitting her and she gathers me up in her iron arms like I'm an empty uniform of salt-and-pepper cords and white, short-sleeved shirt.

I'm crying now and afraid as Sister Mary Annunciata shoos the recess crowd. Another nun helps Jesse Montoya up and takes him to the school office. Sister Mary Annunciata holds me tightly in her arms and carries me across the playground to her classroom.

She opens the door and switches on the fluorescent lights. They buzz like those mosquitoes that drive you crazy when you go camping. She drops me on the floor. We're alone. I focus my blood-blurred eyes behind her black-and-white shape. A crucifix hangs ominously on the wall. The dying Jesus looks down on me. He hates me, too; he's disappointed in me. I force myself to look at Sister Mary Annunciata. I know she's disgusted with me. She breathes noisy, gaspy wet sucking sounds through her mouth. The shiny white triangle chest cardboard rises and falls. I expect her to yell at me, maybe even smack me with one of her yardsticks. But she does nothing except stare. There's no expression on her saggy face; she just stares. That's even scarier.

We face each other for what seems like an hour. Her breathing slows, but she still doesn't say or do anything. We have a stare-out. I'm about to ask her what she's going to do when she grins. It's the scariest smile I've ever seen.

"You're a very evil boy, Roger."

"Yes, Sister Mary Annunciata. I'm very evil."

"Jesus doesn't like evil boys."

"No, He doesn't, Sister Mary Annunciata."

"Jesus says all evil boys should be punished for their evil."

"Yes, Sister Mary Annunciata. Jesus is right." This is going to be worse than I thought.

"It isn't that I object to you and Jesse Montoya fighting. After all, evil little boys will be evil little boys." For the first time since we got back in the classroom she moves away from me. She turns her back and gazes up at the crucifix. I consider making a run for it, but decide that would only make things worse.

"Jesus suffered. Jesus hung on the cross for three hours to forgive our sins. Jesus suffered more than any human who's ever walked on earth, and yet he did nothing to deserve his suffering. He never," she spins back toward me like a ballet dancer, "would have tried to strike a holy woman, he never would've tried to punch and bite his mother!"

I'm confused. Is she saying that she's the Virgin Mary? I'm about to ask her what she means when time runs out for me, because now she's hitting me with a yardstick, and it hurts worse than anything Jesse Montoya did to me, and she's screaming that she's the bride of Christ and no evil little boy can ever strike her without going to hell.

I drop to the floor and curl into a ball; the blows continue as she screams about holiness and virginity and a lot of other things I don't understand. The white flash, where is it? If I could get it back maybe I could defend myself. I pray to Jesus, if He still loves me, to send the white flash so I can save myself from Sister Mary Annunciata. But it won't come. And even if it did it'd probably be too late. As her shoe hits my head and I drift off into dark dreams, my last thought is that Sister Mary Annunciata is going to be in big trouble for killing me.

* * *

I awaken to the reassuring gurgle of my ten-gallon aquarium. It's dark and I can't see them, but I know my guppies are gently swaying in the filter current, floating between the plastic shipwreck and the bubbling scuba diver. I smell the familiar odor of my room. The spicy Lincoln Logs stashed in the toy box mix with smells of the aquarium, dirty socks and me. It's good to be home. I feel safe again.

I try to move but I hurt all over. Between Jesse Montoya and Sister Mary Annunciata there's not an inch of my body that isn't sore. My head, and especially my eyes, feels bigger than usual. One eye barely opens. I remember now. That's where Sister Mary Annunciata landed a really good punch.

Sister Mary Annunciata. Wait till I tell Mom and Dad what she did to me. They'll get her. They'll make her pay. They can't deny the bruises on my body or that a crazy nun beat me up! They'll get her.

"Mom!" I call out. I can't wait to tell her the story. I hear muffled footsteps hurrying down the hall, the door opens, and Mom and Dad peer in. The shaft of brilliant hall light hurts my eyes; it slashes across my room into the aquarium. Through my one good eye I see that the light scares my dozing guppies.

"Roger, honey, are you all right?" Mom asks. *Good old Mom.* I sure do love her.

"Sister Mary Annunciata," I say through puffy lips. Talking hurts.

"We know, Rog. She told us what happened," Dad says, reassuring me. Dad's a great guy, friendly and nice and a pal. He doesn't spank me, and he only yells once in a while. He saves his real anger for my big sister, Mary Frances. She makes him mad. Most of the time when I get in trouble, it's Mom's job to deal with me.

Dad's always been my best buddy. But sometimes I wonder how much he really cares. From watching my friends' dads I know that dads aren't always supposed to be buddies. They get mad and scold and hit. But not my dad. I guess he's just a little different, or maybe I'm a better kid than my friends are. Except now I'm confused. What's he mean that Sister Mary Annunciata told him what happened?

"Sister Mary Annunciata tried to kill me," I gasp. There. I've said it. Now let them punish her.

I see the confusion on my parents' faces as they exchange looks and I know that something's wrong. Mom whispers to Dad, "Poor baby. He's delirious. Confused."

"That damned Montoya brat really kicked the hell out of him. I hope the nuns get the monster tossed out of school. He's a little felon."

No! They don't understand. Jesse Montoya's no saint, but now he seems like my best friend compared to Sister Mary Annunciata. I have to make them understand!

"Jesse Montoya didn't hurt me so bad! It was Sister Mary Annunciata! She wants to kill me!"

They don't say anything. They look at me and then at each other. Maybe, just maybe, I've gotten through to them that Sister Mary Annunciata—

"Is poor Roger frightened?" Sister Mary Annunciata asks. She pops up from behind my parents like a Jack-in-the-box from hell and grins at me with cardboard holiness.

Help me! I scream to myself, she's in my house, ten feet from my guppies, *she's at the door to my bedroom!* And she's grinning. It looks genuine, too, something I've never seen before. I kick and scream, the covers go flying, I've got to get away from her, she's worse than Wolfman, the Mummy and Frankenstein combined.

Mom hurries over and hugs me. I calm down. Sister Mary Annunciata can't hurt me as long as Mom's holding me.

"Roger, honey, it's okay! Sister Mary Annunciata just dropped by to see how you are. She rescued you from that awful boy. She's your friend."

"I'm sure he just connects me with the fight. Poor boy's confused and frightened," Sister Mary Annunciata purrs. Her beady little black eyes actually look concerned. This is a nightmare. She's lying and they believe her. Fine. I'm on my own. I do nothing. I stare at Sister Mary Annunciata and try to make my truth guilt her into confessing. She smiles at me like one of those pastel pictures of the Virgin Mary.

"Go back to sleep, darling. You need to rest. You were hurt but you'll be okay." Mom kisses me on the forehead and tucks me in. I keep my one good eye on Sister Mary Annunciata at all times. They turn off the light and are about to close the door and leave me in the safety of my room when Sister Mary Annunciata hesitates.

"Would you mind if I prayed over Roger for a moment? I have some patron saints who might help calm his fears."

"No, Sister, that'd be great. Can't beat prayer, I always say. Especially from holy people like yourself," says Dad. I assume she'll stand at the door and mumble some of the holy stuff she mumbles at school. But I'm wrong.

She thumps across the worn carpet to my bed. The wood floor underneath the worn carpet squeaks and groans from the stress. My guppies dart wildly, like they're about to be eaten. She kneels at the side of my bed and leans her elbows on it. The whole thing sags toward her; I grab the sheets to keep from rolling into her.

I stiffen my body like a board. Oh my God, this can't be happening, she's kneeling inches from me, in my bedroom, I can smell her Vapo-pee breath, the edge of her chest cardboard cover cuts into my cheek.

"Blessed Mother Mary, protect your child Roger from harm. Holy Jesus, you know how much we love you, and need you to love us, help Roger." She leans closer. "And little Roger knows what happens to evil little boys when they tell lies to their parents about their nuns, doesn't he?" she whispers, so low and threatening I can hardly hear her. She sneaks one arm under the covers and pinches my arm so tight it feels like she's ripping the skin off, but I don't do or say anything because I'm too scared.

"Amen," she smiles and lets go of my stinging arm.

"Amen," I say, blinking back tears.

She gets up and waddles to the door. My parents smile at her and she smiles back.

"Thanks, Sister. Sure do appreciate it," Dad says. I decide I like him a lot less than I used to.

"Yes, thank you so much, Sister Mary Annunciata," Mom says. "Thank you for rescuing him from that boy."

They close the door and ignore me. I listen to them talking in the hall.

"It was just an unfortunate schoolyard fight. The Monsignor and I will have a talk with Jesse's parents. I know they feel bad about what happened. Although," Sister Mary Annunciata's muffled voice punches through the thin walls, "from what I understand Roger did start the fight."

Silence. "Oh," Dad says. That's it. *Gee, thanks for sticking up for me.*

"Well, I should be off to the convent now."

I hear some mumbled good-byes and then she's gone. The devil is gone from the house.

I lie awake for hours, dull aches and pains stabbing me with every move. I want to always remember how I feel right now, because I know that someday I'll make Sister Mary Annunciata pay.

The aquarium bubbles and my guppies calm down. The Lincoln Logs give off their familiar smell. I stare into the darkness, hating Sister Mary Annunciata, hating myself for being picked on, hating everything and everybody that makes things so unfair.

Someday, I'll get even with her.

Chapter Two

Usually, the playground is a lumpy gray expanse of crumbly asphalt. Today it's a brown, smelly pond of floating turds and toilet paper shreds.

A bunch of Mexican guys with a big tank truck are trying to vacuum up the water and turds, but it's not working. Monsignor O'Callahan is yelling at them. Jesse Montoya said he heard Monsignor O'Callahan say, "Damn it!" earlier when he was yelling at the Mexican guys to hurry up. I'm not sure if I believe him, because I'm not sure about Jesse Montoya.

Jesse talks to me all the time and is slowly becoming my best friend. We even hang around together at recess and lunchtime. Ever since I hurt him so bad in the first grade, he's stopped being mean to me and wants to be friends. He still has a bald spot where I smashed his head against the asphalt, and I feel guilty every time the wind blows his hair and the pinkish-brown scar is exposed. At first our friendship was based on me feeling guilty; now we're just becoming plain old friends.

"We're going to have to send the children home if you don't hurry up and get this out of here!" yells Monsignor O'Callahan. "There could be a disease problem!" The Mexican guys suction up dirty brown puddles, but more just gushes up from the broken sewer pipe under the playground.

We all mill around, watching Our Lady of Perpetual Sorrows' new lake grow. It's recess and instead of playing we're trapped by sewage. We giggled and made stupid jokes at first, but now we're bored and cranky and it stinks. I watch Monsignor O'Callahan. He's surrounded by clucking nuns, like he always is, including evil Sister Mary Annunciata and my teacher now, Sister Mary Pius. Sister Mary Pius is small compared to Sister Mary Annunciata, but she's every bit as vicious. She's a big believer in collective punishment. When the person at the front of a row does something bad like talk or not know an answer, she not only hits them with a yardstick, she goes down the entire row and hits everybody's palm. I can't figure out what good it does, but I do know my palm is always sore because somebody always messes up.

She stands next to Monsignor O'Callahan and watches the Mexicans. "Perhaps we should find out how to shut off the sewer, Monsignor."

"I know that, Sister!" he snaps. Her feelings are hurt and the other nuns all look down at the ground, embarrassed for her. The nuns act weird around Monsignor O'Callahan. They're quiet and respectful; sometimes they act like they're afraid of him. It reminds me of the way I act around girls I like.

Sister Mary Pius glances up and catches me looking at her. She frowns, and I know the look. Maybe she has to be nice and respectful to Monsignor, but she doesn't have to with me. I rub my sore palm because I have a bad feeling Sister Mary Pius will take it out on me later.

I'm bored and I cough. My throat hurts. The mountains behind the school are shrouded in smog. Even though Mount San Antonio is huge and gets snow on it in the wintertime, the smog that blows over from Los Angeles makes it disappear a lot of the time. When I was real little I used to think that the mountains disappeared because a giant knocked them down and all that was left was dust. But now I know better. I know that it's smog and I know it's what hurts my throat after I've played outside. My throat really hurts today.

"Wanna ride our bikes to the wash after school?" Jesse Montoya asks. I shrug. The wash is a dry, junk-filled, concrete-lined riverbed that has water in it once or twice a year. We ride our stingrays down there and mess around. But today I'm not in the mood with the smog and turds and all. Jesse annoys me sometimes. Just because I almost killed him doesn't mean I want to do *everything* with him.

Things have been strange lately. Last Friday the President got shot. It was the only time I've seen nuns cry. Even Sister Mary Annunciata was sad, although I heard later that she beat one kid unmercifully because he said his parents thought President Kennedy was a communist.

After we got home from church last Sunday, we turned on the TV and saw the fat guy shoot Oswald. It was kind of neat, knowing it was real and all, not like the fake shooting on stuff like *Maverick* or *Bonanza*. Mom cried and made me leave the room, but I snuck back and watched from the doorway as the news showed it over and over.

"You know the damn Russians are behind all this," Dad said. He hates the Russians and thinks everything bad in the world is because of them. "Or Castro. Goddamn communists. Should've whupped 'em when we had the chance back in forty-five. Hell, I was there, I know we could've kicked their butts."

Mom blew her nose in a shreddy Kleenex. "It's not like Eisenhower was interested in your opinion, Patrick. I'm sure they did what was right." She snorted and blew her nose some more. Dad looked mad.

"Just because I spent the war running alongside a tank doesn't mean I'm an idiot. Hell, grunts like me in the trenches won that damn war!" He was getting hot like he always did when he talked about the war. I didn't really understand all the war stuff. It just seemed like something that was part of him, like the color of his eyes or the way he fell asleep and snored while he watched TV. I knew that there'd been lots of wars in history, but the way he talked about The War made it sound like it was the only one that counted.

They argued about The War while the news showed the fat guy shoot Oswald again. Mom pointed out that trenches were in World War I. Dad grumbled at her, saying she was just a woman and would never understand The War. The news showed the shooting again. I got bored. You can only watch a guy get shot so many times, even if it is real.

Everything had been strange in the week since the President and then Oswald got shot. My parents were grouchy and Mom cried a lot. Dad complained about Russians. The nuns were especially violent. And now the playground is flooded with turds.

God is angry.

"Send the children home, Sisters," Monsignor O'Callahan sighs, unconsciously tugging on gray hairs curling out of his nostrils. Jesse's smiling and so am I as we run back to the classroom to get our bookbags and green uniform sweaters. We run out to where our bikes are locked up, get knocked out of the way by eighth graders who are in an even bigger hurry to leave than we are, and finally get our bikes unlocked and ride away from our sewage-covered school.

It's almost December but it's warm and the balmy air soothes me as I pedal my stingray. It feels good even if the air is full of throat-hurting smog.

We ride past orange groves and lemon groves and neighborhoods. Our town is a checkerboard of healthy, green rows of trees and beige rows of new tract houses. I think the houses are starting to win, though. Every week another grove gets bulldozed, the huge piles of trees are burned in ash-spewing bonfires, and the next crop of tract houses is planted. Just since I was in the first grade the grove across the street, where I used to chase after rabbits and pretend that kid-eating coyotes hid in the trees, is gone, replaced by stucco houses on 90 foot lots Dad calls "crackerboxes" but that look just like ours.

Jesse leads the way through an orange grove, maneuvering between the smudge pots like a race car driver. We come to the edge of the grove and overlook the wash.

"C'mon!" Jesse yells, and he roars off down the sloped concrete bank. He's excited and I'm not sure why. We've been here a million times and there's nothing any different today. Maybe it's because we got let out of school early.

I follow him down to the sandy bottom, and he leads me further, to a tangle of brush and abandoned washing machines and other household junk. He hops off his bike and runs to a big pile of weathered cardboard boxes. He lifts one up and gestures me into the cavern behind.

"C'mon!"

I peer inside. "What's in there?" All I see is darkness. I smell the faintly sweet odor of damp cardboard.

"A fort! I built a fort!" He ducks inside, and of course I follow. I've built lots of forts in my time, and it's just good manners to visit other people's forts when you're invited. I bang my head on overhanging box flaps and begin to wonder if I'm doing the right thing by going into this dark place with Jesse. For all I know he's going to kill me to get even for the first grade head bashing. I hear him shuffling in front of me, and I'm about to back out, when I hear the *slitch* of a match lighting, and now the fort is lit by a flickering yellow glow. Jesse touches the match to an old candle stub (like the ones in church—I think he stole it), and I get a chance to look around.

"Whataya think, Roger?" he asks, his voice begging for approval. I inspect the fort. It's a basic cardboard box fort, nicely furnished with pieces of metal junk and an old tire.

"Neat," I say. And I mean it. Jesse smiles proudly. I study him in the flickering candlelight. He couldn't be more different from me. Where I'm blonde and blue-eyed and a pasty-looking scrawny kid, all bony legs and knees and ears, Jesse's dark and thick and strong. His hair is shiny black and sometimes looks carved instead of combed. His black eyes are almost slanted. Sometimes he looks Chinese. His face is a little flattened, like pictures I've seen of real Indians, and he's bigger and much faster than any of the other kids. I think it was a good thing I attacked him when I did. He's so much bigger than I am now that even with my angerflash I might not be able to beat him.

He's breathing heavily, excited. He lifts up the old tire and pulls out a crumpled lunch bag.

"I'm gonna show you something." Every once in a while the Mexican sneaks out when he talks, and "show" sounds like "cho".

He carefully opens the bag and reaches in like whatever's in there is alive or sacred. It reminds me of the way the Monsignor reaches into the tabernacle to take out the chalice, like he's half expecting it to explode or Jesus to yell at him.

"What, what is it?" I want to know. He hesitates, grinning with a knowing smirk. I reach over and grab at the bag, but he's too quick and jerks it away.

"You gotta promise not to tell anybody, ever, what I'm gonna show you."

"Okay, okay, what is it? Show me!"

He smiles and pulls out underwear.

Black lace ladies' underwear.

I gasp. This *is* serious. He holds them up for me to inspect. A lacy black bra and lacy panties. My heartbeat quickens and I feel movement in my pants. I realized long ago that ladies are something special. The girls at school are mostly disgusting, but I like the older ones, like the high school big sisters of some of my friends. I can't wait to get older. I have a feeling that I'm going to like girls a lot.

But right now I'm gazing at black lacy underwear and I'm starting to breathe faster.

"Where'd you get those?" I whisper.

"My Aunt Yolanda left Uncle Ernesto and she came to stay with us. I borrowed 'em from her suitcase."

"You stole your aunt's underwear?!" I'm horrified. I'm not sure if it's a mortal or venial sin, but I do know it's big trouble.

"She don't care. All she does is cry and call my Uncle Ernesto a *cabron* and a *joto.*"

I'm no expert in Spanish, but I know those are two very bad words.

I gaze at the bra and panties as he dangles them tantalizingly in front of my nose. I try to picture a lady wearing them, but the image is too exciting for me to stand and I feel guilty, so I try to erase it from my mind. I think of the nuns at school and that calms me down instantly.

"Wanna hold 'em?" he asks. I hesitate and then nod. I can't say no to the fires inside me. I reach out, gently touching them and taking them from him. I'm mildly disappointed in the bra—the lace makes it feel rough, and there's a big wire underneath each cup. I inspect the strap and hooks. It's very complicated.

"Wow," I say to be polite as I hand it back to Jesse. I don't want him to know the black lace bra hasn't lived up to my expectations. Now I turn my attention to the panties. These are something special. Lace along the edges, smooth, cold satin everywhere else. These feel good. "Wow," I murmur again, and this time I really mean it.

I reluctantly give them back to Jesse, and he replaces them in the bag, caresses it closed, and hides it back underneath the tire.

"What if your aunt finds out?"

"She won't. And even if she does, she won't think I took 'em. She likes me. She thinks I'm just a little kid."

I'm about to say, "You are a little kid" when another thought smashes its way into my brain. "Is your aunt at home right now?"

"Yeah."

"What's she look like?"

"Like an aunt."

The next words are out of my mouth before my brain realizes it. "Let's go to your house!" I lead the way out of the box fort. I'm running.

We ride to Jesse's house. I pedal my stingray faster than I ever have. Even Jesse, who's so strong and can pedal his bike with much bigger legs, can't keep up.

We speed through neighborhoods on the way to Jesse's house. The houses here are older than my neighborhood, and almost everybody who lives here is Mexican. This part of town, where we go to school and church, is on the other side of Mountain Avenue, which is the official dividing line between where white people live and where Mexicans live. Most of the Mexicans work in the big orange and lemon packing plant or in the orchards. Sometimes I don't understand why it's okay for the white people and the Mexicans to go to the same church and for their kids to go to the same school but it's not okay for them to mix the rest of the time. Mom worries and Dad just gets mad when he finds out I'm riding bikes with Jesse.

"Roger spends way too much time over there with all those beaners," Dad said once. "Especially the Montoya kid. Christ, the little taco bender beat him up that time, what the hell's he doin' being friends?"

"Oh, stop it, Patrick," Mom said with a small giggle. She acts like it bothers her when he calls people names, but I don't think it really does. She always giggles when she corrects him.

We ride up and dump our bikes on the dying grass in Jesse's front yard. Other bikes and broken toys litter the lawn. An old Chevy is up on blocks in the driveway. Jesse's big brother Mando is always working on it, but I don't think it will ever run. I've never really seen any part of Mando other than his legs. He's always underneath the car, banging away. Today he's beating on something metallic with a wrench, screaming, "*CABRON!*"

Jesse leads me inside. The house is small and dark and always overflowing with people and noise and good times. I'm not sure how many brothers and sisters Jesse has, because there's a constant stream of cousins and other people who come and live for awhile, then move on to be replaced by someone new.

I like Jesse's house because it's so different from mine. Mine's quiet and predictable, except when my sister Mary Frances is crying for no reason. But Jesse's house is always so alive and friendly. Even though I'm just a kid everybody's pretty nice to me, especially Jesse's mom. She's a big, fat, smiling lady with a duplicate of Jesse's face. Whenever I come in the front door she wraps me up in her warm, flabby arms and says nice stuff in Spanish. She's like a spare Gramma.

This time is no different. As she's hugging me and murmuring in Spanish, I notice a couple of little diapered kids I haven't seen before playing on the floor in front of the blaring TV. They're busy tugging on the tail of a beat-up and disinterested old cat.

"How are you, Roger?" his mom asks. Her English is hard for me to understand.

"Okay," I smile. She lets me go and waddles back out to the kitchen to continue with her endless cooking. Another lady walks into the living room. She snaps at the kids to leave the cat alone, then plops down on the worn couch. *The Roadrunner* is on the TV. She watches it like it's the most important thing she's ever seen.

Jesse elbows me in the side and whispers, "That's her."

I study Aunt Yolanda. She's young and kind of tired-looking. She has a big black beehive hairdo, and she's wearing heavy eye makeup that almost reaches back to her ears. My eyes move away from her face and down her body. I try to imagine how the black lace bra would look on her. *Not bad. Not bad at all.* My eyes move lower, and though it's hard to tell since she's slouching on the couch, I decide that the black lace panties would be great.

I like Aunt Yolanda. I like her a lot.

But as I stare at her something strange happens: she begins to cry. She watches Wiley Coyote, and tears begin to trickle down her cheeks. The tears pick up some of the eye makeup along the way, so that by the time they reach her jaw they're oily black skid marks. She's so pretty all of a sudden. The crying makes her look soft and sad. I want to go over and hug her, tell her everything'll be okay, just like Mom does to me when I wake up in the middle of the night with a fever or a bad dream.

But before I get the chance, she jerks her head up and glares at Jesse and me.

"Whachew lookin' at?"

I look at Jesse terror-stricken. I don't say anything, figuring she's his aunt and he knows how to handle it. Jesse doesn't waver.

"How come you cry so much?"

"Because your Uncle Ernesto plays around with *putas*, that's why. Because I'm stuck with his two kids and he don't even care about nothing, so I gotta live here with underwear stealing nephews, that's why!"

My head swings toward Jesse. He looks scared and maybe even pale, although it's hard to tell since he's so dark to begin with. I look back at Aunt Yolanda. She wipes away the dirty tears and then smiles. She looks at me closely for the first time, and her smile grows. I'm both terrified and exhilarated. I'm remembering the underwear. And how she'd look in them.

"He show 'em to you, *flaco*?"

I shrug and look at the floor. When I look up she's still staring at me. Smiling. Finally, she shakes her head and goes back to watching cartoons with her kids. One of the diapered babies begins to cry.

"I better go home," I whisper to Jesse. He nods silently, unable or unwilling to move. I think he's afraid what's going to happen when Aunt Yolanda tells his mom. I slowly tiptoe to the front door, and I'm just about outside when Aunt Yolanda looks up from her squalling baby.

"Hey!"

I freeze.

"You like 'em?"

At first I think she's talking about her kids but then I realize she means the underwear. So I do the only thing I think is right: I tell the truth.

"Yeah," I mumble. She doesn't say anything but gets a weird smile on her face, not like something's funny, it's more of a smirk that's covering up something else. Like maybe she enjoys that we were messing with her underwear.

The smirk vanishes when she looks at Jesse. "Don't never take nothin' of mine ever again." She picks up one of the play blocks littering the floor and tosses it at Jesse. It bounces off his head. "Little *pendejos*," she grumbles.

It's late, and I'm in bed and wide-awake. I hear muffled sobs through the wall. Mary Frances is in her bedroom weeping about some new zits that sprouted today.

I think about Aunt Yolanda. Dad would call her a beaner and Mom would say she's cheap, Mary Frances would make a face and say she's a skaggy hard chick, but they'd all be wrong. She's a nice lady. She could've told on us, but so far she hasn't. She didn't even get as mad as she should've. And the way she looked when she was crying, I could tell that beneath the beehive and the makeup was a nice lady. She needs somebody to be nice to her.

But all my tender thoughts vanish when the black bra and panties work their way back into my brain. All I can think of is Aunt Yolanda wearing those. And nothing else.

I don't think I'll be able to sleep tonight.

Chapter Three

"Prepare to die, Protestant bastard!" Dad growls as he pulls his sword from the scabbard and waves it threateningly.

"Patrick, please, we're trying to watch television," Mom says. Dad stands by the fireplace all dressed up in his new Knights of Columbus costume. He's been voted king or something, so he gets to wear a cheap tuxedo, a black Dracula cape, a feathered hat like they wear in old pirate movies, and a big shiny sword. He likes the sword the best.

Mom and Mary Frances exchange glances and roll their eyes like bad actors. Dad's feelings are hurt; I can tell. He looks at me for reassurance.

"Whataya think of your old man, Roger?"

"Neat, Dad. You're not going to wear that anywhere, are you?"

"Ten-thirty mass this Sunday. Me and Manny Arellano will lead the procession. Protecting the holy sacrament from Protestant infidels." He stabs at an imaginary Protestant and then slides the sword back into the scabbard.

"Be careful with that thing, Patrick. You'll hurt yourself," Mom says. She shakes her head at him the way she does with me when I do something spectacularly stupid.

Mary Frances picks at a fresh pimple on her chin. Her eyes well with tears and she hurries out of the living room to her bedroom, slamming the door behind her. Dad takes off the pirate hat and sits down on the couch. His sword clangs and a couple of stray hat feathers float on the living room air currents.

"What's wrong with her?"

Mom shakes her head. "She's a teenager." Mom's been saying that a lot lately.

I don't know my sister very well. She's nine years older than me, and when you're that far apart you might as well not be related.

When I was really little, Mary Frances played with me like I was a toy. She paid me lots of attention and was nice and fun. We played games by the hour, and she always had the time to be my friend and substitute mom. I was a living, breathing, peeing doll. Much more fun than something plastic that could only say "Ma-Ma" when you pulled the string.

But once she got into high school, everything changed. I wasn't little and cute anymore, and she had other things to occupy her time. New friends and new *boys*. She was obsessed with how she looked and how she sounded and what people thought of her. Her parents and her little brother made her look bad, at least in her own self-conscious eyes, and she didn't want the rest of the world to know that we existed. She was always crabby and mad, arguing with my parents about everything, important or not. Now that she's starting her junior year and getting her driver's license, things have only gotten worse.

I think she hates us.

"Maybe I should go talk to her," Dad says, standing up and looking ridiculous in his cape. His sword bangs against the side of the couch.

"You're wasting your time, Patrick. It's just a phase she's going through. She'll outgrow it eventually. Hopefully before we die of irritation."

"No, no, it's my duty as her father to counsel her through her tough times. She needs the firm guidance of a loving father." He struts off down the hall with his feathered hat under his arm and his cape flying. Mom and I watch him. We start to laugh.

He comes to Mary Frances's door and knocks loudly. Her weepy sobs get louder. "Mary Frances, this is your father."

"I *know* who you are! Leave me alone!"

"Let me in, honey. I want to help."

"You can help by leaving me alone!" she shouts. Her sobs become wails. Dad stares at the door, unsure what to do next. Mom and I watch. He looks back down the hall and sees us watching, then apparently decides that since he's in uniform he can't lose his Knights of Columbus' honor, so he knocks on her door again.

"Open this door right now, young lady! I want to help you!" But her crying just gets louder and the door stays shut. Dad stands, looking like a dummy. I wonder if he's going to draw his sword and really let her have it, but instead he just sighs and looks at the floor. Mom takes pity on him, walks down the hall, and gently takes his arm.

"Nice try, Patrick. She just needs some time alone."

"All I want to do is help her. Is that so bad?" Through the door the occasional words, "I'm so ugly," and "I hate my face" break Mary Frances's sobs. I know how she feels. I hate her face, too.

"It's just growing pains, all girls go through it," Mom tells Dad.

"Did you?"

"Ask my mother about it some time. I think she wanted to sell me to

Gypsies. C'mon." She guides him from the door.

"I'll never understand women," he mutters.

"You're not meant to. Why don't you and Roger do something?"

As they come back into the living room Dad's eyes lock onto me. He may not understand teenage girls but he sure remembers what it was like to be a boy—at least he thinks he does. He's got that look in his eye and it worries me. I pray that he won't say the one word I dread more than any other.

"Lemme get out of this monkey suit and we'll go work in the garage for awhile."

Garage.

Dad's garage is a holy shrine. Every tool hangs on pegboard over his spotless workbench, its outline drawn in red so that not even the biggest fool could ever hang the vise grips where the hammer goes. He reorganizes the garage monthly, and he's even hung old curtains over some of the shelves so that everything looks tidier. His big power tools line one side of the garage, next to our blue, '56 Ford. He has a drill press and a radial arm saw and a bench grinder. The reason I know all his tools so well is because whenever he says, "Let's go work in the garage," what he really means is, "I'm gonna go work in the garage and you're gonna follow me around and clean up after I use my power tools."

I hate working in the garage.

The radial arm saw *screeches* as he rips an old piece of plywood. I hate all the noise and the flying sawdust.

"You can't do good work without good tools, Roger," he tells me as the saw whines to silence. He tells me the same things every time we work in the garage. "Safety first, Roger. A one-handed carpenter once told me that." He laughs like it's the first time he ever told me the dumb joke. I smile politely as I sweep up the sawdust.

"So whatcha making, Dad?" I ask.

"Dunno. Just thought I'd get this plywood ripped," he says. Dad never makes anything; he just cuts up wood and thinks about what he might make someday. On the few days in the winter when it gets cold, we end up burning some of the wood he's cut for pretend projects in the fireplace.

"Wood. Wood is good." He rubs the cheap piece of plywood like it's a priceless jewel. "When a man works with wood it brings him closer to his very being."

I have no idea what he's talking about and keep sweeping up the sawdust.

"Do you like wood, son?" he asks seriously, as if it's not the weirdest question in the history of the world.

"Sure."

"Good. We've got a lotta years left together working in the garage."

"Great."

He runs his hand over his radial arm saw. "We need to do a big project."

"You mean like a chair or a shelf or something?" I ask, hoping that maybe he'll actually build something so I can sweep sawdust for a reason.

"Bigger. Yep, we need to take on a really big project. I think we're ready."

"We are?" I'm puzzled since all we've done is cut up scrap wood.

He says nothing for a moment, gazing dreamily up at the garage rafters. He's far, far away from our little suburbia house; he's dreaming of great projects to be built by the master craftsman Patrick Donnelly and his loyal son/apprentice Roger. He sighs and comes back to earth, then reaches over to a large cardboard box on the workbench.

"Hungry?" he asks. I shrug. He pulls out a bag of stale Fritos and tosses them to me. Dad's job is the Frito truck driver. He delivers Fritos and Lay's Potato Chips and Wampum Corn Chips to all the grocery stores in our area. One of the benefits of the job is that he swipes old bags of overripe chips and brings them home.

I've learned to hate Fritos. Especially stale ones.

I rip open the bag and take a few chips. I hand the bag back to him and he munches. Frito fragments fly, some sticking to his chin and the front of his shirt. He's back in dreamland. He takes another handful of chips and stuffs them in his mouth. I'm about to ask if we're finished working so I can go in the house and watch *The Flintstones* when his face lights up with a huge grin.

"I got it!"

I wait as he takes another handful of Fritos and stuffs them in his mouth. He munches, grinning. "We're gonna do it!" he says. He's spraying Fritos and Frito breath everywhere.

"What?"

"We're gonna build an addition to the house. A family room! Paneled, big sliding glass windows, we can keep a Ping-Pong table up year 'round, put the TV in there, a wet bar, have parties, it'll be great!"

"Isn't building a new room kinda hard?"

"Not for us! We're already building pros."

He's so happy with his new idea that I don't say anything. I just smile and nod and watch my father eat stale Fritos and dream of his new family room.

"He took the bread into his holy hands and said, 'Take this all of you and eat it. This is my body, which will be given up for you.'" Monsignor O'Callahan holds up the host, then sets it down and genuflects. Mom thumps her chest with her fist.

"My Lord and my God," I whisper, hitting my chest with my fist just like Sister Mary Pius taught us to do. Monsignor O'Callahan stands back up and does the same stuff with the chalice of wine.

They just changed things around so that the priest faces us. It used to be they did all this stuff with their back to the audience, and I always used to think they were doing some kind of magic I couldn't see. I'm disappointed to see that what I thought was holy mumbo-jumbo is just regular mumbo-jumbo. The whispers and mumbling in Latin have been replaced by boring prayers in English. Somehow, even though I had no idea what the Latin meant, it seemed more important, more...holy. Since they've changed it to English I realize it's just more of the same dull meaningless stuff the nuns cram down our throats. At least *Dominus vobiscum* and *Ectum Spirtu tuo* sounded funny. I liked answering the priest's prayers with stupid-sounding responses. Now it's "The Lord be with you," "And also with you." Boring, boring, boring.

I look around the church as Monsignor O'Callahan finishes up the consecration. Dad and Mr. Arrellano are standing by the sides of the front pews in their Knights of Columbus costumes, swords held upright in front of their noses. I wish a Protestant would wander in; a swordfight might wake things up.

I glance down the pew at Mary Frances. She stares at the altar, but I can tell she's a million miles away, dreaming of boys and zitless skin. She half-kneels, slouching with her butt against the pew. Mom's always pestering her about her lousy posture, since stooped shoulders and a swayback make her look even uglier than she already is. But she just ignores Mom and cries when Mom suggests ways to make herself more attractive. It's strange. Sometimes I think Mary Frances imagines she's the most irresistible girl in the world and she doesn't need to do anything to look better. Other times she acts like she thinks she's a troll. I can't figure her out.

Mom watches Monsignor O'Callahan intently. Her lips move silently with the prayers. Mom's real religious. She loves being a Catholic and all the stuff that goes with it—tuna casserole on Friday nights, holy days of obligation, pagan baby collections and every weird Catholic tradition me and Mary Frances go through. She says her rosary every night, right after she reads the bible. She goes to classes whenever the church offers them, and she's President of the Altar Society. She loves the Pope and distrusts non-Catholics. She worries about dead babies in limbo and dead relatives in purgatory, and she prays for the redemption and conversion of Russia.

As I watch Mom devoutly pray, I realize that even though Dad's the one standing in front of the church wearing a pirate hat and holding a sword, Mom's the real soldier of Christ. She's a true believer, the kind of person who keeps the church going and tries to pass her belief on. Dad's just in it for the costumes and good-old-boy, back-slapping, "Good to see you" social stuff. I'm not even sure he really believes in God.

We stand to say the *Our Father.* I look to the side and see Jesse and his extended family. They take up two pews. His mom and dad are dressed up in their Sunday best, and every female has a black mantilla covering her head. Most of the white ladies in the church wear hats. The Mexican ladies all wear mantillas. I catch Jesse's eye and we smile at each other. He looks funny. They make him dress up in a white shirt and a tie and his thick black hair is greased back. As I'm smiling at him I realize who's next to him. Aunt Yolanda.

Even though I shouldn't, I stare at her. She's saying the *Our Father* and looking straight ahead, and I figure I can look at her without getting caught. So I study her. Her hair is teased into a huge Sunday beehive, but the eye makeup isn't as thick as before—maybe she tones it down for religious occasions. Her two little kids squirm in the pew beside her, busily ripping a missal apart. I examine the curves of her body. She wears a plain white dress and a white mantilla. She looks very innocent and chaste. But as I'm looking at her, I begin to imagine the black lace underwear, and I superimpose it on her body. I'm horrified that I'm in church, about to receive the blessed sacrament of Holy Eucharist, and I'm imagining my friend's aunt in her underwear, but I can't make myself stop. The harder I try not to think of it, the more I do. I know impure thoughts are a sin, and that I'll have to confess them next Saturday, but I wonder if even Monsignor O'Callahan has the power to forgive impure thoughts that happen during mass. My soul's stained with a big, fat mortal sin. Nobody can ever forgive me. So I decide that as long as I'm in this deep, why not go all the way? I try to picture her skin showing through the lace.

As if she can feel my thoughts, Aunt Yolanda jerks her head toward me and eyelocks me. I try to look away but I can't. She won't let go of my eyes. At first she's expressionless, as if she recognizes me but can't exactly remember where she's seen me before. Then, it dawns on her. She smiles. Not a friendly smile, not a funny smile. It's a dirty smile. A smile that says, *I know your secret*, one of those tight smiles that means something far deeper. I try to smile back, but I think it comes out looking more like I'm sick. Her smile gets even bigger and dirtier, and then she winks at me.

I'm humiliated, excited, embarrassed and confused. She turns away from me and faces the altar again, mouthing prayers like a good Catholic lady.

I feel like I've been kicked in the stomach. Aunt Yolanda smiled dirty and winked at me. I have no idea what it means.

After church, the congregation mills around the front doors, doing the post-mass ritual of socializing, kissing up to Monsignor O'Callahan, and seeing what everybody else is wearing so they can gossip later. Dad and Mr. Arrellano stand near the Monsignor, laughing with K of C buddies. Mom stands by Dad, chatting with some of the wives, while Mary Frances has found a friend from school and stands off to the side, making fun of Dad's costume and everything else that has to do with the adults. I stand alone, watching them all and bored to death.

Jesse comes up behind me and gives me a friendly punch in the kidney. "Wanna do something later?"

"Sure," I say, looking around for Aunt Yolanda. She's nowhere to be seen. I feel guilty. "Did you ever get in trouble that time?"

"What time?"

"Remember? Your Aunt Yolanda's...you know."

"Oh, that. Nah, she never said nothin' to nobody."

"Will she be here long?" I ask. Aunt Yolanda drops in every few months after she has a fight with Uncle Ernesto.

"I dunno," Jesse says, losing interest. "I think she's leaving next week."

"Oh." I'm disappointed, and I'm not sure why. I'm terrified of Aunt Yolanda, but it's a pleasant terror.

Jesse stares off at Dad and doesn't say anything for the longest time. He has a strange way of getting hypnotized by something and standing absolutely still while he stares at it. It looks like he isn't breathing.

"What're you looking at?" I ask.

He is rigid for a moment, then his Indian's face softens into a smile. "Can you borrow your Dad's sword?"

I start to say no.

But when he looks at me I say yes.

We ride our bikes through the warm Southern California sunshine. It rained last night, so all the smog was washed out of the air and the big mountains loom behind our town and look dangerously close. Puffy clouds float by. It's my favorite kind of day, when my throat doesn't sting from smog and the world seems safe and beautiful.

We speed down San Antonio Avenue. When I first moved here, San Antonio was just a bumpy road with rock curbs that led through endless orchards. Now, every year, more orchards are torn down and more houses are built, and San Antonio Avenue is just another busy street.

I'm having a hard time keeping up with Jesse because it's hard to ride a stingray bike and carry a bundled-up sword at the same time. The beach towel I wrapped it up in keeps unraveling, and I'm afraid the towel's edges will catch in the spokes and I'll go flying onto the sword and die young.

Dad was busy designing the new rec room at the kitchen table when I borrowed the sword. He was telling Mom all his big plans, and she was nodding and saying the right things, but I could tell she was just being nice and playing along. She doesn't think he'll ever get beyond the design stage, or maybe cutting up some old pieces of lumber.

I snuck past them as they hunched over his scribbled sketches, grabbed the sword from its special place on the shelf in the closet, wrapped it in a beach towel, and tip-toed out of the house.

Parents can be amazingly stupid sometimes.

And now I'm starting to think I can be, too, as I try to ride my stingray and carry the sword. I have no idea what Jesse's planning, if he has anything planned at all. I've just dumbly gone along with him again. That seems to be happening a lot lately.

Jesse has a power. Even though *I'm* the one who beat him up in first grade, and our friendship was based on that, things have changed. Now I go out of my way to hang around him. I'm willing to try whatever he wants, no matter how weird it might be. Jesse has a quiet power that works on everybody—even the nuns.

Our nun this year, Sister Mary Innocent, is less vicious than our earlier nuns, but in her own way she's even scarier. She hits less often, but she humiliates more. If you mess up a spelling test, she tells the whole class your mistakes and tries to make you feel bad. If you talk in class, she just stops everything until you tell the whole class what you were saying. And she has a sixth sense about lies. If you lie about anything, you're dead. That's when she opens her closet of brand-new yardsticks and rulers, selects one that looks like it will inflict the most pain, and then she'll bring you up in front of the class and let you have it. Over and over. Until you cry. That's the worst part: crying in front of your classmates. Sister Mary Innocent knows what really hurts.

Sister Mary Innocent has never picked on Jesse. Even though he's been just as bad as the rest of us, she lets him get by. I think she's a little bit afraid of him. I'm starting to wonder if I'm afraid of him, too. It's not just because he's so much bigger than me, either. With Jesse, there's never the feeling that he'll beat you up if he doesn't like you or if he gets mad. He's not like that anymore. Jesse's different from the rest of us. He's not mean, he never gets into fights, he doesn't even seem to have a temper. He's always even and calm. And by being that way he's the most feared and respected kid in the school. The eighth graders don't even bother him. They smack scrawny kids like me around, but they treat Jesse like a friend.

Jesse leads the way, and I realize that we're going back to church. I catch up to him, and try to talk but it's almost impossible because I'm so out of breath. "How come we're—"

"I'll show you." He coasts into the deserted church parking lot. Once the Sunday masses are over, the church is the loneliest place in town. Monsignor O'Callahan plays golf with the rich men in the parish, and the nuns take the afternoon off to do whatever nuns do when they're not terrorizing children.

We park our stingrays off to the side of the main entrance. Jesse tries the front door. It squeaks open. "C'mon. Bring the sword." He slips inside and I follow, looking around to make sure nobody sees us, because I already feel guilty.

Empty churches scare me. They're dark and quiet and filled with too many memories of black-and-white nun monsters. When the church is filled and we're saying the prayers of mass or the choir is singing, I feel safe. The crucifix above the altar with Jesus writhing in bloody death doesn't bother me at all when everybody's here. But when the church is empty, I imagine he's moving, moaning in agony, begging somebody for relief, and the statues of the Blessed Virgin on one side and Joseph on the other are staring at me, blaming me for letting this happen to their son.

The red votive candles at the far side of the altar flicker menacingly, reminders of the fiery depths of hell that await me. A dark, eerie church always reminds me that even though I'm just a kid, I don't love Jesus enough and I'm too filled with sin to think about going to heaven. Even purgatory's doubtful.

Jesse never has doubts. He moves confidently to the front of the church and stands at the communion rail, gazing up at the crucifix.

"What're you looking at, Jesse? Let's get outa here, if the nuns find us we're dead!" Jesse ignores me and gets that frozen look on his face as he stares at Jesus. "Will you come on," I beg, "we're gonna get in trouble."

Jesse turns and smiles at me. His eyes are wide. "We have to help Jesus," he says. "Gimme the sword."

"Why?!"

"We have to help Jesus."

He takes the sword from me and unwraps its beach towel shroud.

"Geez, Jesse, what're you gonna do?!"

"I had a dream last night."

"So did I, I dreamt about your Aunt Yolanda's underwear, let's get outa here!"

"I dreamt that Jesus was on the cross."

"That's where He always is!"

"And I dreamt that He was calling my name," Jesse says, his voice low and calm. I stop complaining and listen. He's so serious that I'm afraid to try and stop whatever it is he's doing. It's that quiet power thing again.

"He asked me to stop His pain. Mary was there, too. She was crying that her son was up on the cross and no one would help Him. So after He asked me to stop His pain, Mary asked me, too."

"Really?"

Jesse nods, serious and grim. The beach towel shroud is on the floor. Jesse holds the sword up in front of him, and the reflections of the red votive candles dance on its shiny surface. Jesse looks majestic holding the sword, like an Aztec king. Seeing him makes me realize how dumb Dad looks carrying it around.

Jesse turns toward the crucifix and raises the sword up toward it, but he's only tall enough to get the sword point up by Jesus' knees. He looks around, then points at the wooden chair Monsignor sits in during mass.

"Push that over here." I obediently do what he says, even though this whole thing is scaring me and turning my stomach inside out. I'm afraid of being caught by the nuns and I'm afraid Jesse's going to do something weird and get us both in trouble with God.

He hops up into the chair, then climbs and balances on top of the backrest. He steadies himself against the wall behind the altar, face to face with the crucified Jesus.

"Jesse!" I whine, "Get down from there, if Monsignor O'Callahan—"

"Say an *Our Father*," he interrupts. "That was in my dream, to help stop His pain. We have to say the *Our Father* while I'm doing it."

"Doing WHAT!?"

"'Our Father, who art in heaven, hallowed be thy name,'" he says. "Say it with me, Roger. You have to for it to work, for us to help Jesus out of His pain."

I'm willing to do anything to make him finish whatever he's going to do and get us out of here. I start to say the *Our Father*, and Jesse mumbles it with me, staring into the glassy, statue eyes of Jesus. He leans away from the wall, brings the sword up, and when I realize what he's going to do I stop saying the *Our Father* and start to scream but it's too late.

Jesse pushes himself away from the wall, and hangs airborne for a second. He waves the sword with both hands and then plunges it into the chest of the statue Jesus.

"I LOVE YOU, JESUS!"

I'm screaming as Jesse falls backward on top of me and we both crash to the floor with a *thud!* The sword clatters harmlessly away on the altar.

I'm lying on the cold marble, staring up at the ceiling. There is silence. I blink, waiting for Jesus or God the Father or the Holy Ghost or Mary or somebody to say, "Time's up, you're dead, you're going to heaven," or "You're evil sinners, go to hell, go straight to hell!"

Instead, nothing. I breathe again. "Jesse?" I whisper. Nothing. "Jesse?!"

"Nnnghgnn." He's got me pinned to the floor. He's heavy.

"Jesse, get off of me!"

"Oowww."

I squirm out from under him, and he starts to mumble and come around. I try to focus, because my head's a little fuzzy and I'm not sure what just happened.

Jesse's curled up, holding his right hand. He's writhing and his moans are getting louder. I look up at the crucifix, expecting to see a big gash where Jesse finished off the suffering Jesus. Instead, I see only a tiny chip out of His holy wooden chest.

"Are you okay?" I move back to Jesse and look down at him.

"I cut my hand with the sword!" he says, sitting up. "I hit my head when I fell, and I saw stars and stuff." He pauses, like he's thinking, trying to remember. "Shit...."

"What?" I ask, afraid that he said a bad word in church.

"I saw...a miracle!"

I help him sit up, and he uncovers his hand. He has a small cut across his palm that's already starting to dry up.

"There wasn't any miracle," I say. "You stabbed the crucifix and you fell off the chair and almost smashed me. That's all that happened."

"No, no, I saw it! The sword went in and blood sprayed out all over the place, and I heard Him die and I think He even thanked me for helping Him!"

"Nuh-uh. Nothing happened."

"I saved Jesus, just like He wanted," Jesse says proudly.

"You stabbed a wooden statue!"

Jesse stands and gazes up at the crucifix. With a dreamy smile he says, "I love you, Jesus. Thank you for letting me help you."

This is crazy. Jesse's crazy. And he's going to get us in huge trouble. When the nuns find out about this we're dead.

He keeps staring at the crucifix. I look up at it. From this angle the little chip out of Jesus' chest looks much bigger. "Wow," Jesse whispers. "I'm glad I could help you, Jesus."

We both stand, Jesse gazing up in reverent silence, me with fear and disbelief. Miracles. He's crazy.

The church's front door *creaks* open, and our heads snap back to see who it is. An old Mexican lady dips a finger into the holy water font and blesses herself, then readjusts her black mantilla. Jesse and I scramble off the altar, I grab the sword, and we run out the side door by the flickering votive candles. I glance back at the old Mexican lady; she's frowning at the noise, trying to focus on us, but her weak eyes don't work in the dim church and we're out the door before she can see us.

We jump on our bikes and race back to Jesse's house.

Jesse shoos a little brother out of his room and slams the door. We sit, gasping, saying nothing. I stare at the floor. I can't catch my breath. Jesse takes a deep breath, and the dreamy smile returns. He's completely calm again.

"I know what I saw. It was a miracle. The blood of Jesus was all over me. It was like a geyser or something."

"How come I didn't see it?" I ask.

"I dunno. Maybe you don't believe enough."

"Are you gonna tell the nuns? Or Monsignor?"

"Uh-uh. Jesus and Mary said not to. They said the nuns don't have real faith."

This is too strange. My best friend is suddenly talking to Jesus and Mary and seeing things. I think maybe I need to find new friends.

"How much have they been talking to you?"

"A bunch."

Yeah. Right.

"I'm sure what I saw, Roger." "Sure" sounds like "chure". He's trying too hard to convince me. I wonder if he's trying to convince himself.

"You can't prove it," I say.

"The miracle proved everything."

"There wasn't any stupid miracle!"

He closes his eyes and breathes deeply. "All the time I dream about Jesus and the Virgin Mary. They tell me stuff."

"What kind of stuff?"

He shrugs and licks the cut on his hand. "Stuff."

"C'mon, Jesse. I'm your best friend, you gotta tell me what they say to you. You made me go to church with you and watch you stab the crucifix, I could've gotten in big trouble. You owe me." I don't say I think he's crazy.

Jesse sits silently for a moment. His little brother peeks back in the room and Jesse throws a deflated football at him. It *whumps* the kid in the head and he runs squealing down the hall.

"I don't know. What if they get mad and don't visit my dreams anymore? I don't think they want me goin' around telling everybody what they say."

He doesn't trust me. I can't believe it. "Fine," I say, heading for the door. "I'm the one you dragged into it, but if you think they don't trust me, then forget it."

I'm out the door when he gives in.

"Okay. But you can't tell nobody." I come back in and sit in the clutter of dirty clothes and broken toys on the floor. "Promise you won't ever say nothing about this to nobody."

"Yeah."

"Okay...they show up at night in my dreams. I think it's my dreams, I think I'm asleep. Anyway, sometimes it's Mary by herself, sometimes it's Jesus, sometimes it's both of them. And they tell me I'm special."

"That's it?"

"When Jesus and the Blessed Virgin Mary tell you you're special, it means something."

"What else do they say?" I ask, getting more annoyed. I don't believe him.

"Well, last night Jesus told me I had to prove I really loved Him, that the world made Him sad and I had the power to stop His pain. So when I saw your dad's sword and then looked at Jesus on the cross in church, I knew what I had to do. And I did it, I saw the miracle."

"But I didn't."

Jesse frowns, troubled for the first time. "I wonder why?" He thinks for a minute. "I'm sure I saw it. But it's like a dream now, you know? The more I try to remember the harder it is."

That proves it. Jesse's either pretending he saw the blood and stuff—why, I don't know—or he's crazy. Either way, nothing happened.

We sit for awhile and don't say anything. Jesse's lips start moving and I think he's saying *Hail Marys*. I wait for him to tell me more, but he's somewhere else. I finally get bored and head for the door.

"See you."

"You know what's really weird?" he says without looking at me.

"What?"

"In my dreams, Jesus looks kinda like my Uncle Ernesto."

I'm about to ask when he answers for me.

"And the Blessed Virgin Mary...she looks kinda like Aunt Yolanda."

I pedal home, balancing the towel-wrapped sword on the handlebars. What a day. Jesse tried to kill a wooden crucifix, he claims he's on a first-name basis with Jesus and Mary, and if he's not lying there's a chance that Jesus and Mary are Mexicans. Wow. The only problem is that I don't believe anything he said, and I've got a bad, scary feeling inside. I don't know why it bothers me so much. He's just being weird, and it's not my fault. But it feels like it is. He really seems to believe it. I think Jesse is crazy.

I ride toward home, and now, instead of concentrating on miracles and Jesus and the Blessed Virgin Mary my mind wanders back to—

Aunt Yolanda's dirty smile.

Chapter Four

"'Bless me Father, for I have sinned, it has been two weeks since my last confession, these are my sins: I've lied three times and I didn't pray after communion last Sunday.'" I recite it so fast it comes out as one giant word.

I hate confession; it makes me feel stupid and scared. It doesn't help that Monsignor O'Callahan, the scariest man in the world, is sitting on the other side of the screen. I bounce on the kneeler to make sure that the *occupied* light is working. A skinny old man once walked into the confessional right when I was in the middle of confessing lying to Mom. It was like having somebody walk in on you in the bathroom. I don't want that to happen again. The soft *click* as I move on the kneeler reassures me that my privacy is protected by the little red light above the door. I spend more time at confession wondering how the kneeler light switch works than I do examining my conscience.

Monsignor O'Callahan doesn't say anything. I know he's in there, I can see his outline through the wicker screen and I can smell his tobacco breath. I lean closer to the screen and squint. I'm not sure, but I think he's reading the sports page. My shuffling around finally rouses him, and he looks up from his paper.

"Anything else?" he growls. I'm startled, because he doesn't usually say anything except, "Three *Hail Marys* and make an *Act of Contrition*."

"Huh?"

"Do you have any other sins to confess?" he asks slowly, like I'm a retard.

"Well...."

"Yes?"

"I had...have impure thoughts."

"Really?" He sounds mildly interested. "What kind of impure thoughts?"

I'm horrified. Confessing stupid things like little lies and not praying enough is one thing. But telling Monsignor O'Callahan about my impure thoughts, well, there's some things you don't confess to anybody, especially crabby old gray-haired monsignors.

"Answer my question, young man," he orders, and I feel my guts turn to water. Now I'm in deep and I can't get out.

"Um, girls...ladies," I whisper.

"Speak up, I can't hear you!"

I close my eyes, mortified, swallow hard and confess my deepest, darkest grammar school sin. "I have impure thoughts about ladies, Monsignor."

"I see. Impure thoughts can take you away from God, you know that, don't you?"

"Yes, Monsignor."

"And women, *ladies*, they're the biggest source of temptation you'll face throughout your entire life. You have to be strong, you have to resist them."

"Yes, Monsignor."

"Eve's weakness in the garden led to the downfall of mankind, and men have been paying the price ever since. Don't start now, even at your young age, being led by them, being deceived by their charms, *don't let them control you*!" He's almost yelling at me, his breathing is labored, and tobacco bad breath spews through the screen. "Do you understand?!"

I've never been yelled at in confession before and I don't know what to do. I'm afraid I might throw up.

"Well?!" he demands.

"Um, I understand, Monsignor."

"Good. We must respect women, after all, the Blessed Virgin was a woman, but we must also be very careful. Impure thoughts lead to mortal sins of the flesh. You don't want to commit mortal sins, do you?"

"Nosir!" Mortal sins are the biggies, the eternity-in- hell sins, and no way I want one of those stuck on me. I pledge to myself that I'll never have anything to do with women as long as I live. Maybe I'll become a priest.

"For your penance say ten *Hail Marys*, five *Our Fathers*, and three *Glory Be's*. Now make a good *Act of Contrition*."

Ten *Hail Marys*? I'm stunned by the enormity of my sins. I've never been hit with more than three. Monsignor O'Callahan mumbles the absolution while I say the *Act of Contrition*, but my mind is reeling with guilt and I forget the words. "'But most of all, because I have offended thee, my God, who art, uh, who art....'" I'm dead. I can't remember the rest of the prayer.

Monsignor O'Callahan finishes the absolution and the confessional is filled with dead silence. I gulp.

"Well?!" he says. He seems to be saying "Well?!" a lot today.

"I forgot the rest of the *Act of Contrition*, Monsignor."

He sighs disgustedly. "*'Because I have offended, thee, my God, who art worthy of all my love.*'" I remember now, and say the rest of it with him in a strange little duet. "'I firmly resolve with the help of thy grace to sin no more and to avoid the near occasions of sin.'" Monsignor roughly grabs the little sliding door behind the screen. "Next time you come to confession, come prepared! And stop thinking about women!" *Bang!*

"Thank you, Monsignor," I whisper to the dark screen. It doesn't matter, because Monsignor's either back to reading his sports page or attacking his next victim in the other confessional.

I stand on Gumby legs and wobble to the communion rail to say my penance. I gaze up at Jesus on the cross as I speed through the *Hail Marys.* The tiny chip in his side where Jesse stabbed him is a beacon of my sinfulness. Nobody's noticed it in the months since it happened, but I know somebody will, and when they do, I'm going down. I've thought a lot about it, and I'm sure now that there wasn't any miracle. Jesse's nuts. But nobody, not even Monsignor O'Callahan, can ever forgive me for helping Jesse to stab Jesus. It's between me and Jesus, and it's a worse sin than impure thoughts could ever be.

"*Ten Hail Marys and five Our Fathers?!*" Jesse can't believe it. We're in the vestibule behind the altar, putting on our altar boy robes before mass.

"And three *Glory Be's,*" I remind him. I'm starting to like being a big sinner; it impresses people.

"You didn't tell him about the sword?" He looks around to make sure Monsignor isn't lurking.

I shake my head. "Just impure thoughts. Are you going to confess stabbing—"

"*Sssshhh!*" Jesse waves his arms. "That wasn't a sin, I did what they told me to do!"

I don't want to argue with him. I think he might be a little crazy and his dreams—if he really has dreams where Jesus and Mary talk to him—might be the work of the devil. The nuns have been spending a lot of time lately warning us about Satan's tricks; he sounds like a sneaky guy.

But I don't say anything to Jesse because Monsignor O'Callahan sweeps into the vestibule, crabby, red-eyed and feeling mean. We've been around him long enough to know his moods. Jesse and I stand, shuffling, our eyes glued to the floor while Monsignor pulls on his green cassock. Watching Monsignor get ready for mass makes you feel like you're doing something wrong, like peeking at your girl cousin taking a bath or listening at your parents' door on those nights when they lock it and make strange grunting noises. Watching a grouchy old monsignor get dressed for mass makes you feel dirty.

Monsignor coughs up a deep, phlegmy hack and spits into the trash can. He glances at Jesse and me and notices our existence for the first time.

"What's your name?" he barks at Jesse.

"Jesse Montoya."

"Ever served mass before?"

"Yes, Monsignor."

"Make sure your sidekick doesn't mess up."

"Yes, Monsignor," Jesse smiles.

I can't believe it. I've been an altar boy two weeks longer than Jesse has! I've even worked a funeral, I know what I'm doing, I've served at least twenty masses with the Monsignor, how can he treat me this way?

"He looks like the kind who'll mess up," Monsignor grumbles as he turns away and walks to the front of the church for the entrance procession.

Tears sting my eyes. I'm sensitive; I don't like being picked on for no reason. Kids like Jesse just shrug off insults or pound their tormentors, but I can't. Except for the time I attacked Jesse and Sister Mary Annunciata, I've always been a doormat. Maybe I should attack Monsignor and see if the white anger-flash zone will kick in, where I can be something stronger and meaner than I really am. Yeah, maybe I should. Maybe....

Jesse slaps me on the back. "Don't worry, he didn't mean nothin'." He walks off, unfazed by the fatal insult thrown my way. I wish I could be so casual. Of course, it's easy for him to be casual; he wasn't the one who was insulted.

The mass is like any other mass, mostly boring, especially Monsignor's sermon. He reads word for word, never pauses or adds anything, just a droning, crabby monologue, this Sunday about how everybody needs to sacrifice and give more money to the church. He spends a lot of time in his sermons complaining that the parishioners are cheap. Dad says Monsignor sounds like a Jew the way he scrounges for money. Mom giggles and tells him to stop, but I think she agrees with him. Even if the Monsignor isn't hounding everybody for more money or being grouchy, he's still boring. I don't think he likes being a priest.

During the mass, I make sure I do all my stuff perfectly from opening the bible to the right pages to folding the altar linens with perfect corners to pouring just the right amount of water for the hand washing. The glamour duty of altar-boydom is ringing the bells during the consecration. When Sister Mary Victor was teaching us how to be altar boys, she made sure we realized that the bell ringing was the centerpiece of the mass.

"When Monsignor elevates the host, it's just bread, but at the MOMENT you ring the bell, it becomes the body of Christ." She stopped speaking, choked with emotion, and her watery eyes closed in awe. "The consecration, the holiest and most mysterious time of the mass, the time when bread and wine becomes the body and blood of our Lord Jesus Christ, is the time that YOU, as altar boys, join with the priest in the holy mystery."

We were all impressed. Mass could be dull, we could be falling asleep during the sermon and yawning through all the prayers, but when the big moment came during the consecration to ring the bells, whoever was on bell duty fluttered with excitement and anticipation. Some guys give a late-starting, weak little jingle that sounds scared and uncertain, hardly living up to the supernatural transformation occurring on the altar. Jesse and I ring the bell like we mean it, like we understand that Jesus is here and you'd better pay attention. The times I get to ring the bell, I ring hard, loud enough to wake up the dozers in the back rows, but not so loud that people get mad and forget about Jesus and glare at me. My bell work is the best.

But today, Jesse and I flipped a coin before mass and I lost. Not only does Monsignor think I'm a loser, I won't even get the chance to redeem myself with a rousing bell ring.

I daydream through mass and suddenly realize we're at the consecration. Monsignor coughs wetly, then takes the host and prepares to change it from bread into Jesus.

"He took the bread into his sacred hands and said, 'Take this all of you and eat it, this is my body which shall be given up to you.'" Monsignor raises the host and holds it above his head. I expect to hear Jesse's bold bell ringing, but instead there's silence. Monsignor holds the host, waiting. I look over at Jesse. His eyes are glazed and dreamy, and his thick-lipped mouth is slightly open. He holds the bell, but does nothing. His breathing is wheezy, like he's got a cold and his nose is stuffed up. But then I realize what's happening. He's listening.

Oh no. He thinks *they're* talking to him.

"Jesse!" I hiss, "the bell, ring the bell!"

Monsignor still holds the host over his head, but now he's glaring at us. He's not putting the host down until Jesse rings and Jesse's not ready to ring yet. He's somewhere else. Monsignor clears his throat and kills Jesse with his eyes. Then he locks eyes with me and the message is loud and clear: *Do Something!*

It's my chance to prove I'm not a loser, that I'm a competent altar boy who deserves to be noticed and praised, not insulted and treated like a moron. I reach over to take the bell from Jesse, and my hand even manages to grip the handle, but then he jerks it away and starts to ring.

Loudly.

Relief floods the church and the monsignor gratefully lowers the host and sets it on the altar. He genuflects and is about to do the same stuff with the chalice of wine. There's only one problem.

Jesse won't stop ringing the bell.

At first everyone pretends not to notice, but Jesse's ringing so loud and hard and with such a look of crazed devotion that a low murmur quickly buzzes through the church. Monsignor glares at him, but Jesse doesn't see. He's gazing into space, seeing things the rest of us can't. And he keeps ringing the bell, his arm swinging wildly, like he's swatting at mosquitoes the size of birds.

I shrug helplessly at Monsignor, whose face reddens with irritation and anger. Jesse's still ringing the bell like a possessed Salvation Army Santa, and Monsignor moves toward him, along with Mr. LaCava, the lector, and I drift away from Jesse because I get a feeling of dread, something bad's going to happen, and I want to escape, the air seems thick and chewy and I can't breathe, it's too heavy, and suddenly I'm gasping and choking and then I see something—

A flash. Blue. Something out of the corner of my eye. Movement. I turn to see what it is, and silence closes around me and I still can't breathe. The ringing stops, the murmuring stops, even the sound of Monsignor's footsteps stops. I am looking at the statue of the Blessed Virgin Mary by the altar. She stands on a pedestal, dressed in blue, her arms outstretched in soothing welcome. What moved? I turn and look at Jesse. He's still ringing the bell, even though I no longer hear it, and Monsignor and Mr. LaCava are angrily moving toward him, and I can't hear them either. But Jesse's eyes, I hear them, at least I feel them, and then I understand, he's staring at the statue of the Virgin Mary, and my head swings back to the statue but this time I don't see movement. It's just a statue.

Something isn't right. I can't tell what the feeling is, but I know things have gotten unstuck, and for the last few seconds what's real and what isn't has blurred. Jesse stares at the statue, I try to talk to him but I can't make sound come out, and then I feel a rush of cool air and sound roars back, Jesse still jangles the bell, his eyes roll back in his head, only the whites remain.

I hear a *thud* and gasps and turn to see Monsignor O'Callahan sprawled on the floor, moaning.

Chaos overruns the church as people rush to the altar to help Monsignor, but everybody ignores the still-ringing Jesse. I push through the crowd and go to him and pull the bell out of his hand. At the instant I do, he collapses to the floor, but nobody cares. I cradle his head. "Are you okay?!" I ask. He moans back at me, and his eyes flutter open, not just the whites but gaping, dazed pupils.

"Mary...." he gasps. I remember and turn toward the statue. It's as it always is, frozen and friendly and not particularly realistic. No sign of movement. Was it moving? I didn't see what it was, but I thought— What am I thinking?! Statues don't move, Jesse's rubbing off on me and making me crazy! Nothing happened. Whatever moved, it wasn't the statue.

"Mary! I saw her, Roger, I saw her point at Monsignor, she was mad!"

"I think Monsignor's had a heart attack!" shrills one of the blue-haired old ladies who always sits in the front row clicking rosary beads during mass. The altar is more crowded than I've ever seen it, with people running around trying to help Monsignor, but nobody's really accomplishing anything.

"She told me to ring the bell," Jesse whispers, "she told me that Monsignor wasn't a good man, that she'd smite him. What's smite mean?"

"I dunno, but I don't think it's something good." Someone yanks me away and people surround Jesse to see if he's okay.

I squeeze through the crowd and climb over the communion rail. Mom and Dad and Mary Frances are there.

"What happened?!" Mom asks, breathless with concern and the excitement people have when something bad happens and they don't want to admit that it's kind of cool.

"I dunno," I say. I don't know what's going on anymore. The statue didn't move. I'm sure of it.

"Looks like the Monsignor had a seizure when your friend wouldn't stop ringing the bell," Mary Frances says. The way she says it, she sounds like she's accusing Jesse of murder.

"Be quiet!" Dad snaps. It doesn't happen very often, but Dad can be stern when he wants to be. Mary Frances shuts up.

"The ambulance is on the way," someone shouts, and we all stand around, waiting. I catch a glimpse of the Monsignor and he doesn't look good. His skin is gray, and one side of his face is floppy; drool leaks out from the side of his mouth and pools on the floor.

I turn and look again at the Virgin Mary statue. She's a friendly looking, five-foot tall painted plaster Mother of God, tucked in an altar alcove. She's probably identical to lots of other plaster Marys in Catholic churches, Marys who look down with love and understanding on the faithful. Marys who don't move, Marys who don't hurt Monsignors.

Just plaster statues.

I'm afraid Jesse's making me lose my mind.

It's Saturday and *Chiller* is on. Today they're showing *The Crawling Eye* and me and Jesse watch with absolute concentration. We live for Saturdays and the scary movies they show on *Chiller*. *The Crawling Eye* is one of my favorites, especially the part right now where they find the severed head under the bed. I close my eyes and so does Jesse, but then we open them because we just have to look. *The Crawling Eye* gives me the same uneasy feeling I've been getting lately about Jesse.

After the strange business with Monsignor O'Callahan, I realized I couldn't deny that something weird was going on. Jesse might be crazy or lying, but *something* happened to Monsignor.

A couple of days after, Jesse said, "I figured it out. You're supposed to be around when stuff happens."

"Why?"

"I dunno. They haven't told me yet. But things won't happen unless you're there. We're a team."

"I don't think I want to be on your team," I said, feeling queasy. This stuff was starting to scare me. "What happened at church?"

"I was praying, and then I looked at the statue of the Blessed Virgin Mary, and she started to move!" he said, amazed. I said nothing. *The statue didn't move.* "And she told me Monsignor was an evil, unholy man, and she would smite him for his sins, and then she lifted her hand and pointed at him, and then he fell down."

"Oh." I was sorry I asked.

"Anyway, from now on, you don't have any choice. Jesus and Mary want you. You're chosen just like me."

"Great," I said. The last thing I wanted was to be Jesse's miracle helper. Who knew what other weird stuff was coming up?

"God wants us, can you believe it? He wants us, out of all the people in the world, He's using us!" Jesse was breathing heavily, his thick black hair falling over his face. His eyes were wide; the eyes of a true believer.

"If Jesus and Mary are so nice, how come they zapped Monsignor? I thought they were supposed to forgive you for stuff?" My parents said Monsignor'd had a stroke and was paralyzed on one side. They said he'd probably never be a real monsignor again.

"Mary said he was bad, so who knows? It's not up to us. We just do what they say," he said. End of conversation. Jesse was sure of everything; I was along for the ride and I guess he assumed I'd believe everything he said.

The scary severed head scene ends and *Chiller* goes to a commercial. Chick Lambert and his dog Storm walk through the car lot of Ralph Williams Ford, trying to sell used Fords. Storm, a big, droopy German Shepherd, jumps up on a '63 Fairlane. I don't think I'd want to buy a car with dog toenail scratches on the hood.

Jesse's mom peeks into the living room and says something to him in Spanish.

"*Si, mama*," he says, getting up. He heads to the kitchen. "I gotta take my medicine," he grumbles.

After the bell-ringing thing, the nuns insisted that he go to the doctor and get tested. "He went into some sort of trance!" Sister Mary Victor told his parents. "He needs to be checked." She acted like Jesse was a demon or something. The school paid for his tests and the doctor said he wasn't sure but he thought Jesse might have epilepsy, so they gave him some medicine to keep him from having seizures.

At first, Jesse was afraid the medicine might interfere with his dreams, but so far he still has the same dreams every night and talks to Jesus and Mary, and he's sure another miracle is coming. I don't say so, but I wish the medicine would make it all go away.

Jesse returns from the kitchen, trailed by one of his little brothers. I think his name is David, but I'm not positive. There are so many people in this house, and so many little kids—brothers, sisters, cousins—that I never know who's who.

They both flop down on the cluttered floor just in time for *The Crawling Eye* to start again. The little kid pulls a saggy cushion from the sprung green couch and props up his head. Jesse gives him a withering look.

"Get outa here, *mijo*," he says. The little kid doesn't move. "Me and Roger are watchin' this."

"No," the kid says firmly. I'm pretty sure his name is David. "I don't have to. You can't make me. I'll tell Mama you talk to Jesus at night."

Oh-oh. Jesse's mad. I didn't think anybody besides me knew the secret.

"How do you know about that?" Jesse asks.

"You talk in your sleep," says David. "I hear you every night talk to Jesus and Mary. You're *loco*, Jesse."

Jesse says nothing for a moment. He stares at the TV with total concentration, as if David and I aren't in the room. And when he finally speaks, it's without his eyes ever leaving the screen.

"Don't ever tell nobody, David. What you think you're hearing isn't about you. You say anything to anybody, and Jesus and the Virgin Mary will punish you. I'll make sure they do." He says it with absolute calm and assurance—and menace. When he finally turns toward David, David's little kid's chin is quivering, and when Jesse's black, hawk eyes drill him, little David doesn't have a chance. He bursts into terrified tears and runs out of the room.

Jesse calmly turns back to the TV and *The Crawling Eye*. I say nothing. I've never seen Jesse be so mean. The fear I've been feeling is about his dreams and his visions, but not him. He's always seemed harmless. Now, after watching his cold threat toward his little brother, I wonder what exactly Jesse Montoya is capable of—and whether I could ever be his target.

We watch the rest of the movie in silence, and it's not fun anymore.

"Here's the plans!" Dad shouts, slamming the papers down on the kitchen table. The lime Jell-O we were dishing up quivers. Mom made pot roast tonight, which I call string roast because instead of slicing it shreds into wiry, individual muscle fibers. But it was worth choking down because now we get the Jell-O payoff.

"Plans for what?" Mary Frances asks, bored and annoyed. She has a date with Freddie Montgomery later and she's cranky. Freddie's zitty and has a huge Adam's apple, and Mary Frances's friends make fun of him. I don't know if she really likes him, but she's glad for any chance to get out of the house. When she's home she stays locked in her room for hours listening to Beatles' records and dreaming of Paul McCartney.

Her dates with Freddie never seem to be much fun, and she's always grouchy before a date because she suspects it won't be any good, and she's always grouchy afterwards because it wasn't any good. But, date with Freddie Montgomery or not, Mary Frances is always cranky, and Dad's noisy excitement doesn't help.

"The addition," Dad says proudly. "It'll be a combination family room, rec room, and it'll even have a wet bar!" Mom clears the table. Whenever Dad gets real excited about something stupid, she just smiles a sly, weary smile and does Mom things like dishes or vacuuming.

"Woo, neat," Mary Frances says, snotty and sarcastic. Dad's goofy, but when Mary Frances makes fun of him I want to pop her.

If Dad's feelings are hurt, he doesn't show it. "Now it's gonna take awhile, 'cause it'll just be me and Roger building it." My head snaps up at the sound of my name. Mary Frances throws me a vicious grin.

"What?" I ask. The lime Jell-O is turning on me.

"You betcha, Rog, you and me, general contractors. It'll be great!"

I look helplessly at Mom as she comes back in from the kitchen. She just smiles. No help there. I look at Mary Frances. She leers at me. I look at Dad. He's grinning from ear to ear. I'm trapped and nobody's going to help me. Then I get an idea.

"Maybe Mary Frances could help, too," I say with an angelic innocence. Mary Frances's leer evaporates. Her spoonful of quivering lime Jell-O stops in midair right in front of her fat, ugly mouth.

Dad's smile never wavers, but I can tell by the tone of his voice that the idea won't fly. "Sure, maybe," he says, and then he runs his hands over the crudely drawn plans. "It'll be so great, I can hardly wait to get started. Of course, it's gonna take some time, we can't afford to do it all at once, but that's the great part, building it will be like a five year hobby!" Five years! I can't conceive of such a huge amount of time. That means it won't be finished until I'm in...*high school*! "And the great part is we'll be able to buy a Ping-Pong table and leave it up year-round!" he adds.

"That'll be wonderful, Patrick," Mom says, supportive and helpful as always. Mary Frances gobbles her Jell-O, happy in the knowledge that she's off the hook. It'll be me and Dad, cutting wood and hammering nails the rest of our lives. I'm no construction expert, but I know Dad well enough to know that this addition will never be finished; he'll lose interest and want to build some other useless thing, like a tower or a barn or a stagecoach.

I finish my lime Jell-O in despair. The doorbell rings, and Mary Frances leaps up, knocking a spoon to the floor. "I'll get it!" she yells, as if any of us are in a hurry to let Freddie Montgomery in the house. Mom picks up the spoon and finishes clearing the table while Dad studies the plans.

I sit, glumly gumming my Jell-O, when Dad whispers, "Must be pizza face, huh? Only thing in the world that'd make your sister move that fast." He looks up at me and smiles. I decide Dad's okay.

Freddie Montgomery follows Mary Frances into the kitchen. He stumbles over an imaginary bump on the smooth linoleum floor. Freddie has trouble with his body; it's bigger than his brain thinks it is. He has huge, size thirteen triple-E feet, long, bow legs, and scrawny arms. He got into a fight last week because somebody on the football team called him a pencil-necked geek. The football player won.

Freddie stands, nervously shuffling from size thirteen to size thirteen. He rubs an oversized hand across his butch-waxed flattop; there's so much crud in his hair I'm surprised his hand doesn't stick. His zits look especially hideous tonight, angry and red, with ready-to-pop whiteheads mixed in with new bumps and old scabs; there's not a patch of normal skin anywhere on his face. The only smooth spot above his shoulders is his flattop. The soles of his hightop Keds are split, probably because his feet grew an inch or two today. His jeans are too short, and his shirt too baggy.

Freddie's a very impressive sixteen-year-old.

"Uh, hi, Mr. Donnelly," Freddie mumbles. Mary Frances's excitement at his arrival has quickly worn off. She looks at his lumpy face with the same irritated expression she uses with Dad and me. I think everyone in the world annoys Mary Frances, including herself.

"Hiya, Freddie. What're you and Mary Frances doing tonight?" Dad asks, still studying the addition plans.

"Uh, we thought, um," his voice creaks like there's something dead in his throat, "we thought maybe miniature golf or something?" Freddie speaks with hesitation and uncertainty, like he's been smacked a few too many times for speaking out of turn and now he's permanently scared. Mary Frances hurries to her room.

"Lemme get my sweater, we can go."

Freddie nods and stands, nervous and unsure what to do with his hands, a terrified, zit-faced Bigfoot trapped by hunters. I feel bad for him and smile, but it doesn't seem to help him feel better. Dad continues to study the plans.

"Haven't seen you at church lately, Freddie."

Freddie panics. His eyes dart from side to side, and his zits blush. "I'm...not Catholic, sir."

Dad looks up from the plans, innocently puzzled. "Really?" He rubs the back of his neck, thinking. "Huh. Could've sworn I used to see you there. Must be thinking of somebody else." He looks over at me and winks. "Oh, I know who it is, it's the *pizza* delivery guy, he looks just like you." Emphasis on pizza, Dad grins at me, proud of his mean little joke. I feel sorry for Freddie. Not only does he go out with my disgusting sister, but Dad makes fun of his zits and he doesn't even know it. I decide here and now to always be nice to this guy.

Mary Frances wanders back just as Mom comes out of the kitchen and makes all the nice mom noises at Freddie. Mary Frances grabs him and yanks him out the door.

"Back by ten, honey!" Mom calls out after them. Mary Frances doesn't bother to answer, and Freddie's too terrified. The front door slams and they're gone.

"He's very shy, isn't he?" Mom says.

"With a complexion like that I'd be shy, too," Dad mumbles, then he pulls me over next to him. "This is gonna be so great, Rog," he sighs, proudly looking at his plans, "I can't wait to get started. Bet you're pretty excited to help your old man build the addition, huh?"

Woo, neat.

Chapter Five

Rhonda Fairly smiled at me a two weeks ago, and I still can't make my heart slow down.

I've been aware of Rhonda Fairly since kindergarten. Aware that she existed and sort of aware that she was cute, but I didn't really pay much attention. There are lots of girls in school I feel that way about.

When you're in school, you see kids every day, and a lot of them are just there; they don't make an impression. Maybe you play four-square or dodgeball with them, or sit across from them at lunch, or kneel next to them at communion, or stand behind them in line at confession, but you don't really pay any attention until something about them—or you—changes.

It was like that with Jesse. Things changed and we became best friends. Of course, I had to smash his head against the pavement before our friendship grew, but that made it all the more interesting.

It's not like that with Rhonda Fairly. She was there for a while, and I didn't care. Then, all of a sudden and for no apparent reason, I do care. A lot.

None of us will admit that we might like girls—especially girls in our class. We'll look at naked pictures in swiped Playboys, and we'll be interested in ladies like Jesse's Aunt Yolanda, but our own age...there's just something kind of creepy about them. At least I thought there was until Rhonda Fairly smiled at me.

It was during recess. I was playing dodgeball with Jesse and some of the other guys. Getting slammed in the side of the head with one of those soft, red rubber playground balls is one of my favorite recess things to do. It hurts and stings a little, but it wakes you up and makes you feel alive and free after sitting in class and listening to a nun drone about Jesus and Mary and the commandments and reciting the Baltimore catechism until the words don't mean anything anymore. When Sister gets mad and starts smacking people's hands with rulers things perk up, but it's nowhere near as fun as slamming or being slammed with the big red rubber ball.

I had just gotten smashed in the face by Jesse, and was trying to shake the stars out of my head when a jack bounced at my feet. The girls play jacks and hopscotch on the asphalt next to the dodgeball court, and sometimes their stupid games spill over into our important ones. I shook my head and the cobwebs cleared, although I could feel a big red welt puffing on my cheek. Mom would be crazy when she saw it; she hated it when I played rough games. She doesn't understand boys, she doesn't understand the need to run and hit and punch and throw things.

I picked up the jack, ready to toss it at whatever dopey girl had invaded our boy-space. I looked up and was face-to-face with Rhonda Fairly. I'd never *really* looked at her before; our eyes had never met. I was about to toss her the jack and go back to the dodgeball game when she smiled at me. It wasn't just a polite, "Can I have my jack back" smile. It was a smile that made me forget about the welt on my cheek, forget about the dodgeball game, forget about everything in the world except her smile. I stood there on the asphalt playground, surrounded by screaming kids playing all sorts of games, and the only sound I heard was the music of her smile. I couldn't move. Her smile grew bigger and warmer and she held out her hand.

"Hi, Roger. Can I have my jack, please?" she asked. Her voice was clear and sweet. I must've heard her talk in class, but I'd never noticed before. Maybe it was because this was the first time I'd heard her say my name. "*Roger....*" It sure sounded nice the way she said it. I held out the jack and dropped it into her outstretched palm. "Thanks," she said, before she ran back to her impatient friends.

I stood, staring. Until Jesse bounced the ball off the back of my head. "What's the matter with you?"

"Nothing."

"You look like me when I'm talking to...Them."

I just stared at him. Maybe Rhonda was a miracle.

For the last two weeks I've been spending a lot of time looking at and listening to Rhonda Fairly. At first she didn't notice, but then a few times I'd keep looking even after she'd glance my way, and now it seems that we keep exchanging smiles.

I'm not sure what it all means, whether I should do anything other than look at her and smile and hope she says my name again. I don't know the rules. Mary Frances goes out on dates and follows a lot of social customs and regulations. There aren't any rules for us, we're just dumb kids who play dopey recess games and try not to get beat on by the nuns. But even though I'm confused and puzzled, I can't help thinking about Rhonda Fairly. All the time.

I've done a little checking on Rhonda to find out about her. She's the youngest kid, and the only girl. Her brothers are at college and they don't live at home anymore. Mom and Dad know her parents, which doesn't surprise me since it seems like they know everybody in the parish. I'm sure Dad has slugged down booze with Rhonda's Dad at church parties, and I'm sure Mom has giggled and gossiped with her mom.

The more I study Rhonda, the more I like the way she looks. Her hair is black and shiny, almost like a Mexican's. But her skin is white, really white, so transparent that you can see tiny blue webby veins right below the surface of her forehead. She's skinny, like most of the girls are, but the more I study her the more I realize she's really cute. I like her eyes and her smile, I like the way she sits at her desk and intently listens to Sister, and I like the way she plays hopscotch and eats her lunch. I haven't found anything about her I don't like.

I go out of my way after school to ride by her house, hoping to accidentally-on-purpose see her or have her notice me. She lives in another housing tract a couple of miles from mine. It's newer here, and the houses are bigger and nicer than my neighborhood, with lots of swimming pools and fancy patios. Even the TV antennas on their roofs are bigger and better than my neighborhood. Nobody here needs to add on rec rooms to the back of their houses; they already have all the space they need.

I slowly pedal my stingray past Rhonda's house. A couple of high school guys are out in the street, throwing a football around. They glance up at me as I pass, but they pay no attention. I'm younger than they are, so as far as they're concerned I don't exist. I ride on down the street, disappointed that I didn't have a Rhonda sighting. Maybe I'll ride over to Jesse's and we'll do something. He's got a new GI Joe one of his aunts gave him, and it has the cool diving helmet and water commando accessories.

I turn the corner onto Mountain Avenue and head toward Jesse's. It's only a little smoggy today, and I can still see the faint outline of the mountains, although I can feel the first twinge of pain in my throat. On bad days, if I inhale too deeply, the stinging smog throat hurts so much that I'll give up riding my bike and hide out inside for the rest of the day. It's lousy to be a kid and not be able to play as much as you want because it might hurt.

As I ride down Mountain Avenue, I hear the sound of a bike behind me. I turn, thinking it might be Jesse. It's Rhonda. Pedaling as hard as she can to catch up to me. I slow down, my heart starts pounding, I don't know what to say or do. She rides up on her pink stingray. Girls' stingrays usually have little white baskets hanging on the handlebars, and hers is no exception. I always thought the baskets and their fake flowers on the front were stupid.

I think Rhonda's is sort of cute.

"Hi, Roger!" she says, breathless and smiling. I've rolled to a stop by the curb and she stops next to me. She's still in her school uniform. "I have to go to the store and get fish sticks for dinner tonight, my mom forgot to get them. Wanna come with me?"

Before I have a chance to answer, she rides off. I follow. "Sure!" I finally say; but my voice is drowned out by the traffic. She doesn't look back. She assumes I'm right behind her.

We ride into the parking lot of the Shopping Basket grocery store. Mom shops here, and I usually come along with her to make sure she gets all the stuff I have to have, like Cocoa Puffs and Sugar Smacks. I also try to stop her from getting the ingredients for Friday night creamed tuna, the most disgusting puke ever put on a plate, but I never have any luck with that. Sometimes, "As a treat!" she says, she makes tuna casserole on Fridays instead, but that's even worse. She tops it off with some of Dad's stale Fritos and then overcooks it until the stale Fritos turn to charcoal.

I dread Friday night dinners.

We park our bikes by the door, and I follow Rhonda inside. The store is packed with Friday night shoppers, mostly moms who look like my mom pushing shopping carts and dragging along kids who look like me. I've spent so much time here that this place feels like a comfortable, second home. Except now I'm following Rhonda Fairly down the frozen food aisle and I don't know what to say to her.

Rhonda, however, doesn't have any problem talking. "Do you like fish sticks, Roger?"

"Yeah. We don't have them very much, though."

"What do you have on Fridays?"

"Creamed tuna. Or tuna casserole."

"Yuk! My mom used to make that but my dad threw up once, so now we get to have fish sticks."

I nod. Being alone with her makes me feel stupid and clumsy, like I'm Freddie Montgomery. I have even more sympathy for him now. I tag along with Rhonda as she pulls four boxes of fish sticks out of the freezer. She seems happy and calm; it's not fair that she's so calm and I'm so nervous.

"Since you like fish sticks maybe you could come over to my house for dinner some time, Roger."

My hair tingles. My face gets hot. Speech is impossible. She looks at me, smiling, waiting for me to stop acting stupid and say something.

"Would you like to come to my house for dinner?" she asks. She's got my eyes locked and I can't look away. I put my hands in my pockets and nod stupidly. I don't know what to do. I'm not sure, but I think I'm too young for this. Girls in grammar school aren't supposed to ask boys over for dinner. She grins and hands me the fish sticks. "Wanna carry these for me?"

I cough and then I'm finally able to croak a feeble, pathetic "Yeah." We walk to the checkout stand. She chatters the whole way, although I'm so stunned by her invitation I'm not really hearing what she's saying.

I don't hear anything until a familiar voice booms, "Hi, Rog. Who's this?"

I spin. It's Dad. Dressed in his Frito uniform and pushing a dolly loaded with Frito cartons. I've seen him in uniform a million times, but this is the first time I've noticed how silly he looks. He stands there, grinning at Rhonda and me. At Rhonda, mostly.

I'm humiliated.

"Hi, Dad," I mumble.

"Hi, Mr. Donnelly," Rhonda chirps. "I'm Rhonda Fairly. I go to school with Roger. He was helping me buy fishsticks."

"Is that right? What a helpful guy." He's grinning like the Cheshire cat, making me feel even more stupid. Then he makes it worse. He winks at me. "See you at home for dinner, Rog. Your favorite tonight. Tuna casserole. Got some old bags of Wampum Chips to top it off," he adds cheerfully. My stomach flops. My fingers are going numb from holding the frozen fish stick packages. He stands there, smiling. Why won't he go away? He winks at Rhonda, "Nice to meet you, Rhonda."

"Nice to meet you, Mr. Donnelly," she says, way too friendly. Kids aren't supposed to be this friendly with strange grown-ups. Dad, still grinning, pushes his chip-loaded dolly down the aisle. "I like your dad, Roger," Rhonda says, "he's nice."

"Yeah. Most of the time, I guess. Except when he makes me help him build things."

"Like what?" she asks.

I spend the rest of the time in line and then riding our bikes home telling her about Dad and Mom and me and Mary Frances, and by the time we get back to her house I've forgotten why I was nervous. She feels like a friend. Like another guy.

And I like her even more.

I stare at the gloppy tuna goo on my plate. The creamy monotony is broken only by shriveled peas and charred crumbled Wampum chips. I'm not sure I can make myself eat it.

Dad digs in, shoveling in forkful after forkful. "Very good, dear," he says to mom, exactly forty-five seconds into the meal. He always says, "Very good, dear" after forty-five seconds no matter what he's eating. I don't think he notices or cares, so long as he's being fed. He's like a big shaggy stray dog that eats garbage, cat crap, lawn clippings and whatever else fits in his mouth.

Mary Frances gums some of the tuna goo, then tosses her fork down with a clank. "I don't see why we have to eat fish on Friday."

"It's a sacrifice, honey," Mom says soothingly. "It's just one little way to show Jesus we love him."

"By eating tuna casserole?"

"Just eat, Mary Frances," Dad snaps. "I don't feel like having religious arguments after a hard day at work." He gets grouchy when his feeding frenzy is interrupted by non-essential conversation. He seems disinterested in talking anymore until he looks at me. Then my worst fears come true.

"Rog was in Shopping Basket with a little friend tonight," he says, eyes twinkling with amusement.

"Oh," Mom says, "who, Jesse Montoya?"

I stare at my tuna glop and wish I could dive in and become a pea. Mary Frances is prodded out of her pouty Friday night tuna whining and looks at me with malicious interest.

"Who was he with?" she asks, smelling fresh blood.

"Cute little girl named...what was it, hmm, oh, yeah, Rhonda. Rhonda Fairly."

My cheeks burn and I don't look up. Mom giggles annoyingly. "Really? Ann and Bob Fairly's little girl? I remember her at your first communion,

Roger. She's adorable." I look up. Mom's gazing at me with that irritating "Isn't he precious" look that I used to like but now that I'm older am starting to hate.

Mary Frances makes kissing noises and they all laugh at me. I'm about to throw my plate of tuna glop in her face when Dad finally notices my embarrassment.

"All right. Just kidding you a little, Rog," he grins, then he gives me a friendly guy punch in the arm. I won't give him the satisfaction of forgiveness, so I just dive into my nauseating tuna crud and eat up. They seem to have enjoyed my humiliation, because now they're talking and laughing about all kinds of things and having a wonderful family dinner. Even Mary Frances is suddenly merry, although she's still not eating.

I'm glad they're feeling better and closer. I'm embarrassed and mad. But I still can't stop thinking about Rhonda Fairly.

It's Saturday, and Jesse and I are riding our bikes around town. We went downtown earlier and got a malt and some fries at the cafe across the street from the pet store, and then we went over and looked at the puppies and the fish. Now we're just riding around aimlessly, waiting for three-o'clock: that's when *Chiller* starts, and today it's a Godzilla movie. Saturdays are the best. If I can escape from Dad's projects and chores and just hang around with Jesse, every day could be Saturday and I wouldn't care. It's the day I live for.

"Where you wanna go now?" Jesse asks as we ride through downtown, past Rio Linda High School. I look up at the cheesy statue of a snarling panther by the entrance to the high school's parking lot. Every year during the week of the big game with Santa Theresa, they have to guard the statue or somebody will steal it or bust it up. Last year they caught a couple of Santa Theresa guys painting "Fuck Rio Linda" on the panther. Mary Frances says Freddie tells her that this year some of our guys are going to go over to Santa Theresa and burn swear words in their football field with gasoline. I'm looking forward to high school.

I stop riding and dig some Sweet Tarts out of my pocket. "Want some?" I ask Jesse. He nods and I dump some into his outstretched brown palm. As we munch the sour candy, I look up and see smoke in the distance. "Hey, look, something's burning over there!" Without saying anything, we know what to do.

We start riding. When there's something cool like a fire or a car crash or any kind of unnatural occurrence, a kid on a stingray has to be there to observe. It's just the way things are.

We ride, following our noses and the columns of billowing smoke. We're not too far from my neighborhood; maybe about a mile further up toward the mountains. It's smoggy again today, and the thick smoke makes the air even gooier. I'm coughing as we get closer.

We round a corner, and then we see what it is: burning piles of orange trees. A huge orchard has been bulldozed, and the trees pushed into enormous, thirty-foot tall mounds. There are at least twenty piles of trees, and several have been lit on fire and burn roaring hot.

"Aw, man!" says Jesse disgustedly. "They're burnin' down another grove."

We sit on the curb and look out across the vacant but soon-to-be tract house-covered lot. It looks strange without trees; we've spent a lot of time fooling around in this grove, knocking over smudge pots, building forts, or trying to catch imaginary rabbits and Gila monsters. Well, the rabbits weren't imaginary; we just never caught any. We've climbed a lot of the huge orange trees that now lie uprooted in jumbled piles like so many piles of gigantic, useless weeds.

"This was a good grove," I say, feeling nostalgic for the fun times we had here.

"My dad says if they keep tearing out the groves the packing house'll close down and he won't have no job. He says every place around here will just be new houses full of *gringos*, and all the oranges and lemons you buy will be from someplace else." He says this matter-of-factly, with no anger. Even though I'm a *gringo* in a tract house, I'm not offended. I know he's not mad at me.

We watch the burning for a few moments. Huge plumes of gray smoke spiral into the smoggy sky from each pile, blending with the L.A. smog into an eye-stinging cloud. Showers of feathery ashes fall around us.

"Let's get outa here," I say, and I start to turn. But Jesse doesn't move. He's staring at something. "What?" I ask.

"Look over there." He points at one of the piles near the street, a pile that hasn't been lit on fire yet.

"Yeah, it's a pile of dead trees."

"Look at the bottom. On the side. It's like a cave."

I see a small opening, a random space left between the trees when they were bulldozed into a pile. "So?"

"Let's go look, maybe we can climb inside and make a fort or something."

"What if they light it on fire?"

"They won't. They never burn all the piles at once, it makes too much smoke."

Jesse's right. It usually takes a week of burning to finish off a whole orchard. We lay our stingrays down on the soft, bulldozed dirt and go over to investigate the pile of dead orange trees.

Up close, the mound of trees looks even taller. I look up at the limp leaves, rapidly drying out and browning. The twisted trunks and branches poke out through the leaves at crazy angles, like broken legs and arms. The resins and oils from the snapped branches smell strong and sweet, their odor almost overpowering the smoke of the nearby burning mounds.

Jesse crouches and looks up into the small opening in the pile. I feel uneasy and I don't know why. It's just a Saturday and we're doing stuff like we always do: exploring where we live and goofing off. On any other day a find like this would excite me; today, for some reason, it gives me the creeps.

"So?" I ask, hoping there's no space inside and we can just ride away.

Jesse squints into the darkness. "I think we can climb up into the pile. There's like a passageway to the top. Let's go!" I'm about to object, but he's already disappeared up into the tangled dead trees. The only thing I can do is follow.

Mottled sunlight pierces the dying leaves, but deep inside the tree pile it's mostly dark. I hear Jesse scrambling up and I follow, poking through the topsy-turvy ripped up trees.

Gravity tells me I'm climbing, but the trees themselves confuse me. I'm used to starting at the bottom, where the trunk is thick and strong, and working my way to the top of a tree where everything's thinner and scarier. In this mess I climb from a sideways trunk to a tiny branch, back to another trunk. I climb from the top of one tree to the dead roots of another, I squeeze through narrow passages and get scratched by branches and bathed in dirt knocked loose by Jesse above.

I don't like this. I don't like it a lot. Something's not right, I'm gasping, the smoke outside is overpowering the nice woodsy-leaves smell, I'm afraid, and then something brushes against the back of my head and I turn and in the dim light I scream—

A dried-out dead possum dangles from a dusty branch. He's the consistency of crispy paper, his mummy lips curled back from razor teeth into a permanent snarl. My heart's pounding against my skinny ribs. Somewhere far above, I hear Jesse stop climbing. "You okay?" he calls out, his disembodied voice drifting down through the broken trees.

"Yeah! There's a dead possum down here!"

"I know, I saw it! Isn't this great?"

I mumble "Yeah," and brush dead possum dust off my head, then continue to climb.

As I slither further up, the branches and roots seem to grab at me, they wrap dirty wood fingers around my arms and legs and chest as the passage narrows, and I feel the breath going out of my body. I gasp but it doesn't seem to do any good, the branches and leaves close in on me, and I can't hear the reassuring sound of Jesse climbing anymore. I'm beginning to panic and I climb faster, out of control, but I'm not sure if I'm more afraid of climbing up into the unknown or going back down into the depths of the pile where I've already been. I don't want either; I just want out of here.

Just as I'm sure I'm going to scream and begin crying, I burst through a roof of branches and leaves and I'm in blinding daylight. I gulp the suddenly fresh, sweet air. I've reached the top of the pile. Jesse sits on a curved, bare trunk, looking at the view. He's calm and peaceful, as usual. He turns to me and grins.

"Look, Roger. We're on top of the world."

I pop up out of the passageway and wobble from branch to branch over to Jesse. My heart slows, and I'm catching my breath, but as I do I realize something's weird. From up here, the view is clear and unshrouded by smoke or smog. I can see the mountains behind our town as clearly as I can on the days that the Santa Anas blow. And the air smells...clean. I turn and look across the field at the burning tree piles. Their smoke still rises, but from up here it looks like it vanishes when it reaches our level. Something's not right. It doesn't feel real up here. The smog and smoke disappear, the air is funny, and I'm not sure if I'm even home anymore.

Jesse notices, too. "I think this is a present from Them, Roger."

"Who?" I ask, even though I know what he's going to say.

"Jesus and Mary."

He's got that look again. He's sliding into a miracle dream. I may not believe in it, but he sure does, and I know the look.

"What's going to happen, Jesse?"

It's too late. He's gone. His eyes glaze over and he's staring into the clear, blue sky.

"Jesse?" I ask, knowing he won't say anything until he decides to come back. His eyes are milky and gone. I wait. The view's nice up here, and the sensation is pleasant. Maybe nothing bad or scary will happen. I lean back on a broken trunk and try to relax.

I've never noticed the detail of the mountains before. Mount San Antonio is carved with deep canyons and white granite gashes, and from my treetop perch I can see individual pine trees atop the mountain. I've never noticed them before. And the sky directly above us—bright blue with occasional lumpy, pure white clouds—it's never been so pretty. I'm more aware of being alive and feeling the world than I've ever been. I'm beginning to calm down and enjoy it. I glance at Jesse. He's still staring into something I can't see, his dreamworld of Jesus and Mary. He's crazy but it's okay; he's my best friend and I feel safe.

Until I smell smoke.

At first I think it's just stray smoke from the other burning piles that's blown over our perch. But then it gets stronger, and I begin to lose the good feeling, the feeling of calm and safety. I look out over the edge of our tree pile and see wispy swirls of white smoke. I'm confused for a minute, and then I realize: *our bulldozed pile of obsolete orange trees is on fire!*

Panic slams my throat shut. I think I might throw up, but it passes quickly and now I'm shivering. The smoke thickens, and our platform changes from clear, peaceful safety to smoggy, burning hell. I pull on Jesse's shoulder, but he's paralyzed, still staring upward into the swirling, smoky brown sky.

"Jesse, we gotta get outa here!" He doesn't respond, he just stares with that idiotic, saintly smile. He may burn to death, but at least he'll die smiling. "JESSE! JESSE WE'RE IN TROUBLE!" I give up on him and try to balance on a broken trunk. I wave at passing cars on the street and scream "HELP!" as loud as I can. The fire is all around, it licks the trees below us, the branches and leaves boil into crackling smoke and flame. Smoke curtains my view of the road, and sickeningly sweet burnt orange chokes my lungs; I'm coughing and gagging and I retch ashy puke. My eyes stream tears, it's almost impossible for me to blink enough to see, but I do and I catch a glimpse of cars stopping and people running toward us across the field, but I know it's too late, I can tell by my body that there's no way we can last up here, the flames are almost on top of us—

I inhale a last breath of smoke, close my eyes, and collapse on a bed of broken branches and leaves. I'm gone; I think I'm dreaming. I dream of cool, clear air. In my dream, I turn toward Jesse. He's still in the exact same miracle position, except the air around and above him has cleared. I see a cylinder of clear blue sky above him, and instantly the cylinder expands, and I'm in it, too. I can breathe again, and I no longer feel the heat or smell the smoke. I look behind me, and just a foot or so away is a wall of smoke and lapping, angry flames beyond. It's like the flames and smoke are on TV, and they can't possibly come through the glass screen and hurt us. They're not real anymore.

A wet drop *splats* of on my forehead, and I look up into the sky. Soft, gray clouds are now above us, and they begin to drip refreshing, warm rain. I lean my head back and the rain rinses me. The fear and smoky grime wash away. I know I'm safe now. In the dream, I close my eyes and relax. I know it's a dream, and it's okay.

"Roger?" I hear Jesse's voice, and I reluctantly open my eyes, but I know I'm still in the dream. He's grinning at me. "Some miracle, huh?"

"The first part was scary, but I like this."

"They want us to be safe, Roger. And this time They want us to tell everybody what happened."

"Okay. But can't we stay here for awhile longer? It feels so...good." The warm rain is the nicest sensation I've ever had. Jesse looks back toward the sky. Like he's asking.

"Yeah," he says, looking back at me, "but not too much longer. The fire department's gonna come and get us. And then we have to start telling people."

I rub the leftover smudgy ash from my face. I don't want this rain to ever stop, it feels so good. "What if nobody believes you?" I ask.

"Then I'll just have to keep telling them until they do, I guess. Jesus and Mary said I have to." He hesitates for a moment. "*We* have to."

I nod. Nobody's going to believe us, but if that's what they say we have to do, then that's what we have to do. Besides, I know this is all a dream, so who cares? I'll agree to anything, as long as they let me stay in the dream and this rain a little longer.

I hear a noise and turn just in time to see the end of a huge ladder punch through the cylinder's safe curtain, suddenly the rain and clear air are gone, and I smell smoke and feel nearby heat. I'm not safe and relaxed anymore, and the helmeted head of a fireman appears at the top of the ladder, he grabs me with rough-gloved hands and pulls me from the perch.

I'm awake now, the dream is over, and I'm scared but I'm so filled with smoke and so dizzy that I don't think I'll last much longer, the fireman carries me down the ladder, I don't want to be awake, another ladder appears and Jesse is yanked to safety.

We've been saved, but all I can think about is how much I miss the dream and the soft, warm rain…

"Que pasa contigo? Como pudiste ser tan pendejo? Te podian haber matado!" Jesse's dad is yelling at him as the emergency room doctor finishes checking us over. Jesse's mom and his big brother Mando stand quietly behind Mr. Montoya. When Jesse's dad gets mad, everybody shuts up and waits for him to say what he needs to say. He's usually pretty nice; it's just not a good idea to upset him.

Jesse's putting his T-shirt back on while the doctor listens to my lungs. I watch Jesse closely as his father yells at him. Jesse is calm. A small smile creases his dark, round face, which makes his dad even angrier. Jesse's mom dabs little tears away. I can't imagine her ever being mad. She's nice and friendly and loves everybody, especially her kids, no matter how stupid they are.

"Lungs sound fine," says the bald-headed doctor. He smiles at me like I'm supposed to be reassured. I pretend that's good news, but I already knew I was fine. Once I finished coughing up a bunch of ashy snot and puked again everything was okay. Mom and Dad stand at the side of the examining table. They haven't said much to me yet, but I've got a feeling I'm in for a yelling session like Jesse's getting right now.

"Thanks, Doc," Dad says, in his best man-to-man voice. "These kids, they're always getting into something." He laughs a fake laugh and tousles my hair a little too roughly.

I'm a dead man.

The doctor tells them to let me take it easy for a few days, that I've had a bad time, and then he's off to tend to other more important problems. Dad grabs my shoulder and steers me out of the ER.

"We'll talk on the way home, Roger." His voice is icy.

"I'm so glad you're okay, honey," says Mom. She bursts into tears.

We pass by Jesse and his parents, and Mr. Montoya stops yelling at him long enough to mumble with Dad off to the side of the hallway. Mom and Mrs. Montoya sniffle and commiserate, while Jesse's big brother stands watching, looking cool and scary.

I go over to Jesse. "Sounds like your dad's pretty mad."

He smiles like it doesn't matter. "Yeah. Especially after I told him what really happened."

"About Jesus and Mary?" I whisper.

He nods. "That part made him *really* mad. I don't think he believes me." Jesse just smiles. "But he will. They said it might be hard to convince people."

"What's he gonna do?"

"Yell some more. You tell your mom and dad?"

"About what?"

"The miracle."

"There wasn't any miracle. We climbed up to the top of the tree pile and almost got barbecued."

"But we didn't. You saw the rain."

I feel light-headed again. "What rain?" I whisper.

"I know you saw it, Roger. They saved us to prove Their love for us."

I don't know what to say. That was a dream. I passed out, the smoke got to me, and then I had a dream. He couldn't know what I dreamed.

"I...didn't see anything."

Jesse smiles at me. "Okay. So, you gonna tell your parents?"

"There's nothing to tell!"

Jesse smiles. I'm quickly getting sick of the smile. The way he looks at me gives me the creeps. It's like he can read my mind.

"Hey, they talk to you, not me," I mumble. I think he's crazy but I still feel like Judas.

"Jesus and Mary said you're part of it. There's no miracles without you."

"There's no miracles anyway!"

Great. According to crazy Jesse, Jesus *and* Mary know my name and they expect me to do things. Why can't I just be a normal kid in grammar school?

"You're gonna tell them, aren't you, Roger?" he asks, more insistently. I look into his eyes. The smile slowly fades, and his eyes become blacker and harder. "You're gonna tell your parents," he says, and this time it's not a question.

I nod. I have to. Jesse's my best friend, and even if I don't believe him, sometimes you have to do stuff for your best friend.

Dad finishes talking with Mr. Montoya and he and Mom whisk me off down the echoing, antiseptic hallway to the parking lot. As we go outside I hear Jesse's dad yelling, "Jesus don't talk to little *pendejos*!"

I don't think he believes what Jesse's telling him.

"Jesus Christ!"

"Don't swear, dear," Mom soothes. Dad's driving us home from the hospital and I've just told him. I guess he's not convinced. It's okay, neither am I.

"Roger's been through a trauma, Patrick. He's still frightened. Aren't you, honey?"

"Yeah. I guess."

"But he's saying the Jesus and Mary talk to him, for Christ's sake! That's gotta be some kind of sin!"

"They don't talk to me, Jesse says they talk to him."

"Jesus...." Dad shakes his head so hard I'm afraid he's going to hurt himself.

We drive home from the hospital in our blue, '56 Ford. It's noisy and bumpy, but it's the only car we've had since I've been alive and it feels like home. Mom looks back at me, forcing a smile and trying to understand what's wrong with her little boy. Dad throws angry glances at me in the rearview mirror. I feel like I'm shrinking under their eyes as the giant back seat swallows me up.

Mom's fake smile wobbles. "You're just tense, honey."

"Mom," I say in my best "don't talk to me like I'm a two-year-old" voice, "I'm not saying I believe this stuff. Jesse's the one who says he does."

"I've never liked that kid," Dad says. "Ever since that fight you had with him. Damned lemon picker."

"I started the fight, Dad," I say, "and don't call him names. He's my best friend." *Even if he is crazy*, I want to add, but don't.

"So, Jesse talks to Jesus and the Blessed Virgin. What do they tell him?"

Mom's talking down to me, but I decide to go ahead and tell them everything Jesse claims: the stabbed crucifix, Monsignor's stroke, the rain today.

Mom's smile melts and her lips begin to quiver. I think she's going to cry again.

Dad goes nuts.

"It's all that trash you kids watch on TV, it's putting sick garbage into your head, all those monster movies and God knows what else. That's it, no more TV! From now on you spend your time reading or doing homework or helping me build the rec room!"

Mom stares at me like I'm covered with snot. "Crucifix, blood, Monsignor's stroke...Roger, my God, what are you talking about? It's evil!"

"Mom, it's what Jesse says, I didn't say I believe it!" I think Jesse's crazy, but it makes me mad they think he's crazy. "Besides, miracles happen sometimes. I know you believe in them."

"Of course I believe in miracles, but those are church miracles like Fatima and Lourdes, and they don't happen anymore. Miracles are always a long time ago." She sniffles and snorts and keeps staring at me like I'm a stranger. I could kill Jesse. Telling them was a waste of time and all it's going to do is get me in trouble and make them think I'm nuts, too.

Mom turns back to Dad. "Maybe he needs to talk to a child psychologist or something."

"He doesn't need a damn shrink, he's just a knucklehead kid with a wild imagination. He spends too much time watching the idiot box and too much time with that damn taco bender."

I want to punch him. Dad knows Jesse's name. He's just being mean because he's mad. Whenever he gets mad and there's Mexicans involved he starts calling them names.

"Patrick...." Mom warns. She knows he's gone too far. He grumbles but doesn't say anything else. Mom turns back to me and tries to smile again. "Do you feel okay, honey?"

"Yes."

"You won't say anything more about this miracle nonsense, will you?"

I hesitate. Of course I don't want to say anymore about it; it makes me look stupid. But Jesse asked me. I'm torn. Right now my mother is looking me in the eye and telling me to keep quiet. If there's one thing the nuns have beaten into us over the years, it's honor thy father and thy mother. I feel bad for Mom. Her eyes are red from tears and worry, and her shaky smile isn't going to last much longer. Forget Jesse. I decide to follow the commandments.

"Okay. I won't say anything."

She breathes a huge sigh of relief. I'm relieved, too. I'll tell Jesse I had to follow the commandments, not his nutty dreams. Jesse can do what he has to do. Just leave me out of it. And Jesus and Mary can find somebody else to help Jesse. I quit.

"And stay out of bulldozed orange trees, for Christ's sake," Dad says, "you're old enough to know better than that. Climbing around in a burning pile...."

"It wasn't burning when we climbed it!"

"The firemen said some embers must've blown over from another pile and started it, Patrick. It wasn't the children's fault."

"It was still damned stupid, if you ask me."

We turn onto Mountain Avenue and head for home. We go by the bulldozed orchard and the smoldering piles of burned orange trees. Dad has to slow down because there are dozens of cars parked along the street, and I see lots of people walking out into the vacant lot. There's a huge group of people standing in front of the tree pile me and Jesse climbed. The firemen put out the fire when they rescued us, so the pile is scorched but still there.

"What the hell?" Dad says. He slows, then pulls over and stops. The people walking out in the field are mostly Mexicans—Mexican ladies. They wear mantillas and some carry rosaries. "What in the hell?" Dad says again, but his voice trails off into a whisper and he pales.

"What is it, Patrick?" Mom asks, but Dad doesn't answer. He opens the car door and stands, staring open-mouthed at the orange tree pile. Mom gets out of the car, and so do I. Several Mexican ladies brush past us, and one turns and acts like she recognizes me and gets all wide-eyed. She starts chattering excitedly in Spanish to the other ladies, and they all drop to their knees and make signs of the cross. I think they're either praying to me or for me. Either way, I don't know whether to laugh or to run. Mom is absolutely horrified. "My God, what—"

Dad gently touches her elbow and points at the tree pile. Mom looks up at it and so do I, and then we both understand.

Dozens of people are kneeling in front of the charred pile, praying and fingering their rosaries. The sides of the pile are burned, just like I remembered from being up on the top. But down the middle and along the upper sides the pile is untouched. The leaves are as green and healthy-looking as they were before the trees were bulldozed. They stand out against the burned part of the pile as if they're still growing.

The unburned leaves are shaped like a crucifix.

A huge, green, perfect crucifix. If somebody had spent weeks carefully burning away the leaves around the edge they couldn't have made it more precise.

Oh boy. The secret's out.

"Jesus...." whispers Dad. I've heard him say "Jesus" more in the last half hour than in the last year.

Mom starts to cry.

The kneeling Mexican ladies reach out to touch me like I'm one of the Beatles; they have a scary, awed look in their eyes, a look of hunger—it's as if they want pieces of me to hang by their Our Lady of Guadalupe statues in their living rooms. It scares me, and I back away from them. They mumble prayers in Spanish.

I look between the Mexican ladies and the crucifix tree pile and my frightened parents and all the people milling around and kneeling and praying and I panic. I don't want to be part of this anymore.

I turn and run away; my parents shout after me but I don't stop. I brush past newly arriving faithful pilgrims and sprint down the street, and I don't stop running until I get home. I lock the door and collapse on my bed, crying and scared and yelling at Jesus and Mary that it's not fair to make me go through this, especially since I don't believe in it.

I stay home from school for the next few days, and the fear slowly fades. Mom and Dad have been strangely quiet; even Mary Frances hasn't given me a hard time. She had a date with Freddie Montgomery last night, and Freddie treated me like I was something special. He was friendly and went out of his way to talk to me. I get the feeling people aren't sure if I'm part of a miracle or just a disturbed kid. Either way, everybody's being really nice.

Rhonda Fairly called and said everybody at school missed Jesse and me and couldn't wait until we came back. Jesse's parents are keeping him home, too. I want to talk to him, to see what he thinks about all this, but my parents won't let me call. I tried to sneak a call to his house anyway, but Mrs. Montoya said it would be better if we didn't talk until things settle down and we go back to school.

The day after the supposed miracle, the green leaf crucifix vanished, and within an hour the leaves were as crispy and dead as the rest of the pile. In spite of a lot of complaints from the holy people who thought the pile should be left alone, the guys in charge of tearing down the orchard were in a hurry to get rid of it and all the praying Mexican ladies on their property, so they burned the pile as fast as they could. People who saw it said they've never seen an orange tree pile burn as fast and as hot as that one did. And the smoke didn't smell as bad as usual—it smelled like fresh orange blossoms.

It's late afternoon and I'm watching *Superman* when the doorbell rings. Mom already gave in on Dad's TV ban, as long as I only watch it during the day and don't tell Dad. I quickly turn off the TV, even though it's getting to a good part where Superman is getting sick from Kryptonite hidden in a drainpipe. I grab a religion book and pretend to read it.

Mom answers the door. I hear voices, but I don't pay much attention. People have been ringing the doorbell and bringing food over ever since the tree pile fire. There was an article in the local paper about the fire and the leaf crucifix, although they said they thought the crucifix was just a coincidence, probably from the firemen spraying water to put out the fire. For some reason people who read about it seem to think I'm not getting fed, so they bring covered dishes to our house.

Adults are very strange.

Mom walks into the living room, trailed by Father Quinn. Oh no.

"Roger, Father Quinn came by to see how you're doing. Isn't that nice?"

I nod, trying not to look too dismayed. I don't like having religious people in the house. Ever since Sister Mary Annunciata dropped by to threaten me, I prefer my dressed-in-black holy monsters to be on the altar or in front of a classroom—not in my house.

"So, how are you feeling, Roger?" Father Quinn asks.

"Okay," I say, hoping that's enough and he'll go away. Father Quinn is the replacement for Monsignor since Monsignor's stroke left him so sick. Father Quinn is lots younger than Monsignor; I heard Mom say he was her age, which makes him old to me but not grandparent old. I have to admit that he's seemed pretty nice so far, he hasn't terrorized us when we serve mass, he doesn't say weird stuff in confession, and he doesn't growl and yell at us on the playground the way Monsignor did. But he is a priest, and he's in charge of the church and the school...and the nuns. So that makes him the enemy. He's tall and muscular—somebody says he used to play football in college—and he reminds me of James West on *The Wild Wild West.* I've noticed that Mom and a lot of the ladies at church giggle and act stupid when Father Quinn talks to them after mass. I wasn't sure why until I heard Dad complain to Mom on the drive home from church one Sunday that, "You women treat the new padre like he's a movie star or something." Mom just giggled and turned a little red. I think she likes him.

I sit on the couch and wait for Father Quinn to leave. But he doesn't. He stands there, smiling at me like I'm his best friend and he's waiting for an invitation to come in and watch cartoons. His eyes bother me, and I look away.

"Well. I'll let you two talk then," says Mom, and before I can object she's gone. I'm alone in the room with a priest and I don't like it.

"Okay if I sit down?" he asks, and I nod. I have no choice. I look up as he walks over. He moves like the football players I've seen at Rio Linda—loose yet strong, sure of himself and sure of the fact that a scrawny kid like me is no threat to him. He sits on the couch next to me and I wait for him to do or say something. I'm not going to help him by being friendly.

"You think you're ready to come back to school?"

"Yeah. I was never not ready."

Father Quinn smiles. "True. I guess staying home wasn't your idea, was it?"

I retreat into a pout and shrug.

"What happened to you and Jesse Montoya was a frightening thing. Fire's so...well, it's bad. I used to work in a hospital when I was in the seminary, I saw what fire can do. Must've been pretty scary."

"It was."

"Until the miracle?" he prods. I decide this is going to be bad. Father Quinn sighs loudly, like he's suddenly tired or bored. "Why don't you tell me about the miracle."

"Have you talked to Jesse?"

He ignores my question. "Tell me about the miracle, Roger."

I hesitate. Should I clam up, just play stupid and hope he goes away? Or should I do what Jesse wants and tell him? Jesse's probably already told him all the junk about Jesus and Mary anyway. As much as I want to, I can't lie to a priest. That's got to be about as big a sin as there is.

"We were on top of the pile," I begin, hoping I'm not making a huge mistake, "and Jesse went into one of his miracle spells—"

"What's a miracle spell?"

"He gets all dreamy, kind of, you can't talk to him because he says he's talking to Jesus and Mary."

"You can hear this?"

"No. But he stares off into nothing and he says he can hear them. So anyway, we're on top of the pile and he goes into a miracle spell, and then I smell the smoke and see the pile's burning and I try to get him to come back but he won't and I'm really scared that we're gonna burn up or something." I'm getting scared all over again telling him about it.

"Did you faint? Or get dizzy and confused or forget where you were?"

"Yeah. I think so. Then I had a weird dream about rain." I don't tell him about Jesse being in the dream, or that Jesse knew what I was dreaming. I still haven't figured that out myself.

"Rain, huh? Probably the water from the firemen's hoses. I'll bet you were panicked, overcome by the smoke, strange things happen to your mind when you're scared."

I hadn't thought of that. Sure, the rain dream had to be water from the firemen. It makes sense. But how did Jesse know what I dreamed? I put it out of my mind.

"Whatever," I say. "You should talk to Jesse. He's the one who talks to

Jesus and Mary. He says they want him to tell everybody about the miracles and stuff."

"Miracles? There've been others?"

I guess he hasn't talked to Jesse yet. "Yeah, there's others. That's what Jesse says." I tell him about the stabbed crucifix and Monsignor O'Callahan's stroke. He looks worried. Maybe he's afraid Mary's statue might zap him, too.

After I finish, Father Quinn sits quietly and stares at the floor. I suppose he's thinking, but I wish he'd say something. He finally looks up and now he's dead serious.

"Some people say you and Jesse started that fire yourselves, that you put some gas or something on the trees to make the crucifix shape."

"We didn't!—" I start to object, but he holds up his hand.

"And other people think what happened to you guys was really a miracle. That you and Jesse are chosen by God. My problem is that everybody's coming to me for the truth. And I don't know what to tell them. Can you help me out, Roger?"

I realize that Father Quinn is just as confused and scared as I am. He may be big and strong and look like James West on TV, but inside he's puzzled and I think he's afraid of Jesse and me and I think he's afraid of miracles.

"Maybe you and Jesse have vivid imaginations, maybe you guys got each other all worked up and you thought it might be fun to fool people into thinking a miracle happened," he offers helpfully.

"I don't know what happened, Father Quinn. I don't think there was any miracle, but I know we didn't do anything wrong. I don't know why the cross showed up on the trees and I don't know why Jesse thinks he can talk to Jesus and Mary. But I can't help it if some people want to believe in this stuff. It's not my fault. You need to talk to Jesse. He's the one who believes in miracles."

Father Quinn rubs his hands through his thick brown hair. "I'd like to think that miracles happen in our smoggy little parish, Roger. I'd like to think that in the suburbs Jesus and Mary could appear to a Catholic school kid and do miracles and give messages. I'd like to believe all that, I truly would. But I need more to go on than these stories. Because what it sounds like to me is a couple of buddies telling lies to get attention."

I'm not going to get anywhere with this guy, so I don't bother. "I don't know what else to say. You need to talk to Jesse." I pick up the religion book and pretend to read. Father Quinn gives up, stands slowly, and walks to the door. He stops by a shelf of Mom's cheap ceramic knick-knacks hanging on the wall.

"You can talk to me any time, Roger."

"Okay."

He turns to leave and is halfway out the door when it occurs to me to ask him a question.

"Do you believe in miracles, Father Quinn?"

The strangest thing happens. He looks smaller and scared. His movie star good looks slowly collapse into wrinkles and frowns. He begins to say something, then stops. I watch and wait for his answer.

"I don't know what I believe, Roger," says Father Quinn, and then he turns and leaves without another word.

Chapter Six

"HEY, MIRACLE BOYS!" somebody yells across the playground. Jesse's eating a banana and acts like he doesn't hear the taunt. We're on a bench near the playground fence, finishing our lunches. "C'MON, MAKE A MIRACLE!" somebody else yells, laughing. I lose my appetite for my stale Fritos. I toss the bag back in my lunchbox and close the lid on the box's sour-smelling interior. Mom needs to wash it; I must've spilled some milk inside.

"I hate this," I say, as I stand and gaze through the chain link fence to the freedom outside. "Don't you?"

Jesse shrugs. "They said it would be hard to convince people. They said we'd just have to keep trying."

I look down at him with annoyance. He calmly eats his banana. Nothing seems to bother him anymore; he's got this unnatural calm that's bugging me and bugging everybody else in school.

When we first came back after the fire, everybody was excited to see us and wanted to hear what happened. We were heroes for awhile, and we liked all the attention. Even some of the nuns were impressed; well, maybe not impressed, but at least friendly. Kids crowded around asking questions, and everybody seemed to believe Jesse.

But then Jesse pushed too hard. He started talking about "Jesus and Mary" this and "Jesus and Mary" that and pretty soon the other kids at school got sick of hearing it. The nuns began to get mad, especially when Jesse would talk about having conversations with the Son of God, and they started telling him to stop, and then they started smacking him with rulers to *make* him stop. Our teacher this year, Sister Mary Victor, lost her patience with what she called his "sacrilege" and started looking for reasons to whack him with her yardstick.

Our time as celebrities was short.

Rhonda Fairly is still friendly, but she doesn't mention the miracle anymore, and I don't bring it up. But even with her there's a weird feeling, and I wonder if she thinks this whole thing was a made-up lie to get attention. Worse, I wonder if she thinks I'm crazy. At least she still talks to me.

Jesse swallows the last bite of his banana and tosses the peel over the fence. "Wanna play catch or something?" he asks. Since we've been shunned, our presence in dodgeball games isn't welcomed anymore.

"Nah." I gaze toward hazy Mount San Antonio. I wish school was out for the summer. We need to get away for awhile. Just to be a wise guy, I ask, "When's there gonna be another miracle, Jesse? I'm getting bored."

"Not for a long time. Jesus and Mary said They're not even gonna talk to me in dreams for awhile."

"Oh yeah?" I'm not sure why, but this news bothers me. I don't believe Jesse talks to Jesus and Mary, but his crazy stories make life interesting.

"They want to test our faith."

"How come they need to give us a test? Everybody we know already thinks we're stupid and crazy, haven't we proved that we've got faith?"

"Jesus said faith is hard. Sometimes it even hurts. He told me back in the olden days people got killed for their faith, so if we have to be by ourselves at lunch and recess and not play dodgeball, I guess we don't really have it so bad."

I don't bother to argue. It doesn't make much sense, but then, none of Jesse's miracle vision stuff does.

I'm tired of talking. We need to *do* something. "Okay, let's play catch," I say, and I run over to the ball bag and dig out a squishy football. We stay off in our corner of the playground and toss it back and forth, the throws getting longer and longer. Jesse's strong and can throw it a long way; I'm uncoordinated and my throws are weak and wobbly. I'm at the limit of my throwing range, so we start to punt it to each other. Jesse boots it high and long, and it sails over my head and rolls near the convent. I run to get it, and just as I round a juniper hedge by the side of the cracked stucco building I come face to face with Sister Mary Annunciata.

Sister Mary Annunciata still teaches first grade, and from what I hear she still terrorizes little kids for Christ. I've been able to avoid her most of the time, and the few times we've crossed paths she's glared threateningly and I've been able to scurry away unharmed. Whenever I see her I still get that sick feeling in my stomach, a feeling of dread and fear and humiliation—and I still want to get even with her.

The football slowly wobbles to stillness at the toes of her scuffed, black shoes. I stare at the football, afraid to look at her. The gentle lunchtime breeze rustles her shiny black habit. If I'm smart I'll turn and run away, and I'm about to do that, but—

No. I won't. I'm bigger now, she can't hurt me, and I want my football back. I'm about to say, "May I please pick up my football, Sister Mary Annunciata," when I hear a gaspy/wet snort. It's disgusting, like the sound a dog makes when it's barfing. I look up, surprised that even someone as awful as Sister Mary Annunciata can make a sound like that, when I realize she didn't make the sound. It came from behind her, and I lean to my right and look past her fat, billowing habit.

Monsignor O'Callahan sits in a wheelchair, staring at me through droopy eyelids with wet, milky eyes. He snorts again and creamy gray goo dribbles from the paralyzed side of his mouth. Unseen claws pull the left side of his face toward the ground, while the right side looks normal. His lower lip flips outward, the moist, pink flesh flabby and soft. The drool that dangles from the dead lip is slowly filling a little glistening pool on his lap. He looks much thinner now, his hair sparser, his skin gray. It's hard to imagine that he ever roared sermons during mass or yelled at us on the playground. I stare at him, fascinated.

He's almost horrible enough to be in a monster movie.

I'm jolted back into attention when Sister Mary Annunciata slams a meaty hand on my shoulder and squeezes hard enough to make me cry out in pain. She pulls me close to her and leans into my face.

"Hello, Roger."

"*Hi*," I squeak.

She squeezes harder. "Seen any miracles lately?"

"No, Sister!"

"You've lied about everything, haven't you, Roger?"

It's time for me to make a choice. I can go along with her, do and say whatever it takes to get away from her and survive, or I can be a smart-ass and pop off to her. I look at her round, splotchy face. Her eyes are bloodshot and wide. She has the same horrible medicine breath I remember from first grade. She scares me to death, but even though she does, I find strength in my fear and I do what Jesus—or at least Jesse—would want.

"Jesse Montoya says he talks to Jesus and Mary, Sister Mary Annunciata."

I say it calmly and with certainty. I don't believe in Jesse, but I don't have a problem telling Sister Mary Annunciata what he says. If it makes her mad, too bad. And I feel good about it.

Until she slaps me hard across the face.

"Blasphemous little liar! Pray for forgiveness!" She slams my shoulders with both her hands and forces me to the asphalt. Monsignor O'Callahan watches and groans, but I'm not sure if he wants her to stop or he's encouraging her to continue.

I refuse to let her get the best of me, and I try to get up, but she keeps forcing me down. "Repent your sins before God almighty, Roger Donnelly, repent your lies or Satan will drag your soul to hell!" She holds me down and I'm about ready to bite her ankle when I hear Jesse's calm voice.

"Leave Roger alone, Sister."

Sister Mary Annunciata, startled, looks up. Jesse's standing a few feet away, a vague half-smile creasing his round, brown face. I scramble away from horrifying nun-creature. They should use her as a monster on *The Outer Limits*.

Sister Mary Annunciata is silent for a moment, then she grins at Jesse. It's not a friendly grin. "Well, it's the other miracle boy. You and your friend Roger need to start telling the truth, Jesse Montoya."

"We have been, Sister. Jesus and the Blessed Virgin told me to tell everybody about the miracles, so that's what me and Roger are doing." Well, not really. I haven't been saying much to anybody about Jesse's delusions, but now's not the time to argue about it.

She glares at him, but she doesn't make a move to touch him. It makes me mad. She has no problem using me as a human punching bag, but she respects Jesse enough to hate him from a distance.

"You're evil," she says, her smile fading. "Neither of you belong in a Catholic school. If Monsignor still ran this place you'd both be gone."

Monsignor groans loudly. He sounds like Frankenstein. Jesse steps closer and looks at Monsignor curiously.

"The Virgin smote you, Monsignor. When you got sick at mass that day. I looked it up in the dictionary, it means to strike down; the Blessed Virgin struck you down. Did you do something to make her mad?"

Monsignor roars to life, the muscles that still work propel him out of the wheelchair and he hits the asphalt with a gravelly *thud*! Sister Mary Annunciata rushes to him, he flails, groaning and gagging in his best Frankenstein imitation, and as he whips his head wet tinsel drool strands fling into the sky.

Jesse calmly walks over, picks up the football, and leaves Sister Mary Annunciata struggling to get Monsignor O'Callahan back into his wheelchair. I watch the whole thing, terrified; I can't believe any of this is happening. Why am I involved with these people? My life isn't supposed to be this complicated.

Jesse brushes by me, tossing the football from hand to hand. "C'mon, let's play some more catch." He wanders away, oblivious to the two holy people who, if they had the chance, would love to kill him. I turn and run after him, leaving Sister and Monsignor wrestling on the asphalt.

I hope this is my last dealing with Sister Mary Annunciata and Monsignor O'Callahan; deep down inside I know it's not.

It's almost Easter, and Jesse's orange tree cross miracle has been forgotten by most people. A few old Mexican ladies still treat Jesse like he's a direct link to God, and some of the nuns still grumble and yell at us, but for the most part, our lives have gotten back to normal.

Jesse's parents—especially his dad—won't let him talk about Jesus and Mary or miracles, but I don't think it bothers Jesse all that much. Jesse says the dreams have stopped, and he's lost interest and gotten back to being a normal kid. I think maybe he's decided that making up stories about miracles and talking to Jesus and Mary isn't as much fun as it used to be. People have stopped paying attention. I wonder now if the cross on the trees was something Jesse set up ahead of time, like Father Quinn suggested. I don't believe in any of this stuff, and I can't see how that cross could've ended up there unless Jesse went ahead of time and did something to the trees. It's a bad thing when you don't trust your best friend, but I can't help it.

My family never mentions the miracle stuff. I think the idea of their kid being involved with miracles scared them, and they didn't know what to believe, so they figured it was best to ignore the whole thing. My family's good at ignoring. It was okay with me, though, since Jesse was the preacher and I didn't believe in it anyway. But I did notice a change in the way they treated me. It was like I had suddenly gotten older. They talked to me more, and they treated me like I was something other than just a stupid kid. Respect would be too strong a word, but they seemed to treat me with more consideration. Sometimes I even notice Mary Frances giving me odd looks, like she's trying to read my mind and figure out what's different about me. She's wasting her time. Since things have gotten back to normal, I'm just another kid who watches monster movies, reads comic books, and rides his bike around. I don't think my family realizes that yet.

I help Dad every night and every weekend with the rec room. He's really serious about it—I think it might be one project he'll actually finish. So far we've dug out the area where they're going to pour the slab, and once that's done, he says we can start framing. I kind of hate having to help him, but I am learning how things are built—even if it is from Dad, who has to get every home improvement book in the library to figure out how to do the simplest thing.

"Yep, Rog," he says as we dig, "we're having a great time doing this together, aren't we?"

He's in one of his "I love having a son" moods. "Yeah, Dad," I gasp, trying to lift a big shovel full of rocky dirt.

"You know," he says, lowering his voice, "I could never get your sister to do something like this."

"She's a girl." It makes perfect sense to me. "Girls don't do stuff like this." *They're too smart,* I think.

Dad leans against his shovel and wipes sweat off his forehead. I look at him as he gazes at the almost-finished hole we've dug. I smile. He's looking at the ragged backyard pit with such pride and joy that I can't help but love him. It's the essence of Dad—goofy pride in stupid things.

As I continue to shovel and Dad admires his hole, I notice for the first time that he's changing. Or maybe he's always been changing but I've never paid attention. He looks older. Gray hair streaks his temples and things are getting a little sparse up top. His chin is slowly sagging, and the body I've always thought of as strong and lean is getting thicker. Flab pushes against his belt. The years of gobbling up stale Fritos and Lays potato chips are starting to take their toll.

For the first time ever I realize that my dad is a living, breathing person. That may sound strange, but before he's just been...DAD. The guy who's always there, never-changing, the guy who brings home money and makes me do things I don't want to do and sometimes smacks me when I have it coming. But I've never thought of him as being a real person, somebody who gets scared, or happy, or sick. Or somebody who's going to die someday.

The realization that Dad's not just Dad but also a person surprises me so much that I stop shoveling. My eyes fill with tears and I can't make them stop. Dad stops admiring the hole and looks at me.

"What's wrong?"

"I hurt my elbow."

"Take a break. Gotta keep you healthy, Rog. We've got a long way to go on this baby."

I nod and turn away so he won't see the tears leak from my eyes. I pretend to cough and roughly rub my wet cheeks dry, then massage my elbow and pretend like it hurts.

I feel like an idiot.

"Hey, I didn't think Irishmen were smart enough to dig a hole without Italian supervision!" a big, boomy voice yells.

Dad and I turn and see our neighbor Joe Fanucci hanging over the block wall. As usual a huge, dirty grin covers his face.

Everything about Joe is big. He's a truck driver like Dad, but instead of delivering feather-light chip boxes, Joe delivers furniture. Joe has huge biceps and shoulders, and even the veins that run through his wrists and forearms are ropy and strong. His head is anvil-shaped and topped with a mass of curly black hair. Mom teases Dad sometimes, saying that Joe's a "real man". Dad laughs, but I think he wishes he was just a little bit more like Joe.

"Know what sound an Italian helicopter makes?" Dad asks, his voice deeper than usual. Whenever Dad talks to Joe he lowers his voice and sucks in his gut.

"Yeah, yeah, tell me, you dumb mick." Joe's the only person I know who can get away with making fun of Dad's Irishness.

"Wop, wop, wop."

Joe throws his big head back and hoots; it echoes through the neighborhood. Joe loves being alive, and no matter what he's always laughing and having fun. Mom says it's because he drinks a lot, but Dad says it's because he's a big, dumb, happy wop.

"Good one, Pat," he says when he finally stops laughing, "Gotta tell Shirley that, she'll love it." Shirley is Joe's wife. She's a nice little lady who's as tiny and quiet as Joe is burly and loud. "The old man working you pretty hard, Rog?" he asks. The thing I like about Joe is that he always notices me and takes the time to talk to me like an adult. Most grown-ups can't be bothered. Joe's like a cool uncle—an adult you can call by his first name and not have to worry about him pulling parent rank on you.

"Yeah, Joe. I'm doing most of the work, though." They both laugh at that, and it makes me feel good, like I'm one of the guys.

Joe and Dad shoot the breeze while I continue to dig at the edges of the hole. A warm wind whips up dust, and as it rustles and swirls around me, I realize I'm not the same anymore. I'm starting to feel differently about things, like the strange, sentimental moment when I began to cry thinking about Dad. Maybe that's what happens when you get older.

Lately I've been feeling like I'm part of the world around me, like I might have a reason to be here. I'm beginning to notice things—things about people. I wonder if I'm weird, or if every kid goes through this? I'll probably never know, because it's not the kind of thing you talk about with your friends during recess.

I keep digging as the wind whips harder, and Dad and Joe continue to laugh and talk. Even though I'm digging rocky ground for Dad's stupid rec room, right now I don't want this feeling to stop. I'm outside being soothed by the warm beginnings of a Santa Ana, accepted by a pair of pretty neat grown-up guys—even if one of them is my own dad—and I feel secure and safe.

I'm happy.

"'*Saint Perpetua and Saint Felicity.*'"

"'*Pray for us.*'"

"'*Saint Basil.*'"

"'*Pray for us.*'"

It's Holy Saturday, and Jesse and me—for the first time since Monsignor's stroke—are serving a mass together. Holy Saturday's service is at night, and it takes forever. There are a million readings, and they chant the "'*Pray for us's*'" to a bunch of strange-named saints. We have to keep lighting up the incense for Father Quinn so he can shake smoke over everything in sight, and there's a bunch of stuff he does that doesn't usually happen at regular masses. Holy Saturday is the Catholic church version of a Saturday in the suburbs: chores get done. They baptize and confirm new converts, they bless the holy water for the upcoming year, they break in the great big candle they use at baptisms—they do lots of housekeeping stuff. Although Holy Saturday takes forever and the readings get boring, at least it's different from regular masses. That's probably what gets me the most about going to mass: it's always the same. Same beginning, same middle, same end. The sermon is the only thing that changes, and who listens to that?

Last week, Father Quinn pulled Jesse and me out of a basketball game at lunchtime. We thought we were in big trouble, since Father Quinn has ignored us since the miracle stuff faded away, and I had a brief, horrible moment of gut-wrenching horror that he was bringing us to Sister Mary Annunciata and Monsignor O'Callahan. But no, Sister Mary Annunciata was off near the rectory, reading the bible to Monsignor O'Callahan. She always rolls Monsignor O'Callahan out at lunchtime to let him bake in the sun, and while he sits and drools she reads to him.

Father Quinn guided us over to a lunch bench and sat down. "C'mon, don't stand there and stare at me like I'm gonna kill you, sit down."

We sat, not sure what was coming. Even Jesse's usual calm seemed a little shaky. Since his Jesus and Mary delusions had gone away, he wasn't quite as sure of himself.

"I'm thinking about letting you two serve mass again," said Father Quinn.

Jesse and I exchanged surprised glances. "But I need to know something first."

"What, Father?" asked Jesse.

"I need to know I can trust you to not disrupt things." We said nothing. "You know what I mean," he added.

"Jesus and Mary haven't talked—" Jesse began.

Father Quinn held up his hand. "I don't even want to hear about that. If I'm going to let you guys rejoin all the activities of your class, I have to know I'm not making a mistake. There are people who don't want you two in this school anymore, let alone serving mass. But I'm willing to take a chance. Can I trust you?"

Jesse and I looked at each other. It was up to him. I never claimed Jesus and Mary talked to me.

"Okay," Jesse finally said. I nodded along.

"Good," said Father Quinn, relieved. "I'd like you to serve Holy Saturday."

And so now we're on the altar again, waiting for the "'*Pray for us's*'" to end. The sickeningly sweet incense is beginning to make me queasy. It smells like burning dirty socks soaked in maple syrup. I blink my eyes, trying to clear them of the thick, stinging smoke. Jesse kneels next to me at the side of the altar. He's watching Father Quinn attentively, being a good altar boy.

The "'*Pray for us's*'" end, and we finally get to the regular part of the mass—the consecration. Father Quinn's going to turn bread and wine into the body and blood of Jesus, and we get to help. We are at the hand-washing ritual, and I'm holding the bowl and Jesse has the crystal jar with water. Father puts his hands over the bowl, and Jesse carefully pours a little stream of water over Father Quinn's fingers. We've done this a bunch of times, it's no big deal. Except this time, I notice a swirl of red in the bowl along with the water. It looks like blood.

At first I assume Father Quinn must have a cut on his fingers, or maybe some wine got into the water, but then I see another red drop splash into the bowl. Father Quinn sees it, too, and we stare into the bowl, confused. Another drop. It swirls and mixes with the water. Father Quinn pulls his hands away from the bowl, and then we see where the blood is coming from.

Jesse's hand. A trickle of bright red blood flows down Jesse's palm and drips into the bowl. Father Quinn leans close to Jesse and whispers, "Are you okay?"

Jesse nods, but as he looks at the blood on his hand I notice he's pale. "I guess so," he whispers back. "I must have a cut or something."

Father Quinn tells him to go back into the vestry, that I can finish the mass alone. Jesse nods and quickly walks off the altar, rubbing his hands.

After the mass is over, Father Quinn and I go back and find Jesse sitting in a battered old chair. He's still dressed in altar boy vestments, and he sits with his knees pulled up to his chest. He stares at the floor.

Father Quinn hurries over to him. "What's wrong?"

Jesse says nothing. He doesn't move, and I begin to think he might be in the miracle zone, but then he finally looks up at us with frightened eyes. He holds out his hands, palms up.

There's a bloody hole in each palm.

"Jesus!" Father Quinn gasps. "Did you do this to yourself?!"

"Uh-uh," Jesse says in a dreamy voice. "It just happened." He straightens out on the chair and looks down at his feet. We follow his glance. There are bloody stains on his Keds high-tops. I'm beginning to understand what's going on, and my eyes immediately go to his chest. Blood seeps through his robe in a small spot on the right side of his chest.

"Stigmata...." Father Quinn whispers in awe.

"What's that, Father?" I ask.

"Stigmata happens sometimes to people around Easter. They get the same wounds as Christ, they just appear. I've always thought it was some kind of hysteria, or a scam. You didn't do this to yourself, tell me the truth, Jesse," Father says sternly.

Jesse sits there, bloodstained, looking helpless. "No, Father. Will it go away?"

Father Quinn is completely bewildered. He looks like I do when I'm caught doing something bad. He finally gathers some composure and stammers, "I don't know what's going to happen. But you can't tell anybody about this. It'll just stir things up, and you don't need that. I don't need that."

Jesse nods and looks down at his bloody palms.

Nobody says anything else.

We're all scared.

Easter comes and goes and I don't hear from Jesse. He doesn't show up at school for a week, and when I call his house his mom says he can't come to the phone, but he's okay, don't worry.

I see Father Quinn around but he avoids me. Yesterday I saw him outside the rectory during recess, and I went over to ask him if he'd heard anything about Jesse, but when he saw me coming he ducked back inside.

I don't think Father Quinn was taught how to deal with people like Jesse when he was learning to be a priest. They know how to do easy stuff like make communion and give out *Hail Marys* at confession, but dealing with miracles and stigmatas, well...

The more I think about all this, the more confused I get. The nuns have told us stories about saints, and of visions and miracles like Fatima and Lourdes, but that stuff happened a long time ago, and the people involved were holy. Okay, so the kids at Fatima were just kids like us, but still, from what the nuns told us, they were holy kids. Not like Jesse and me. I know we're nowhere close. We think about naked ladies, we lie when we need to, I've even stolen candy from the Shopping Basket store a few times. There's no way that either of us is holy enough to be part of anything religious.

But Jesse believes we are.

He thinks we're chosen. Chosen out of everybody. I can't believe in any of it, but I can't explain it, either. It was one thing to shrug off Jesse's fantasies about killer Virgin Mary statues and the orange tree cross, but I saw his bloody palms. I don't understand it, and it scares me. I want some answers. Things don't make any sense to me, and I want explanations.

I'm watching Bugs Bunny when the phone rings. Mom's at the store, Dad's at work, and Mary Frances is out making life miserable for somebody, so I force myself to get off the couch and answer the phone. I'm annoyed because Bugs is getting ready to make Elmer Fudd look stupid again; I love it when Elmer Fudd gets fooled. But now I'm going to miss it because the idiot phone's ringing and it's probably for Mary Frances anyway.

"Hello?"

"Roger," Jesse whispers, "I gotta talk to you, come down to the wash tonight after it gets dark."

"Why?"

"Just be there!" he whispers urgently, and then he hangs up.

I put the phone back in the cradle. It's got to be something holy. I'm worried. There was something in his voice I haven't heard before: the sound of fear.

It looks like I don't get to be a regular kid. Jesse's sucked me back into his world of Jesus and Mary and miracles. I'm not holy, I don't want to be holy, and I don't think he's really holy either. There must be lots of people like Jesse, people who want to be religious, who feel (or imagine) that Jesus and Mary are in their lives. I wish I could change places with them; Jesse needs a friend who wants to be part of his fantasy.

I'm not the guy.

After dinner I tell Mom I'm riding my bike down to the library to look for some books.

"Okay, be careful riding home, it'll be dark," she says as she bustles around the kitchen, cleaning the charred remnants of pot roast off our plates. Dad's in the living room watching the news and reading the paper. One distracts him from the other, and sometimes I think he ends up not getting *any* news because he tries to get too much.

I pedal up Mountain Avenue, toward the dry wash where we ride our bikes and build forts. There's light smog today, just enough to make the fading orange sun reflect softly on the mountains. Sometimes smog makes the world prettier than it really is.

I coast down into the wash and ride along the sandy, junk-strewn bottom. Since the wash almost never has water in it, thick brush grows out through cracks in the dusty concrete. It looks like a big concrete planter box filled with weeds.

I ride up and down the sloped walls of the wash. No Jessie. I ride back to where I started and make up a slalom course to kill time.

The sun goes down and the orange glow fades away; the mountains darken into sharp silhouettes. The warmth leaves with the light, and I'm beginning to get cold as I swoop my stingray down one side of the wash and back up the other. I wish Jesse would show up. It's going to get scary out here if it gets much darker and I'm all alone.

Just as the twilight fades and gives way to darkness, I see Jesse pedaling furiously toward me. I ride up toward him, grinning. Seeing him again makes me feel safe.

"Hi!" I call out as we skid, spraying roostertails of dirty sand.

Jesse hops off his bike. He's winded and looks very serious. "I don't have much time, if my dad finds out I'm gone he'll kill me."

I look at his hands. It's hard to see in the dim light, but the wounds seem to have healed and are now just faint red marks.

"What's wrong?" I ask. I've never seen him so agitated.

"I talked to Them again."

"Jesus and Mary?"

He nods. "Last night in a dream. It was about you."

It feels like the temperature drops twenty degrees. Hairs on the back of my neck tingle. "What about me?" I ask. My voice sounds small and tight.

"They wanted me to warn you, to tell you that your life's gonna change, and that you have to have faith to get through. But They also said that They'll always be there for you, no matter what. All you have to do is ask Them for help, and They'll help you."

"What's gonna change?" I ask. My stomach's fluttering and my head feels spinny.

"I dunno. They didn't tell me. But I think it's important, and maybe it might be scary or something."

I look at Jesse. I lean toward him and look for the truth in his big brown eyes. I don't know why his stupid fantasies bother me. I know his chats with Jesus and Mary are just pretend, his miracles aren't really miracles, the holes in his hands and his feet are some weird psycho thing—none of this stuff is true or real. But tonight, for some reason, his warning scares me. He's gone too far this time.

I study him, and he looks back at me, unflinching.

"So what's gonna happen to me, Jesse?"

"They didn't tell me. They just said you have to be strong, you have to pray when it happens and they'll help you, you have to—"

I'm tired of hearing "I have to's." I'm angry. I don't want to hear any more of his stupid stuff.

"Shut up, Jesse. You're lying and you're crazy!"

"You have to pray, you have to ask Them for help, you have to have faith—"

I lunge at Jesse and knock him to the ground, and I punch him and swear at him and then I feel that white-hot shot of anger I felt before, when I attacked him in the first grade, and I swing wildly and punch him and punch the dirt and scream and I want to kill him because I don't want to be a part of this anymore, and then the white anger disappears.

I'm hunched over Jesse. His face is bloody, and one of his eyes is already swelling shut. He's gasping and coughing, and his one good eye is wide open and locked on mine. I jump up and stand over him; I don't know what to do next. I'm scared and I'm still mad at him and I don't know why, but I'm mad at God, too.

"It's okay, Roger," he whispers as he sits up, rubbing blood off his face. "I forgive you," he says, trying to smile.

His annoying forgiveness makes me even angrier, and I grab my bike, hop on, and ride away. I don't care that I hurt him, and I don't care that he forgives me. I just want to be away from the guy—I don't ever want to see him again, I don't want to hear about his stupid miracles, I don't want to hear about Jesus and Mary, I just want to be left alone.

I ride up out of the wash and onto Mountain Avenue. The cool air is nice, and as I pedal toward home, I begin to calm down. The faster I pedal and the more tired I get, the better I feel.

By the time I've reached my street, I'm almost ready to go back and see if Jesse's okay and apologize for hitting him. I feel guilty now that I let the white-zone temper kick in and I beat him up. He's bigger and stronger than I am, and he could've wiped me out if he wanted to, but he didn't even try to defend himself. I wonder why? Did he know that if he fought back he'd cream me, and he didn't want to hurt me? Or did he feel so guilty about what he knew—

He knew that something bad was ahead for me anyway, so why should he add to it! My momentary calm vanishes and I'm back to being scared and mad. *Stop it!* I yell at myself. It's pretend, make-believe, nothing's going to happen, it's just Jesse being weird.

I stop trying to figure it out. I'm scared, and I know inside there's no reason to be, but I am, so I'll just have to live with it. I'm almost home, and as I ride the last few hundred feet to my house, headlights hit me. As I get closer I see it's our neighbor, Joe Fanucci, coming home from work. He drives an old, beat-up pick-up, as big and burly as he is. I'm almost to my driveway and starting to feel safe now that I'm close to home. But then Joe's pick-up veers across the street. I assume he's pulling into his driveway, and he's gunning the engine to be goofy. I expect to see his big head thrown back as he laughs his big, hooting laugh. I expect him to turn away from me at the last minute, roll down the window and yell some guy thing like, "Hey, Roger-Dodger, where'd you learn how to drive?!" or "I almost lubed my truck with an Irish kid!" Right now I could use a friendly, good-natured joke from my next door neighbor pal.

But his truck keeps coming toward me, and Joe's face isn't laughing or smiling or even looking at me. I expect him to turn and grin but he doesn't. In a split second I see him try to focus on me, but it's like he can't see me, or he can but he doesn't recognize me. He's shaking his head like it's cloudy and confused, and I realize he's not going to swerve away at the last minute and this isn't a joke.

I try to veer out of his path, but he's moving too fast, he's accelerating toward me, and then for one horrible second our eyes meet and he recognizes me and he starts to scream but by then I'm underneath the truck, I hear my bike get squashed by the tires, I roll and my face grinds against asphalt, then up against an oily axle, then back against the asphalt, then against something metallic and dirty and—

I think I'm about to die, and now I know what Jesse was talking about, and if he knew what this was, why didn't he warn me, why didn't he stop me if he knew this was going to happen, why didn't he do something, the pain flashes through me, I taste blood, I smell blood and oil and now the hot muffler sears my face and I roll more, and through it all I hear Joe screaming, "ROGER!" and the truck accelerates and I'm hooked on something underneath the truck and I'm dragged, asphalt rips my flesh, I'm going to die, I know I'm going to die, *please, Jesus and Mary, help me, you promised, help me....*

And then everything goes black.

Part Two

JFK Junior High School
1968-1970

Chapter Seven

As Bushman slugs and punches me, the only thing I can hope is that the pain and humiliation won't make me cry.

I'm trapped in a stall in the boy's bathroom at JFK Junior High School being beat-up by Frankie Bushman. Some of Bushman's friends crowd around the stall door, laughing and hooting as Bushman punches me in the stomach. It feels like he's punching a hole right through me; I can't even catch my breath. If he doesn't stop soon, I'm afraid I might suffocate.

Frankie Bushman has been my personal monster since the first day of seventh grade. He spotted me after I limped off the school bus, and something about me pissed him off. I hadn't met him or spoken to him or even knew he existed until he tripped me and I crashed to the ground.

"Fag!" he taunted. I tried to focus on his face, but the sun was behind him and all I saw was a halo of red hair. "What happened to your face, asshole, walk into a blender?" He and his friends laughed at me and strolled away. I clumsily got up, tried to salvage some dignity, and limped off into my first day of junior high. Kids were laughing and pointing at me. Junior high hadn't started well.

My parents—like many of the parents of kids at OLPS—had decided that the extra expense of Catholic school wasn't worth it once you learned your catechism, so a lot of us ended up going to seventh grade at JFK instead of Father Serra Jr/Sr High. It had been okay with me, enough of my friends—including Jesse—were going to JFK that I wasn't going to be alone. And I was sick of the nuns, of their crazy rules and crazier discipline, and of all the Catholic stuff shoved down our throats day in and day out. *Wear a scapular and you'll go to heaven; it's not too early to be thinking of a vocation to the priesthood; you need to give more money for the pagan babies.* Being a Catholic was as much a part of me as the color of my eyes; I just didn't want to have to be reminded of it every minute of every day.

But even with fellow OLPS refugees at JFK, the prospect of public school was a little frightening. The very words "public school" conjured up something completely alien, a place where people actually believed different things, and where religion wasn't part of the school day. At OLPS, no matter what our differences were, we were united against a common enemy: the nuns. They were the black-and-white monsters of all our dreams. A school where teachers didn't hit you, where they dressed like humans, where *men* actually taught some of the classes, well, it was exotic and different and it sure wasn't Catholic.

It felt good.

Public school wasn't completely unknown to me. Mary Frances had gone through it, but she was so much older than me—and a girl—that her experiences didn't mean much.

What I hadn't expected was that instead of crazed nuns tormenting me every minute of the day, I'd be the official punching bag of a redheaded asshole named Frankie Bushman.

Over time, I've learned bits and pieces about Bushman, but nothing that would explain why he hates me so much. He was a basic kid, he'd moved to my town when he was in the fifth grade, he had a couple of older brothers who were just regular high school guys—they didn't terrorize innocent cripples like me.

Frankie Bushman is one of those people who are mean for no reason. He'll probably grow up to be a murderer, or he'll go into the army and end up in Vietnam where he can torture and kill and get away with it.

But that's all someday; right now he's torturing me and I hope he stops soon. I try to cover my stomach with my hands to stop the punches, but then he hits my face, so my hands move there, then he hits my stomach again.

"Fucking spaz! Meat face! Where's your ear, veggie boy?!" I can live with the insults, I just wish he'd stop hitting me.

He finally does stop, not out of compassion, but because he's tired. He's gasping and can't catch his breath. Beating up Roger Donnelly every day takes a lot out of you.

He looks at me with disgust, like I'm a cockroach, and he and his friends leave me lying in the stall. They wander out of the bathroom, laughing and hooting. I don't move; I'm not sure I *can* move. I wait for my stomach to feel better, and then I slowly sit up. I lean against the stained, dirty toilet and try to shake the cobwebs out of my head. There's no blood from today's beating, so that's a good sign, and I don't think I'll have a fat lip or a black eye, so I'll look more or less normal, which for me isn't all that normal to begin with, but that's another story.

I slowly stand and test my legs. They work. I shuffle to the sink in my normal halting, stiff walk, and rinse my scarred face off with cold water. Cold water feels strange on my face; the heavy scar patches are insulated, and the thin spots where the skin is red and blotchy are hypersensitive, so any face washing is a tingling blend of dull feeling and sharp stabs. It's like the feeling you have when the novocaine starts to wear off after a tooth filling and you can feel your cheek again.

I look into the cracked bathroom mirror and inspect my face for damage. It's depressing. As my run-over-by-a-truck injuries heal, I'm looking even worse. The wide, thick scars on my cheeks and forehead are spreading out, and the blotchy, skinned red spots blaze angrily. A few trial zits are popping up, and they run along the scar edges like white-topped rivets holding down dead skin plates. My hair's longer, and it covers most of the lumpy scars on my scalp, although the patchy fuzz and training whiskers smudging my sideburns will never fill in completely because of the webby scars.

I blink away a drop of water. My left eyelid droops; the plastic surgeons did their best, but the damage was too much for them to fix. I can still see out of it, but I have a hard time blinking, and it's always bloodshot. Bushman's had a good time making fun of my droopy eye.

But I think the worst part of all of it is my ear. One ear is fine; the other is a gnarled stumpy thing, ground down by asphalt and Joe Fanucci's muffler to half the size of a regular ear. I try to hide it, but my hair is thin and no matter how hard I try, my half-ear shows through. I know people look at me and wonder "What happened to that kid?" It's not like I'm a monster, or so gross that people look away and puke, but I look different enough so that I get plenty of weird looks from adults and taunts from kids.

Like Frankie Bushman.

I was in a coma for several weeks after Joe Fanucci ran over me. I remember strange, scary dreams, the kind where you're in a room and all the lights go out, and unseen arms pull you down into dark pits. Or escape dreams, being chased by something creepy and not being able to move fast enough. I remember one dream where Jesus was talking to me, and I got real excited in the dream that at last I was going to get a chance to talk to Him, to find out if Jesse was really crazy. But I soon realized he was talking nonsense, that he looked like Mary Frances's boyfriend Freddie Montgomery, and then he turned into a flying zebra and I was peeing into a trash can. So much for my Jesus vision.

When I finally woke up, I was sore and scabby and scared. They transferred me to the UCLA Medical Center, and I went through a bunch of skin grafts and plastic surgery and physical therapy for my shattered leg. I came home after two months, but I was too much of a mess to go back to school. I slowly healed, and a tutor came to my house so I was able to keep up with my class. It was actually a better deal for me; when you're the only student, you pay more attention and learn better. There isn't the distraction of psycho nuns, recess, or irresistible Rhonda Fairlys.

I missed most of sixth grade. By the time I hobbled back to school in May, there were only a few weeks left. I'd seen most of my classmates at one time or another, either at church or the occasional visit to my house. The nuns made sure everybody made the pilgrimage to see me; I think it was part of their Lenten sacrifice, to go see old crippled Roger. I didn't mind, I liked having company, even if most of them were wary and nervous and either couldn't take their eyes off my scars or avoided looking at me altogether.

Jesse showed up on a rainy Saturday afternoon a few weeks after I came home from UCLA. I was in the living room, trying to do stretching exercises to keep the thickening scars from turning my arms into useless leather stumps, when Mom peeked in and gave me one of her big, stupid grins, the kind she always has when she's got a surprise.

"Guess who's here?" she asked in a high, giggly voice. She'd been acting weird ever since Joe ran over me. I guess she was so glad I survived that she wanted to raise me from babyhood again. I liked being babied as much as the next guy, but since I'd gotten home she'd gone way overboard, fussing endlessly and asking a hundred times a day how I felt.

"I dunno. Who's here?" I said. I'd been drowned with well-meaning visitors, mostly adult friends of my parents, and I was getting tired of being clucked at.

"Jesse!" She stepped aside and Jesse looked in. I felt my spirits soar. I wasn't mad at him anymore, if I ever really was. I was just glad to see him.

"You okay, Roger?" he asked, taking a tentative step into the room.

"Yeah," I shrugged.

"You still mad?"

"Nah."

"I'll leave you two alone," Mom said as she scurried away.

I looked at Jesse for a long moment. Since I came out of the coma I'd been wondering....

"How'd you know something bad would happen to me?"

He shuffled and looked at the floor. "They told me to warn you."

"I don't believe you."

"I know. I wish you did. You been praying?"

Oh boy. Back to the same old stuff. No matter how hard I tried, I couldn't make myself believe Jesus and Mary talked to him. But I couldn't explain how he knew something bad was going to happen to me, either. Maybe it was ESP; I saw a show about that awhile ago.

Anyway, it didn't matter anymore. A truck had squashed me and there was nothing I could do about it. I wasn't mad at Jesse; Joe Fanucci was the bad guy. I decided to drop it and never mention it again.

"*Chiller's* on at three. It's *The Brain That Wouldn't Die*," I said. It was one of our favorite movies, the one where the woman is decapitated and the mad scientist keeps her head alive in a tray.

"Cool!" He turned on the TV and then joined me on the couch. Our friendship was intact as we watched the crabby lady complain about being a bodiless head in a tray.

After that, Jesse came by all the time, and things were like before, except I couldn't ride my bike or go outside much, so we hung around the house and played endless games of Monopoly and Life. Jesse was my connection to the outside world of OLPS, and he made sure I stayed informed. He didn't say anything about visions or miracles, and I didn't ask. I hoped that was all behind us, that we could just be normal guys. I thought back then that I'd heal and everything would be like it was before. What I didn't know was that I'd never really heal, that I'd be stuck with the scars of Joe's drunken mistake forever.

The night Joe ran over me, he'd stopped off for a few beers with some buddies after work. Being Joe, he bought rounds for everybody in sight—including himself—and he was drunk by the time he climbed in his old pick-up.

The cops arrested Joe after he ran over me, and he later pleaded guilty to everything they charged him with. He got off with six months in jail and a bunch of probation and fines. My parents couldn't believe it. They were furious, Dad especially; they wanted him in jail for a lot longer. When I realized I was messed up forever, I felt the same way.

While Joe was in jail, Shirley had to sell their house and move into an apartment; their lives really fell apart. After Joe got out of jail, he tried to get jobs driving trucks, since that was all he knew how to do, but nobody would hire him.

One Friday afternoon about a year after the accident, while my tutor Miss Nye was showing me how to do fractions, the doorbell rang. Dad was out delivering Fritos, and Mom was at the Shopping Basket picking up tuna for dinner. I hobbled to the front door, and there stood Joe Fanucci, thin and weak-looking, his thick hair stringy, his usually cheerful face pasty and afraid. As soon as he saw me, he started crying.

"God, I'm sorry, Roger. I tried to call you, but your folks wouldn't let me talk to you, I guess I can understand, but...Jeez...." He studied my scarred face, and his eyes wandered down to my beat-up arms. He cried harder.

I was embarrassed. Crying was something I didn't know how to handle, especially from a guy I used to think was a cool grown-up.

I looked at him, and I didn't feel anything other than anger. He'd hurt me, almost killed me, and now he was crying at the door. Too bad. I wasn't going to help him feel better.

"I'm okay, I guess," I finally said. I wanted him to go away.

"No, no, I almost killed you, God, I'm so sorry!" He was crying hard, big wet, snotty gasps, and I didn't know what to do. All the crying and begging for forgiveness wasn't going to change anything now.

I stood there and watched Joe weep. He collapsed against the doorjamb, and Miss Nye came to the door. "Roger, are you okay?"

"Yeah. This is Joe, our old neighbor."

Miss Nye, a young, skinny lady who looked like she would've made a good nun, nodded. "Ah, the neighbor." She pulled me back and stepped between Joe and me. "I think you'd better leave, sir." She slowly closed the door, and the last thing I saw was Joe's tear-streaked face and his panicky eyes as he begged for forgiveness.

"Bastard!" Dad spit out at dinner that night when he heard about Joe. "Drunken asshole almost kills my kid and he's got the nerve to come by here."

"Please, Patrick," Mom pleaded. She didn't like mentioning Joe's name; it upset the carefully constructed wall she put up around the family. Mom wanted to pretend everything was normal and okay.

"He's got a lot of nerve," Dad repeated.

"What'd he say?" Mary Frances asked. She was the first one to ask that question.

"He said he was sorry," I said.

"Bastard!" Dad grumbled.

"What'd *you* say?" Mary Frances asked, ignoring Dad.

"Nothing."

"You should've forgiven him," Mary Frances said. "It was an accident."

"It wasn't an accident! He's a goddamned drunk!" Dad clanged his fork down on his plate and stomped off. I wondered if he was using it as an excuse not to finish Mom's tuna casserole. It was especially nauseating.

We sat in silence and stared at our gloppy tuna. Then Mom looked up at me with that dreary, pitying look I was beginning to dread and started to cry.

"*Mother*," Mary Frances scolded. She had no patience for Mom and Dad anymore. Their existence had always pissed her off; now, sometimes, I think she hated them. "You're not helping things by always crying and acting weird. Rog needs everybody to just be cool!"

Mom looked at Mary Frances like she didn't know her, burst into even bigger tears, then slammed her fork down on her plate almost as loud as Dad did. A tuna goo blob jumped from her fork and splatted against the wall. She ran weeping out of the kitchen.

"How come they're so weird, Mary Frances?" I asked.

She shrugged. "I dunno. Parents, I guess. Catholic parents, especially." She moved the food around on her plate, like she was trying to spell a word or make a tuna sculpture. "I hate it here," she said as an afterthought.

"Are you leaving after you graduate?" She was graduating from high school in a few weeks, and nobody had said anything about what she was going to do. Or maybe they had and I didn't pay attention. But now, the thought of her taking off was something pleasant. I couldn't help it if I didn't like her; just because you're related to somebody doesn't mean you have to like them.

"College, stupid. I'm going to UCLA. Don't you pay attention to anything?"

I shrugged. *Not when it's about you,* I thought.

"What about Freddie?"

"Freddie's going in the Air Force," she said. "He reports the morning after grad night." Grad night was an all-night high school graduation party at Disneyland. It seemed especially cruel to go from Fantasyland one night to a war the next.

"You mean Vietnam?" I asked.

"Probably."

Vietnam didn't mean a whole lot to me, other than it was always on the news and Dad was always complaining about why we couldn't kick the gook's asses like he did to the Germans in the Big One. And I always wondered why they called the bad guys the Vietcong. What was a Cong? I didn't pay much attention to the news, but I couldn't help notice that the weekly body counts were climbing.

"You think he'll be okay if he goes?" I asked.

Mary Frances smiled. "He's too dumb to get hurt." She never treated Freddie Montgomery very well, but she must've had a soft spot for him. I don't know what was in it for him, though. He put up with her pouty moods and snarling fits, and he took her abuse with a goofy smile and unhurt feelings. He was like a big stupid dog that jumps on you and leaves slobber on your face: he's annoying, but you still like him after you've finished smacking him.

Mary Frances and I were done talking. We sat alone at the table in silence. She stared down at the tuna glop. She seemed genuinely sad.

Now, as I look at my ugly reflection in a cracked JFK Junior High School bathroom mirror, the sadness of the last year and a half washes over me, too. I'm tired of being scarred and ugly, I'm tired of my droopy eye and my lumpy ear, I'm tired of stiff arms and gimpy legs, but most of all I'm tired of being noticed. I didn't realize how nice it was to be anonymous. When people noticed I was one of the miracle boys it was a bother, but it faded as soon as their memories faded. But now, I'll forever be "the kid who got run over by the drunk", and the scars will be a permanent billboard so people will never forget. And creeps like Bushman will always make me their target.

I take a deep breath. I need to regain enough strength and dignity to go back outside and face a lunchtime filled with classmates who either ignore me, stare at me, or, in Bushman's case, beat me up.

I walk to the door and bump into the Pendleton-clad chest of Ray Wisma. I've never spoken to Wisma, but he's in my wood shop class so we're aware of each other. He glances up at me—he's short and skinny—with neither surprise nor annoyance.

"Howsitgoin?" he mumbles.

"Okay, I guess."

I'm about to leave when he pulls a pack of Kools out of his Pendleton pocket. "Wanna smoke?"

"No thanks." I just want to get out of here before some teacher wanders in and thinks I'm one of Wisma's smoking buddies.

Wisma's a white guy who wants to be a Mexican. He dresses in perfectly ironed Pendletons, slicks his dirty blonde hair straight back, and talks like a little *vato.* Wisma didn't go to OLPS, but I heard that in public grade school he hung around with the hard guys and got into lots of fights. He seems friendly enough now; at least he offered me a Kool.

"You get beat-up?" he asks, firing up the Kool.

"Yeah, I guess."

"Bushman?"

"Yeah."

"You should kick the *pendejo's* ass."

I can't help but smile. Wisma sounds more like a Mexican than most Mexicans do. "Yeah, I should."

"How come you don't, man?"

"He's meaner than me."

Wisma looks at me through a cloud of smoke. The guy has no expression on his face; it's like his face muscles have been removed.

"I hear he beats you up all the time. Why don't you do nothing?"

I shrug. His questions make me feel like a complete loser. *Yeah*! I want to yell, *I want to kill the fucker! I'd love to slam the redheaded fucker's head into the wall and make it explode, I'd love to be able to punish the asshole for making my life miserable.*

Only I can't. I'm too afraid of him.

Wisma hawks a tobacco loogie into the sink. He looks at me, and then, almost sadly, shakes his head. He stubs out the Kool, stuffs the remaining half of the cigarette into his Pendleton pocket, and brushes past me out the door.

He stops and turns back to me. "How come your face is all fucked up, man?"

"I got run over by a truck."

Wisma studies my scars without disgust. Just detached interest. Then he gives me a little head nod and he's gone.

"Sure you can handle it, Rog?"

"I got it, Dad, okay? I got it."

"All right, don't fly off the handle, just checking."

I'm helping Dad with the rec room. I'm struggling to hold up one end of a 4x6 header while he nails down the other end. The truth is, my arms are screaming and I'm about to drop it, but I refuse to say so. I'm tired of admitting weakness all the time, and I'm tired of being pampered. I just want to be a guy again, like the old days when Joe was still our neighbor and he'd hang over the fence and BS with Dad while we worked on the rec room.

"Almost done, Rog, hold on!" Dad finishes pounding the nail and runs over to my side and starts pounding there. Soon, the header is solidly in place and I let go. "Nice work, Rog," he says, grinning.

Work on the rec room stopped for a long time after I got run over, and only in the last few months has Dad fired up his enthusiasm to go back to work on it. He had the concrete foundation poured a few weeks ago, right after he finished roughing in all the plumbing lines, and now we're working on the framing. Being back at work on the rec room feels good; it's a reminder that I've healed enough for some things to go back to normal.

"Glad we're working on this again, son," he says. Lately he's been calling me "son" a lot. He sounds like a dad on a TV show.

"Me too," I say, and I mean it.

"We'll get the building inspector back out next week to take a look at the framing, I think he'll pass us with flying colors."

I'm not so sure. When the inspector came to look at Dad's plumbing job he laughed when he saw Dad's Mickey Mouse handiwork.

"Last time I checked turds don't float uphill," he said when he showed Dad he hadn't gotten the slope right for the drainpipes. Dad just laughed it off and didn't seem to notice that the jerk was making fun of him. I felt bad for Dad. He means well, it's just that he's kind of a bonehead sometimes.

We work for a while longer, efficiently cutting 2-bys and nailing stuff up.

I'm feeling better and better until Dad asks, "How's things at school?"

I don't want to think about school and Bushman and all that stuff. "Fine," I say, hoping he'll let it drop.

"Not having any problems?"

"No."

"You'd tell me if you were, wouldn't you, son?"

"No."

"Well, I'd hope you would. Your mother and me worry about you, we just want you to be okay."

We're back into the babying mode again, and I don't like it.

"I'm fine," I lie.

"Well, I hope so."

We continue to work on the framing in silence. My good mood is spoiled. Now all I'm thinking about is getting beat up by a redheaded freak named Bushman.

We're in our usual pew at Sunday mass. Dad is waving and nodding to his Knights of Columbus buddies, and Mom is smiling at her Altar Society pals. Mary Frances is home from UCLA for the weekend, and she's reluctantly let herself be dragged to church. I know that on the weekends she doesn't come home she doesn't bother to go to church anymore, but Mom and Dad don't know that. They think she still goes to confession every two weeks.

Mary Frances is in her first year at UCLA, and she lives in a dorm with a strange girl named Mary Anne. Mary Anne is a year ahead of Mary Frances, and she's a hippie. At least that's what Dad calls her.

Mary Anne wears love beads and tie-dyed shirts and says, "Groovy" and

"Far out" a lot. Mary Frances thinks she's great, but to me she seems like somebody who's pretending, like every day is Halloween.

Mary Frances sits next to me in church, mouthing the *Glory to God* but not letting any sound escape. She yawns and twitches through Father Quinn's sermon, and I can tell by Mom's annoyed glances that she's not happy with Mary Frances. To Mom, mass is the true sacrament, a mystical place where Jesus comes to visit and she gets to drink his blood and eat his body. Sometimes she gets so caught up in it that she cries during communion.

I think Mom's kind of strange.

Dad's more like the rest of us: he trudges in every Sunday, mouths the prayers without knowing what he's saying, daydreams through the sermons, and walks out feeling holy and refreshed, all without any effort.

Mom's grumpy on the ride home. "I don't think Mary Frances was respectful during mass, Patrick."

"Oh yeah?" Dad yawns. He's still in his church tune-out zone.

"Oh, Mom," Mary Frances sighs. "I was there, wasn't I?"

"That isn't enough, Mary Frances. You know that. To be a good Catholic—"

"—You need to be a mindless drone," Mary Frances answers.

"Mary Frances Donnelly, I won't allow sacrilegious talk like that!"

"Knock it off, Mary Frances," Dad mumbles. He doesn't understand Mary Frances, but at least he's finally realizing it doesn't do any good to get mad at her. She lives to argue and piss them off.

"You ever think about what it is we're supposed to believe?" Mary Frances asks. "I mean, it's kind of weird when you think about it. We take the word of the bible, which my world civ professor says has had all kinds of grubby fingers rewriting it over the centuries, then we follow the rules of a bunch of celibate old men who hate women and are so conservative they refuse to leave the tenth century—"

"That's enough!" Mom says. "The Roman Catholic church has been here for two thousand years, it's survived every sort of persecution and blasphemy, I think it'll survive a smart-alecky know-it-all college freshman!"

"What about the Inquisition, what about all the bad popes who had mistresses, what about—"

"Nobody's perfect," Dad interrupts. "End of discussion." Dad's tone is final. It shuts everybody up. They stare out at the passing view of another orange grove being plowed under for tract houses. Dad ignores their pouting and looks in the rearview mirror at me and smiles. "Whataya say we work on the rec room when we get home, huh son?"

"Sure."

"You know, you could ask me to help sometimes," grumbles Mary Frances.

Dad just shakes his head. "Women...."

"BE A MAN!" Coach Hawkins yells at a skinny, sniffling kid named McQueen. McQueen just got steamrolled by Jesse, who was leading the blocking, and a bunch of other offensive linemen. McQueen made a weak little effort to grab the running back's flag, but it was obviously half-hearted because when he saw he was about to get creamed by five big Mexicans he tried to dive out of the way and got stomped instead.

Now McQueen's lying on the patchy grass, trying without much success to sniff back tears. A ring of flag football players surrounds him.

"C'MON, MCQUEEN, QUIT SNIVELING, GET UP!" Coach Hawkins screams. Coach Hawkins is a skinny little guy with slicked back hair and a perfect tan. He may be skinny, but he's solid muscle and everybody in JFK Junior High is afraid of him. He teaches PE and math, and he coaches the flag football team after school. Jesse was going to play Pop Warner, but the coach was somebody's dad who didn't know what he was doing, and Jesse decided he wanted to learn how to play football from a real coach—even if it was flag instead of tackle.

Since I couldn't play and didn't have anything better to do, I came along to watch. At first Coach Hawkins said he didn't want me hanging around, but he did want Jesse on the team, so he gave in and let me be the team manager.

For my official duties I get to drag the footballs and a first aid box out to the field every day, and then I relax on the grass and watch the other guys play. It's not bad, except that Bushman's on the team and he gives me trouble. He knows that me and Jesse are best friends, so he doesn't dare pound me when Jesse's around, but he still glares at me, whispers threats, and sneaks in an occasional shove when Jesse's not looking. I don't think Jesse knows about my problems with Bushman, and since I don't want to be a whiny wimp I don't tell him. I'm hoping Bushman gets tired of bugging me and the whole problem goes away.

Jesse pulls McQueen to his feet as Coach Hawkins sputters with annoyance and Bushman and some of the other guys on the team call McQueen "Fag" and "Pussy" under their nasty breaths.

"You okay, man?" Jesse asks as McQueen coughs and tests out his legs.

"Yeah, I guess."

"That's just great," Coach Hawkins says, "I'm so happy I could cry, can we play some football here if you're done trying to win an Academy Award?!"

"He got hit pretty hard Coach," Jesse says.

"It's football, for God's sake, Montoya, people are supposed to get hit hard, that's why we're out here! You think it'll be any easier in high school when you're playing tackle?!" Coach Hawkins blows his whistle. "Let's go!"

They go back to scrimmaging, and I take my usual place on the splintered bench and watch them play. Coach Hawkins yells and blows his whistle for no apparent reason, and the scrimmage continues as I relax in the gentle afternoon sun.

Wisma's on the team too, and as he runs by the sideline he gives me a friendly headwave. "Hey, man."

I nod back. I'm not sure why he's nice to me, but it's kind of cool for somebody to be pleasant without making a big deal about how different you are. Wisma's a hard guy, and I'm surprised he's on the flag football team. Usually guys like him don't do anything extra at school, but I guess for him football's different.

The scrimmage continues and I begin to daydream. This is the best part about being team manager. I can sit in the warm sun, and if it's not smoggy enjoy the fresh air and think about things. Lately I've been thinking about Rhonda Fairly.

Rhonda bailed out of OLPS and came to JFK with the rest of us, and she's fitting in here like she's known these people all her life. Rhonda's like that; she walks into a room full of strangers and leaves a room full of friends. And if they're boys most of them are in love with her. Here at JFK she's already active in a bunch of clubs and the teachers' favorite and it's obvious to everybody that she's special.

Especially me.

"Hi Roger!" she grinned one day not too long after my surgery. She'd come knocking at the door carrying math assignments from school and a big bag of M&Ms. "I'm here to help you get better!"

And she did.

She came by every week, with homework and candy and smiles. Sometimes she would watch *Chiller* with Jesse and me on Saturday afternoons, although she'd scream and cover her eyes during good parts. We didn't mind, though. It was nice to have her around.

During the early months of my recovery, Rhonda never seemed to mind that with my crusty scabs and vividly growing scars I looked far worse than anything on *Chiller.*

"Do...they hurt?" she asked, eyeing my scars one day after a hot game of Monopoly and some M&Ms.

"Nah...well, yeah. Sort of."

She didn't say anything more. She just looked at me with big, sympathetic eyes. And then she smiled. It was a smile so warm and sweet that I knew no smile would ever feel as good.

But as time wore on and it was obvious I wouldn't be back at school anytime soon, Rhonda came over less and less. She still called and seemed to care, and I liked her as much as ever, but I think she just moved on to other things. The novelty wore off of going to see Roger The Cripple. I didn't really blame her, I could understand. If I had been in her place I probably wouldn't have been so nice to begin with.

Now, at JFK, we're in Spanish class together and I get to talk to her every day. She's still friendly and nice, and she gets cuter by the minute. I have a hard time concentrating on *"Hola Paco, que tal? Como estas?"* when I can be stealing glances at Rhonda Fairly. The problem is, I'm not alone. None of the guys in Spanish are doing well; we're all infected with incurable Rhonda crushes.

I figure that since Joe messed me up and I'm ugly and creepy I'll never have a real chance with Rhonda, but at least I can be friends and daydream about her.

I'm sitting on the bench dreaming about Rhonda Fairly and paying no attention to the scrimmage when I hear the sound of thundering footsteps. I look up and Bushman replaces my Rhonda image. He's racing toward the sideline with the ball, red flags flapping on his hips, being pursued by a panting horde of defense. I watch, thinking it will be interesting since Bushman will have to go out of bounds right by me and I hope maybe he'll get knocked down and stomped on by the pissed-off defense. I realize, though, that he's looking at me, eyes locked on mine, and there's a smile on his freckled, evil face. He speeds up toward the sideline, even though there's no chance he can evade the defense. It's like he wants to run out of bounds as fast as he can, and then I realize why he's doing it: he's aiming *for me*! I jump up as fast as my stiff legs will lift me, but there's no way I can escape, he hits the sideline at full speed with a gang of defense on his butt, and he slams into me as hard as he can. I flip backwards over the bench and Bushman lands on top of me. I feel the breath *whoosh*! from my lungs as he squashes me. My vision sparkles as my head slams against the ground, but I'm conscious enough to see Bushman's grinning freckled face inches from mine as he lies on top of me. His breath stinks and I try to turn away, but I'm pinned to the ground and as he scrambles back to his feet, he makes sure to step on my chest and accidentally-on-purpose drop the football on my head.

I'm gasping, trying to suck some air back into my lungs. I look up into the bright sky, seeing the same view McQueen saw a few minutes ago: a ring of faces looking down at me.

"You okay, Roger?" Jesse asks.

"Oohhhh...."

Coach Hawkins pushes into the ring. "The crippled kid okay?" he asks nobody in particular. He can't seem to remember my name.

"I think so, you're okay, huh, Roger?" Bushman asks the question like I'm a baby. "I feel bad, Coach, he just got in the way when I went out of bounds. I hope he's okay," he adds, sounding so concerned it makes me want to puke.

"Don't worry about it, son. He shouldn't be hanging around the sidelines anyway. Get up, Ron."

"It's Roger," Jesse corrects.

I struggle to a sitting position, and finally gasp some air back into my lungs. Jesse and Wisma help me to my feet. Bushman stands, watching closely with phony concern.

"Sure you're okay, man?" he asks, his flaming red hair blowing in the breeze. *Asshole.*

"Catch your breath and then take off, Reggie," Coach says.

"Roger."

"Whatever." Coach Hawkins loses interest in me. He blows his whistle. "Let's go, let's go! Let's play some football!"

Jesse slaps me hard on the back like a true pal and trots back on the field. Bushman waits until Coach Hawkins's back is turned, then flips me off and mouths, "Fuck you". Wisma is nearby, watching everything. As always, his face is a blank; how does he do that?

As Bushman runs back out to play, Wisma wanders over and mumbles so quietly that I'm not sure he's talking to me. "Watch this, man," he says.

I breathe choppy breaths; a hot new pain flares to life in my chest where Bushman crashed into me. I try to stand up straighter but one of my ribs feels like it's stabbing my lung. What I want to do is limp home and get away from this place and these people, but I decide to wait and see what Wisma's up to.

They run a couple of plays and nothing happens. Then, Bushman gets the ball and heads down the middle of the field, dodging would-be flag-snatchers, his red hair flying. He's quick, leaving defensive players sprawled on the grass as they dive for his flags and end up with handfuls of air. Wisma and two other fast guys chase Bushman, and one finally catches him and yanks off a flag.

Bushman stumbles and falls and does an unnecessary show-boaty roll. The other guy stops, but Wisma keeps charging, then he trips and goes flying. To everybody watching it looks like he's doing his best to avoid hitting Bushman, but he doesn't quite make it and ends up kicking Bushman in the side of the head. Hard. Bushman yelps in pain, jerks the football into the air, and spasms into the fetal position, holding his head. He starts to cry. A crowd quickly surrounds him.

"Jesus Christ, can't anybody around here keep from getting hurt today?!" Coach Hawkins yells.

Wisma walks over to me as everybody surrounds the injured, wailing Bushman.

"Too bad that red-haired *maricon* got kicked in the head, huh, man?" He says it without any expression. Or remorse. Then, slowly, Wisma grins. It's the first time I've ever seen the guy smile. I guess he does have face muscles. He tosses me the football Bushman coughed up when he kicked him. "See you around, man." He trots back out onto the field.

Jesse comes over to me. "Bushman's bleeding."

"Too bad."

"Coach says he'll probably be okay."

"Yeah, great."

"Almost looked like Wisma wanted to kick him."

I begin to laugh. The pain in my side seems to have dulled. I feel much better.

I toss Jesse the football and limp off toward home. The sound of Bushman crying carries over the field, floating on the warm afternoon air like a really beautiful song.

* * *

Freddie Montgomery's time in Vietnam will be up soon, and he'll be back home for good—if he doesn't get killed first. He's been writing to my parents and keeping us up to date on the stuff he's doing there. We assume he's writing Mary Frances, too, but she never mentions him.

"Freddie's a good kid," says Dad one hot Saturday afternoon as we nail siding on the addition. "Not like all these long-haired queers smoking drugs and protesting everything that's good about this country. Freddie's doing his duty and he's not complaining. He should be a model for you."

"I don't have to worry about the army, Dad. They won't want me."

"That's not the point. Whether you go in the army or pick lemons, I don't care. Just so long as you're patriotic and you've got honor."

Dad's on one of his America-the-Beautiful-Amber-Waves-of-Grain kicks, so I don't bother to do anything but occasionally nod and grunt agreement. With the war protests on the news every night and rock music and drugs and long hair and all the weird stuff that he can't even begin to understand, Dad's confused and feeling left out. The world he's used to is changing into something strange and scary.

"In my day...." he's saying, and I quickly tune out.

I hammer nails into siding, one after another, and even though it hurts my scarred arm, it feels good to do something constructive and physical. Each hammer blow shoots hot pain through my mended bones, and the white, tough scars stretch tight and tingle.

"...And we had respect for authority...." Dad continues. I give him a courtesy nod and go back to hammering.

An old VW with a black guy at the wheel roars up into the driveway. Mary Frances is with him.

Mary Frances hops out of the still-moving car, waving and giggly. "Hi everybody!"

"What the hell's this?" Dad whispers to me. "She's bringing jigaboos home now?"

"C'mon, Dad," I say, trying to scold him with my best seventh grade social conscience. Dad's a bigot, and it's starting to bug me. He calls everybody names, and ever since the Watts riots he's really had it in for black people. I don't know why he's like this; people who aren't white have always been pretty nice to him. He's friends with Mexicans at church, but when he's home he never hesitates to call them "beaners" or "taco benders" or "wetbacks". I don't get it.

We watch the black guy get out of the bug. He unfolds himself from the front seat and stands—tall, black and out of place—on our white driveway. His Afro and torn Levi's with matching faded Levi jacket are just the 1968 look Dad loves.

"Christ," Dad whispers. "What if he's a Black Panther?"

The black guy folds his arms and leans against the car, watching us from behind wraparound sunglasses.

Mary Frances skips into the backyard, all smiles. "Hi guys!" she says as she hugs Dad and me.

"We didn't know you were coming home this weekend," Dad says. His voice sounds frozen.

"We just decided."

"We?" asks Dad. His voice is suddenly weak.

"Yeah, me and Ken. Ken, c'mere, meet my dad and my little brother!"

Ken pushes himself off the car and strides our way. Dad shrinks back a little, like he's scared. Mary Frances looks at him and then at me and grins. She loves every minute of this.

Ken comes over and stands a few feet away. He doesn't say anything. We just look at each other.

"Dad, Rog, this is Ken Johnson."

"Hey," Ken says in a deep, surprisingly friendly voice. "How you doin'?"

"Okay," I say, since Dad isn't going to say anything. "Nice to meet you." Ken gives me a soul brother handshake and it makes me feel cool, like I'm not just a dumb little white kid.

Dad nods and clears his throat, all serious and grim. "So...." His voice trails off as we all wait for him to say something. "So...."

Mary Frances looks at Ken and giggles. I've never seen Mary Frances so giggly before; she's usually crabby. Ken smiles at her and she reaches over and puts her arm through his. My head snaps back to Dad, because I'm afraid he'll do something crazy like attack Ken with the hammer. But Dad just stares at them.

"Nice to meet you, Ken," he finally manages in a hoarse voice.

"Ken and I are dating," Mary Frances adds.

"That's just great," says Dad, sounding like it's anything but great. He is very pale.

We eat a tense dinner of stringy pot roast and undercooked potatoes and carrots. Dad doesn't say much, but Mom makes up for it by yammering endlessly about stupid things. She interrogates Ken about everything, from his family to his future plans to how good a cook his mom is. Ken's cool, he pleasantly answers all her bonehead questions with humor, and by the end of the dinner seems to have won her over.

Dad's another story. He shovels stringroast and potatoes into his mouth and watches Ken with barely hidden hostility.

After dinner, as we finish off cups of chocolate Whip'N'Chill, Dad perks up when Ken says he's going to try and get into the UCLA Law School after he gets his undergrad degree.

"Lawyer?" Dad says disgustedly, "Why would you want to do that? Bunch of shysters and ambulance chasers."

"My father's a lawyer," Ken smiles.

"Patrick!" Mom chides.

"Just my opinion, Sylvia."

"It's okay, Mrs. Donnelly, a lot of people feel that way. And a lot of lawyers are shysters. But I won't be."

"Ken wants to do legal aid for people who can't afford to hire expensive lawyers, Dad," says Mary Frances. She's annoyingly chirpy.

"Huh. Colored people, you mean?"

Oh boy. A big blob of embarrassment flops onto the table, but Ken's smile doesn't go away. "Any color who needs it, Mr. Donnelly. I might even represent white people."

I laugh and it seems to break the tension. Dad "hrmphs" and Mom starts to chatter again. Ken looks at me and smiles. I think he's going to be a friend.

Ken spends the night sleeping on our cracked Naugahyde couch, and goes to church with us the next morning.

"I'm a devout agnostic," he tells Mom when she asks what religion he is. She laughs nervously. I think she's secretly excited by the danger of her daughter dating a godless black guy.

Mass is boring. Father Quinn gives a sermon that starts out about forgiveness, then veers into giving more money to the church because the rectory needs a new roof. Dad sits, stewing, his arms folded. He's not his usual day-dreamy Sunday mass self. I can see people in church giving us strange glances, wondering what's going on the with black guy. OLPS is whites and Mexicans—that's it. There's never been a black person here before.

After mass Dad cuts short his usual hand shaking and being Mr. Social. He heads straight for the car, dragging Mom along. She can barely keep up in her Sunday best high heels.

Ken and Mary Frances stroll to the VW, holding hands. I stay with them because Ken offered to give me a ride home, and I'd rather be crammed into the back seat of a ratty VW than listening to Dad grumble about "jungle bunnies" the whole way home.

We pass Jesse and his family as they pile into a couple of their beat-up station wagons.

"Hey, hi, Mary Frances," Jesse says. He's looking at Ken as strangely as everybody else.

Mary Frances sneers at him. "Seen any miracles lately?" Mary Frances has never liked Jesse.

"Nah," Jesse says, ignoring her nastiness. "I don't think They like me no more. I must've pissed 'em off."

"Miracles?" Ken asks.

"Jesse says he used to talk to Jesus and Mary. He and Roger almost got burned up once being stupid, and Jesse says Jesus and Mary saved them."

"They did," Jesse says.

This is embarrassing. Ken's a cool guy; we don't need to get into this stuff. Ken looks at Mary Frances like he's expecting her to say she's just kidding.

"No, really," she says. "Jesse believes in it."

Ken folds his arms and levels his piercing brown eyes at Jesse. "I don't believe in miracles. Convince me."

"We should go," I say, but Jesse holds up his hand.

He looks at Ken, studies him, and suddenly gets that dreamy, faraway look in his eyes. *Oh God*, I think, *I know that look*. Even though it's been a couple of years, he's going into the miracle zone, and he reaches out his index finger and moves it toward Ken's face. Ken stands rigidly, watching Jesse. A small, disbelieving smile creases Ken's face, like he's being let in on a private joke.

Jesse gently touches Ken's cheek. Ken flinches, and then Jesse jerks his finger away and his dreamy expression vanishes. Jesse is back in the here and now, and he looks frightened.

"You okay?" Ken asks.

Jesse shakes his head. "They...do you pray to God?" His voice is small and breathless.

"Uh-uh. No such thing."

"You need to talk to Jesus. He wants to save you."

Ken laughs a big, booming laugh. "What if I don't want to be saved, my man?"

"Then you'll die."

"Jesse!" Mary Frances says with annoyance, "Stop being so weird, shit, you sound like a psycho!"

Ken shakes his head, laughing, and climbs into the car. "Don't sweat it, Mary Frances. You do the prayin' for me, okay, Jesse? See you."

As we drive down the street I look out the back window.

Jesse watches us drive away. A queasy knot ties up my guts; I don't want the weird stuff to come back. But as I watch Jesse watch us I know it's starting again.

We turn the corner and are far from the church parking lot, but I can still see Jesse standing there, looking small and alone.

Chapter Eight

Freddie Montgomery got home from Vietnam two weeks ago, and last Monday night he killed Mary Frances's new boyfriend, Ken.

It's weird that a guy I've talked to and gotten to know, who's hung around the house with my sister, is dead.

Murdered.

Of course, I'm not stupid, I've been aware of death for a long time; I realize it's all around and that we all die someday, but when you're in the seventh grade you don't really think about people dying. Occasionally a classmate's grandfather will have a heart attack, or somebody's uncle will crash his car, but all in all, my only experience with death has been guppies getting stuck behind the plastic shipwreck and mysteriously croaking or a pet chameleon forgetting to wake up.

I wasn't prepared for Ken.

Things had been okay for Mary Frances and Ken. In the four months we knew him, Ken had begun to feel like a part of the family. He came by on weekends and slowly was breaking down the black/white weirdness that had been so uncomfortable at first.

Mom came around the quickest. Ken was nice and polite and smart and he treated Mary Frances good, and, in Mom's unbelievably stupid comment that made Mary Frances scream at her for half an hour, "He almost seems white."

Dad was a different story. Even though it looked like Ken and Mary Frances loved each other, Dad didn't trust him.

"What if he's just after money?" he mumbled at dinner one night.

"We don't have any money, Patrick. Besides, his parents are very well off. I can't believe you said that." Mom was getting tired of Dad's potshots at Ken.

"Maybe he wants free stale Fritos," I added helpfully. They both ignored me.

"I just don't understand," Dad grumbled.

"He cares for Mary Frances."

Dad pondered that for a moment, looking perplexed, and then asked, "Why?"

After awhile, though, even Dad weakened and began to tolerate Ken—if not like him.

Ken lived to argue and loved to provoke Dad, which didn't take much. If Ken hadn't died he would've been a good lawyer, because he could smilingly pull opinions out of you, then, with little effort, pull them apart and show you—nicely—that you were an idiot.

"I don't know what it is that you colored people want," Dad argued one night after dinner. "In this country you can be or do anything you want. Hell, look at your dad, he's a big money lawyer, you're in college. You're living the American Dream."

"Uh-huh." Ken smiled his cobra smile. Dad was about to get bit. "Four hundred years of slavery and oppression, institutionalized racism, murder, 'colored folks' just want to be respected for who we are and what we are. That first day I drove up your driveway, you weren't sure whether to run or call the police or hit me with a hammer. You didn't know me, all you saw was a black man and it scared you. Admit it, Mr. Donnelly. That's the attitude black people have to deal with all the time from white folks. So no, man, in this country we can't do or be anything we want. And until white people stop being racists—which I don't think they ever will—then we'll have to demand equality. It won't be given to us. We'll take it."

"Jesus. You *are* a Black Panther, aren't you?" Dad said.

"Nope," Ken laughed. "Not yet, anyway."

So they'd argue and discuss, sometimes with Mary Frances joining in, sometimes just man to man. I think Dad was even starting to enjoy Ken; Dad's not a real deep thinker, and Ken was so much smarter than him that Dad felt flattered to be discussing stuff. A Frito driver doesn't get much chance to talk about more than the weather or how the Dodgers are doing.

So the Donnelly family—even Dad—was slowly getting used to the changes.

Then Freddie Montgomery came home.

Freddie had been in the Air Force, and he was stationed someplace near Saigon. They had him doing number-crunching accounting stuff in a supply unit on base, so he didn't stomp through rice paddies or have to worry about getting killed. In some of his letters he told us about going into Saigon for fun, and that sounded like it was the most dangerous part of being there.

Freddie was discharged, none the worse for wear, and came home to go to JC and pursue Mary Frances. They'd dated off and on all through high school, and it must've seemed natural to him that they'd take up where they left off.

He hadn't expected Ken.

When Freddie came home, he still looked military: buzzed hair, the careful, disciplined way he moved. He stood out from the average 1969 longhaired, bellbottomed, tie-dyed, love-beaded guy so much that it was hard to believe he was real. Freddie had always stood out anyway—tall, gawky, big-footed, acne-covered; now he stood out all the more. He was an ex-military misfit to his peers; people called him a baby-killer. Nobody bothered to notice that all he did in Vietnam was paperwork. He hadn't fired a gun since basic training.

Freddie showed up at our front door two weeks ago, all smiles. My parents, especially Dad, treated him like a hero. They had a barbecue for him and his parents, and he even helped Dad and me work on the rec room.

The only problem was that Mary Frances refused to see him, or even answer his phone calls. He went down to UCLA a couple of times and snuck around the dorm, but friends warned her he was there, and he never saw her.

Freddie was helping me and Dad nail shingles to the roof of the rec room last Monday afternoon. He had been down to UCLA that morning looking for Mary Frances, but she had dodged him again, and now he was depressed and confused.

"How come she won't talk to me, Mr. Donnelly?" Freddie sounded pathetic, like I sound when my parents make unreasonable demands, like "Mow the lawn" or "Take out the trash."

Dad exchanged a glance with me. "Well, I don't know Freddie. You know how women can be."

I didn't understand why nobody would tell the poor guy the truth. If they thought they were being nice to him by pretending not to know anything, they were wrong.

Freddie hammered down another shingle, lost in the confusing world of women and love. "I just don't get it, Sir." Freddie was big on the "Sir" stuff. It was another reminder of just how different he was from everybody else.

We hammered shingles in silence. After awhile, Dad went into the house to grab a beer and some stale Fritos, so I decided to tell Freddie the truth.

"She's got a new boyfriend," I said, figuring it was best to tell him straight out. From his reaction, the thought had never crossed his mind.

"No."

"Yeah. Ken. He's cool." I probably shouldn't have added the last part, but I thought he ought to know.

"Ken. Boyfriend." Freddie dropped the hammer and leaned against the sloping roof. I've never seen anybody look sadder. "I thought we'd get married some day. I figured I'd maybe be an accountant or something, I kinda liked doing that kind of stuff in 'Nam, then maybe buy a house here in town, like a nice three-bedroom-two-bath in a new tract, and maybe have some kids and they could go to the same schools we went to...I thought I had it all planned out." He sighed; it was like he'd deflated and now he was flat and saggy. "Ken," he mumbled, shaking his head.

"Well, maybe they'll break up or something," I said too quickly, feeling like the biggest jerk in the world for ruining Freddie's dreams. He shook his head and smiled tightly. "You're okay, Rog," he said. He gave me a friendly slug on the shoulder. "Thanks for telling me. Guess I've looked pretty stupid since I got back, chasin' her all over the place."

Dad came back out carrying Fritos and a couple of beers.

"Here we go, guys, a little something to make our work better, except no beer for you, Rog."

Freddie slowly stood up and gazed up at Mount San Antonio. Its faint outlines were smudged fuzzy against the smoggy afternoon sky. Freddie didn't say anything for the longest time; he just stared at the mountain. His acne had finally stopped blossoming, and now his blotchy face was lumpy and pitted with scars of past outbreaks; the mild sunlight cast tiny shadows in the pockmarks, and he appeared almost...noble. He finally looked down at Dad.

"Thanks anyway, Sir. But I have to leave now. I've got some things to do." He climbed down the ladder from the roof and then walked away. He didn't say another word, nor did he look back.

That night, after Ken and Mary Frances finished studying at the library, Ken walked her back to the dorm. Nobody knows exactly what happened after that, but Freddie must've followed Ken to his car. Some people said they heard them arguing in the parking lot, and then they started fighting. Freddie bashed Ken's head against the roof of the VW over and over until he killed him.

Now it's been four days since Freddie killed Ken, and I can't get over the feeling that it's my fault. My parents, and even Mary Frances, have told me not to feel guilty, that if I hadn't told Freddie about Ken he would've found out anyway. After the funeral, Mary Frances said it was really *her* fault.

"I shoulda talked to him, I shoulda told him about me and Ken. But I never, ever made him any promises, you know? Like getting married or anything, I never told him...I loved him, he just assumed, Jesus, Ken's dead because of *me*...." She collapsed in tears against my shoulder and her body shook violently as she wept. I didn't know what to say. After that she didn't talk to me anymore.

Tonight, after a silent, tension-filled dinner, Mom says, "Hurry up, Roger, you'll be late for catechism."

"Do I have to go?" I can't believe she's making me go; we spent today at Ken's funeral, Mary Frances is in her bedroom crying, Dad's in shock, and I'm feeling so guilty and responsible for what happened I can hardly concentrate on basic life, let alone stupid, boring catechism.

"You need to go, Roger." Mom's eyes are red and puffy from crying and stress. I don't think she's slept much since all this happened.

Dad's sitting at the table, glumly eating a piece of pie. I look to him for help; he'll understand.

"Dad?"

"Go to catechism."

"But—"

"Just do it!" he snaps.

Mom begins to silently weep. Dad looks up from his pie at her and then at me, and I drop my eyes down at the tabletop.

"Go on, Rog," Dad says, this time more gently. "You don't want to be late. Extra time in purgatory, you know."

There's no reason to argue, and on second thought with the way things are in this house, maybe I'd be better off at catechism. I dump my plate in the sink and leave Mom and Dad sitting silently at the dinner table. The yellowish light from the cheap chandelier Dad put up last year bathes their faces in long, sad shadows.

I've recently gotten strong enough to ride a bike again, so I climb on my new ten-speed and pedal over to OLPS.

I hate catechism. It's more of the same warmed-over religious junk that the nuns pounded into our heads through the first six grades. Most of the kids in catechism have always gone to public school, so the classes are geared to them, not the hardcore religious experts like me and Jessie and Rhonda Fairly. We may have bailed out of OLPS, but we're still forced by well-meaning parents to keep up with our so-called religious training.

Mrs. Maldonado is the teacher. She's the mom of one of the kids in catechism, and she tries hard to do a good job, but she isn't able to make it interesting—I don't know if that's possible—and she has trouble keeping the class under control. I don't think she's ever taught before, and trying to teach God to a bunch of rowdy public school seventh graders is beyond her.

It seems weird to be back in an OLPS classroom and not have a nun glaring at you from the chalkboard or coming at you with a yardstick. Some of the catechism grades have nuns, but there aren't enough to go around, so we get Mrs. Maldonado. As boring and bad as she is, I'd rather spend an hour a week sleeping through class with her than with a psycho nun.

I'm locking my bike to the rack when Jesse rides up.

"Hey, man. How was the funeral?"

I shrug. "A funeral. Not like the ones we've served at, though. Ken was a Baptist. They don't even have altar boys."

"Weird."

We walk toward the classroom. I stop. Jesse stops and looks back at me. "What?"

"You knew."

"Knew what?"

"That Ken was going to get killed. You knew."

Jesse looks away, nervous. "I don't know. It wasn't that, it was like...I felt something was bad. I didn't know exactly."

Jesse rubs at fuzzy black whiskers sprouting on his chin. I have to look up at him now; he's growing bigger every day. The high school football coaches have already been sniffing around during flag football practice, and I've overheard them mumbling about Jesse's future as a Rio Linda Panther.

As I watch Jesse hem and haw and avoid answering my question, I wonder again if he's crazy. I've been around when the strange things have happened, but I still don't believe in anything miraculous. The problem is, I don't know what to believe. Maybe he's a good liar, or a lucky guesser, and I'm his idiot, gullible sidekick. Maybe he's not really my best friend, maybe he laughs at how stupid I am, that I'm actually confused by his Jesus and Mary talk and the miracles.

Still—

He knew something was going to happen to me when I got run over, and the orange tree fire, and Monsignor O'Callahan, and now Ken—it can't all be coincidental. Can it?

"If you know bad things are going to happen to people, why don't you warn them?" I ask.

"I do."

"Not the 'Say your prayers' stuff. I mean like, 'Don't let Freddie Montgomery get near you,' or 'Watch out for Joe Fanucci's truck.'"

He shrugs and starts to go into the classroom. I grab his arm and pull him back. He's so big and strong it takes all my puny strength just to hold onto his rock-hard arm.

"How come, Jesse? What's up with you?"

He hesitates for a long time. "I don't know. I don't understand this shit, either."

"How come you don't understand it?"

He smiles tightly. "It don't make no sense to me. Jesus and Mary don't talk to me anymore. I just...feel stuff. Anyway, there's nothing I can do. It's God, you know. You can't get away from God. If *He* wants something to happen, it's gonna happen."

Later, I sit in the too-small desk in the fifth grade classroom and think about what Jesse said. Mrs. Maldonado is valiantly trying to explain the difference between a soul in the state of grace and one that isn't by holding up a bouquet of red roses and a dead potted plant. We all get the point within three seconds, but Mrs. Maldonado is in love with her soul/rosebush comparison and spends ten minutes beating it to death. She's lost the class in a buzz of chatter.

Rhonda Fairly is behind me, and she taps me on the shoulder and whispers, "Would it be possible for Mrs. Maldonado to be more boring?"

"No," I say, turning around. Rhonda's smiling face makes my heart beat faster, and I feel hot little pinpoints of sweat pop out on my forehead.

"Are you okay, Roger?" she asks. "You look sad."

"You know how it is," I shrug.

"How's your sister?"

"Pretty bad."

"It was so terrible," she nods. Hearing her light, sympathetic voice makes me feel better. "I don't know if I could handle something like that happening to my boyfriend."

I look over at Jesse in the next row. He's the only one in the whole class listening to Mrs. Maldonado. He always concentrates, he's always so sure of everything. Jesse's dark eyes never waver—unless I'm bugging him about answers to the miracle stuff—and they laser in on whatever he's observing. Like now. He watches Mrs. Maldonado and her stupid plants like it's the most fascinating thing he's ever seen. It's starting to piss me off.

"Jesse knew what was going to happen, only he didn't warn my sister's boyfriend," I whisper to Rhonda, loud enough for Jesse to hear. He pretends that he doesn't, but I know he does.

"How could he have known?" Rhonda asks.

"God—or maybe it was Jesus and Mary, I don't know—but somebody told him."

"Oh," Rhonda says, sounding dubious. "You guys still do that stuff? I mean, the visions and miracles? Because I don't think anybody believes in it anymore."

I make sure Jesse hears me. "Yeah. I don't believe in it. But Jesse does."

Jesse slowly takes his eyes from Mrs. Maldonado's lame dead plant theology and turns to me. I expect him to be hurt, or angry. But all he does is smile an infuriating, all-knowing Buddha smile.

"Are you having trouble with some of these students, Mrs. Maldonado? I was walking by the classroom and it seemed noisy." Our heads snap back toward the front of the classroom at the sound of that voice.

It's Sister Mary Annunciata.

She stomps into the classroom and stands next to Mrs. Maldonado, glaring in our direction. She's gotten saggy and splotchy the last few years. Her shoulders are hunched and lumpy, like she has a pillow stuffed under her habit. She has to crane her neck up to see straight ahead, but when she locks her black, evil eyes on mine I know that one thing about her hasn't changed: she's still a black-robed monster from hell.

"It's the miracle boys," she says, her voice heavy with contempt.

"Hello, Sister," says Jesse politely.

Mrs. Maldonado stands, confused and embarrassed. "Everything is under control, Sister. I was just explaining to the students the difference between a soul in the state of grace and one that isn't."

Sister Mary Annunciata grins. Her teeth are yellow and crooked. "Perhaps Roger Donnelly could explain to us what happens when you blaspheme almighty God, when you claim to be part of something miraculous when you're really a liar."

I have a choice to make. I can answer her, maybe even yell at her and cuss her out, because I'm furious and embarrassed and it's been a terrible week and I don't have to take this from her, or—

I can be wimpy Roger Donnelly, the scarred-up crippled kid, everybody's doormat; I can sit silently and let her insult me, I can let her—

"God's will always wins out over the sinner, Roger Donnelly. Your 'accident' wasn't any accident. God was punishing you for your evil lies, and He's going to punish you, too, Jesse Montoya, He will as sure as the sun rises every morning, He'll strike you down, and I hope when He does it's something even worse than what happened to evil Roger, because you deserve far more punishment."

"Sister!" Mrs. Maldonado is appalled. She drops her rose bouquet on the desk.

Sister Mary Annunciata throws Mrs. Maldonado a disgusted glance. "Don't be weak, dear, the children need to be led, they need strength. Perhaps I should teach the rest of the class tonight."

Mrs. Maldonado's lip quivers, and her eyes tear up. She grabs her roses and her dead potted plant and rushes out. Sister Mary Annunciata turns back to face the class.

She's grinning.

"Repeat after me," she orders. "'*I am the Lord Thy God, thou shalt not have strange gods before me*'."

Half the kids in the class mumble incoherently, the other half says nothing.

"LOUDER!"

"'*I am the Lord Thy God—*'"

"LOUDER!! JESUS CAN'T HEAR YOU!"

"'I AM THE LORD THY GOD, THOU SHALT NOT HAVE STRANGE GODS BEFORE ME!'"

"Better. *'Remember to keep holy the Lord's day.'"*

"'REMEMBER TO KEEP HOLY THE LORD'S DAY!'"

I look over at Jesse. He's parroting the commandments back at Sister

Mary Annunciata with a huge grin on his face. She continues to drill us, and by the time we get to *"Thou shalt not covet thy neighbor's wife"* I notice that Jesse's smile is slowly freezing into place and his eyes are getting that glazed look.

He's going into the zone.

As we finish the Ten Commandments and go into Baltimore Catechism questions and answers, Jesse raises his hand. Sister Mary Annunciata ignores him at first, but he continues to hold his hand high and motionless. His eyes are far away, although he's staring straight at Sister Mary Annunciata. She finally lets her annoyance get the better of her, and she stops shouting questions and answers. A strange silence descends on the classroom as Jesse, his hand still raised, waits for Sister Mary Annunciata to call on him.

She's wheezing, and her hunchback seems to have inflated in the last five minutes. The air in the classroom is close and warm; clammy. It smells of decay and Sister Mary Annunciata. I look up at the stained ceiling tiles; how many hours did I spend staring at this ceiling when I was in the fifth grade, wishing I was anywhere but OLPS grammar school? And now, here I am, back in a place I wanted to forget, trapped with a nun who's always hated me, waiting for something to happen between her and my crazy best friend.

Sister Mary Annunciata glares at Jesse. He holds his hand up, frozen smile aimed at her, waiting patiently. Her beady black eyes narrow as she tries to decide what to do.

After what seem like hours, Sister Mary Annunciata finally gives in and calls on him.

"What is it?!"

Jesse slowly lowers his hand. I think he's coming out of the miracle zone, because his eyes are back, like he can see the world again.

"Sister?"

"Yes?! Hurry up, you're disrupting the class!"

"Watch out for Joshua."

"What?" There are a few muffled laughs in the class. Sister Mary Annunciata's iron gaze immediately shuts them up.

"Who's Joshua?" Rhonda whispers. I shrug. I have no idea, unless he's talking about the guy in the bible.

"Say your rosary, Sister. Because the Lord will smite you."

There's that smite word again. Sister Mary Annunciata trembles with fury. Her face reddens and she strides toward Jesse. He sits, smiling impassively. She comes to his desk and stands over him.

"Watch out for Joshua," he repeats.

She raises her hand to hit him, but she doesn't move. She stands, arm ready, palm open to knock the hell out of him, she shakes with anger, I turn away because I don't want to see it, I wait for the *smack!* of flesh or the *crack!* of breaking bone, waiting, and—

Nothing.

I look back at them, and Sister is frozen in her pre-hit pose. Jesse smiles at her.

"Watch out for Joshua," he says again.

She slowly lowers her hand. Fury is replaced by fear.

"Get out," she whispers.

Jesse gets up, nods pleasantly like they're the best of friends, and strolls out of the classroom.

Sister Mary Annunciata hesitates, then, in a shaky voice says, "Repeat after me: *'I am the Lord thy God...'*"

Freddie pled guilty to second-degree murder and was sentenced to fifteen years at Chino State Prison. Ken's parents objected, saying that a cold-blooded murderer deserved more punishment, but the judge said that since it was a crime of passion, and Freddie didn't have any prior record, fifteen years was fair. I felt bad for the judge, because no matter what he did, somebody would be mad.

My parents and I went to Freddie's sentencing hearing; Mary Frances refused to go and spent the day at Laguna walking along the beach. As I watched Freddie stand before the judge to be sentenced, I realized that because of Mary Frances's power, one guy was dead and another's life was ruined. To me, she was just a crabby sister. But to Freddie Montgomery she was his only reason for living, and if he couldn't have her, nobody would, and he willingly killed another person and then flushed his own life down the toilet forever because of his Mary Frances obsession.

I can't imagine any person, any girl, having that kind of power over me.

It's been a couple of months now since Freddie went to prison, and life is slowly returning to normal. School's almost over, and I'll be glad when summer gets here and I can have Bushman-free days. He hasn't beat me up in the bathroom lately, or even touched me, but he's always in the background, taunting me, whispering, "Fuck you, cripple fag" in the lunch line, or slamming my locker shut while I'm trying to juggle books with my stiff, scarred arms.

He's become a constant in my life, like the color of my hair or my scars. I've learned to accept that he'll always be here, making me feel bad, threatening me, a red-haired mosquito buzzing around my head that I might swat at but have no hope of killing.

Jesse has settled into a normal—for him—state. He's just a regular, very big Mexican who, in spite of everything, is still my best friend. His last miracle zone was the "Joshua" stuff with Sister Mary Annunciata; he hasn't said a thing about that or any other visions since. We've been hanging out a lot after school, riding bikes, throwing a football around, or just doing nothing together. It's like old times, and it's nice.

The rec room is actually getting close to being finished. It'll seem strange not to have Dad hounding me to help him work on it, and once it's finally done I'll miss it. I think it's been Dad's main reason for living the last few years. He diligently delivers his Fritos day after day, and he takes care of his family and church responsibilities, but the only time he seems really happy is when we're pounding nails or painting new walls that we put up.

"Look at that beautiful sumbitch, Rog," he'll say, lovingly running his hands over lumpy wallboard. "It's almost even! Coat of paint and nobody but us will know it's not quite smooth."

The strange thing is I'm almost as absurdly proud of our amateur work as he is.

We're putting the finishing touches on the rec room now. Dad wants to have it finished by early summer so he can have a big party to show it off to all of his and Mom's church friends. My parents live to party with their church pals; sometimes it seems odd that people bound by religion express their oneness by drinking too much and acting stupid.

When Dad's sucked a few bourbons down and he's around other Knights of Columbus guys, things can get wild and nasty fast. I've even seen Father Quinn join in the party good times. Last Christmas at my parents' annual K of C party, Father Quinn, after having a whole bunch of Dad's spiked eggnog, started telling nun jokes. He also hugged people for no apparent reason. The women loved it, since they all have crushes on him, and he hugged Mom more than anybody else. Every time he saw her he'd hug her and slur, "Great party, Sylvia. Great party." Mom would giggle and turn red, and sort of pretend to push him away. But I noticed their paths seemed to cross more than anybody else's, and I think Mom wasn't trying too hard to avoid him. "Great party, Sylvia," he'd mumble-hug again and again.

I don't think he gets out much.

Today Dad and I are hooking up the final plumbing connections for the wet bar. The wet bar is the crown jewel of the rec room. We built it from plywood and walnut paneling, and Dad made a cabinet behind the bar to hold all his booze. Everything's a little crooked and rough, and gaps filled with putty and plastic wood are the norm for every joint, but it fits in the with homemade, learning-on-the-job quality for the whole addition.

"Shit!" Dad's just gouged his finger trying to hook up a garbage disposal to the little bar sink. When I asked him why he needed a garbage disposal on a sink he'd almost never use he said, "Because *I'm* building it and I can do whatever I want."

"You okay, Dad?" I ask. He shakes his hand and swears under his breath. He's lying on his back underneath the bar, trying to attach the electrical hookups to the garbage disposal. I stand above him, helpfully holding a screwdriver and offering moral support. Blood trickles down his index finger. He wipes it on his T-shirt.

"No problem, the bastard wrench slipped, gouged my finger."

One thing I've learned from the rec room project is that any problem, injury, or screw-up is the fault of the tools or the building materials.

Dad sucks the blood off his finger and finishes up the electrical connections. He slowly wiggles out from underneath the sink, still shaking his nicked finger. As Dad gets older, these kind of "crawl-under" jobs get harder and harder for him. He grunts and groans, rubs his tight, sore muscles, and complains about getting to be an old fart.

He turns on the water and it hisses and burps out of the faucet, but it runs! He beams proudly at the bubbling, brownish water and flips the switch for the garbage disposal. It groan-gargles to life, and we stand there together, father and son, admiring the final big job of the years of our labor.

I'll admit that I thought the whole thing was stupid when it started, that I had my doubts whether Dad could pull it off. But he did, with my help, and I feel proud that our tacky, poorly built little addition is finally finished. It's not perfect, but it's ours; we did it together.

As we stand, watching murky water go down the drain and listening to the *gurgleroar* of the new Lady Kenmore one third horsepower automatic garbage disposal, I feel emotion close my throat and my eyes mist. Dad must feel the same way, too, because he leans over, puts his beefy arm around me and gives me a guy-hug.

"We done good, Rog," he says.

"Yep."

There's nothing else to say.

We done good.

Father Quinn is standing in the center of the rec room reading prayers. Mom, Dad, Mary Frances and me stand behind him, our heads solemnly bowed, as Father Quinn blesses the addition.

My parents, especially Mom, are firm believers in having everything in our lives blessed. Whenever we've gotten a new car, she's taken it over to the rectory to be blessed. When Dad gets a different Frito truck, he gets it blessed. Our house has been blessed, and any time we've had pets—mammals, anyway—they've been blessed. We've had a few cats over the years, but apparently the blessing doesn't work well for them; they've always ended up as road Frisbees or coyote food after a few months. Maybe they need to rewrite the official cat blessing.

Father Quinn sprinkles holy water from his portable, travel sized holy water sprinkler. I know I've heard the official name for the thing, I think it's something Latin, but I can't remember. It's just another accessory that priests get to use, like little holy oil containers and travel crucifixes.

I look over at Mom. Her eyes are tearing up. Almost anything religious makes her cry, even something as dopey as this. Dad stands, head down, staring at the floor. I think he's studying the indoor/outdoor carpet we glued down, looking for the seam. We spent hours making sure it was just right, and now one of his biggest sources of pride is the fact that the seam is almost invisible.

Mary Frances listens to the mumbled prayers as if they're important. Since Freddie killed Ken, Mary Frances has become a different person. She dropped out of UCLA and came back to live at home, and she ditched the whole tie-dyed-pot-smoking-stop-the-war thing that she'd embraced so strongly. Now she goes to mass every day, spends her days reading all kinds of stuff from philosophy and lives-of-the-saints books, and hardly says a word to anybody.

My parents were thrilled when she decided to move home, but as time has worn on, they've started to worry about her moody weirdness and lack of any goals. She has vague plans to go to the local JC in the fall, but I don't think she's serious about it; she just tells them that to keep them off her back. She doesn't say much to me, either. She's not crabby and mean like she used to be, now she's just pale, thin and sad. I think she's lost and alone, and she doesn't have any idea what to do. I know the feeling.

Father Quinn finishes with the blessing, and puts his holy water sprinkler in its black leather case.

"You and Roger have done a remarkable job, Patrick."

"Thanks, Padre. We're pretty proud of it." Dad points down at the floor. "Bet you can't find the seam."

Father Quinn leans over, squinting. "Huh. You're kidding, right? There's no seam in this carpet."

Dad beams his best proud little-kid-who-got-an-A-on-his-science-project smile. Even Mary Frances manages a wan smile.

"Don't encourage him, Father," Mom says. She dabs a leftover tear from her cheek. It takes her awhile to come down after religious ceremonies.

"Remarkable job," Father Quinn repeats. He repeats himself a lot when Mom's around. She seems nervous and twitchier than usual.

"Well," she says, trying to be the perfect social hostess. "How about a drink, Father?"

"Please, Sylvia, after all the years we've known each other, call me Steve."

Mom blushes. "Well, I don't know since you're a priest and all, I just feel—"

"Belly up to the bar, Steve, let's give 'er a trial run," Dad interrupts. He proudly pulls out a scotch bottle from the cabinet and pours Father Quinn a glass. "It'll taste better since you're drinking it in the official Donnelly watering hole. Now, you'll be at the party Friday night, won't you?"

Father Quinn looks between Dad and Mom. For a moment it looks as if the faint breeze of panic crosses his face, but then, looking at Mom, he grins his movie star smile.

"I wouldn't miss it for the world," he says softly.

The party is like all my parents' parties: loud, smoky and boozy.

I perform my usual slaveboy party tasks, wandering through the partiers, offering them trays of cocktail weenies and bowls of chips Dad stole from work. I get to listen to drunken ladies from church tell me how big I'm getting, and what a nice young man I am. The guys give me "How ya doin', kid?" smacks on the shoulder and swear good-naturedly about what a half-assed job Dad and I did on the rec room. I smile courtesy smiles, and try to be friendly, but the social thing is something I don't enjoy and am not very good at. I've noticed that as people get older, they seem to be able to stand around and amiably yammer for hours on end about nothing. I don't know how they can do it. It must be the booze. Normal people couldn't laugh and talk this much without chemical help.

For a bunch of good Catholics, it amazes me how nasty they are. I catch snatches of conversation as I make my rounds, and much of it is filled with "Goddamns", "Shits", and even the occasional "Fuck". Father Quinn floats around, drink in hand, touching base with his flock and telling semi-dirty jokes. As always, the parish women spend a lot of time near him, and he doesn't seem to mind. As I watch him, I notice he's more ill at ease around the men than the women. That seems strange; girls—women—are what scare me. I've always liked them, and as I get older I like them more and more, but there's something about them that's intimidating. I'm beginning to think I like them so much *because* I'm afraid of them. Sort of like enjoying scary movies.

Mary Frances disappeared for the night, leaving me as the only Donnelly kid to service our drunken visitors. She can always use the Ken/Freddie excuse to weasel out of things. I know it was horrible and she's having a hard time, but I'm beginning to wonder if she uses her mourning to get out of doing shitty stuff.

The noise rises as the boozy good times wear on, and pretty soon Dad has five K of C buddies on their hands and knees trying to find the seam in the indoor/outdoor carpet.

"Wait, I think I see it!" says Rhonda's dad, Mr. Fairly. He's loud and kind of annoying, and he drinks a lot. It's hard to believe Rhonda's related to him. "Naw, never mind. Wasn't it, must've been the line in my bifocals!" The rest of the seam-searchers laugh uproariously, like it's the funniest thing they've ever heard.

I look over at the knot of cackling, smoking women. There's so much haze in the rec room it's hard to see from one side to the other. Neither of my parents smokes, but most of their friends do. I watch the women talk and puff.

Most of them are old, like Mom, but they don't look as good as she does. They all have yellowing teeth and skin that's creased and saggy. Their hair is too done—all big and poofy. These are the same women I see at the Shopping Basket during the week wearing scarves over spiky hair rollers. They're noisy and screechy, and seeing all these good Catholic moms, the backbone of the parish, tipsy and silly and aging, makes me wonder why I find the opposite sex so appealing. But then I picture Rhonda Fairly and I know why. Will she end up like them some day? I can't imagine.

As the party wears on, the people get wilder. The noise and yowly laughter grate on me, and I can't wait for it to end. Mom and Dad are both drunk, and it bothers me to see them acting like fools. But since everybody else is drunk and acting like fools, too, I guess it's no big deal.

Mom, who's usually demure in a lovably goofy way when she's sober, is acting weird—even stranger than usual for a party. She's manic, her piercing shrieks of laughter shoot through the underlying party noise. Her face is flushed, and she throws her head back every time she laughs, teeth bared, like a howling beagle. As she talks and laughs her eyes dart around the room, watching her guests, wary with anticipation or fear. I can't tell which.

Her eyes keep coming to rest of Father Quinn. No matter what group he's latched onto, her eyes eventually find him. She laughs and talks with other people, but her interest and concentration are obviously with him. He occasionally makes eye contact with her, and when he does, he smiles and raises his drink. Mom smiles back shyly, and looks away. This happens enough that I'm beginning to wonder what's going on. I'm no expert in this stuff, but I think their interest in each other might be something more than just priest and parishioner. I look at Dad to see if he's noticing, but he's too busy showing off bumpy drywall seams or semi-plumb doorjambs to his buddies.

There's a break in the feeding frenzy, so I fade to the side of the rec room and watch the party. Especially Mom and Father Quinn. They move around the room in a slow-motion ballet, accidentally-on-purpose ending up in the same conversational group every ten minutes or so. It's interesting to watch how people float from group to group; it's like they're driven by some invisible tide. A batch of partiers will clump together, laughing and talking, and then after a few minutes people will start to drop off and latch on to other groups. In a little while, the group has completely broken apart, and all the talkers have joined other groups. Then these groups break apart and form new groups. There's a natural order to this, like rhythms that can't be changed. I wonder if there's a math formula or some kind of biological law that explains it. I'll have to ask at school.

Dad is mixing drinks behind the bar, being Mr. Social, and spilling more than he gets into the glasses. He's entertaining his crowd of fat K of C guys when he sees me sitting off by myself, watching.

"HEY ROG, C'MERE, GIMME A HAND!"

Damn. I've been spotted. Back on the cocktail weenie/Frito patrol. I reluctantly weave through the crowd toward the bar. As I get closer, I see Dad dumping some lemon rinds into the bar sink. He turns on the water, and proudly shows the guys that it "Even has a garbage disposal!" to a chorus of "Sonuvabitch Patrick" and "Goddamns". He flips the switch and the Lady Kenmore disposal roars to life. His drunken buddies have never been more impressed with a garbage disposal in their lives.

Dad casually reaches toward the faucet to turn up the water. His finger touches the faucet handle, and the instant it does, something goes wrong.

Dad's laugh becomes frozen, and his smile gets unnaturally huge. A throaty, choked sound comes from his chest, and his eyes widen.

The tipsy K of C buddies laugh with Dad, not noticing yet, but I can tell something's terribly wrong. I rush toward the bar, push through fat smoking women, brush against Father Quinn and knock his drink on the floor, but it doesn't matter, something's wrong with Dad and I have to help him, I get closer—

And now the K of C buddies start to understand, Dad's standing, his hand on the faucet, smile stretched taut, a grimace, and he starts to shake violently, he's trying to pull his hand away from the faucet but he can't, he's stuck, and now a horrible scream unlike anything I've ever heard bursts from his chest and his eyes bulge out, pushing his eyelids, he looks like a bug, his face reddens—

"You okay, Pat?" asks Rhonda's dad.

Dad shakes and screams, it's some kind of seizure, and the alcohol-dulled partygoers finally realize there's a problem and the laughter and talking stop, and everybody stands stupidly and watches Dad scream and shake to the sound of the running faucet and the Lady Kenmore garbage disposal.

I finally push my way to the bar. "Dad! Let go of the faucet!"

He screams and shivers and tries to talk but he can't. Father Quinn leaps over the bar and grabs Dad. He doesn't have a chance to help because something knocks him to the floor.

"IT'S ELECTRICITY!" shouts Father Quinn. "HE'S BEING ELECTROCUTED, SOMEBODY SHUT OFF THE POWER MAIN!"

I'm the only one who knows where the panel is, so I run outside and flip the main switch off. The house goes dark and Dad's screaming stops. I run back inside and see a big group of people in the dark clustered around Dad's body on the floor. His arms and legs are twisted into crazy positions.

"Call an ambulance!" someone yells out.

There's confusion and fear in the darkness, and I hear Mom sobbing, "Patrick, are you okay?! Patrick!"

I stand outside the clump of people. The alcohol-fueled good times have evaporated and now all I hear are gasps and sobs.

I back away from them.

I feel it.

I know it.

Dad's dead.

I stagger backwards and bump against the new Naugahyde couch Dad bought especially for the rec room. I collapse into the cold, squeaky upholstery.

I glance outside through the sliding glass door Dad and I installed. A full moon bathes the yard in eerie blue light, and shafts spill into the dark rec room, casting soft shadows. I'm crying, and as the commotion fades from my hearing, my eyes adjust to the dim light. I blink back tears, and then I see it.

If I squint, I can just barely make out the faint ridge of the seam in the indoor/outdoor carpet.

Chapter Nine

"Patrick died doing what he loved most: being with his family and friends. I was privileged to have known Patrick, to have called Patrick a friend, for the entire time I've been here at Our Lady of Perpetual Sorrows," says Father Quinn.

The church is full for Dad's funeral. There's a bunch of people here I've never seen before, so I assume they must be people from his work or Knights of Columbus guys from other parishes. I vaguely remember Dad going off to funerals in other churches, but I didn't pay any attention at the time; it was just Dad doing whatever he needed to do and it didn't concern me. Now that he's dead, I can appreciate having a church full of people. It doesn't seem quite so scary when there's a crowd. The K of C's realize the importance of sending you off to heaven with a full house.

I sit in the front pew with Mom and Mary Frances. Mom hasn't cried much since the night Dad died, but her eyes are still red and puffy from stress and lack of sleep. Mary Frances has retreated into sullen silence, beyond crying, beyond emotion. There's been too much death around her recently, and she's absorbed all she can take. She is cold and numb, and I wonder if she'll ever make her way back out.

"The tragedies that have beset the Donnelly family have tested their faith," Father Quinn continues. I can feel my neck and ears reddening. *I'm* one of the tragedies he's talking about. "But, through their prayers and steadfast devotion to God, they've persevered. And they'll persevere this, too, but not without pain, not without tears, not without memories, both happy and sad, of Patrick." Father Quinn pauses for a moment and a wistful smile crosses his face.

"I have a vision of Patrick, laughing and very loud, because, let's face it, to all of us who knew him, he *was* loud." There is scattered, knowing laughter in the church. "And I see Patrick in heaven busily at work building some new dream rec room." The laughter this time is a little tentative, because, after all, the rec room is what killed him.

The building inspectors who used to enjoy making fun of Dad and his less-than-professional building skills weren't laughing when they came out the day after Dad got electrocuted. He had messed up the electrical connection for the garbage disposal, and when the garbage disposal was running and he touched the faucet, *bam*!, that was it. The building inspectors were very sober and respectful until Father Quinn—who had stayed with us after Dad died until the afternoon of the next day—pointed out that they should've caught Dad's screw-up during the final inspection.

"Hey, you can't pin the blame for this on us!" protested the head building inspector, the one who had been the biggest asshole when it came to making fun of Dad. "The guy had no business trying to build something like this, it was way outa his league."

"I'm just thinking Mrs. Donnelly might have an actionable complaint here since her husband was depending on your inspections to catch his mistakes."

The inspectors left a few minutes later, sputtering that it wasn't their fault. I don't think they'll be making fun of home-improving homeowners anytime soon. Seeing Father Quinn defend Dad made me realize he's an okay guy for a priest; he was our family's friend and protector, and it was nice to know that even without Dad we wouldn't be completely on our own.

Father Quinn continues with his sermon, reassuring us that even though bad things happen God still loves us and the power of faith and prayer and *blah, blah, blah.*

I'm not even sure I believe in God anymore. I don't see how anybody with a brain can buy the "God will provide" stuff force fed to us by the Catholic Church, and, I assume, all the other churches too. The nuns taught us that God was all good, all holy. If He's so good and holy, why'd He create weak little creatures like us, give us impossible rules to follow, make us scared of dying and being hurt and alone, put assholes like Hitler and Bushman and Sister Mary Annunciata on the planet to torment us, and then expect us to be obedient little prayer slaves who thanked Him all the time for letting us put up with all of it? As I sit here in church at Dad's funeral, staring at the shiny casket and listening to Father Quinn's well-meaning but empty sermon, I can think only one thing: God's a jerk. He's mean. Does He enjoy sitting up there watching us run around like a bunch of confused ants, afraid and angry and mean? If He does, He's got a strange sense of humor.

While Father Quinn wraps up his eulogy, I turn around and scan the church. Jesse and his family sit a few rows behind us. All his brothers and sisters are there, hair freshly washed and combed, dressed in their best clothes. They occupy an entire row, and I first nod at Jesse who smiles back, then look down the pew at the rest of his family. Mr. Montoya is wearing a suit; it's the first time I've ever seen him dressed up like that, and he looks great, gallant and dashing like he'd be a Mexican gambler or something. Mrs. Montoya tries to smile at me and nods, wiping away a tear. Seeing her here sharing our pain is soothing; everything about Mrs. Montoya is soothing. When she wraps you up with a soft, squishy hug, you feel safe from any problem in the world. God should be like Mrs. Montoya.

Aunt Yolanda sits at the end of the pew. When my eyes meet hers, her usual tough expression softens a bit. She's had a couple of more kids in the last few years, and she's back to living at Jesse's house because she finally left her husband for good. Jesse told me he beat her up one too many times, so she grabbed a knife from the kitchen and cut off his ear. He was pretty pissed off, but he didn't touch her again or call the police. He wrapped his ear in a Kleenex and found a doctor to sew it back on and everybody got on with their lives.

Aunt Yolanda intrigues me. She's still the classic hard chick, with big hair and too much makeup, but I can't deny that she's great looking in a scary way, and that the swells of her body fire up my seventh grader's passion. I know it'll only get worse. I've spent enough time watching other guys to know that the desire for women will eventually take over my life. It's just the way guys are. It wouldn't be so bad if I thought I could do anything about it, but since I'm geeky cripple boy I've got a bad feeling that girls will probably exist only in theory for me.

I continue to stare at Aunt Yolanda; I don't want to look away. She's wearing a tight black sweater, and I like the way it clings to the curve of her shoulders. My eyes move down to her breasts, and before I realize what's happening, I feel my dick stirring to life and heat flash across my face. My eyes snap back up to Aunt Yolanda's eyes, and she's still watching me, a puzzled expression shadowing her dark, heavy eyes.

I quickly turn back toward the altar, and now I'm looking at Dad's casket. *Oh Jesus, I'm a psycho-sinner, sitting in church at my Dad's funeral staring at tits and getting a hard-on.* If there is a God, He's sending me straight to hell—and that's where I belong.

I try to listen to Father Quinn, but my mind soon wanders. I'm thinking about women, about Aunt Yolanda and Rhonda Fairly and anonymous imaginary creatures with large breasts and pretty faces.

I force the images out of my brain and concentrate on Dad's casket. Now I really feel terrible; Dad's dead and I'm a pervert and life will never be the same. My eyes blur with tears, and soon I'm weeping. Mom notices and puts her arm around me; she thinks I'm crying because of Dad, and maybe I am a little bit, but mostly I'm crying because I'm a creep and a loser and I know I always will be.

The wake is a strange thing, a hazy, boozy get-together that starts off sad but soon seems like any other drink-too-much-laugh-and-feel-good party. People are packed into our house—more bodies than I've ever seen. They spill out into the front and back yards, drinks in hand, nibbling on cold cuts and cheeses from trays people brought. I've never seen so much food in my life. Dad's Frito co-workers have bowls of chips sitting on every conceivable flat surface, and a couple of his K of C friends pour drinks from behind the rec room death bar. I notice that none of them dares go near the sink; if they need water, they go to the kitchen. Cowards. Father Quinn fixed it the day after Dad died.

I understand the idea behind wakes, that everybody needs to mourn together and remember the dead person, but I don't think it's right that they're having such a good time. Maybe they're sad inside and they're trying to hide it by drinking too much and laughing it up, but it still doesn't seem respectful to Dad's memory. Of course, I'll bet when Dad went to funerals he always boozed it up and had a good time.

Maybe that is the best way to remember him after all.

I wander through our packed house, dodging soothing clucks and hair tousles from everybody I pass. I soon tire of their sympathy and go outside.

I wander around to the side of the new rec room and sit on a pile of left-over scrap lumber that Dad and I never got the chance to take to the dump. I can hear the party/wake, but at least I'm alone now and don't have to be social. I close my eyes a let the warm sun soak in. My scars and damaged bones have ached lately, and my doctor told me it was a combination of the healed injuries and growing pains. I wonder now if it's punishment for being evil.

A hand touches my shoulder and startles me. I don't want to open my eyes and acknowledge whoever it is, because I'm sure it's some tipsy K of C guy who wants to do the right thing and tell me if I ever need anything to give him a call, or it's a flabby old lady with streaky mascara who's going to give me a shivery hug and sob about how sad it all is. I keep my eyes tightly closed and hope they go away.

"Roger?"

My eyes instantly snap open. It's Rhonda Fairly.

"Hi," I say, the doomed mood lifting like early morning fog burning off.

"Are you okay?"

I shrug. "I didn't see you at church."

"We were in the back. We almost couldn't find a place to sit. Your dad sure had a lot of friends."

"Yeah. He was pretty cool." My voice cracks on "cool" and my eyes tear up. I look away, feeling like a fool that I can't control my emotions, but I can't make my eyes stop crying.

Rhonda sits next to me and says nothing. The board we're sitting on shifts under her added weight, and it pitches her toward me. I can smell the fresh sweetness of her skin and hair. Being so near her makes me cry even more.

I'm humiliated and mortified that she's seeing me like this. I'm about to jump up and run away when she puts her arm around me and pulls me toward her. I bury my face in her long, silky hair. I have no control over my actions, I go along like a rag doll, and now my crying gets deeper, I'm gasping for breath, and she hugs me tightly with both arms, and I hug her back.

"It's okay, Roger, it's okay," she murmurs. "I'm here, it'll be okay, your Dad's in heaven."

Being held by Rhonda Fairly is the sweetest sensation I've ever had. Her small, strong body presses against me, and as I hug tighter, she hugs back; I don't ever want to let her go.

Gradually, I'm able to gulp back the sobs and the tears stop. My crying has made her hair wet, and as I sniffle the sudden horror strikes me: what if I've gotten snot in her hair? I abruptly pull away from her and study her glistening hair. It's wet, but no sign of anything else.

"What? What's wrong?" she asks. "Did I say something wrong?"

The concern in her voice rips my heart in half. *She's* afraid of offending *me*? Her big brown eyes gaze into mine, unwavering, caring. She has a few light freckles around her nose; they make her so cute that I can't resist her. I wipe my still-wet cheeks against my sleeve and look away, because if I don't I'll lean over and kiss her, and I don't think that's the right thing to do. She'd probably scream and punch me.

"You can tell me, Roger. I mean, we've known each other forever. You can tell me anything. You know that, don't you?"

I look up at her smiling, beautiful face. She's so nice I can do nothing but tell her the truth.

"I was afraid I got snot in your hair."

Her first reaction is shock, then she begins to laugh, a warm, friendly laugh. "Well—did you?!"

"Naw," I reply, feeling better. "Just tears."

She continues to laugh, then she does something that absolutely shocks me. She leans over, hugs me tight, and gives me a sweet, soft kiss.

"Roger," she says quietly, pulling away, "you're the best."

"Uh, thanks," I say, feeling stupid. "You're okay, too!" I add as an afterthought.

She just laughs. The fact that I'm a nervous geek doesn't seem to bother her. But sitting so close to her makes me self-conscious of my scarred face. Even though I know she's sincere and wonderful, I can't help wondering if she's looking at my scars and being secretly grossed out.

But my doubts fade as she hugs me again. This time I cling and relax into being part of her.

I don't ever want to let her go.

The first time I saw Danny Robledo, the front of his perfectly pressed Pendleton was covered with Randy Schilling's blood.

Robledo—who'd been in school less than a week—had just beat Schilling up, and nobody was quite sure why. Schilling was lying on the sidewalk in front of the cafeteria, groaning softly as a pool of blood haloed around his head.

A big crowd of kids surrounded them, including me, but we all scattered as teachers and coaches came running over. I later heard that Robledo had knocked out four of Schilling's teeth and put a four-inch gash in his scalp.

Randy Schilling soon transferred to another junior high.

Danny Robledo is tough and he's mean. He showed up at JFK around Thanksgiving, unnoticed until he started beating people up. Nobody had the guts to ask him where he came from, and even if they had he would have just pounded them and not answered. He seems older than the rest of us seventh graders—he's one of the few who shaves, and he already has a wispy black goatee. Some rumors say he's really fifteen but he was held back a couple of classes in grammar school. He's short and stocky, and it's hard to tell for sure, but hidden under the baggy Pendletons probably lurks solid muscle. His thick hair is always perfectly slicked back; it's more like a solid black helmet.

As Danny Robledo strolls down the halls, it's obvious he owns the school. Other students, and even teachers, get out of his way, and he moves with assurance and power. He never bothers to make eye contact unless somebody's pissed him off and he's about to pound them. A couple of *vatos* follow him around like little slaves, *yessing* him and helping him intimidate the rest of the school.

So far this year, Robledo's been in five fights—he's won them all—and he's been suspended twice and threatened with expulsion. But he keeps coming back to cream other poor unsuspecting slobs for imaginary offenses.

The only class I have with Robledo is PE, and I always keep my distance from him. Since I'm messed up, they make me dress out but if I don't want to participate in whatever they're doing, I can just hang around and watch. I'm not bad enough to be in adaptive PE playing chess with the asthma geeks.

We're playing basketball today, and I'm hobbling around the court, following the action and being useless, but I enjoy being out with the guys and feeling part of the world.

Every so often Jesse tosses me a sympathy pass, which I promptly throw up at the basket and miss completely. The closest I've come is hitting the corner of the backboard. Nobody dares give Jesse shit for giving me a shot because he's bigger than all of them and they know we're friends. It's thoughtful little things like this that makes me appreciate Jesse's friendship.

Today, however, Robledo is on our team. He doesn't show up for PE that often, but when he does everybody is on edge and afraid they'll be his next victim.

He's a surprisingly good basketball player for a short guy, and his game is helped since nobody is willing to guard him. It's okay for us since he's on our team, but it still annoys me because it messes up the game when one guy has free range on the court. When Robledo plays defense, whoever he's guarding usually gives him the ball. It's the smart way to survive.

The game is going along uneventfully until Jesse feeds me a pass under the basket. I make a weak, sloppy lay-up that drops off the side of the rim. Robledo comes crashing in for the rebound, grabs the ball, and then stops. He holds the ball and glares at Jesse.

"How come you keep givin' this *pendejo* the ball, man?"

I'm the *pendejo* he's talking about.

"Just play, man," Jesse answers disgustedly. Jesse's usually a pretty tolerant guy, but Robledo's viciousness pisses him off.

Robledo doesn't move. "Don't give the fucker the ball no more, man. He's fucked up, he don't play no good."

Everybody on the court slowly steps back away from them.

"You don't wanna play, Robledo, then gimme the fuckin' ball. But don't tell me what to do, man. If I want to pass the ball to Donnelly, I'll pass it to him."

Robledo and Jesse stare each other down. Nobody breathes. It's going to be an ugly fight, and even though Jesse's huge and I know he can be mean, I'm not sure he can beat Robledo.

Coach Hawkins is over at the sideline of another game, busily massaging his flattop, but he sees that something's up on our court and trots over.

Jesse and Robledo don't move, don't blink. I'm tempted to jump between them and volunteer to get out of the game, but it's too late for Roger the peacemaker, and I'm afraid if I get caught in the middle I'll be ground into hamburger.

Coach Hawkins gets closer, and somebody needs to do something fast, because if we're just standing around when he gets over here, we're all going to be doing wind sprints and ten-count burpees for goofing off.

Robledo finally relents. He gives Jesse a cobra smile and bounces him the ball.

"Let's play, *puto.*"

There is a sigh of relief and we all move back to play. Coach Hawkins arrives at the court just as we restart the game.

"Hey! What's goin' on down here?!"

"Just playin', Coach," Jesse answers as we sprint down the court.

Coach Hawkins is smarter than most PE teachers, and he doesn't believe Jesse but there isn't much he can do but stand there and watch us play.

Jesse steals the ball and runs back down court, and I limp along behind him. He can easily make the lay-up, but instead he feeds the ball back to me. I pull up and take a shot that actually drops!

"Nice shot, Donnelly," Coach Hawkins yells, and I try to pretend it's nothing but inside I'm as proud as can be.

Robledo hangs back, not really playing offense or defense, until the other team takes a shot that bounces off the rim and flies high. Jesse leaps up for the rebound, and it seems he'll be the only one going for it, but then Robledo comes out of nowhere, blindsides Jesse to the asphalt and grabs the ball. Jesse crashes to the ground and slides along the loose asphalt.

"Hey, Robledo, take it easy out there, he's on your team, for Christ's sake!" Coach Hawkins yells.

Jesse slowly gets up and picks pieces of bloody asphalt gravel out of his skin.

"You okay, Montoya?" Coach Hawkins asks, more with boredom than concern.

"Yeah," Jesse says.

Robledo smirks, "You okay, man?"

Jesse doesn't say anything; he turns his back on Robledo and the game goes on.

There's no more payback for the rest of the game, but I notice that Jesse doesn't pass me the ball anymore.

Summer's here and it's just in time. School was starting to get me down, and with all the bad things that have happened to us in the last year, I need a summer vacation to try and straighten myself out.

It's not that I'm in trouble, like being suicidal or anything. It's more confusion. Freddie Montgomery kills Ken, Dad dies, Bushman uses me as his personal punching bag, Rhonda Fairly kisses me—it's way too much for a scarred-up, going-into-eighth-grade crippled kid to figure out.

I've decided I want to get a perfect tan this year, so I'm lying out in the backyard every day for a couple of hours. I think that the sun, in addition to browning me, will warm me inside, make me feel safe, make me understand why my family and my life are so confused.

I'm baking on a beach towel; sweat trickles down the side of my chest, tickling like crawling bugs. Mary Frances gave me her portable radio—she doesn't listen to it anymore—and I have it blaring to KKLA—Boss of the Beach. They just played *In the Year 2525* and next up after the commercial is *Ride, Captain Ride.* I love lying out here, cooking in the smoggy summer sun, listening to the radio and drifting away. The red sunlight glows through my eyelids, and if I let my mind idle and my body absorb the heat and the music I feel like I'm floating above it all, above my smoggy subdivision, above the killer rec room, above Bushman, above my scars and my stiff, damaged limbs, above it all.

Floating above everything with Rhonda.

After The Kiss every time I saw Rhonda my knees would Jell-O out and my forehead would sweat. She was always friendly and warm, with a big smile and easy chatter. She never mentioned anything more about The Kiss, and neither did I. I figured it was our secret, and the depths of our love would hold us together forever. I had pleasant little fantasies of being married someday, even of having sex. Rhonda was still kind of skinny and kid-like, unlike some of the blossoming girls at school, but she was definitely the cutest—and as she got older, I could see she'd be utterly irresistible and sexy.

Once school was out I didn't get to see her every day, which disappointed me. It's been a few weeks now of summer idleness, and I usually see her at church, and a few times I've ridden by her house hoping I'd get lucky. I did, once, when she was out mowing the lawn, and we chatted pleasantly for a half-hour while streaks of salty sweat dried on the sides of her face. Otherwise, I only see her in my dreams and in my afternoon tanning sessions when we float together above the smog.

"Roger?"

Mom's voice breaks into my fantasies, and I reluctantly open my sticky eyelids. I turn to face her. She's standing at the sliding glass door to the rec room, squinting out at me. I blink, trying to clear the glowing aftervision of the sun and floating Rhondas and focus on Mom. She's gotten skinnier since Dad died, and more gray strands streak her blonde hair. She doesn't laugh nearly as much as she used to, and she seems older and tired.

Dad had a hefty life insurance policy, so money isn't a problem, although Mom has talked about trying to find a job. I think she's more bored and out of sorts than anything else, and she realizes the job of dealing with weirdo Mary

Frances and goofball me isn't enough to fill her life.

I feel bad for her, but I don't think there's much I can do. I'm wrapped up in being me, and even though I'd like to help her out, my own problems are more important.

"How's your tan?" she asks. It's one of those stupid, unanswerable mom questions.

"Fine. Brown. Except for the scars. They don't get brown, they just get whiter."

"Oh." She stares off into the yard.

I watch her, but I don't know what to say. I'm not good at small talk, especially with close relatives, and anyway, I'm not sure that talk is what she wants. I wait a few minutes, watching her stare at a crow as it flaps along the power poles. She watches for the longest time, entranced by the shiny, squawking black bird. It hops from wire to wire like an acrobat. I find myself staring at it too, wondering why it doesn't get electrocuted standing on the power wires. But at the thought of electrocution my thoughts U-turn back to Dad, and I look away.

Eventually, I hear a *flap-flap* and the big bird goes *cawing* off into the distance.

Mom watches it disappear, then reluctantly looks back at me. "You should come inside soon. You'll get burned."

"Okay. Just a little while longer." I can't bear the thought of getting out of the sun. I wish she'd leave so I can get back into the dreamzone and float with Rhonda.

Mom turns and slides the door shut. Then, she remembers something and opens the door again. It squeaks horribly. Dad meant to oil it after we put it in but he never got the chance.

"Roger?"

"Yeah, Mom?"

"Father Quinn's coming over at two-thirty. Will you be here?"

"Sure. I guess."

Father Quinn comes over all the time to see if we're doing okay and to do Mr. Fixit house stuff. He's good with tools. Better than Dad ever was.

"Good," Mom answers absently. A blank, confused look washes over her face. "Oh. Did I tell you?"

"About what?"

"I thought I told you."

I know Mom's having a hard time with Dad being gone, but her weirdness is starting to bug me.

"Told me what, Mom?"

She frowns, like thinking is hard and painful. "Mary Frances," she murmurs. I'm not sure if she's actually talking to me or mumbling to herself.

"Mary Frances?"

And as soon as I say Mary Frances's name Mom's head snaps up and her eyes focus. She's back from the Twilight Zone or wherever she was.

"Mary Frances is going to become a nun," she says, smiling. And then she closes the squeaky sliding glass door.

I'm too stunned to even attempt to try and recapture the dreamzone and float in the sky with Rhonda Fairly.

The visit from Father Quinn isn't the usual "How's the toilet working, is there anything I can fix?" visit. Usually when he comes by he's wearing normal clothes and tennis shoes. Today he's in his priest uniform, and he's more serious.

He's acting like a priest, not a friend of the family.

Mary Frances has emerged from her room and the four of us sit at the kitchen table having milk and cookies. Mom made a batch of chocolate chip cookies, but she forgot to put in the salt and baking soda, so they taste funny. Nobody mentions it, and we all munch our scorched, strange-tasting cookies in strained, overly polite silence.

Mary Frances nibbles at her cookie as if more than a bite will make her explode. She hardly eats anything anymore, and since she spends most of her days holed up in her room reading and praying she's pasty-looking—like a vampire.

As I watch her gum the cookie, I try to picture her dressed in a black-and-white Sister Mary Annunciata habit smacking little kids with yardsticks.

Somehow I don't see it happening.

Father Quinn finishes choking down half of an icky cookie and then clears his throat.

"Well, Mary Frances. Your mom tells me you're interested in the religious life."

"I think so," she answers in a small, weak voice. Mary Frances has become fragile and delicate. It's hard to remember her being noisy or annoying, or having any vigor. She's shrunken, like an elderly, worn-out aunt.

"Why would you like to become a nun?" Father Quinn asks. I detect a note of disbelief in his voice. I'll bet he's really thinking, *Why would anybody in her right mind want to be a nun?*

"I...want," she hesitates. "I need to know God."

"That's what all Christians and Catholics should want, Mary Frances. But do you really think you're called to serve?"

"I'm not sure. I think so."

"A vocation is a very serious commitment to God and to yourself. You should think long and hard about it before you act."

"I have. I'm sure," she says, sounding none-too-sure at all.

Mom looks at her, eyes filled with concerned tears. "We just don't want you to rush into something because of what's happened and then regret it later."

For the first time since Freddie killed Ken, Mary Frances's eyes flash with anger. Her voice is suddenly hard and certain.

"I know what I want, Mother." She turns to Father Quinn. "Why are you trying to talk me out of becoming a nun, Father? You're supposed to encourage me, aren't you? I've heard you give sermons about how much the church needs vocations and all. Well, here I am."

"I'm not trying to discourage you, it's just that when you make a life-changing decision, you should be as certain as you possibly can. Especially in regards to God."

"Were you sure?" Mary Frances asks.

Father Quinn sits back from the table as if she just threw a cookie at him. "Well...."

"Were you?"

"Mary Frances, it's not polite to interrogate Father, especially after all he's done for us since your father passed away, he's here to help you figure out what's best for you. He's trying to help."

"Did anybody try to talk you out of being a priest, Father?" she continues, ignoring Mom.

"Sure."

"And you didn't pay any attention to them, did you?"

"No, I didn't." Father Quinn leans forward across the table and grabs another cookie. He takes a bite, and doesn't seem to mind that it tastes terrible. Mom watches him closely. I can't read her expression, but she watches him so intently it's like she's eating the cookie with him.

"How come you became a priest?" I ask. I know this isn't really any of my business, but as long as they're making me sit here and listen, I might as well ask questions.

"I thought I could save the world. I wanted to help people love Jesus as much as I did."

Okay. Seems like a good answer. I'm satisfied, but Mary Frances isn't.

"Do you still love Jesus as much?" she asks, her voice rising because she thinks she's caught him.

"Faith gets harder the older you get, Mary Frances. You'll see."

We sit silently for a moment, and Father Quinn squirms nervously. Mom hates silence, so she starts to chatter.

"Is there anything else Father can help you with, Mary Frances? Questions or anything?"

Mary Frances levels her gaze at Father Quinn. "I don't know. Can you help me, Father?"

Father Quinn returns her look, and a tight, fake smile creases his face. His good looks take on a mask-like quality, as if pulled tight over something not nearly as attractive.

"Well," he says finally. "You have to do what you think is right, Mary Frances. Sometimes God shouts at us, sometimes He whispers." Nobody is satisfied with that non-answer, but neither Mom nor Mary Frances pushes it.

After a long silence, Father Quinn asks Mom, "How's everything been working, Sylvia?"

Mom brightens at the question. "My faucet's been dripping lately, do you think you could take a look at it?"

Father Quinn grins broadly. Fixing a leaky faucet, that's what he really wants to do, not give holy advice.

"Let's go have a look," he says, and Mom leads him to her bathroom. Mary Frances disgustedly tosses cookie remains back on the plate.

"He's no priest," she grumbles. "Not really. He's not holy. I'd be surprised if he even believes in God."

I nod. I think she's right. "Yeah. He's just a nice guy."

"I need to talk to somebody who *really* believes, who's really close to God."

"What about the nuns at the school?"

"I already have. That's why I'm going into their order. But it'd be nice to talk to somebody else who feels like I do, whose faith is as strong."

"Oh." Nobody tells me anything. The horrible thought occurs to me: *she's going to be in the same order as Sister Mary Annunciata!* That's as sickening as it gets. "If you want to talk to somebody who thinks they're holy, why don't you talk to Jesse?"

"I said holy, not psycho."

I consider standing up for Jesse, but on second thought I can't defend something I don't believe myself.

"Be careful of Jesse, Roger," says Mary Frances. She actually sounds concerned. "He's on the wrong track."

"He hasn't said anything about miracles or talking to Jesus lately."

"Good. Maybe he's grown out of it."

Even though they don't taste good, I have another cookie. They *are* chocolate chip, after all.

"Don't be a nun, Mary Frances. They're weird and scary."

"*I* won't be. I'll be something special." She gets a dreamy look in her eye. "Someone holy like Terese of Avila, somebody who spends her life getting closer to God, somebody whose prayers get listened to and who makes a difference. And maybe if I pray hard enough, I'll understand why things happen."

That's all she wants. To understand why Freddies kill Kens, why Dads die, why any of this stuff happens. She must think becoming a nun will put her closer to the answers, but I think she's wrong. It'll probably take her farther away. Unless there's some kind of super holy nun school I don't know about, I think she's making the biggest mistake of her life.

But I don't say anything to her because nobody cares about my opinion.

Jesse's big brother Mando has an old weight set, and he's gotten Jesse started lifting. I'm spotting for Jesse as he grunts and strains, trying to bench press two hundred pounds. If he has a problem I'm not going to be much help, but at least I'm offering moral support.

"You can do it, man, you can do it!" I say as he strains and tries to lock out his elbows. The most he's ever done is one-eighty, but he set that record last week and at the rate he's bulking up twenty pounds a week isn't unusual. There are a lot of guys in high school who can't bench press that much; Jesse's going to be a monster by the time he gets there.

"C'mon, Jesse, push, push!!"

He groans, gives it everything he's got, one last mighty push, locks out his elbows, he's made it! I help him guide the weights back into the rack and he sits up, grinning and sweaty.

"Fuckin' A, Rog. That was easy. I'm doin' two-twenty next week."

Jesse's got a blue bandana tied around his thick, unruly hair, and he's not wearing a shirt. His chest and arm muscles are well defined and hard; he looks a lot older than he is, and seeing him makes me more self-conscious than ever of my crippled wimpdom.

"Wanna run with me?" Jesse asks. He's been running a couple of miles a day and I usually follow along on my bike to keep him company. The high school coaches told him he might start on varsity as a freshman if he was in good enough shape, and he's been training like crazy ever since.

"Yeah, I guess. It's kind of smoggy, though."

"So what? Smog makes you strong, man, makes your lungs work harder, makes you tough."

"You're so full of shit, *mijo.*" Aunt Yolanda stands on the front porch, leaning against the house, her arms folded and a sly smile on her face. She's wearing tight jeans and an old T-shirt. I don't know how long she's been watching us, but seeing her immediately makes me nervous and self-conscious. Whenever she looks at me, I feel like I'm naked and she's on the verge of hysterical laughter.

"Yeah, well, shut up, Yolanda," Jesse says, not unkindly. He and Aunt Yolanda yell and swear at each other all the time, but I think it's because they're friends.

"Yeah, little *puto*, muscles won't do you no good, no girl's ever gonna look at you."

"*Pendeja*," Jesse mutters.

"Now your little honky friend Roger, girls gonna love him."

My face flares red-hot.

"He's different," she continues, amused at my embarrassment. "He's mysterious."

"Don't listen to her, Roger. She just likes to fuck with you."

Aunt Yolanda watches me, smiling. "Yeah, he's mysterious. Girls like mysterious."

"Yolanda's in college now, she thinks she's smart," Jesse says to me in a low voice. Yolanda overhears him and comes to the edge of the porch. She's suddenly angry; I guess she didn't like the way Jesse talked about her brains. She begins yelling at him in incredibly fast Spanish, and he yells back, and the only words I can make out are the cuss words. I'm glad they're fighting, though, because at least the attention is off me.

I wonder how long it'll be before Aunt Yolanda doesn't scare me.

"Mary Frances is gonna be a nun," I tell Jesse, pedaling alongside him while he runs. We're headed up Mountain Avenue, past the place where we got caught in the orange tree fire. It's all tract houses now. The place where we almost got barbecued is now a beige three-bedroom rancher with a swimming pool and a swing set in the back yard.

Jesse stops running. I brake to a stop as he mops sweat from his forehead and looks at me like I'm nuts. "What?" he asks, as if what I said is so absurd he must've misheard me.

"She wants to be a nun."

"Why?"

"I dunno. Something about getting closer to God."

"Maybe I should talk to her."

I shrug. I don't want to tell him what she thinks of his religious powers. I've been wondering if he still believes in the miracles and stuff, but I haven't wanted to ask until now.

"Do you talk to them anymore?"

He shrugs. "Yeah. Once in a while."

"When?"

"Dreams, mostly. And sometimes when I glaze during a boring class. They talk to me then." He looks down and stares at the road. "They're bugging me again. Especially Mary. She wants me to start preaching."

My stomach sinks. If he fires up the miracle stuff again, I'm sure to be included. "Preaching about what?" I ask, not really wanting to know.

"Jesus. God. All that stuff. They keep telling me that I'm blessed and chosen, that I don't need faith to believe because They've proven to me that They're real, now it's up to me to show the rest of the world that God exists."

I'm sorry I asked.

"But I told Them I don't wanna do it," he continues. "I mean, fuck, man, I just wanna get through the eighth grade and play football in high school, I don't wanna be a preacher or nothing."

Jesse's tales of talking to Jesus and Mary were easier to listen to back when I was a kid. Now, hearing him speak matter-of-factly about divine conversations, I realize that he's gone too far. He needs to stop.

"This is crazy, Jesse. Maybe you need to go to a psychiatrist or something."

Jesse looks up from the road and smiles at me. It's his infuriating "I know you don't really mean that smile". He wipes away more sweat trickles; it's oppressively hot and smoggy today, the kind of nasty Southern California day that makes you want to leave forever, to escape to a place with snow and seasons and air that isn't brown and doesn't smell chemically stale. But as Jesse smiles at me, I get the bad feeling that I'll be trapped here forever with him.

"You believe, Rog. You know you do."

"Yeah, right. So, what, you're gonna go out and be a preacher?" I ask. I try to sound contemptuous, but he doesn't catch it.

"Nah, not yet. Maybe I can talk Them out of it. I don't think I'd be no good at it." He turns and jogs off. "I just wanna play football."

I can't believe it. He claims that Jesus Christ and the Blessed Virgin Mary are speaking to him in dreams and visions, they're telling him to do things, but he's going to ignore them because he'd rather play football?

As I pedal alongside Jesse, I decide I need to get away from this guy, he's absolutely out of his mind, he's going to drag me into more crazy miracle garbage, I'm crazy to even hang around with him.

But, as always, I stick with him. We continue along Mountain Avenue, toward the invisible, smog-shrouded mountains. We're the ultimate odd couple: a solid-muscle mystical Mexican running smoothly and powerfully toward his varsity letter, and his trusty sidekick, a skinny, scarred, crippled kid wobbling alongside on his rickety ten speed.

School starts next week, so Jesse and I are taking advantage of the last few days riding our bikes around and savoring every second of smoggy freedom. Our destination: The Mall.

The town's population has grown, with tract house subdivisions sprouting all over from the remains of bulldozed orchards, so a couple of years ago some local businessmen decided it was time to build a mall. The guys who owned stores downtown screamed that a mall would ruin the town, that they'd all be driven out of business, but the developers didn't care. They bought up some orchards, plowed and burned the trees, and a covered mall with a Sears at one end and a Broadway at the other soon sprawled on the land. The new mall opened a few weeks ago, and it's changed our lives. For any kid in town, the mall is the best thing that's ever happened. We can hang out in air-conditioned comfort, wandering around free of parents and responsibilities. We can see friends, dodge enemies (I saw Bushman there last week), buy junky stuff—but most of all, it gives us a place to *go.* A destination. Everybody needs a destination.

On this hot, late summer day, Jesse and I lock our bikes out front and head inside to cool off and prowl.

Everything looks and smells new; the displays of 1969 fashions in the shop windows remind us how great it is to be growing up in America, in Southern California. There's so much *stuff*; it's reassuring to see what we could buy if we had the money. The mall makes me feel safe.

"Where you wanna go?" Jesse asks.

"I dunno. The record store?"

Jesse nods. We like to waste time there, thumbing through albums we can't afford, listening to Jimi Hendrix or something else noisy blaring over the store's speakers.

We head down the wide central atrium, past big indoor palm trees and a display of new Fords from the local dealer. Muzak purrs from hidden speakers, and the rhythmic movement of shoppers and strollers pulls us along. It's like an unseen force is controlling everybody: wander, shop, buy.

We come to the Groovy Vibes record store. Some unidentifiable acid rock blasts out the doors, drowning the Muzak in the mall, and the screechy electric guitars and yowling singing draws us in. Black light posters glow on the walls, and being here makes me feel like I'm getting away with something. Mom would hate it; so would Dad.

Dad. The thought of Dad makes me sad. He's been gone a few months, but already I'm beginning to forget what it was like having him around. The sharp edges of my memories are beginning to blur, and when I think about him, his face seems like a stranger's, or someone I saw on TV but never really knew. Sometimes, though, the very thought of Dad can make my eyes water and my throat close up. I don't think I'll ever be able to eat another bag of Fritos, especially stale ones; it's too painful a reminder of good old Dad.

Jesse and I wander the aisles, looking at album covers, always searching for the ones with semi-dressed, sexy women. It's amazing how many albums put women on the cover, but when you think about it, it's sensible; it makes me want to buy them.

As I round the album bins and go over to look at the singles I come face to face with Rhonda Fairly. I smile at my good fortune; my breath quickens and sweatbeads pop on my forehead. My exhilaration is short-lived, though, because when I finally pull my eyes from her cute, smiling face I see that she's not alone.

She's with Bushman.

I blink. Maybe it's a hallucination, maybe he'll go away. Nope. He's still here. Looking at me with a disgusted, hate-filled expression .

"Hi, Roger!" says Rhonda, all cheery and friendly. She spots Jesse a couple of aisles over and waves to him.

I'm too stunned to say anything, so I stand like an idiot and stare at them. Bushman smirks, and Rhonda looks at me with her usual interested, cheerful expression.

"Are you here with Jesse?" she asks. I nod, and then she nods, and then I nod again. There is a strained silence, then Rhonda chirps, "Me and Frank are going to see *Butch Cassidy and the Sundance Kid* later."

"It's rated R but my brother can get us in," Bushman adds, smugly.

I'm too thunderstruck to reply. Rhonda's going to a movie with Bushman?! Has she lost her mind? The guy's a red-haired living penis. And anyway, I'm the one she kissed.

I stand, stupidly, nodding for no apparent reason. Bushman contemptuously shakes his head and starts browsing through record albums.

"Are you okay, Roger?" Rhonda asks.

"Yeah," I manage, but I say it too loud and it comes out like a beagle's bark.

Jesse wanders over and makes small talk with Rhonda. I stand, staring at Bushman's back as he's bent over an album studying the cover. If I had something sharp I could sever his spinal cord and he'd never be able to take anybody to a movie again.

If only....

"You wanna go, Rog?" Jesse asks. I snap out of my murder fantasies and look at him.

"Go? Where?"

"To the movie with these guys."

Rhonda smiles expectantly. Panic chokes me. I'm not going anywhere or doing anything with Frank Bushman. It'd be like hanging around with Satan.

"No!"

Bushman looks up from the albums, and Rhonda and Jesse pull back from me, startled by my loud "No!"

"I mean, I can't go to an R-rated movie," I stammer. Bushman laughs at me. I feel like a complete fool.

"Okay," Rhonda says, being nice.

"C'mon, let's go," Bushman says. Rhonda smiles apologetically and then she and Bushman head out into the mall.

"Not cool, Rog," Jesse says.

I watch Rhonda disappear into the swarms of summertime shoppers with my archenemy. My eyes get heavy with tears; I try to blink them back. I feel so betrayed, so stupid. Of course she wouldn't care about a guy like me. I'm skinny and scarred and crippled and I'm turning zitty and I'm a loser.

"Hey, man. She's still okay, maybe she just ran into Bushman and he asked her to the movie and she was being nice and said yes," Jesse says, trying to help. "Everybody knows what a *pendejo* he is, man, she's just too nice to say no, that's all."

"Yeah."

"What do you wanna do now?"

"I dunno." I'm too drenched in self-pity to care.

We wander through the mall, past the theaters where Rhonda and Bushman are. I can't even bring myself to look at the ticket window; she's in there with him. In the dark, sitting next to his glowing red hair, breathing the same air he's breathing.

I feel sick.

We leave the mall and ride around aimlessly. Jesse tries to cheer me up, but I'm not paying attention and he finally gives up.

"See you," he says as he rides off for home. Even Jesse only has so much patience for a pouty, betrayed almost-eighth-grader.

I ride my bike for hours, until I'm sweaty and exhausted; I cover almost every street in town—except Rhonda's street. It's getting dark by the time I finally get home; the sun is setting into the smog-sea, and a beautiful burnt orange light bathes the neighborhood.

As I ride up my driveway, I see Father Quinn's car parked in the street. Mom's been complaining about a light switch that doesn't work, so I assume he's here to do his parish handyman thing. Our old Buick's gone, and at first I wonder where it is, but then I remember that Mary Frances was going out with some old high school friends since she'll be locked up in a convent soon.

I barge into the house with my usual, "I'm home, Mom, we got anything to eat?"

There is no reply, but I hear a scuffling sound out in the living room, so I go to see what it is. I expect to see Father Quinn fiddling with the light switch, I expect to see him turn and smile and say, "How you doing, Roger?", I expect to see Mom close by, watching him be Super Repair Priest.

What I don't expect to see are Mom and Father Quinn jumping up from the couch, straightening clothes and looking like the two guiltiest people on the face of the earth.

"Hi, Roger!" Mom chirps, shifting her shoulders so her blouse hangs right; she tugs at her mussed hair.

Father Quinn rubs a smear of Mom's lipstick from his chin and smiles weakly. He's dressed in his handyman clothes, so maybe since he's not wearing a priest's collar it's okay to be making out with lady parishioners—but I don't think so.

Mom stands by the couch, Father Quinn sits on it, and they both smile at me. Their smiles are grimaces, like a terrible moan is about to escape. I can think of absolutely nothing to say, so we continue to stare at each other.

Finally, Mom breaks the silence. "Want some dinner, honey?"

I just shake my head and go to my room.

This day has been too much.

I lie in bed, staring at the ceiling. My aquarium gurgles; I've been neglecting the guppies lately, but I think they're still breeding. It's hard to tell because the algae is so thick. I reach over and turn on the aquarium light. The glass is crusted with green and brown slime, and even with the light on all I can see are dim outlines inside. There are occasional darting movements, so some life form survives.

I'm lost. My own life is surrounded by a slime-covered shadow. Nobody can be trusted; no one is who or what they seem. Mom, Father Quinn, Rhonda, Mary Frances: mourning widows who kiss cheating priests, girls who trick you into thinking they're in love with you when they're really after red-haired dicks, and a weirdo sister who wants to be a sister.

I can't understand any of it. When Dad got electrocuted I thought, *okay, this is terrible, but I can deal with it. I have to deal with it. I'm the man of the house now, I'll have to grow up and take charge, help out, be....a man.* But instead all that's happened is everyone's gone crazy. And maybe I have, too.

I start eighth grade in a week and high school looms beyond. I'm supposed to start understanding things; life should be coming into focus. In five years I'll be considered an adult, I'll supposedly be prepared to go out in the world and survive. Unless I can start figuring out what's going on, unless I can even begin to understand people, I'm not going to have a chance.

Does anyone, I wonder? Maybe everybody just bumbles along, and the people who are supposed to know the answers—the priests, the politicians, the teachers, the parents—maybe they're all faking it. The crabby Sister Mary Annunciata who's so sure Jesus is on her side, the grouchy teacher who hates kids, the parent who's supposed to behave like an adult but doesn't—they're all liars, all fakes.

But maybe that's the point. The understanding that people—even the ones who are the most sure of themselves—are scared, confused liars, is the key to growing up, the key to dealing with it all.

As depressing as that thought is, it gives me comfort. If I can convince myself that the world is as afraid and confused as I am, I won't feel so alone.

I drift, the soft green light and low gurgle from the aquarium lulls me into a daze. My eyes flutter shut, and soon my brain flits from thought to thought, between dreams and reality. I'm thinking about Mom and Father Quinn one minute, then stepping off a curb and into the sky the next. I drift for awhile, then an image burns into my brain and I'm instantly awake.

Aunt Yolanda. I try to force her out of my mind but she won't go. Almost immediately, a hard-on stirs and I can't stop myself from fantasizing about her. My hand is on myself—I've only done this a few times because it gives me such a guilty conscience—but I can't stop. I don't want to stop.

Aunt Yolanda. Naked, wanton, she inhabits my feverdream of confused sex, with my eyes closed I see her, uninhibited, and she wants *me.* An annoying, intruding thought of Rhonda Fairly threatens to interrupt, but I push it aside and concentrate on Aunt Yolanda. She's warm, soft, and nasty—and then it's all over.

I lie perfectly still, a thin sheen of sweat evaporates quickly, and I wilt back to my puny, limp state. My breathing slowly returns to normal, and I savor the memory of my Aunt Yolanda fantasy. I have a mess to clean up in the sheets, but I'll worry about that later. Right now, all I want to do is think about Aunt Yolanda and forget about Rhonda and Mom and everything else.

But as I finally drift off to sleep, Aunt Yolanda fades away and I spend a troubled night tossing and turning and dreaming of priests and nuns and monsters with red hair.

Chapter Ten

As Mom says, "I do" I notice that the white paint on the gazebo is peeling.

Brother Charlie, pastor of the Third United Congregational Church of the Divine Light, has just finished marrying Mom and Father Quinn. Brother Charlie is an old hippie friend of Father Quinn's; I think they were in the seminary together, but Brother Charlie bailed out to be a full-time beatnik. When the hippies came along, he blended right in. His braided gray hair hangs down to his waist, and his bushy beard is speckled with tiny, freshly picked wildflowers. His tie-dyed caftan flaps gently in the breeze.

We're standing in a park not far from home; it's not too smoggy today, and the air is warm and soothing.

It's a good day to get married.

After I walked in on Mom and Father Quinn that night, they decided it was time to bring things out in the open. Father Quinn took a leave of absence from being a priest and started working as a counselor, and he continued to come over to fix things and make out with Mom.

Mary Frances was furious that Mom dared take a holy man away from Jesus, and on the day she stomped off to the convent she refused to say good-bye to either of them. It didn't seem like a real good way to start a religious life to me, but that's Mary Frances. Even though she's turned toward God, she's still a crabby grouch. Maybe the nuns in the convent can change her, but I doubt it. They're just as crabby; she'll fit right in.

It's taken a long time to get used to Father Quinn not being Father Quinn anymore. Now he's the guy who's married to Mom. I don't know what to call him. Father Father?

Mom is smiling radiantly; she looks happier than I've ever seen her— happier than even when Dad was alive. She's wearing a casual, flowery dress and a big floppy hat. She doesn't look like the Mom I know. Since Dad died and Father Quinn started hanging around she's changed a lot. She seems younger.

Father Quinn is big into social causes, and he's gotten Mom to go to anti-war rallies and ban the bomb marches. She was reluctant at first, because when Dad was alive she didn't ever express political opinions; she reacted to Dad and agreed with him. He did the talking and complaining, and he spoke for the both of them. Or so it seemed.

But with Dad gone, and Father Quinn on the scene, Mom suddenly changed into a person with real opinions and ideas. She said the war in Vietnam was wrong; I never knew she felt that way. She'd never said anything before. And she hated Nixon; when Dad was alive I assumed she liked the guy as much as he did. She never said she didn't. And now, along with her new ideas, she looks different. The middle-class generic mom look is fading away and now she seems softer. Seeing her lately, I've begun to realize how pretty she is. Even Jesse noticed.

"What's with your mom? She's lookin' good, man," he said a few days before the wedding.

"Shut up," I mumbled. The idea of Mom being noticed by guys bothered me. Jesse just laughed, but I could see why he asked. Mom was kind of foxy-looking lately.

Father Quinn took me out to dinner shortly after I caught them on the couch. It was one of those "man-to-man" things; we both ordered steaks and he tried to explain why he was ditching the church and kissing Mom.

"I'd really hoped Mary Frances would come with us," he said. She'd gone into the convent and they wouldn't let her leave since part of being a baby nun is staying away from your family. But she probably would have refused to talk to any of us anyway. "Since she couldn't be here, I still wanted to try to put all this into perspective for you."

I carved off a chunk of T-bone. For a skinny wimp, my appetite was huge lately. I didn't want to make this too easy for Father Quinn, so I just chewed and stared at him.

"Well," he continued. I felt bad for the guy, because this was obviously hard for him, but it was nice to have a feeling of power over an old authority figure, so I didn't give in to the urge to be nice. "What's happened between Sylvia—your mother—and me is, well, wonderful."

"Uh-huh."

"Love is something so special, so strong, that we shouldn't ever resist it."

Geez, he was slipping into a sermon. If this was all he had to say, I wasn't interested.

"I think you liked my mom before my dad died. I saw the way you looked at each other."

Father Quinn blushed. The noises in the restaurant—clangs of silverware, bursts of laughter and talk—made things even more uncomfortable between us. Something about the sound of everybody else having fun made it feel like we were talking about something illegal or dirty. Father Quinn sat there looking desperate and lonely.

"I want you to know," he said, leaning over the table, his voice low and serious, "that I never, never, did anything disrespectful while your dad was alive."

"Sometimes you don't have to *do* anything to be disrespectful," I said .

He leaned back and sighed. After a few embarrassed moments he said, "You're right. But I couldn't help it. From the first day I saw your mom I was in love with her."

Now it was my turn to be uncomfortable. I didn't want to hear this. Mom, love—it was too much. Father Quinn had known our family for years; during all those Sundays he gave communion to Mom was he having Aunt Yolanda-style fantasies about her? My appetite vanished and I pushed my plate away.

"I know it's hard to understand. It'd be hard for you to accept anyone falling in love with your mom, but it's especially hard when the person who loves your mom is your old parish priest." *No kidding,* I thought. "And I don't know how to make you more comfortable with the idea. I think we all need time to adjust."

"Are you going to get married?" I asked, hoping that the blunt question would make him squirm and say no.

"Yes. After a little more time has passed."

Someday I'd be calling Father Quinn "Dad". It was just too weird to imagine.

Time passed and things did get a little easier. Just having Father Quinn around all the time—and seeing how happy Mom was—helped calm my fears.

I was still a little uneasy around Father Quinn, because, to me, he'd always be a priest. I couldn't picture him sliding into a dad role; I kept expecting him to show up in his collar, or see him on the altar at Sunday mass, dressed in vestments and raising the chalice during the consecration.

Instead, he was at home with us eating stringy pot roast and passing the ketchup.

A good-sized crowd is at the park watching Father Quinn give Mom the official, just-married kiss. There are even a couple of priest friends of Father Quinn's, although they're not wearing their collars. He'd said they had to come undercover or else they'd get in trouble with the bishop.

Everybody applauds and laughs as they kiss and Brother Charlie holds his hands above them to bless the union.

I'm standing with Jesse, and he's clapping and laughing along with everybody else. I'm trying, but I just can't get excited about this. I'm the one who's going to have to live under the same roof with a new priest/dad, knowing he's in the bedroom with Mom doing...whatever.

"This is cool, man," Jesse says. "A priest married to your mom."

"Ex-priest."

"He's always a priest. That's what the church says. Even if he quits and gets married."

Great. I have visions of communion at the kitchen table and confessions in the rec room.

"Jesus and Mary tell you about this happening?" I ask, feeling grouchy.

"Nah. But I'll ask 'em next time if they're mad at Father Quinn. Maybe they'll tell me if he's gonna go to hell."

Jesse's smiling like it's all a big joke; I'm never sure how to take him. Sometimes he's just screwing around and being weird, other times he's dead serious. It's impossible to tell the difference. For someone who's supposedly a messenger for God, he doesn't take his role very seriously. He can be talking about tits one minute and holy miracles the next.

Mom and Father Quinn come down from the gazebo into the crowd of well wishers. Mom hugs me and gives me an embarrassing wet kiss on the cheek, and Father Quinn shakes my hand so hard it tingles with pain.

They've rented a banquet room at a restaurant next to the park, and everybody strolls over in the shade of the park's canopy of droopy pepper trees. It would all seem fun and romantic to me if it were somebody besides Mom and Father Quinn.

The wedding guests are giddy and happy, but I notice that they're not the usual crowd of people I'd expect to be hanging around Mom. There aren't many people from church; most of the old boozing party crowd hasn't shown up. Mom and Father Quinn are a parish scandal, and people who had been friends for years have shunned Mom and treat her like a leper.

We still go to church, but when we go, whatever pew we choose quickly empties out. We're always alone, even if the church is crowded, and nobody will turn and shake hands during the sign of peace. It's embarrassing and humiliating, and at first Mom cried every Sunday after we got home from church. Father Quinn doesn't go to mass anymore, so he'd take us out to brunch someplace and try to cheer Mom up by being perky and pumping her full of champagne. He finally convinced Mom that if people wanted to be jerks and act like unholy five-year-olds, it wasn't her fault and she should be defiant.

"Fuck 'em," Father Quinn said after Mom had a particularly grueling time at mass. He immediately blushed bright red. "Ooops, sorry, didn't mean to cuss." But it was just what Mom needed. She laughed and stopped crying and from then on she slowly got used to her role as parish slut.

The only church people who still treated Mom well were Rhonda Fairly's parents and Jesse's family. Maybe they're all nice to Mom since I'm such a great guy. It's a respect thing.

Well, it's a thought.

The wedding reception is kind of fun. A noisy band plays a weird combination of normal music like Rolling Stones and Beatles, and then they veer to goofy old stuff that Mom likes.

There's lots of food and booze, and the wedding guests suck up plenty of both. The guests are a mixture of pals Father Quinn has made over the years—priests know a lot of people—and new friends from anti-war marches and other places. Father Quinn has a talent for making friends, and in the few months they've been together they've met more people than Mom and Dad did during their entire marriage.

Jesse and I sneak champagne in paper cups and load up on cold cuts and *hors d'ouvres*. The champagne gives me a buzz; I like the feeling. I've had a few drinks before, but never enough to feel really happy. This time I'm guzzling champagne and I understand why people like it so much. I feel light; my worries drain away. I'm actually happy that Mom and Father Quinn are married, and I'm looking forward to him moving in. The world's a great place, I'm happy, nothing bad will ever happen—

"Shit," says Jesse, breaking into my good mood.

"What?"

"Fuckin' Yolanda's here."

I pivot on feather-light feet toward the door. It takes a minute for my eyes to catch up with my body and the room spins. I squint and wait for the dizziness to pass, and then my eyes lock on Aunt Yolanda.

She's standing at the entrance to the banquet room, surveying the scene, looking cool and bemused.

"Wow," I say to Jesse, my tongue sluggish and thick. "She's beautiful, man."

Jesse looks at me like I'm crazy. "Yolanda?"

"I love her."

Jesse bursts into laughter. "You're fuckin' drunk!"

Maybe I am, but his words hurt me. "You just don't see 'cause you're related to her. She's...special."

Jesse drains his champagne cup and shakes his head. "'Love her'. Shit."

I can't pull my eyes away from Aunt Yolanda. She's wearing tight Levi bellbottoms, a too-tight fuzzy white sweater, and way too much makeup.

She looks great.

"She's beautiful, man," I repeat. My words are slurred.

"She's twenty-eight. She's old and she has kids and she's my aunt. You're crazy. You need to beat off more."

Beating off has become a main topic of conversation lately. When Jesse isn't talking about talking to the Virgin, he's talking about sex and masturbation. I need to read some of Mary Frances's lives of the saints books to see if this is common to all saintly people. It seems to me that maybe Jesse's on a strange track to holiness.

I watch Aunt Yolanda stroll over to Mom and Father Quinn's table. I can't hear what she says over the din of the band, but she smiles and hugs both Mom and Father Quinn. It surprises me, because she doesn't know either one of them very well and she wasn't invited to the wedding, but they don't seem to mind. They're so caught up in the festivities I don't think they care who shows up.

"She likes wedding receptions," Jesse says. "She hears about weddings and just shows up, even if she don't know anybody."

"Why?"

"Dunno. Maybe because she never had one. She never goes to weddings, though. She hates those. Just receptions."

I watch her and wonder. Why wedding receptions? Free food and booze? Maybe. Or maybe she just likes the crowded closeness of happy people. I can see why she might; I like the feeling myself.

She moves through the packed banquet room toward the dance floor. People are stuffed into the small area, some couples bouncing and moving to their own personal beat, others clinging tightly as if the music gives them permission to make out standing up. Aunt Yolanda disappears behind a group of people and emerges with an older, longhaired guy and heads to the dance floor.

How she managed to grab a stranger so quickly amazes me, but then, I guess if other guys see her the way I do, it isn't that surprising.

They dance, the guy jerky and spazzy-looking like most guys are when they dance, Aunt Yolanda moving with the music, oblivious to the guy, lost in the music and her body. I can't look away from her; she moves sensuously, her eyes heavy and half-closed, I don't think she hears the music so much as she feels it. The guy she's dancing with stares at her with wide, horny eyes. I know how he feels.

The song ends, Aunt Yolanda reluctantly stops dancing, gives the guy a courtesy smile and wanders over toward Jesse and me. When she sees me she smiles—not a fake smile like she gave her dance partner, but a real, friendly, and, to my drunk eyes, eager smile.

She pours herself a cup of champagne and gulps it down. Her eyes never leave mine.

"So how's Roger?" she teases.

"Roger's drunk," Jesse says with a snort.

"Go make a miracle or something," she says with a wave.

"Fuck you, Yolanda." Jesse isn't used to being dismissed by anybody. Aunt Yolanda slowly turns to him and gives him a withering look of such scorn that it blows him out of the room. He stomps off, muttering, then looks back. "Roger says he loves you even though you're a *puta*. Ask him about it."

I could've done without that. I'm sweaty and weak-kneed enough as it is from the combination of cheap champagne and Aunt Yolanda lust. I don't need to add embarrassment to the mix.

Aunt Yolanda ignores Jesse and looks back at me, her annoyed expression instantly replaced by a dazzling smile.

"I dunno why you're friends with that little *pendejo*."

"We go way back."

"Old buddies forever, huh?"

I tell her about almost killing him back in first grade and how we ended up being friends. It might be the champagne, but Aunt Yolanda seems easy to talk to. She reminds me of the way Rhonda Fairly used to be, how I could talk to her about anything and she'd listen and be friendly and make me feel like what I was saying was the most important thing in the world.

Aunt Yolanda leans close to hear me when the band starts to play again, and I'm momentarily distracted by the way she smells. It's some kind of orange blossom perfume, and it's so sweet it makes me want to dive into her and not let go. She's close enough that I can see the pores in her skin and dangling flecks of mascara on her huge, false eyelashes. Up close her black hair is really more brown, with dozens of different, subtle shades that reflect the light into sparkling highlights.

I lose track of what I'm saying and sputter into dopey silence.

"Huh," she says, smiling, politely ignoring the fact that I'm an idiot.

"Wanna dance?"

My heart smashes against my ribs, every fiber of my being screams "NO!" since I've never danced before and I'll look like a clown and I'm still afraid of Aunt Yolanda.

But I don't get the chance because she grabs my arm and yanks me out onto the dance floor. The band is doing *Yesterday* and it's slow dance, cling-to-each-other-like-you-really-mean-it time. I'm horrified and exhilarated when she pulls me close and holds me tightly against her. I'm as tall as she is; our eyes are on the same level and I can't look away. She leads, and I stumble along. I'd like to say I'm a bad dancer because of my gimpy leg, but I think it's mostly because I'm a spaz.

I accidentally step on her toe. "Geez, I'm sorry!"

"It's okay. You're a good dancer."

"No I'm not. I'm a dork."

She laughs, tosses her head back, and her soft hair brushes against my cheek. She holds me close as we move to the music.

I see Mom and Father Quinn, guzzling champagne at their table, watching and grinning. Mom's grin is especially infuriating, because it's her "Isn't he cute?" look. If she only knew that at this instant—

I'm getting a hard-on! Oh shit. I don't want this to happen, please don't, my body's betraying me, but there's nothing I can do because this is the first time in my life that I've been held so tightly against a woman—a woman I've had the hots for since I was a little kid. I can feel her soft breasts against my chest, and my hands are holding the small of her back. My body is tight against hers, I can feel her hips move against mine as we dance, so a hard-on is only natural. There's nothing I can do. You can't wish them away.

I pray that she doesn't notice and that the song will end and I can get away, because no matter how exciting and good this feels, the fear and humiliation of getting caught are worse. The lead singer is just about to the end of the song, and I try to pull away to keep my hips from touching hers, and just as I think I've made it she makes a sudden turn, pulls me close, and *bam*! I've been discovered.

"Oooh, you like to dance, huh?" she whispers. She leans close to my ear and gives my earlobe a quick bite. "Anytime, Roger boy, anytime." The song ends and she lets me go. I try to smile, but it comes out a grimace, and I try to talk but I can't do that either, so I just nod and walk off the dance floor, partly bent over to hide my rapidly deflating dick. I hear Aunt Yolanda laughing in the background.

In bed tonight I furiously beat off. It's the best ever.

Later, as I calm down and drift off to sleep, I'm surprised to find that I'm thinking not of Aunt Yolanda, but Rhonda Fairly.

Eighth grade has been strange. It's March 1970, and I'm at a loss to explain what's happened with Rhonda Fairly lately.

After seeing her with Bushman at the mall, I did my best to avoid her. When school started, I was relieved to find we didn't have any classes together. I decided that since she stomped on my heart, the best way to get over it was forget she existed.

Easier said than done.

I'd still see her at school, or at church, and she'd always be perky and annoying and say, "Hi!" or try to make chitchat in the hallway. I was never rude, but I didn't go out of my way to be friendly because it hurt too much.

She never mentioned dumping me for Bushman, or the kiss we'd shared after Dad died. To her, it was like neither had ever happened, although I guess she didn't really dump me; it's not like we were going out or anything. But we might have. If Bush-dick hadn't showed up.

She was still with the jerk. Rumor had it that he'd given her a necklace and they were going steady. That news was bad enough, but the fact that Bushman still tormented me made it even worse. I think he knew how I felt about Rhonda, and he liked rubbing my nose in it. I was stuck in PE with the asshole, and he always made sure I heard him brag about how he'd felt Rhonda up or French-kissed her the night before. My anger would rise, and my face would turn red, but I never said anything because I knew he'd pound me if I did. I was pretty sure he was lying, because even though Rhonda had betrayed me, I knew her well enough to know that she wouldn't be sleazy with anybody, especially Bushman.

"Yeah, I got to third base," Bushman bragged one day in the locker room, after we'd all showered and were getting dressed. I wasn't really sure what third base was, but I knew it involved female flesh and I also knew it was a place I'd probably never go. "Yep, home run coming up," he grinned, and I wanted to smash his face in.

Bushman's little band of jerk followers snickered knowingly with him, but nobody said anything until Wisma, my white guy *vato* savior, slammed his locker shut.

"Fuckin' *joto*," Wisma muttered. Everybody shut up, because he'd just called Bushman a queer. Everybody knows what a *joto* is. "You ain't shit, Bushman. Only thing you ever gonna fuck is your right hand."

Bushman's a bully, but bullies only pick on weak guys like me, so when Wisma challenged him, he knew better than to fight back. He laughed nervously and mumbled, "Fuck you."

"What'd you say, fucker?!" Wisma was pissed. This was getting interesting; I was liking Wisma more and more.

"Nothin', man."

Wisma glared at him, finished buttoning his Pendleton, dragged a comb through his slick hair, and walked out of the locker room. I made the mistake of getting caught smiling by Bushman.

"What're you smilin' at, fag?!"

"Nothing."

Bushman moved toward me, followed by his buddies. I straddled the bench between the lockers and tried to prepare myself for the inevitable beating. Jesse wasn't in the same period PE this year, and with Wisma gone and the coaches outside sneaking cigarettes, I was on my own.

Bushman was almost to me, and I quickly buttoned my shirt because somehow it seemed faggier to get beat-up being half-dressed. He was reaching out to shove me when he slipped on a water puddle underneath the bench. His shove turned into a wild arm wave as he tried to regain his balance, but it was too late, he was going down, and he smacked the concrete floor with a satisfying *crack*. His ugly red head bounced like a basketball, and his eyes rolled back so only the whites were showing. His pals froze, waiting to see if he was okay. They never acted on their own, Bushman had to lead them, so with him out cold, they were helpless.

I had a choice. I could've run away, taken advantage of the distraction, and scurried out of the locker room like a cockroach trying to outrun the can of Raid, or I could wait for him to come to and take my medicine.

Actually, I had a third choice, which was to take advantage of the situation and kick him while he was down.

I decided I liked that idea.

So I kicked him; in the head, in the chest, in the stomach, with my good leg and my bad leg, the blind white rage I hadn't felt in a long time returned and I couldn't stop, couldn't think, I wasn't aware of anything but hate and anger. I kicked him for being Bushman, for tormenting me, for taking Rhonda away and making me feel like a fool, I kicked him for everything rotten that had happened to me from being run over by Joe Fanucci to Dad getting electrocuted, I wanted to kill him, if I did that everything would be okay.

But the white rage vaporized away, and the kicks became half-hearted, and I became aware again as his dull-witted pals finally acted and pulled me away.

It was my bad luck that the coaches decided to wander back into the locker room right then, just in time to see me land one last kick to the side of Bushman's head. They started screaming at me to stop, and before I knew it I was down at the vice principal's office and Bushman was in the school nurse's office getting bandaged and cooed at.

As I sat in the hall I heard Bushman bellowing and whining about how hurt he was. Even though I knew I was in big trouble—the stern, angry expression on the vice principal's face as he ushered me into his office said that I was a dead man—I couldn't help but smile.

It felt good.

I got a week's suspension for beating up Bushman. Right after I tried to kill the ugly, carrot-topped pig, they called in Mom and Father Quinn for a conference, and everybody acted shocked and amazed that I'd done something like that.

"You know, Jesus spoke often about forgiveness against our enemies," Father Quinn said on the long ride home after the conference. He couldn't help slipping into priest mode even though he wasn't one anymore.

"I know," I sighed.

"What on earth got into you, Roger?" Mom asked. "You've always been such a sweet boy. To attack that other boy the way you did, it's so unlike you."

"You don't understand, Mom," I said, weary but still elated that I'd finally got even with Bushman.

"Well, I guess I don't understand how you could kick somebody while they were down."

"Bushman's done it to me plenty of times," I said.

"Then why didn't you tell me? I could've spoken to his mother."

I didn't bother to answer. If she didn't understand why eighth grade guys had to deal with bullies and psychos their own way, she never would.

"It's the code, Sylvia," said Father Quinn. "You know, guys. We take care of our own problems." He glanced back up in the rearview mirror and smiled. At least *he* understood. "Which isn't to say it's right," he added quickly. "That's just the way it is."

"I'll never understand males," Mom sighed. She turned back and looked at me. "I want you to write what's his name?"

"Bushman."

"Does he have a first name?"

"Frank."

"I want you to write Frank an apology note and then deliver it to him personally, do you understand?"

"Mom!"

"Just do it!" she snapped. There was steel in her voice, so I didn't argue. I looked to Father Quinn for help, but since he was the new kid on the block he was staying out of it, for the most part, except to drop in Jesus quotes.

"Blessed are the peacemakers," he said, and we drove the rest of the way home in silence.

I stalled as long as I could, but Mom stayed on me and made sure I wrote Bushman an apology letter.

"Are you finished yet?" she demanded.

"Yeah. I guess."

"Then go over to his house right now."

"Mom...."

"Now!"

I got on my bike and rode to his house. The few steps to his front door were the longest of my life. I felt like I was walking into death; I knew how people felt right before their execution.

I hesitated, considered running away, then sucked up what little courage I had and rang the doorbell. I heard the sound of someone shuffling to the door. I hoped there wasn't a gun in the house.

The door opened a crack and a woman looked out. "Yeah?" she said in a raspy voice.

"I'm Roger Donnelly."

The door opened further. Bushman's mom stood before me in a ratty bathrobe. Her hair was rolled in big, spiky curlers; they made her head look inflated. Her eyes were puffy and red, and her skin was an unhealthy yellowish-gray. She was unusually ugly. I couldn't see any resemblance between her and Bushman, except for the ugly part. Maybe he was adopted.

"You the kid who beat him up?" she asked, her voice slurred slightly. It reminded me of the way Dad sounded during his Knights of Columbus parties.

"Yeah," I mumbled, secretly pleased at being known as "The kid who beat him up". "Is he here?" I asked, wanting to get this over with.

"C'mon in." She turned and I followed.

The inside of the house was dark and messy; all the drapes were closed, and it smelled musty and sour. A couple of mangy cats sprawled on the couch, and the TV blared a soap opera. An ironing board sat in the living room, clothes mounded on top. They looked like they'd been there for months.

Mrs. Bushman led me into the kitchen, which was even grosser than the rest of the house. Dirty, crusted dishes towered on the sink; the trash overflowed.

"Frankie beat you up?" she asked, plopping down at the cluttered kitchen table. She sipped from a full glass; I think it was wine. She motioned for me to sit.

"Sometimes," I said.

"All my boys are bullies, they're like their father."

"Uh-huh."

"Bastard," she muttered. She took a long guzzle and lit a cigarette. "The boys' father left me. No word, no alimony, no child support, no nothing. We're gonna have to move soon."

I didn't know what to say. I just wanted to get out of the depressing house and away from this drunken lady.

"Frankie's a lot like his father. Too bad. Probably deserved whatever you did to him."

I felt bold. "He did," I said. "He deserved more than he got." I handed her the apology note I'd scrawled. "Can you give this to him?"

She grabbed the note, scanned it with bleary eyes, and smiled. "Your mom make you do this, hon?"

"Yeah."

"You're not sorry one bit, are you?"

"No."

"Good. Being sorry's for losers. Don't ever be sorry for mean people. Frankie may be my son, but I don't like him very much. And I don't blame you for not liking him, either."

"Is he here?" I asked, suddenly worried that he might be overhearing the conversation and taking notes on new ways to pound me. I may have gotten him once, but it was cheating, and I knew that there would be payback.

"He's out with his brother somewhere doing god knows what." She crumpled the apology note and tossed it toward the overflowing trash can. It bounced onto the floor. "I won't tell him you came by. It'll be our little secret."

She may have been drunk and ugly and Bushman's mom, but I liked her. I got up to leave, and she held up her glass in a toast.

"Cheers, Ray."

"Roger."

"Roger. Don't take anything from anybody. And feel free to beat up Frankie anytime. He's just like his father."

I left her sitting in her filthy kitchen, sipping wine and mumbling about her sons and their no-good father.

It's our spring field trip, and we're going to the beach to pick up trash for Earth Day. It's cool and foggy as the four busloads of eighth graders roll into the parking lot, and as we pile out of the busses I see that our school isn't the only one who had the idea to pick up beach trash. Hundreds of kids from all over Southern California are fanned out on the sand; some pick up junk, but most just goof off, splashing each other in the foamy surf or running around for no apparent reason. The beach does that to you.

"Man, this is bullshit," Jesse complains as he picks up a black banana peel and disgustedly tosses it in his plastic garbage bag. I'm shuffling along next to him with my garbage bag, but I'm more interested in the way the sand feels between my toes than in picking up trash.

"It's Earth Day," I say. "You're supposed to feel good about it."

"Shit. I ain't no janitor."

I scan the beach for Bushman and Rhonda. I haven't spoken to Bushman since I talked to his mom; the few times I've seen him at school he's avoided me, almost as if he's afraid of me. I was amazed at first; now I like the feeling. It's power.

"*Cabron*," Jesse mumbles. He's found a used rubber. "Look at this, man!" A small crowd gathers around and studies the wrinkled, gummy-looking thing as if it's an archaeological artifact.

"Gross," says one guy, bending closer to inspect it. Most of us have never seen a rubber close up, and I have a feeling some of us are only dimly aware of its use and purpose.

"I'm not pickin' this shit up," Jesse complains, and then he stomps off down the beach, kicking dead kelp leaves out of his path. The rest of us stand, gazing down at the rubber, lost in our dreams that someday, we too will get to wear one. The only thing that worries me is that it looks so big; it would fall off me. Great, another thing to be concerned about: a tiny dick.

Our inspection team slowly dissipates, although nobody picks up the rubber and puts it into their trash bag. I wander along the beach, watching the waves splash and foam. I feel good now, better than I have in a long time. I've earned Bushman's fear, though I don't know how long that will last, and for some reason the Rhonda problem seems far away and silly.

At least it is until I hear: "Roger?"

I turn. Rhonda stands behind me, holding her full trash bag. Of course. Always the over-achiever. My bag flaps empty in the cool sea breeze.

"Hi."

"Can I talk to you?"

"I guess." My heart pounds and the sweat beads pop on my forehead.

Will it always be like this when I'm around girls? I hope not; it's really annoying.

She sits down. Her long hair hangs down her back and brushes against the wet sand. As I sit next to her, I'm aware of how small she seems. Maybe I'm growing and I don't know it, but suddenly she seems thin and frail. She pulls her knees up to her chest and stares out at the gray ocean. She shivers.

"Why don't you talk to me anymore, Roger?"

Using my stunning conversational skills, I say nothing and shrug.

"It's like you avoid me. Did I do something?" she asks, her voice quiet and hurt-filled.

Yeah, you did something, you started going out with that fucker Bushman, what do you think?! But I don't say that. No, I'm not honest enough to tell the truth, so instead I mumble, "You didn't do anything."

"Then what's wrong?"

"I dunno."

We sit in silence for a moment, both staring out at the waves. Squawking seagulls flap around on the beach behind us, fighting over an old hot dog bun. They start to bug me and I toss some kelp scraps at them. They don't even bother to look at me as they continue to squawk and fight.

"I thought we were friends," she says.

"We are."

"If we're friends then we should talk. If we're—"

"How could you hang around with him?!" I blurt out, finally fed up that she doesn't understand.

"Who?" she asks, startled.

"Bushman!"

"He's nice."

"Nice? He's an asshole, he's been trying to kill me from the minute he first saw me, he talks about you like you're some kind of...well, he doesn't talk about you like you're a good Catholic!"

Rhonda looks at me with wide, disbelieving eyes.

"And he's a liar, and he's...." I sputter and run out of names to call him. Rhonda looks so utterly shocked that I have a hard time continuing. I can't believe that all this is news to her.

I expect her to start crying or yell at me, but she does neither. "*You're* the one who tried to kill somebody, not him. At least that's what I heard."

"Did he tell you that?"

"Everybody says you're weird, Roger. They say you and Jesse are still into all that miracle stuff, and that when you got run over it messed up your head. I always try to stand up for you, because you're my friend and we've been friends forever, but then you go and try to hurt somebody that I like, it's hard for me to make excuses for you."

I can't believe it. All the shit I've had to take from people, especially Bushman, and somehow it's my fault?!

"You don't understand, Rhonda. He's...Bushman's crazy, he's mean. You wouldn't believe the stuff he's done to me, and then the other day, he tried to beat me up, I got a chance to fight back so I did and I'm the one who got in trouble, it's not fair!" There's an annoying whine in my voice that even I can hear.

"I don't know what's wrong with you, maybe what people say is right."

"But—"

"Maybe we shouldn't be friends anymore. Until you get normal again."

She stands, grabs her trash bag, and heads off down the beach.

So much for my good mood. Jesse wanders back, still grumpy about having to pick up trash. He plops down on the sand next to me.

"What'd Rhonda want?"

"Not to be friends anymore."

"Because you kicked Bushman's ass?"

I nod. "She says people think I'm weird."

"You are."

I look sharply at him, and he gives me his best Jesse Montoya crooked grin.

"Shut up," I mumble, trying to hold back my own smile. "She also said people talk about you and me and the miracle stuff."

Jesse's smile fades. "Yeah, I've heard. Nothin' I can do about that. Except maybe do some more stuff to prove to everybody it's true."

I get that old familiar feeling of dread. "Like what?"

"Dunno. They been talking to me, but I don't know what They want to do yet. But I think something's coming up."

"And I get to be there when it happens."

"That's the deal, *ese*." He jumps up and offers me his hand. I grab it and he pulls me up. His good mood has returned. "Let's go pick up some fuckin' trash, man. Fuckin' Earth Day, right on!"

I feel something wet on the palm of me hand.

Blood.

But it isn't mine.

"Hey, Jesse?"

"Yeah," he says, heading down the beach searching for beer cans and used rubbers.

"Is your hand bleeding?"

He looks at his palm, then drops his trash bag. I go to him and look. The stigmata marks are in his palms, oozing thick, sticky blood.

"Easter-time," he sighs. "Fuck."

He clenches his fists tightly, then opens them and rubs the blood on his Levi's. "I don't like this shit. They don't tell me what I'm supposed to do, like if I'm supposed to show it to everybody or what."

I don't know what to say. This stuff gives me the creeps.

"Fuck," he says again, softly. He picks up his garbage bag and slowly shuffles off down the beach.

I hope Jesus and the Virgin aren't easily offended, because Jesse sure says "Fuck" a lot.

"Hey Rog, wanna go outside and throw the old Frisbee around?" Father Quinn asks.

"I guess," I say, trying to sound interested.

"Groovy." He bounds out of the house like a puppy, and I limp along behind him.

Father Quinn's been trying real hard to be a substitute dad to me, and I appreciate the effort. I really do.

But he's beginning to get annoying.

After I caught him and Mom making out and they announced to the world that they were a couple, Father Quinn stayed in the background and didn't try to push the new dad business. He understood that I was uneasy about all this, and that he needed to keep his distance and let me adjust.

But now that he's living in the same house, and the familiarity of being under one roof has worn down the feeling that you're sharing a house with an amiable stranger who'll eventually leave, Father Quinn's shifted into DAD mode and I get to be his target.

First it was the good-natured jokes when Mom was being weird and we'd share a raised eyebrow or a witty wisecrack. I didn't mind that, it's kind of fun to have somebody to laugh at Mom with. And she didn't mind either, because it meant she was getting attention, and she always likes attention. But then Father Quinn started to pry into my life.

"How *are* you, Roger? Really?" he asked one day, appearing at my bedroom door while I was trying to finish some math homework. His voice was insistent and serious. As if how I *really* was mattered more than anything in the world. I knew this voice. I'd heard it before. In confession.

"*Really* okay, I guess."

"Really?"

"Really."

Father Quinn came in and sat down on my bed. He gazed into my aquarium, fascinated by the bubbles and green algae/scum-covered glass.

"Do you pray, Roger?"

Actually, I'd just finished praying. I couldn't figure out my math homework and we were having a test the next day, so I'd asked God for some help. But I didn't see any reason to tell Father Quinn the details.

"Sure," I said, hoping he'd go away.

"That's good." His voice trailed off as he leaned toward the aquarium. "Are there any fish in here?"

"Guppies. They breed like crazy."

"That's good. Good." He wasn't listening and I didn't know what was going on. I wished he'd leave.

"So. I'm just trying to do some homework."

"Uh-huh." He finally took his eyes away from the fish tank and looked at me. "It's important to be happy."

I didn't know what else to say, so I just looked at him.

"And I think happiness is the people in your life, don't you agree?"

"Sure."

"I'm one of the people in your life now, Roger. I want you to be happy with me as your stepfather."

"Okay."

"So if there's any man kind of stuff you want to talk about, I'm here. Or anything, for that matter."

"Okay."

He got up and went to the door. "I'm glad we had this little talk." He smiled and left.

I had no idea what the point of all that was, but it must've been important to him, because soon after he started acting Dad-like. I think he got his idea of Dad-dom from movies and old TV shows, because he was always suggesting that we go outside and throw something. Footballs, Frisbees, whatever, it was always, "Hey, Rog, let's go outside and throw the old *fill-in-the-blank* around."

So now, I'm outside, reluctantly tossing a Frisbee. I've never mastered the art of Frisbee, and most of mine immediately go sideways and crash, rolling along the ground like plastic wheels.

"Nice toss, you're getting the hang of it," he says helpfully as he runs after the rolling Frisbee. I appreciate that he's trying to be positive, but sometimes when you're bad at something, it just makes it worse when somebody lies and says you're doing okay.

As he throws a perfect floater back to me, I hear the telltale rumble of a rotten muffler coming down the street. It has to be a Montoya car. I turn just as Jesse hops out of his brother's growling sixty-five Impala. He says something in Spanish to his brother, waves, and the car roars off, sputtering and missing and as noisy as a rocket.

"Hey man," Jesse says as he jumps and intercepts the Frisbee from me. He expertly tosses it back to Father Quinn, flicking it backhand and making it look simple. I hate it that Jesse can master any physical thing so easily; even if I weren't crippled I'd still be clumsy and throw like a girl. It's in my genes.

"Man, I'm glad to see you," I whisper. "Father Quinn's driving me nuts with the Dad stuff."

"Huh," Jesse says, not interested. "Hey, Father Quinn, can I talk to you a minute?"

Father Quinn walks over to us. He's sweaty from the Frisbee throwing, and his hair flops over his forehead in a manly way. I'm not a fag or anything, but I have to admit, the guy's great looking.

"I'm not Father Quinn, anymore, Jesse. I keep telling you guys that."

It doesn't make any difference to me; he'll always be Father Quinn. So now I don't call him anything. When I want to talk to him, I just start talking and hope he realizes I'm talking to him.

"Call me Steve," he says.

Jesse nods, but I can tell he's not listening. He's got that look in his eye. Something important is going on.

"See, Father Quinn, it's like this. Jesus and the Blessed Virgin have been talking to me in my dreams again, and they want me to start preaching. So I figured I'd talk to you about it, like how hard it is to do and stuff, since you used to preach."

Father Quinn looks queasy. He hasn't asked about Jesse's visions and miracles in a long time; I think he'd hoped it had all gone away. Ever since that day a long time ago when Jesse had the stigmata during mass, Father Quinn has gone out of his way to avoid the subject.

"There's more to preaching than just preaching, Jesse. You have to have something to preach about. You need training, you need to understand the scriptures. Have you even read the bible?"

"Nah. Don't need to. I get my information from the source. Besides, they told me a lot of the stuff in the bible's wrong. It got messed up when people rewrote it and stuff."

Father Quinn looks even queasier. "That's going to be your message? That the holiest of holy books is 'messed up'?"

"Yeah. Sort of. And other stuff, too. Whatever they tell me I have to say. You can't say no to Jesus and the Blessed Virgin."

"I guess not."

"So what I'm thinking is that at school, during lunch, you know, maybe trying to preach, see if I can do it."

"I think you're in for a rude awakening, Jesse."

Jesse looks at him without comprehension. Jesse just assumes that he'll be successful.

"What if people make fun of you?" I ask, always sensitive to *that* issue.

"Fuck 'em."

I look to Father Quinn for help, but he's staring off into space looking bothered.

After a long pause, Father Quinn looks back at Jesse. "You should do what you have to do," he says simply, and then he takes the Frisbee and goes back inside the house.

"They're gonna kick your ass, you know," I tell Jesse.

"Nah."

"They will. When you're different people don't like it. Take it from me, I know."

"I'll just convince 'em. Jesus and the Blessed Virgin will tell me what to say and what to do."

"Don't you have to be holy for this to work? I mean, like pray all the time, and stop cussing and looking at girls?"

"What's that got to do with being holy?"

"Everything! The pope doesn't say 'fuck', and priests don't dream about tits. At least I don't think they do," I add quickly, realizing that my new stepfather probably *did* dream about tits. Mom's tits. I feel sick.

"Who says those guys are really holy?" Jesse asks.

I don't have an answer for that one. Maybe he's right. Maybe the holy people really aren't. But it's hard to change your image of saintliness from pasty, haloed statues of holy perfection to a foul-mouthed, girl-crazy Mexican eighth-grader.

Mary Frances sits in silence at the dinner table. The mother superior was horrified by Mom's marriage to an ex-priest, but she gave Mary Frances special permission to come home anyway, probably so she'd see the marriage as a good example of mortal sin.

I can't get used to seeing Mary Frances in her baby nun habit. She's not a fully covered black-robed monster yet; they let her wear a funky-looking long black skirt and a modified veil. You can still see a glimpse of her hair, and she looks somewhat human, although I'm sure the old nuns will grind that out of her soon enough.

Father Quinn has made a couple of attempts to break the ice, and Mom has chattered and laughed and generally acted nervous and silly. I don't know why she's trying so hard; it's not like Mary Frances is anybody special, but the nun get-up and Mom's lingering guilt over stealing Father Quinn from the church conspire to make her act stupid.

After we finish a lukewarm meal of Mom's tamale casserole and I've cleared the table (I hate special family gatherings; I always get stuck doing the shit-work), Father Quinn turns on the charm and starts talking religion with Mary Frances. She's a little more animated once the talk turns to Jesus and vocations.

"I feel the presence of Christ every day," she says in answer to Father Quinn's question about how life is at the convent. "We start praying at four-thirty in the morning, and I'm filled with Jesus by breakfast."

I laugh out loud, and the three of them throw me dirty looks. "Well," I protest, "it sounded funny. I mean, 'filled with Jesus by breakfast'?"

"Finish the dishes, Roger," Mom says coldly. I look to Father Quinn for help. He tries to be stern, but I see a small smile cross his face. At least *he* understands.

I go out to the kitchen and scrape gooey, corn-filled tamale casserole into the garbage disposal. It hungrily consumes the glop; the garbage disposal is the only thing that enjoys Mom's cooking. Mixed in with the garbage disposal's roar, I hear Mary Frances yammering about how holy she is and what a difference going into the convent has made.

The chunky water swirls into the drain.

God.

Jesus.

The Virgin Mary. Holiness. Love thy neighbor, impure thoughts, pagan babies, the Pope, "Eat his body, drink his blood"—my life has been filled with this stuff, and not once, not *once*, have I ever felt anything that makes me think there even is a God. The nuns told us Jesus and our guardian angels were always around, ready to help when we needed it, if only we believed enough. Well, I believed, at least I thought I did, and I've never felt them. How come people like Jesse and Mary Frances and the nuns and the priests all claim to feel the presence of these guys and I don't? What've I done wrong? Are they all mistaken, or, worse yet, liars? I feel like the last kid in dodge ball, that horrible "Everybody else has been through it and they understand but I don't" feeling of being left behind.

I'm sick of the pious mumbo-jumbo. It means nothing to me. If I go to church and stand/kneel/sit/stand/kneel, mumble prayers I memorized a million years ago that no longer even sound like English, can I expect to wander back out into the sunshine after an hour, filled with grace and holiness and feel the presence of God? I don't think so.

Or can I kneel in a stuffy confessional, tell a cranky old priest that I lied and beat-off, say a couple of *Hail Marys* and be off the hook, to lie and beat-off again next week? I don't see the point.

But maybe no point is the point. The priests and nuns always say we're not supposed to understand. Even Father Quinn gave sermons saying everybody just had to put up with what's thrown at them and not try to understand what God is thinking. But it makes me mad that some people—even if they're deluding themselves—have this feeling that God and Jesus and angels and the Virgin are hanging around, making things easier for them.

It's not fair.

I go back into the dining room and sit down. Mary Frances is still going on about how holy she feels, and I look at Mom. She's listening intently, with a fake, pasted-on smile. It's obviously forced; I've seen her do it too many times before. It's more of a painful grimace, and she won't let it go, as if she's trying to keep it frozen in place because if she lets it slip for a second her face will flop like pudding and she'll never smile again. Mom's holy—at least she seems holy to me—but I can tell that Mary Frances's newfound religious zeal has Mom completely perplexed—and maybe a little frightened.

Father Quinn, on the other hand, isn't smiling. He's listening to her intently, his eyes boring in on her like she's the most important person on earth. I've noticed that about Father Quinn: when he's listening, he makes you feel important. That's probably why people liked him so much when he was a priest. When you're in trouble, spilling your sins and fears to a priest, you want him to care only about you and your problems. As I watch Father Quinn I assume he's completely fascinated by Mary Frances's religious quest, until she looks over at Mom to make a point and Father Quinn glances at me. In the instant that Mary Frances isn't looking, Father Quinn rolls his eyes at me, then snaps them back to rapt attention as she yammers on.

It's now that I realize the truth: Father Quinn doesn't believe in this stuff any more than I do. He's been through the seminary, ordained a priest, preached, counseled, made up fresh batches of communion every day, done all the holy/priestly stuff, and now, at the end, he's just as confused and cynical about it as I am.

"And what do you plan to do once you take your vows?" Father Quinn asks.

"I want to spend the rest of my life in prayer."

Father Quinn nods seriously, Mom says "Mmmmm" and her perma-smile falters but doesn't fade, and I look at the tabletop and shake my head.

Mary Frances sees me. "What?!"

"Seems like a waste of time to me."

"What do you know," she says, a whine slipping into her nun-calm voice.

"It just seems like a waste of time, that's all. I mean, you could be out doing something to help people instead of sitting around some old convent praying all day long."

"Roger, please, you're not being supportive of your sister's calling," Mom scolds.

I shrug. "I'm just saying what I think."

"The contemplative orders serve a purpose, Roger," says Father Quinn, slipping into priest talk. "They pray for the rest of us, they talk to God and take the time to pray deeply where the rest of us can't."

"Then how come stuff never gets any better?"

"Shut up, Roger, you don't know anything," Mary Frances snaps.

"Real holy, Mary Frances," I shoot back.

Father Quinn ignores the squabbling. "That's the holy mystery, why bad things happen to good people in spite of prayer, why God allows evil to triumph over good. We won't know until we're with God."

Yeah, yeah, yeah. I've heard all that before. Mary Frances listens to him intently, nodding along. I think Father Quinn has won her over and she trusts him, even if he did ditch the priesthood and marry Mom.

"Well, who's ready for Whip 'n' Chill?" Mom chirps, eager to change the subject from deep philosophical prayer talk to safe subjects, like dessert. "Give me a hand, Roger."

I dutifully follow her into the kitchen. She closes the door between the kitchen and the dining room and nails me with an angry glare.

"What are you trying to do in there?!"

"What?"

"Don't interfere with the relationship Steven is trying to build with your sister!"

"We're having dinner and everybody's talking, so I talk, what's wrong with that?!"

"This night isn't for you. You've had plenty of attention over the years, now it's your sister's turn."

That hurts. It wasn't my fault I got run over and everybody decided to make a big deal about it. They could've just left me alone and I would've been fine. Anger rises in me, and I try to decide if I should argue with Mom and make her feel bad or just shut up and take it. But I don't get the chance to say anything else because she grabs the bowls of mucky chocolate Whip 'n' Chill and heads back out into the dining room.

"Here we go, everybody," Mom says, instantly cheerful. It's obvious she's still mad at me, and her smiley camouflage can't hide it.

We eat our dessert, and Mary Frances is deep in conversation with Father Quinn about holy stuff, so I tune out. Mom watches them, beaming, she's thrilled that Mary Frances has warmed up to him. As I watch them talk I notice the expression on Mary Frances's face. It's more than holy interest.

Father Quinn has suckered her. Even though he doesn't believe all the holy junk he's saying, he's saying it anyway to make her like him. And it's working. Mary Frances is like most women, and when Father Quinn turns on the charm, she can't resist.

It must be nice to be so good-looking and slick that it's easy to win over women—even ones who don't like you at first. I hope Father Quinn doesn't get sick of Mom some day and turn his charms on somebody else. I'd feel bad for her if he did, because it'd be real easy for him to get just about any woman.

The night drags on, and I don't say anything else. We move to the living room, and by the end of the evening Mary Frances and Father Quinn are sacred soul mates, Mom's smile has become real and joy-filled, and I feel like shit.

I think I'll become an atheist.

* * *

I'm standing in line at the school cafeteria, waiting to get a soggy, oatmeal-enhanced hamburger, when I first hear the mumbled comments about Jesse.

"He's crazy, like he thinks he's a preacher or something," the girl in line behind me says to her friend.

I whip my head around. "Who?!"

"Your friend, that guy Jesse." She talks to me like I'm a moron for not knowing.

"What's he doing?" I ask.

"Preaching. Saying stuff about going to hell. He's gonna get in big trouble."

"When did he do this?"

"He's doing it right now."

"Shit. Where?!"

"Over by the gym. There's a crowd watching him and stuff, and Mr. LoBianco's there."

The vice-principal. Jesse's dead. I run over toward the gym as fast as my stiff legs will take me. As I get closer I see a big crowd of kids standing by the side of the gym; I slow, then stop. Do I really want to see what he's doing? I might be better off to just turn around, forget about it, and let him deal with whatever mess he's gotten himself into.

I'm about to go back and get my oatmeal burger, and I actually take a step toward the cafeteria. Then I stop. I can't. Like it or not I'm tied up with Jesse, I always have been, and I want to see what's going on.

I walk slowly toward the crowd.

As I get closer, I see that Jesse has climbed up to the top of a basketball backboard on one of the asphalt courts. Mr. LoBianco stands at the free throw line, looking up at Jesse with alarm and disgust. Jesse is shouting, waving one arm while he holds onto the backboard. The metal pole holding it up sways under Jesse's weight.

"JESUS TOLD ME YOU GUYS GOTTA START PRAYING, YOU GOTTA START BEING GOOD."

"Mr. Montoya, get down from there right NOW!" Mr. LoBianco yells. He's a short, bald guy who's in a perpetually bad mood. I think he hates his job.

"IT GOES FOR YOU, TOO, MR. LOBIANCO. JESUS AND MARY WANT EVERYBODY TO BE BETTER."

"We'll talk about it after you come down from there!"

The coaches are watching, bemused by it all. Coach Hawkins chews his gum furiously. "Sumbitch," is all he says.

"THE RELIGIONS YOU BELIEVE IN ARE ALL WRONG, THEY'RE LIES, YOU'VE GOT TO GET BACK TO THE TRUTH, AND IT'S NOT IN THE BIBLE EITHER, BUT I HAVE IT, THEY TALK TO ME, I'LL LEAD YOU TO THE TRUTH!"

Wow. This is something new. He's talking like he's some kind of god or prophet or something. He's going to get in big trouble.

The gathered kids are strangely silent. I'd expect them to be laughing at him, or heckling him, but instead they watch him with odd expressions. Almost like they're afraid.

"JESUS IS THE WAY, BUT NOT THE WAY YOU THINK. I'LL TELL YOU THE RIGHT WAY TO SEE GOD, 'CAUSE WE'RE NOT GONNA LIVE FOREVER OR NOTHING, AND WE ALL GOTTA LOVE JESUS—" Jesse gestures wildly and the metal pole sways even more. First there's an ominous creaking metallic groan, then the backboard snaps away from the pole and Jesse crashes to earth with it.

Mr. LoBianco and the gathered kids scramble out of the way of the falling backboard/Jesse, and his big body *thuds* on the asphalt.

I rush over and help Mr. LoBianco grab the heavy metal slab and pull it off him. Jesse lies still; a gash on his forehead dribbles blood. I can't tell if he's breathing.

"Somebody go get Mrs. Hahn!" Mr. LoBianco yells. Mrs. Hahn is the school nurse.

"Is he dead?" a kid asks.

"Everybody just back away!" Mr. LoBianco says as he kneels next to Jesse. He touches the side of Jesse's neck. I guess he's checking for a pulse the way they do on TV cop shows.

I should be scared, watching my best friend and chosen-by-God miracle buddy bleeding on the asphalt. But I feel strangely calm and I'm not sure why. Maybe I believe in all of Jesse's miracle stories; maybe I believe God won't let anything bad happen to him until he does whatever it is that God wants him to do. Or maybe I don't believe any of the God stuff and I'm just sure that someone as strong and tough as Jesse can't die.

Whatever the reason, he starts groaning and his eyes flicker open. At first he squints up into the sky, unfocused and dazed, then he sees Mr. LoBianco's concerned face looking down at him.

"Hey, Mr. LoBianco," Jesse whispers. "How you doin'?"

"Don't move, Mr. Montoya. You might've broken something."

"Donnelly 'round?"

"I'm right here." I come close and squat down next to Jesse.

He moves his head in my direction, grimacing as pain shoots through his neck. "Hey, man."

"Hey. You okay?"

"They just talked to me."

"Who?" I ask, knowing full well what the answer is.

"When I hit the ground, there was this flash of light, brighter than anything I've ever seen...and they started telling me stuff."

"Yeah. Why don't you stop talking and wait till the nurse gets here, you're bleeding pretty bad."

"Now I know what I gotta do. It ain't just preaching, I mean that's a big part of it, but not all."

"Uh-huh."

Mr. LoBianco stands and starts to pull me away. "He's delirious, son. Why don't you step back."

Sounds good to me. I start to stand, but Jesse reaches up and grabs my arm.

"They want me to heal the sick!" Jesse whispers. He slaps his bloody forehead with his palm, and blood spatters from underneath his hand. He holds his hand against his forehead for a moment, then slowly takes it away.

Everybody watches, but nobody except me seems to notice that when he removes his palm, the wound seems to have stopped bleeding. It may be my imagination, but the cut looks smaller, too. I *must* be imagining things.

"Healed...." Jesse mumbles, and then his eyes roll back in his head and he passes out.

Part Three

Rio Linda High School
1970-1974

Chapter Eleven

It never gets very cold here, and the change in seasons is subtle. You have to watch the weather closely to sense the move from summer to fall. Around the end of August the light gets different; it pierces the smog with less strength, and the shadows seem dimmer.

The Santa Anas kick up, and fall heat waves spark huge brushfires, but the falling leaves and frosts of autumn are alien here. In Southern California, our only exposure to that kind of stuff is on TV commercials.

It's fall, 1970, and as I stand at my bathroom mirror dabbing Mom's gooey Dippity-Doo on my imitation sideburns, I'm filled with excited anticipation. The weather may not change much, but there's one sure sign that fall's here: football.

Tonight I'm going to my first high school football game as a genuine high school student. It's the coolest feeling in the world. Even though I'm usually depressed about being me, tonight I feel good and hopeful. I tease long hair from behind my ears and glue the strands to the side of my face with the Dippity-Doo. In a little while it'll harden to a crust, and I'll have crispy imitation sideburns. I wish I could grow real ones, but between my scars and the fact that I haven't sprouted much facial hair yet, real sideburns aren't possible. I think they look pretty realistic, though, especially from a distance.

After I finish with the sideburns, I squeeze a couple of zits and dab Clearasil on the oozy bumps. If I'm lucky, they won't refill while I'm at the game. I can live with zit bumps, but a big whitehead ready to be zapped isn't cool. I guess it doesn't matter, though, because there isn't much about me that *is* cool.

I put on my best pair of ratty Levi bellbottoms and my back-to-school pair of Wallabies. They're still a little too new for my taste, but they're all I have. I'll try to scuff them up on the way to the game. Now, the shirt. I've got an old T-shirt that Mary Frances tie-dyed before she got holy, and I've got an orange, long-sleeved shirt with huge collars. It's a tough call, but I choose the long-sleeves. They cover my scrawny arms, and, I hope, make me more of a stud.

I check myself out in the full-length mirror in Mom and Father Quinn's room. Not bad. The zits have been worse, the scars aren't too red and angry, just pale and smooth, and the body...well, I need to work out more. But all in all not bad.

"Well, don't *we* look nice," Mom says in that annoying voice she has when she's feeling Mom-ish. I didn't realize she was watching me from the hall.

"You think?" I ask.

"I think all the cute little girls at Rio Linda High School will fall in love at first sight."

"Mom...."

"They will! You're adorable."

That's not what I want to hear, but I smile anyway. Mom's so goofy that I can't take her seriously or stay mad at her. She's just Mom. She thinks I'm irresistible. Too bad the rest of the world doesn't see me that way.

She continues to smile the goofy smile.

"What?" I ask.

"Oh, nothing, it's just...." Her eyes squint strangely and she suddenly begins to cry. "It's just that you're growing up." She wipes tears away and sniffles. "My baby...."

"Aw, Mom."

She sobs and then comes over and hugs me. I hug her back, feeling stupid; I don't know how to act when somebody's crying.

"I just want you to know I love you, honey," she sniffs.

"Loveyoutoo," I mumble. Father Quinn is out at a candlelight war vigil tonight, so he's not here to rescue me from Mom's out-of-control Mom eruption. She hugs and whimpers until a car honks outside. "Must be Jesse, see you later!" I say. I pull away from her and hurry to the front door.

"Don't be too late!"

"Yeah, okay!" I'm out the front door, free of her weirdness, and on my way to a FOOTBALL GAME!

The air is warm and soft tonight; it's like a caress. Jesse and his brother Mando are parked in front of my house. Mando's finally got his rumbling, sixty-five Impala lowrider looking good, with sparkling new purple paint and black tuck-and-roll upholstery. It seems like he's been working on it forever. *Chapel of Dreams* is painted on the back window in that weird angular lowrider writing they like so much.

Jesse opens the door and leans forward so I can get in the back seat. His brother stares straight ahead, expressionless, as if the thought of actually having to let a skinny, crippled honky ride in his treasured lowrider is too disgusting for words. *Tears of a Clown* plays on the radio; when Smokey Robinson hits a high note it makes my neck tingle.

I squeak as I slide across the seat. Jesse's brother looks up in the rearview mirror at me.

"Don't fuck nothin' up, *pendejo*."

"Okay. Sure," I say politely, ignoring the insult.

"Fuckin' FOOTBALL, man!" Jesse yells, and we both grin stupidly at each other.

"*Jotos*," mutters his brother, turning the tiny chain steering wheel as we slowly drive off.

Jesse's as pumped up as I've ever seen him. Tonight he's starting his first varsity game for the Rio Linda Panthers. He's the only freshman on the team, and the local paper says he's the first one to start on varsity in the history of the school. When football practice began in the summer, the varsity coaches made him work out with the freshman team for a few days, but after he put two of his scrawny teammates in the hospital with big-time tackles, they decided to hop-scotch him over JV and straight to varsity.

Within a few practices, they could see he was something special, and he quickly beat out a senior for the starting middle linebacker spot. I've watched a few scrimmages; Jesse's a Mexican Butkus, tossing offensive players out of the way like they're annoying little bugs, and squashing the ball carrier with no mercy. I have a feeling he'll be causing a lot of fumbles.

"Fuckin' Santa Susanna gonna die," Jesse says. "We're gonna kick their asses."

"Yeah!" I say, feeling like I'm part of the team.

"What you gonna do, *ese*? Piss on 'em?" Mando smirks.

"Shut up, man," Jesse says. I don't dare pop off to Jesse's brother. He's a *vato loco* who's been in jail and he's welcome to say whatever he wants to me. He and Jesse argue in Spanish for a minute, then Jesse turns back to me.

"Tonight, man, I'm gonna hurt somebody," he says, dreamy and expectant. Then, he changes direction without missing a beat. "I'm gonna preach at the mall tomorrow. Be there at eleven."

I nod. I'm getting used to this. Since Jesse's fall from the basketball backboard in junior high, he's been on a preaching blitz.

They threatened to throw him out of school because of the disruption, but since only a few weeks were left they gave in and let him finish out the year. He continued to preach at lunchtime and bother anybody he could corner—but he didn't climb up on things anymore.

"I've got important stuff to tell you, man," he'd say to some poor, unsuspecting loser. Then he'd pin the guy up against a wall, get in his face, and preach his "God tells me what to tell you" sermon. The victim would usually listen politely, especially since Jesse was so big and intimidating. There were few people at that school who would dare tell Jesse to back off; the only ones who did were the dopers but they were too stoned to care—and why bother preaching to them, they'd never remember, anyway.

Jesse would usually say, "I know this is hard to believe, but Jesus and Mary talk to me. All the time, man. And They tell me shit you wouldn't believe. What religion are you, man?" The victim would stammer whatever he or she was. "Ah, man, you're on the wrong track," Jesse would say to whatever they answered. "The religions, they're all bullshit, man. Me, myself I'm a Catholic. I still go to church and communion and all that stuff, but they're just as wrong as everybody else. See, the thing is, there was a Jesus and the basic story, you know, that's right. It's just that afterwards, man, people got hold of it and fucked it up. Bad, too. I mean, you don't have to follow stupid rules and stuff, you know? Like Catholics, man, they got so many rules and stuff that's sins you can't do nothing. You know how you're not supposed to beat off?" he'd ask. "Bullshit, man. How do I know? I asked Jesus and Mary. They said as long as you ain't hurting nobody it's not a problem. Hey, I don't have to tell you that beating off is a whole lot more better when you don't have to worry about going to hell because of it.

"It's stuff like that," he'd continue. "They tell me what's wrong and what's right. It isn't hard, you just gotta do what's right, be good to people, don't hate too much. Pretty easy. Wanna stick with me? I'll tell you more."

Sometimes the person would nod nervously, probably fearing that if they didn't agree the giant crazy Mexican might kill them. Others just said, "No thanks" and Jesse would leave them alone.

"Losers," he'd mumble after somebody blew him off. "I can make salvation easy for 'em and they don't wanna hear it."

"They've got their own religions, Jesse. If they go home to their parents and tell them they're not going to church anymore because some Mexican guy at school talks to Jesus, what do you think they're gonna say?"

He shrugged. "Then their parents oughta listen to my message."

"Hey, I've listened to you from the start, and even I don't know what the message is," I said. "Are you supposed to get people to follow you and start your own religion? Or are you just supposed to tell them beating off is okay and not to worry about stuff and be nice? That's pretty basic, man."

Jesse pouted for a minute. "I'm not sure. They haven't told me everything yet. Just, 'Go out and spread the word'."

"What if they don't tell you? What if you keep on doing this stuff and they leave you hanging?"

"They won't," he grumbled, sounding none too sure.

So Jesse went on preaching in his own *vato* style. During the summer we'd hang around the mall, and Jesse would hunt for believers. At first, he always picked scared-looking white kids, skinny ones like me who wouldn't dare not listen, but after awhile his confidence grew, and he'd hit up just about everybody—including adults. Some people treated him like a bum, as if he was going to try and roll them for a quarter, others listened politely, and a few cussed him out. But it didn't faze him that he got through to no one. He'd just move on to the next person and pitch his weird mix of Jesus, Mary and Jesse. As was bound to happen, the mall security guys finally got fed up with Jesse ignoring their friendly warnings to leave shoppers alone, and they started to throw us out as soon as they caught Jesse bothering people.

I tagged along with him every day, mostly because I didn't have anything better to do, but all I did was stand off to the side and watch him unsuccessfully work his flock. I don't know why I didn't just tell him to waste his own summer and let me enjoy mine, but as usual with Jesse, I caved in and dutifully followed him around like a little puppy. It was even more boring than I had expected; he never did any miracles and nothing strange ever happened. All he did was talk.

When Jesse got hold of some nice person who didn't have the heart to tell him to get lost, I'd disappear into the B. Dalton book store and browse the Playboys or wander into Radio Shack and look at stereos. After the victim finally wiggled away, Jesse would come looking for me.

"C'mon, man, They said you gotta be with me all the time."

"What for? It's boring."

"You're like an apostle or something. I dunno. They just told me you got to be there."

I'd whine, Jesse would guilt me, and in the end he'd get his way.

I was glad when summer was over and we went back to school. Three months of loitering around the mall with Jesse and being at home with Mom and Father Quinn was about all I could take.

I was used to Father Quinn; I didn't have a problem with him being married to Mom. It's just that since he's moved in they're always making out. If

Mom's in the kitchen whipping up a batch of Hamburger Helper, Father Quinn will sneak up behind her and start kissing her neck. Or I'll walk in on them feeling each other up on the couch with the local news blaring away unwatched on the TV. It's like living in a big make out zone, only I'm not getting any. So besides mall preaching with Jesse, I spent my summer trying to avoid Mom and Father Quinn's runaway hormones. I can't imagine seeing Mom as anything but Mom, but Father Quinn sees her as the ultimate fox. All those years of being a priest must have changed reality for him.

So, when my endless, lousy summer finally sputtered to a finish, I started high school with great expectations. In the two weeks I've officially been a freshman at Rio Linda High School, I've begun to feel the difference of sliding from being a kid to being, well, not exactly grown-up, but older. Junior high still had a grammar school feel; lots of skinny, high-voiced boys and little girls who were still little girls. There were a few early bloomers, but until high school they were few and far between. Now that I'm in the big leagues, it's hard to get used to being around juniors and seniors who seem to have more in common with adults than with us. I watch the big, hairy GUYS, and girls with breasts and good bodies, sitting around on the senior patio at lunch, self-conscious in their cool, grown-up way, ignoring the pathetic little freshman (like me) in their midst. And the divisions between different groups are far more pronounced than in junior high. The lettermen jocks stake out one spot by the gym at lunch and look cool; the *vatos* in their Pendletons and perfectly creased pants gather near the parking lot to talk about lowriders; the dopers in their baggy, assless bellbottoms and tie-dyed T-shirts meet out in the far corner of the field to smoke pot and exchange opinions about the comparative highs of different kinds of dope; nerdy chess-players, easy girls, cheerleaders, wussy freshman, geeks, losers, you name it, they've all got territory staked out and the walls between them are obvious and understood by all.

High school also seems faster somehow, as if time is compressed now that we're older and it's just the beginning of having to hurry and catch up with the rest of the world. The easy days of childhood are over.

Tonight will be the best part of high school. The air is filled with football expectation. It takes forever for us to get to school because Jesse's brother refuses to drive more than twenty miles an hour.

"C'mon, man, Coach'll be pissed off if I'm late," Jesse pleads as we crawl down the street.

"Too fuckin' bad. *Chapel of Dreams* don't go fast...it goes slick, *cabron.*"

We finally arrive at the high school and Jesse's brother eases the lowrider into the parking lot. It's just getting dark, and since it's still two hours before the game there aren't many cars here yet. Jesse and I hop out and his brother slowly rumbles off into the dusk.

"I'll fuckin' walk next time," Jesse complains as he hurries off to the locker room. "Gonna kick some ass tonight, Roger. Be watchin'."

I give him a high-school-guy-see-you-after-you-kick-ass head nod as he goes into the locker room. I wander over to the field, show the shop teacher who's manning the gate my shiny new ASB card, and walk up into the bleachers.

I've been here lots of times before, on weekends when Jesse and I were wandering around town, or on the Fourth of July when they have fireworks, and even a couple of football games when Mary Frances went here. But it's different now. Now I'm a part of it, I'm a Panther, I'm friends with the starting middle linebacker. It's the coolest feeling in the world.

I climb up to the top of the stands, right below the press box. Each step makes booming thumps through the metal structure; my footsteps echo across the field. When the stands are full in a couple of hours, they'll reverberate with the stomping feet of a thousand fans.

I sit, savoring the warm fall air. The smoggy sunlight fades away, and

Mount San Antonio disappears into a hazy black outline against the sky. The field lights switch on, and soon thousands of moths encircle them, mindlessly smacking the lenses, to be crispy-fried by the heat and sent spiraling down onto the stands like bug snow.

The lines are freshly painted on the field, and the cheerleaders busily put up banners along the sides of the stands. "SMASH THE SPARTANS!!" and other goofy sayings splashed in dribbly red paint on paper banners.

The team starts straggling onto the field to warm up, and I see Jesse, number forty-eight, trot out with his defensive squad. The punter and field goal kicker boot balls into the sky, and the quarterback loosens up by throwing long passes. Since we run the wishbone he probably won't throw many tonight, but I guess it's good to be warmed up just in case.

It feels good here. The air, the mood, even the dead moths—I love it all. As more people show up and the stands start to fill, anticipation buzzes; laughter, good times, a warm fall night and a bitter school rivalry. It doesn't get any better.

My first high school football game.

A group of the hardest of the hard guys strolls up into the stands. Danny Robledo, the king of the lowrider *vatos*, leads them, the guy people whisper about and don't dare make eye contact with. Since he and Jesse went head to head over letting me play basketball, I've made it a point to avoid him at all costs. Tonight he's with six of his friends; they're dressed identically, in brown Pendletons buttoned at the neck, perfectly ironed pants and slicked back hair. As they stomp up the stands toward me, I lower my eyes and hope I can fade into the bleachers. They sit a few rows below me. Wisma, the white-guy *vato* is with them, and as I look up he looks back. Wisma was cool to me in junior high, and I hope that since he's started hanging around the really hard guys he won't turn on me. Our eyes meet, and he gives me an almost imperceptible head wave. Whew.

I decide to go down and get something from the snack bar, so I walk along the top of the bleachers and go back down as far away from Danny Robledo as I can. After I buy a greasy corn dog from the stand underneath the bleachers, I go out to the dark, grassy area between the parking lot and the field to eat. I start to feel a little lonesome all of a sudden; my best buddy, who I'd ordinarily be hanging around with, is on the team, so I'm here alone. The crowd has started arriving for the game; everybody comes in groups. They may be cool groups or geek groups, but nobody is here alone.

Except me.

I'm about finished with my corn dog, gazing up at a few bright stars that flicker through the evening-thin smog, when a sudden searing pain shoots through my back and something slaps my head. Before I realize what's happened, I'm on the ground and my corn dog has vanished into the long grass.

I hear a voice, and my first thought is, *Shit, it's Danny Robledo and he's gonna kill me!* I try to crawl away, but powerful kicks smash my side.

"Fucker!" the voice hisses. More blows.

The voice. It's familiar but my mind is fuzzy and I don't know who it is. My attacker is hidden by darkness, I can't see the person's face, the only thing I know is that I'm getting the crap kicked out of me and I can't do anything about it. A strange metallic taste and odor floods my senses, and my thinking is disjointed. A foot kicks the side of my head and I black out.

It's sometime later. I open my eyes. I'm cold. People yelling, clapping, shouting. I can't remember where I am. What happened to me?

"T..O..U..C..H!" girls' voices spell out, punctuated by claps. "D..O..W..N!" Clap, clap, clap. "GOOOOO PANTHERS!!" A band plays *Twenty-five Or Six To Four*. Stomping feet, thunderous crowd roars, oh yeah, the football game. I slowly sit up in the grass; my head aches, and the feeling I have is the same horrible sensation of pain and disorientation I had when Joe Fanucci ran over me.

Crusty blood blocks my nostrils and painful lumps throb on my chest. I touch one and wince; whoever kicked me really meant it.

Wild cheers roar out of the stands. The cheerleaders go crazy, and barely audible over the crowd I can hear the public address announcer screaming "Touchdown!" I slowly move to my knees and consider the possibility of standing up. My legs seem okay, so I wobble to my feet. My head aches and my side aches but otherwise I'm all right.

I slowly walk to the bathroom underneath the stands. Some people look at me curiously as I go in, but nobody says anything. I look at my face in the mirror. One eye is almost swollen shut, and dried blood smears my nose and chin. I rinse the blood off and clear out my nose. Red-tinted water runs off my scarred face; in the cruel fluorescent light, the patchy scars look stiff and hard, like bleached leather. I'm about to dry off when Danny Robledo and a couple of his pals stroll in. I freeze.

Robledo glances at my dripping face. I feel a fresh trickle of blood roll out of my left nostril, but I don't dare move; I'm afraid he might take it as a threat if I lift my hand to wipe it off.

Wisma trails in behind them, and he watches curiously. I'm hoping they're just in here to pee and nobody'll mess with me. Robledo glances back at Wisma.

"Shut the fuckin' door," he snaps. Wisma closes the door and stands leaning against it.

I decide they're going to kill me.

Robledo reaches into the pocket of his baggy Pendleton and pulls out a huge joint. He glances in the mirror into my eyes. "Turn around, man."

I turn slowly toward him. He fires up the joint and takes a hit. He looks at me through the haze of smoke, neither threatening nor friendly.

"Somebody fuck you up, *joto*?"

"Yeah."

"Who?"

"I dunno. They jumped me."

Wisma folds his arms and watches me. A small smile crosses his face. I wish I knew what's so funny.

Robledo takes another hit. He holds the smoke in for a long time, then blows it out in my face. His buddies laugh. They move closer to me. I'm surrounded. I start to say *Hail Marys*, because the nuns always used to tell us you had a better chance of going to heaven if you died with a prayer on your lips, and I'm suddenly feeling religious.

"You smoke, man?" Robledo asks.

I start to say no, but then I catch a glimpse of Wisma and he gives me a little nod.

"Sometimes," I mumble quickly.

Robledo holds up the joint. "Take a hit."

I don't know what to do. I'm afraid of drugs, but I'm more afraid of Robledo. So, with shaking hands, I take the joint from him, inhale, try to hold it in but instead blast the smoke out in a huge, choking cough.

They laugh at me. Even Robledo smiles. He takes the joint back. "You need practice, asshole. Don't wanna waste good shit on a *pendejo* like you."

I smile sickly, trying to be cool and one of the *vatos*. That's a mistake.

"What's so funny?" Robledo asks, suddenly icy and threatening.

"Nothing."

Robledo studies me. He's shorter than I am, but he's strong and seems years older. He has a crude teardrop tattooed under one eye.

"How come your face is fucked up?" he asks.

"I got run over by a truck when I was a kid."

"Fuck."

"Yeah."

"You friends with fuckin' Montoya?"

I shrug. "Yeah."

Robledo leans close to me. I smell the sweet-strong pot on his breath. "You fuck him?"

I'm smart enough to know this is going nowhere and I'm dead anyway, so I don't say anything. I decide to be bold, so I wipe the drying trickle of blood from my lip. They're all just staring at me.

"Thanks for the hit, man," I say finally, and then I turn to leave. I expect to feel a knife plunge into my back, or a bullet enter my brain. Instead, Wisma opens the door for me and gives me a little nod. I can't believe it; they're going to let me live!

"Hey!" Robledo calls out. Shit, just when I thought I've escaped.

I turn. "Yeah?"

"Tell Montoya to start prayin'. Just 'cause he's a fuckin' preaching football player don't mean he can't get fucked up by somebody."

I nod and say, "Okay," stupidly, and then I'm back out into the night. The game has just ended, and the crowd streams out of the stands. I walk back over to the field. We won, 28-21.

I wish I could've seen it.

Our players move toward the locker room, surrounded by backslapping parents and cheering students. I spot Jesse and go over to him. His uniform is stained with grass and mud, and his formerly pristine helmet is scuffed and beat-up.

He pulls off the helmet when he sees me, and grins happily. He's got a cut on is forehead, and dried blood streaks his sweaty face. He looks terrifying.

"That was great, man! What'd you think of the fumble I got?!"

"Far out," I say, hoping he won't notice I'm lying.

He slaps me hard on the shoulder and almost knocks me down. He's gotten so strong that he's unaware of how powerful he really is.

"Man, when Coach called a blitz on that third-and-twelve and I snuffed the QB's ass for a loss, it was so cool!"

"Yeah."

As I walk with Jesse people I've never seen before come up and congratulate him on his game. He's like a celebrity all of a sudden.

I fade away from him as some older Mexican guys surround him and excitedly talk in Spanish. I think they're alums who've been out of high school for quite a while but can't let go. Jesse realizes I've disappeared, turns around, spots me, and yells out, "Remember, the mall at eleven!"

I nod. A sea of people washes around me. Everybody is laughing, having a good time, and reliving high moments of the game. And I stand alone, sore and scabby and feeling stupid.

I scan the faces, looking for someone familiar. At first I don't see anybody of interest; then—

Rhonda Fairly. She's with Bushman. They're walking toward me. She's holding his disgusting hand. It makes me want to puke.

I try to step off to the side and melt into the crowd, but it's too late. Rhonda sees me and waves.

"Hi, Roger!"

I'm trapped. They come to me, Rhonda grinning, Bushman strangely expressionless.

"Hi," I say, specifically looking at her and ignoring him.

"Wasn't the game great?!" she gushes, caught up in the spirit and excitement that I'd hoped to experience.

"Yeah. Great."

"And Jesse! Could you believe how well he played?"

I smile and nod. Rhonda notices that I don't look too good, but she doesn't say anything about it. Her perky smile falters.

I glance at Bushman. He looks straight through me.

"Well," Rhonda says uncertainly. "See you."

They walk off. I stand for a moment, then, for some reason I don't understand, I turn and look back at them. Bushman's looking at me.

He grins. It's not a friendly smile. It's a "fuck you" smile. I'll never be able to prove it, but I know he's the one who jumped me. He's finally gotten his payback.

I hate him now more than I ever have.

I wait around for Jesse, hoping to get a ride, but he and the team stay in the locker room forever. Maybe they're praying or something.

I call home and Father Quinn comes over and picks me up. He notices that I'm beat-up but he doesn't say anything about it and I don't offer any explanation.

My first high school football game hasn't turned out at all as I expected.

Jesse has come down from his football high and now is in full preach. It's a busy day at the mall, and so far all we've done is play hide-and-seek with the security guys. Jesse hasn't been able to corner any potential converts yet.

We wander through the mall, past the Halloween and Thanksgiving-decorated stores. The window displays are filled with paper cutout autumn leaves and other fake seasonal stuff. Being inside the mall almost makes you forget that it's hot and smoggy out today and fall is only a theory.

"I don't think this mall stuff's working out," Jesse says, sounding tired and disgusted.

"No shit. I could've told you that in the summer."

"I need to ask Them what to do," he says, and I assume he means Jesus and Mary. "They haven't been helping me much lately."

"So why don't you quit for awhile?"

"Can't do that, Rog. It's Jesus—"

"Yeah, whatever. Let's get something to eat."

We duck into Orange Julius and grab a couple of chilidogs. We take them out into the mall and eat by a gurgling fountain surrounded by shiny plastic plants.

Lots of kids from school are at the mall today, and it seems like all of them stop by to congratulate Jesse on last nights' game. He accepts the compliments with humility, and then tries to hustle them into his Jesus and Mary pitch. It's fun to watch their eyes get wary as they make excuses to escape. Jesse's only been in high school a short time, but everybody's already getting the message that he's a great football player and a religious weirdo.

After he's scared away a couple cheerleaders he wolfs down the remains of the chilidog and then he looks at me.

"Who fucked you up last night?"

"Didn't think you noticed."

"You look worse than the quarterback after I sacked his ass."

I tell him what happened, except I leave out the part about Danny Robledo. Maybe I should tell him, but I don't see the point. He'd just laugh; I don't think Jesse's afraid of anything.

"Think it was Bushman?" he asks after I've finished.

I'm surprised because I've never said anything to him about my problems with Bushman. "Yeah. Maybe," I answer. "I don't know who else would want to mess me up."

Jesse nods, deep in thought. "You praying for him?"

"Yeah. I'm praying for his ugly red-haired ass to die a long, painful death from dick cancer."

"Hey, Rog. That's not the way to go."

"Don't waste the holy shit on me, Jesse. I don't believe in any of it anyway."

Jesse daintily wipes his mouth with a paper napkin. For a huge, muscle-bound football player his movements can be surprisingly delicate.

"You don't mean that, man."

"How do you know what I mean? Jesus and Mary tell you?"

Jesse smiles and shakes his head. "You believe. You know you do. God's been good to you."

"He has? Seems to me that everything that happens to me is shitty: I get run over, my dad dies, my sister turns into a crazy nun, my mom marries a priest, a psycho red-haired asshole wants to kill me—have I left anything else good out?"

"I didn't say stuff was perfect. But you're blessed, man. You got a safe place to live, you survived some bad stuff and you turned out okay. People care about you." He pauses. "And you know me," he adds with a smile.

"Great. I get to follow you around while you make an idiot out of yourself. Nobody believes you, Jesse. If you weren't a football player they'd all be laughing at you."

If I'm hoping to hurt him, it doesn't work. He just smiles. That's one of the most annoying things about Jesse. Unless you're a quarterback on the opposing team you can't piss him off.

"They'll see. Someday." He has that dreamy look in his eyes.

I study him. The gash on his forehead from the game last night is scabbed over and black. He's shaving every day now; the weightlifting and football practices have made him older. He could easily pass for twenty. Though he's stopped looking like a kid, the ever-present hint of a smile makes him young and mischievous.

Jesse's a strange combination of innocence and fierceness. And although I know him better than anybody, he's a complete mystery to me. I've read books in the library about psychology, and I know that people can make things happen to their body by what they think and believe. I'm wondering if that's what's up with Jesse. Since I'm finding it harder and harder to believe in God, a mind-over-body thing makes a lot more sense.

"Don't try to convince yourself that I'm *loco, ese*," he says, reading my mind and slipping into the *vato* slang he saves for occasions when he wants to be threatening. "I'm the fuckin' sanest dude you're ever gonna know." He narrows his dark eyes at me, and for a moment I'm afraid of him. His smile vanishes, and he glares with the intensity of a true believer.

"You got no choice," he continues. "We're in this together. Forever."

Now he smiles.

But I'm still afraid.

* * *

Algebra is stupid.

I don't care about x's and y's and I don't care about "How many oranges does Bob have?" or "When will the trains be fifty miles apart?" Mary Frances used to complain about algebra, and Mom and Dad agreed with her.

"Never saw the point," Dad said one night as he struggled to help Mary Frances with her homework.

"They always told us it was supposed to help us to learn how to think," Mom said. "But I didn't get it either. It seemed more like torture," she added reassuringly. Mary Frances didn't seem reassured.

Now I'm sitting in Algebra I, watching Coach Gutierrez scribble on the blackboard and try to explain to us how this stuff works.

I'm lost.

Coach Gutierrez is the head varsity coach, and for a football coach he seems pretty smart. He always wears gray sweat pants, a Rio Linda T-shirt and baseball cap. His big gut hangs and jiggles with a mind of its own, sometimes staying behind when he turns quickly. He scribbles algebraic formulas with the same intensity he scribbles defensive alignments, and he's surprisingly friendly and helpful when we don't understand what's going on.

He's explaining factoring to us now, and he looks at me and suddenly stops.

"Lost you, huh, Donnelly?"

"Yessir."

"Okay," he says, smiling. He slowly goes over everything again, patiently trying to open our eyes to the wonders of algebra. Once he's finished I'm sort of understanding things, and the bell rings for the end of the period. We file out, noisy and in a hurry for whatever awaits us next. Coach Gutierrez stands by the door.

"Got a minute, Donnelly?"

"Yessir."

After the last of the students have left, Coach Gutierrez closes the door. "I'll write you a pass for your next class." He goes to his desk and sits down. "Have a seat."

I sit in the desk in front of him, worry starting to gnaw at my gut. Am I in trouble? Does he think I'm too stupid for Algebra I? Great, how am I going to explain this to Mom and Father Quinn? Retard Rog, tossed out of college prep into the basic classes with all the losers.

"You friends with Montoya?" Coach asks.

Relief. Just a Jesse question. I can deal with that. "Yeah. I mean, yessir."

He smiles. "You're not on the team, you don't have to do all the 'yessir' stuff."

"Yessir."

Coach Gutierrez laughs and makes me feel at ease. I like this guy. He isn't intimidating like football coaches are supposed to be. But I know from what Jesse tells me that he can lose his temper and scream, so I can't be too buddy-buddy with him. He might turn on me.

"Known him a long time?"

"Since first grade."

"He always been...religious?"

Uh-oh. What's Jesse been doing? I have a horrible image of him accosting Coach Gutierrez in the locker room and trying to convert him to the First Church of Jesse.

"Well," I stall. "We were in Catholic school and all. You know."

"Uh-huh," he says, his smile fading. "You know what I'm asking about, don't you?"

"Yeah."

"He's a hell of a football player. One of the best for his age I've ever seen. I'd hate for him to blow it by being...too different. People don't like different."

"I know."

"I've talked to him already. But it's like talking to pavement. I thought maybe he'd listen to you. Kid like him, if he keeps playing the way he does and sticks with it, he could get a four-year ride at a major college. USC, UCLA, you name it."

I'm not sure if I should do it, but Coach Gutierrez seems so cool that I decide to level with him. "I think Jesse might be crazy, Coach."

He shrugs. "We all are to a certain extent. That's not a problem. Hell, it's healthy in a linebacker. You think Butkus isn't screwy? Doesn't matter what Montoya believes, doesn't matter if he sees pink helicopters flying around his head. He just needs to keep it to himself. Because if he's going to bother people with this religious stuff, if he forces it down their throats, he's gonna flush his future right down the toilet and he'll end up picking lemons the rest of his life."

"What do you want me to do, Coach?"

"Best friends got a lot of power. Use it on him. If this stuff is just a passing thing with the guy, then fine."

"It's not. It's permanent."

Coach Gutierrez scratches his huge belly. "Shit," he mutters. "Do your best, okay? I want to help Montoya out. He reminds me of myself. The only way I got outa being a dumb Mexican chile-picker is because I played football. And I found out I wasn't so stupid after all. Got a free education and a career. I'd like to see him get the same."

I appreciate the urge to help, but I've got my own problems—and I know Jesse well enough to know I'd be wasting my time. But I don't tell Coach that. "Sure," I say, trying to sound sincere. "I'll see if I can do something."

"Thanks, Donnelly." He scribbles a hall pass for me. "Hey," he adds as if a thought just popped into his head. "The team manager's out with mono. You interested? You were manager in junior high, weren't you?"

"Yeah."

"Wanna do it? Requires you to be at all the practices, but you get to go to all the games, and you get a box lunch on the away games. Get to be part of the team."

"Sure!" Some people think being manager is for geeks, but hey, who am I trying to impress? That's what I am. Besides, watching the game from the sidelines sounds great to me.

"Okay," Coach Gutierrez says. "Be at practice this afternoon."

I go to my next class excited and happy. I conveniently put the Jesse problem out of my mind, because I know there's nothing I can do about him anyway.

I can't wait to tell him the good news when I see him at lunch.

When I find Jesse at our usual spot in the cafeteria, he's scarfing down a bunch of the cafeteria's lousy tacos and a couple of oatmeal-extended hamburgers. His dining choices don't surprise me; it's the fact there's a girl eating lunch with him that startles me.

I go over to them and stand next to Jesse. The girl sits across from him, and Jesse leans toward her, shaking a half-eaten taco and making a point.

"See, that's the thing, religions are all bullshit! The ideas are good, but then people fuck 'em up!"

"Right on," she says, nodding.

Jesse senses my presence and looks up. "Hey, Rog, sit down, man. You know...." he looks confused. "Shit, what's your name again?"

"Patty."

"Yeah, you know Patty?"

"No. Hi," I say, annoyed. Another lunch ruined with preaching. I sit down and squirt ketchup and mustard from squeeze packs onto my oatmeal burger.

"Patty believes in me, Rog," Jesse says, trying to keep the excitement down in his voice.

I look up. Believes in him? This is news. I look at Patty. She seems familiar, and now I realize that she's in my English I class. She's one of those skinny, freckly, frizzy-haired girls dressed head-to-toe in hippie stuff—tie-dyed peace-sign T-shirt, patched bellbottoms, floppy leather hat. I've never paid any attention to her. Now, I study her face. Angry freckles spatter her cheeks, and thick, wire-rimmed glasses magnify her eyes. They look unnaturally large, like she's seen something scary. She has a loopy, smiling attitude, like maybe she's not real smart but at least she's pleasant.

"You believe?" I ask, just to make sure Jesse's not mistaken.

"I think," she says in a squeaky, positive voice, "that Jesse might be the guy who like saves the world."

I glance at Jesse. He's beaming. His first convert.

"Now what?" I ask him.

"What do you mean?"

"Do you baptize her? Start taking up a collection, what?"

Jesse's face clouds. "I don't know. They haven't told me what to do when

I get somebody."

"We could protest the war. Maybe Nixon's the antichrist, we could pray for something bad to happen to him," Patty offers helpfully.

Jesse's not listening. My question got to him. So, being the good buddy that I am, I ask it again.

"What now, Jesse?"

He doesn't say anything; he looks at me, moody and annoyed. He wolfs down an oatmeal burger in two bites. Patty chatters about how out-of-sight and groovy Jesse's visions are, and how when they get other people converted they can change the world.

Jesse finishes eating; he doesn't say another word.

Coach Gutierrez juggled my afternoon classes so that I'd have last period PE with all the jocks. They put them in there so they can get a head start on practice before school's out.

I feel special and chosen. Being team manager isn't that big a deal, but being asked to do it by the head coach and being treated with respect by an adult is an unusual experience for me.

I walk into sixth period government class—I'd originally had it seventh period and PE sixth—expecting nothing unusual. Just different faces.

And there *are* lots of different faces. And one familiar one. Rhonda.

Shit.

I find a desk as far away from her as I can. She's talking to somebody, so she doesn't see me slink into the classroom. I slither into the desk and keep my head low. At least Bushman isn't here, too. That would make things impossible. I knew things were too good; neither Rhonda nor Bushman was in any of my classes originally, and it made it easier to forget about them. As I sit, cursing my bad luck, a voice shrills in my ear.

"Hi, Roger!"

I look back. Jesse's new recruit, Patty, has plopped down in the desk behind me. She's all perky smiles; she's found the meaning of life.

"How come you're in this period?"

I tell her, but before I've finished the sentence she's lost interest.

"Can you believe Jesse Montoya would want me to be one of his followers?" she says, dreamy and excited.

"He's not real particular," I say, not meaning to bruise her feelings, but I do anyway. Her huge eyes are suddenly narrowed in hurt. "I mean," I add quickly, "religious people try to convert everybody. That's what they do."

She quickly gets over it, and she's excited once again. "What do you think they'll tell him to do next. I mean Jesus and Mary?"

"Guess we'll just have to wait and be surprised."

"Wow. This is the best thing that's ever happened to me. You're so lucky to have been with him all this time. He told me you were his first believer, that Jesus and Mary talk to him about you. It makes you almost a saint or something."

"Or something." I decide that Patty's goofy. I'm beginning to wonder if the only reason she's so into this is because Jesse's a big football stud and she's flattered he noticed she's alive.

"He says he can heal sometimes. How come he hasn't healed you?" she asks.

The anger that flashes through me catches me by surprise. Hairs tingle on the back of my neck and my face gets hot. Patty looks at me, all innocence. I can't get mad at her; she's just a well-meaning dummy who says whatever pops into her moron head.

I'm mad at Jesse.

Not that I believe all this vision/healing/chosen one bullshit, but what if, *just what if?*, he's not a psycho-liar? What if he might actually have some kind of connection with God and Power? If he really believes in all this stuff he's preaching—and I've been around him long enough to think he does—how come he's never tried to do anything for me? Couldn't he have asked his buddies Jesus and Mary to zap me some night in my sleep and let me wake up with arms and legs that work right and a face that isn't scarred and leathery?

It shouldn't be any big deal if he's got a direct line to heaven. And if he cured me, I'd be his biggest disciple, I'd preach proudly by his side, I'd make him famous—like the pope. So why hasn't he tried to cure me, or even mentioned it? And why haven't I ever asked him to?

Because I don't believe in him. Period. I never have. Even though some strange things have happened over the years, I've never believed. I still don't, and I never will. He's my best friend, and he always will be, but you don't have to buy into everything your best friend believes to be his best friend.

I'm puzzling over this when I realize that Patty is asking me a question. I look at her blankly; her freckles and magnified eyes and frizzy red hair blend into a terrifying clown face. I don't hear what she's saying. She looks at me, curious, confused, waiting for me to answer whatever it was she asked.

I look away from her and immediately lock eyes with Rhonda. She's turned around in her desk and she's looking at me. She smiles; I smile back. At least I think I smile—I'm not sure. I'm in a fog, my heart's pounding, sweat heats my back. I pull my eyes away from her, I stare down at the desktop. I try to catch my breath, I'm having some kind of attack, I'm getting scared now, what's wrong with me?

And suddenly I know. It hits me with a cold clarity I didn't know was possible. Pure understanding of myself and what I want.

I'm looking for a miracle.

"The first aid stuff's in this old tool box," Mr. Clark tells me as he guides me through the training room. Mr. Clark is the assistant coach, and Coach Gutierrez has put him in charge of my care and feeding.

"Make sure you've always got at least ten ice packs," he continues. "We get a lot of sprains and twisted things during practice." He giggles strangely. "Twisted things, heh, heh, heh."

Mr. Clark has the reputation of being one of the creepiest teachers at Rio Linda. He's the head of the English department, and he teaches the seniors in college prep classes. They say he makes them read a lot of strange stories filled with weird sex. He's the line and receivers coach, and from what Jesse says all he tells the linemen is to "Make sure you hold on every play, just don't get caught" and the receivers "If you drop a catchable ball I'll personally cut your *cojones* off." He likes to throw Spanish cuss words in so the guys will think he's cool. Jesse says they all think he's an idiot.

"Be on time," he continues as he leads me around. "The team depends on you. Just keep your mouth shut and don't distract anybody during practice or games. Be seen and not heard."

"Yessir." Mr. Clark is bald with a patch of erect hair right on top, and his head is pointy. I've heard people call him "onionhead" behind his back. A big red scar creases the side of his head, and I find myself wondering if he got run over at some point in his life. I find that seeing another scarred guy is somehow reassuring.

He finishes giving me the tour, and I grab the big, rusty Craftsman toolbox filled with ice packs, tape, and ammonia inhalers and lug it out to the practice field. Most of the team is already there, loosening up and being yelled at by Coach Gutierrez.

"C'MON, MONTOYA, AT LEAST PRETEND YOU'RE STRETCHING!" Jesse's sprawled on the grass, his legs stretched out as far as I think he can make them go. I don't know what it is that Coach Gutierrez wants him to do; maybe he yells even when everything's okay, it gives him something to do.

I put the toolbox by the sideline, sit down and settle in to watch practice.

It's a mild, beautiful day. The mountains are sparkly and in unusually sharp focus; the smog was swept away earlier in the day by Santa Anas which have since died down. Now it's calm and pleasant; the grassy odor of the freshly cut practice field mingles with the fresh, sweet air into a soothing perfume. When it's like this, it's impossible to worry about anything. Life's great, nothing could ever go wrong. It's irresistible.

I've calmed down since my panic attack in class. I've got a plan now. It's good to have plans; it makes life easier.

I sit, watching the team being put through their paces. High school football practice is a lot tougher than junior high was. Coach Hawkins used to make them do a few easy drills, then they got to scrimmage the whole time. It was like recess. Here, Coach Gutierrez and the other assistant coaches take small groups and bust their asses, doing drill after drill after drill. If somebody slacks off or screws up, the whole team has to run fifty-yard wind sprints; it encourages you not to mess up, because you don't want these guys to be mad at you.

It's starting to get dark when they finally run some plays. This part is fun to watch. The quarterback, Benny Martinez, is the fastest person I've ever seen. When you're a defensive guy trying to figure out if he's going to pitch it or run it, you have to think faster and move quicker than he does. Not many people can. Even Jesse has trouble figuring him out. His fakes are smooth and impossible to see; his only weakness is passing, but since they're running the wishbone it doesn't matter all that much.

After three hours of screaming and yelling Coach Gutierrez has had enough. He tells them they're lazy and no good, that if they don't change their attitudes they'll never win another game, and then he makes them run ten wind sprints and four laps around the field. It looked to my untrained eye like they practiced hard and did what they were supposed to do, but I'm not a coach. He must see subtle things.

After they finish running they stagger into the locker room, sweaty and spent. I lug the toolbox back in and put the balls and other stuff away, then wait for Jesse to give me a ride home.

"Fuckin' Gutierrez gonna kill us, man," Jesse moans as we walk out to the parking lot.

"Nothing makes him happy, huh?"

Jesse just sighs and shakes his head. We're almost to the parking lot, where his big brother waits, scowling, in his lowrider. Even though Jesse's brother is one of the scariest people I've ever seen (except for Danny Robledo), I think he's got a soft spot for Jesse. He'd probably kill anybody who said so, and outwardly he treats Jesse with disgust and contempt, but I get the feeling that he secretly likes his muscle-bound, football-star, miracle-working little brother.

Jesse continues to mutter and bitch about coach Gutierrez. I make the appropriate noises, then I spring my trap.

"How come you don't try a miracle on me?" I ask.

"Huh?" he asks, his mind still filled with football.

"A miracle. Ask them to cure me."

Jesse stops walking and stares at me. I've caught him by surprise.

"I...dunno. I can't, man."

"Why?"

"Because...I dunno."

"Have you asked them?"

Jesse looks down, as if he's embarrassed. "Yeah. I asked."

"And what'd they say?"

Jesse's brother honks. "JUST A MINUTE, *PUTO*!" Jesse yells. He looks at me. "They said you don't have enough faith, man."

"I'd have a whole bunch of faith if they'd cure me!"

"That isn't the way it works. You've gotta believe *before* the good stuff happens."

"Bullshit, man," I say, anger rising. "You're just saying that because you don't have any power, all this stuff's crazy bullshit, you're fuckin' crazy!"

Jesse doesn't get angry. He shrugs. "You even believe in God anymore, Roger?"

"What? Yeah, sure I do."

"They don't think so. They're worried about you. They told me you don't even pray or nothing anymore."

"I...I...that's bullshit!" is all I can respond. He's right. I don't believe. But the thought of Jesus and Mary telling him they're worried about me is enough to give me pause.

"There's no such things as miracles without faith, man. You know that. The fuckin' nuns were mostly crazy, but they were right about the faith part. You should've listened to them."

"Bullshit," I mutter. I need to come up with a better response. I sound like a moron.

"You're luckier than most people, Roger. You seen stuff with me. Remember the fire in the orange trees? And Monsignor O'Callahan? C'mon, man, you've got proof and you still won't believe. You're lucky Jesus and Mary don't just give up on you, man."

Jesse's brother honks again and yells some Spanish cuss words at us. He fires up the lowrider and slowly drives away.

Jesse yells back at him and we start to walk to the parking lot.

"Ask 'em again," I say, suddenly pleading. I surprise myself with my longing, whiny voice. But I don't care. I want the scars to go away; I want my legs and arms to work right, I don't want to be the "runover by a truck" geek anymore. So if I have to beg, then I'll do it.

"C'mon, Jesse, ask. Tell them I'll do whatever they want."

We catch up to his brother's lowrider. Jesse opens the door and pulls the seat forward so I can get in.

"It's easy, man. All you have to do is believe," he says with a smile.

Chapter Twelve

Jesse's dad died two days after the citrus packing plant closed. Everybody knew it was only a matter of time before the place went under; since most of the orchards had been ripped up to build tract houses, there were fewer lemons and oranges for the plant to do anything with. The main thing that grows around here now is kids.

It was the night of Rio Linda's last football game when Mr. Montoya died. The team was five and three, with some tough losses. For some reason we could stomp the good teams, but when we played the dog teams they'd beat us by a field goal or an extra point. Coach Gutierrez was going nuts.

"JESUS H. CHRIST," he yelled in the locker room after a particularly embarrassing loss to Father Serra, a wimpy Catholic high school a few towns away. "HOW COULD YOU LET THOSE...THOSE...*PUTAS* BEAT YOUR ASSES?!" The team hung their heads with shame. Even me, the lowly manager, felt like a failure. Maybe I hadn't packed the Gatorade right, or maybe when I helped the trainer tape Benny Martinez's ankle I'd wrapped too tight and he couldn't move as fast as usual. Who knew? We were losers.

"Shit," Coach Gutierrez muttered. "Looked to me like you were out of shape. Looks to me like we need to work on conditioning." One of the guys made the mistake of groaning. "What?! Somebody doesn't want to get in shape?! You're football players, for Christ's sake, if you're gonna win you need to act like men, you need to get your fat asses in shape so you can play all four quarters! Starting Monday, it's hell week all over again! You're gonna get in shape and you're gonna win some games!"

He stormed out of the locker room and left everybody staring at the floor and murmuring "Fuck" to themselves.

Coach Gutierrez was good to his word, and the next week was the worst thing I had ever seen. He ran them and drilled them with no mercy. Guys were puking on the field, and a couple even passed out. I got to run over to them, break open an ammonia capsule, and wave it under their noses. The first thing they saw when they came to was my concerned, scarred face. They weren't thrilled to see me.

Coach also decided that drinking water during practice was for pussies, so he forced them through three-plus hours of gut-busting practice without a drop of water or a rest break. It was the team's bad luck that a Santa Ana was blowing that week, and the air was crispy dry and hot. By Thursday they were praying for death.

They won the next game they played by thirty-six points; Coach Gutierrez had made his point.

We were tied for first in league with our archrival, Kennedy High, and they were our last game of the season.

Things were going pretty good that week. The team was practicing hard, and everybody was confident we could beat Kennedy. I was settled comfortably into my managerial duties, my classes were okay, everything was fine.

Except I was still waiting for that miracle.

Jesse hadn't mentioned anything since the night I'd begged him to help me. He hadn't bugged me to join him on preaching missions, even though I knew he was wandering through the mall on nights and weekends when he had a chance. Patty was his new little helper, and she tagged along, like I used to, giving him moral support or whatever it was he needed. I heard rumors that people thought they might be having sex. I knew better. Jesse was hot for girls—but not girls like Patty.

Jesse and I had been...cordial. We talked, laughed, and acted the same outwardly. But we both realized that things had changed. He had something that I wanted, and he wasn't willing—or able—to provide it. When a wedge like that comes between two old buddies, things can never be the same.

The town hummed with excitement on the night of the Kennedy game. The stands were packed full, and Mr. Cullen, the public speaking teacher who did the PA stuff for games, announced that it was the largest crowd in the history of Rio Linda High.

We won the coin toss and elected to kick off. Coach Gutierrez liked to come across as confident enough not to care if we received the ball first, and usually it worked.

The first quarter passed with no score; so far we were evenly matched with Kennedy. Jesse made a couple of tackles, and assisted in a sack, so he was having a good game. I didn't bother trying to talk to him when he came out during our offensive series; during a game Jesse was in the zone, almost like one of his miracle zones, and talking to him was impossible. All he wanted to do was get back out on the field and hit people.

During the second quarter, I heard a commotion up in the stands. People up near the press box were standing and acting weird; then Mr. Cullen came on the PA system asking if the team doctor could come up. The game went on, but pretty soon the ambulance that was parked near the end zone in case somebody in the game got hurt drove over to the stands, and the attendants hauled someone down on a stretcher and drove away.

A few minutes later, Jesse's lowrider brother, Mando, came down to the sidelines and tapped me on the shoulder.

"Hey, Donnelly."

I turned, shocked. He'd never called me anything other than "joto" before.

"Yeah?"

"Tell Jesse our old man just died."

I couldn't be sure in the light and commotion of the sideline, but his eyes were watery and I think a tear may have leaked out onto his cheek. He turned and hurried away.

I sat, frozen. *Mr. Montoya dead?* I always thought of him as forever. He wasn't soft, like Dad was. He was thin and tough. He never really spoke to me, but he'd nod when I was in their house, and I always felt that he was a good guy. Jesse never talked about him much, maybe because he was always working at the citrus plant and wasn't home that often.

Mr. Montoya was one of those guys who quietly lives his life, takes care of his family, and then dies way too young before he gets a chance to enjoy anything. I wonder why would God do this to people? He's got a mean streak.

Jesse came off the field and flopped on the bench. His uniform was streaked with dirt and grass stains, his helmet with gashes of paint from Kennedy helmets. He sprayed water from a squeeze bottle on his sweaty face, and stared out at the field. I could tell he was itching to get back in.

I got up, walked past the coaches, and squatted down in front of Jesse. He stared past me out to the field.

"Jesse."

He didn't hear me.

"Jesse. Listen to me, man."

He glanced down at me, frowned as if he didn't recognize me. "What?" he said in a low voice.

"Jesse, forget about the game. You have to leave."

Coach Gutierrez overheard me. "Hey, whataya doin' Donnelly?! Don't bother Montoya, he's in the middle of a game!"

I ignored Coach and grabbed Jesse's facemask. "Your dad's dead. You have to go."

When Coach Gutierrez heard that, he didn't say anything. He just stood, staring down, chewing his gum.

Jesse finally focused on me. He didn't look shocked or sad. After a long silence he said simply: "I know."

And then, as the offense ran to the sideline, he got up and trotted back out on the field, the one place in the world he wanted to be.

That night, Jesse Montoya played the greatest game anyone could remember by a high school linebacker. We beat Kennedy by ten points, and after the game Jesse rushed home, still in his dirty, bloodied uniform, to be with his family.

Another funeral. I don't like the way funerals feel. There's a bizarre unreality to them, a feeling that it's a big practical joke, that the person isn't really gone, that the casket lid will pop open and they'll jump out and everybody will get on with their lives.

I'm sitting a few pews back from the front with Mom and Father Quinn. Mr. Montoya's casket is at the altar, and I can't help remembering the way I felt at Dad's funeral. The huge Montoya family fills the first three pews, and most of them are weeping.

Aunt Yolanda is in the pew directly in front of me. Her long, black hair hangs over the back of the pew and when she moves it lightly dances against my knees.

Her kids sit next to her, polite and quiet. Even though they're not very big, they understand the solemnity of the occasion and aren't messing around like they usually do. Aunt Yolanda is living permanently with the Montoyas now; she's busy at college and working part-time at a real estate office. Jesse says when she gets her AA degree she'll start selling real estate.

"How come she needs to go to college to sell real estate?" I had asked.

"She says she don't want to be a dummy any more."

I thought that made good sense. Not that I ever thought she was a dummy. I've also noticed lately that she's looking different. She's toned down the killer makeup and she's let her hair go long and straight—no more of the enormous big-hair beehivey stuff. Even though she's old—she's somewhere in her thirties—she looks better now than she ever has. When I've seen her lately she hasn't tried to terrify me like she used to. I guess with school and all she's got other stuff on her mind. That's okay with me, since I don't like being terrified by man-eating spider-women, but I still think about her sometimes at night and beat off. After all, I'm only human.

The priest does the funeral mass in Spanish, since most of the people here are Mexicans. Father Quinn speaks Spanish, so he's real into it. He's intense about everything. I wonder what it's like for him to be in church but not be the master of ceremonies any more.

My mind wanders, like it always does during mass, but Mom is sniffing and dabbing tears with a linty Kleenex. I think she's crying because she's reminded of Dad more than being sad about Mr. Montoya.

Jesse sits in the front row with his mom and brothers and sisters. Although everyone around him is sniffing and sad, Jesse sits, stoic, staring straight ahead. I can't tell since I'm sitting behind him, but by his rigid posture and lack of movement I'm wondering if he's in the miracle zone. I hope he doesn't do anything stupid to make his dad's funeral a joke; I'm positive now that Jesse's just a deluded fake, not an intentional liar, but somebody who's confused and a little disturbed. I'm considering bugging him again to go see a psychiatrist.

The funeral mass ends, and the pallbearers carry Mr. Montoya's casket out. As we stand watching, Aunt Yolanda turns and looks at me with, I think, a tiny smile. With her new, sophisticated look and normal makeup, she's beautiful. My heart starts pounding. I manage to smile back, but I'm not sure if it's the right thing to do. After all, she is Mr. Montoya's little sister, and I don't know if you're supposed to smile at people who've lost loved ones. But she doesn't seem to mind, so I feel like I did the right thing.

"Damn shame," Father Quinn says as we're driving in the procession to the cemetery. "He was a good man. Works like a dog all his life, is a good Catholic parent and husband, then, boom, his heart quits at a football game and it's all over."

"Did they teach you why it is that God kills good people but leaves the jerks alive?" I ask, grouchy and annoyed.

"Roger! Don't be sacrilegious!" Mom says, trying to sound sterner than she really is.

"It's okay, Sylvia, that's a questions theologians have been asking forever. And I don't know the answer, Rog. We can't know what God's plan really is. No matter what happens all we can do is have faith."

"Yeah. Faith," I say. Faith. Why should anybody have faith in a God that goes out of His way to kick your ass? We'd probably be better off praying to goats or mountains or believing in aliens. But I don't bother to argue. Because what's to argue? You either believe or you don't.

It's windy and unusually cold at the cemetery. The mourners huddle around the open grave as the priest mumbles prayers and sprinkles holy water. Again, my mind wanders. It seems physically impossible for me to pay attention during anything to do with church or God.

I watch the low ceiling of gray fog that seems just out of reach over our heads. It's a lid over us, keeping us trapped down here with trouble and hate and pain. I'm sure there's nobody up there, there's no greater power who lives above the sky somewhere.

It's bullshit.

The priest finishes the graveside service, and the Montoya family leaves roses on top of Mr. Montoya's casket. Mrs. Montoya cries loudly, her big body heaves with pain. I feel bad for her. She's the nicest lady I've ever known, and now God's stuck her with a bunch of kids and no husband. My thoughts keep coming back to the God thing. Mr. Montoya's death has me pissed off; I felt the same way when Dad died. It doesn't make any sense, and priests and crazies like Jesse can yammer about how kind and merciful God is for the rest of their lives but they'll never convince me.

We go over to the Montoya's house for the post-funeral party. They call it a wake, and even though I went through it after Dad's funeral and Mom explained the theory behind it, I still call it a party. People stand around, chat, eat and drink. In my book that's a party.

Rhonda Fairly and her parents show up with sympathy and a covered dish. They didn't make it to the funeral, but they came for the party. I make sure I stay as far away from Rhonda as I can. The last time we got together at a funeral she broke my heart, and I don't need that again.

I cruise the house, sampling bites of all the different foods. Their kitchen table overflows with all kinds of good Mexican stuff brought by their friends and relatives. Fresh tamales wrapped in corn husks, the best salsa I've ever tasted, *menudo* (which I know better than to try), and boring stuff like Jell-O salad and cold cuts that the Anglos brought.

Jesse's big brother Mando, the scary lowrider, (whose name really is Armando—I read it in Mr. Montoya's obituary) walks up behind me and taps me roughly on the shoulder. I turn, my mouth full of tamale. Mando's looking at me with his expressionless, *vato* "I'm gonna kick your pasty white ass" face, and I'm afraid he's going to pop me or toss me out of the house for eating their food.

But instead he just nods, gives me an awkward pat on the back, grabs some food and wanders off. I guess that's his way of saying I'm okay.

Jesse wanders over and inspects the food.

"How you doin'?" I ask.

"Okay."

This is the first time I've talked to him since the night his dad died.

"You gonna play Friday?" I ask. Friday night is our first playoff game.

"Sure." He dishes up some Jell-O salad. All this good food and he picks the whitey garbage. Sometimes I wonder about Jesse. "They said he's with Them," he adds nonchalantly as he gulps down the Jell-O. "And that I shouldn't mourn or nothing. Just keep doing what I'm doing and preaching the word and playing football and all that stuff."

"Oh." *They*. Good old Jesus and Mary. How come Joseph never tells him what to do? Nobody ever mentions Joseph. He's the forgotten loser in the whole deal. I know how he feels.

Jesse savors his Jell-O, a vacant expression on his face. I'm pissed off. Here they just buried his dad and he's standing around, sucking up Jell-O, spewing psycho nonsense about messages from Jesus and Mary.

"Does it even bother you that your dad's dead?" I ask.

"He isn't dead. He has eternal life with Jesus and Mary in heaven. They let him in even though he didn't really believe in me. I think they gave him a break because of me, you know? Otherwise...." His voice trails off. The implication is that his dad would be frying in hell at this instant if Jesse weren't such wonderfully religious guy.

"You're fucking unbelievable, man," I say. Just then Rhonda Fairly walks up, and she overhears what I've said.

She gives me a look that could melt steel, then hugs Jesse. "Are you okay, Jesse?" she asks, her high, clear voice sad and sympathetic.

"Well, you know, it's sad and all," says Jesse, shrugging, but acting a lot more bothered by his dad's death than he did a few minutes ago when I asked him. It's surprising how different a guy's response is when a cute girl hugs him.

"We're praying for him. And your family. My parents are having a novena said," Rhonda says. A novena. Just the right thing.

"Thanks," Jesse says, all humble and appreciative. "'Course, he's already in heaven."

"I'm sure he is," Rhonda says. I can't help it, I know it's bad acting and I should just shut up, but I simply *cannot* stand here and listen to his bullshit. So I roll my eyes. Bigtime.

Rhonda glares at me. "What's the matter with you, Roger?"

"Ask Mr. Miracle."

Jesse looks at me with an infuriatingly condescending smile. "Roger's having a hard time with religion right now. But he'll come around some day."

Rhonda glares daggers at me, then looks back to Jesse. Her expression immediately softens. It's amazing how fast she can change her mood, depending on whom she's talking to. She's almost like an adult when it comes to that.

She gives Jesse a friendly little kiss on the cheek, ignores me, and goes back to her parents. Her dad is talking away to Mom and Father Quinn. He's not even trying to act like he's at a wake; he's loud and laughing and drinking booze. Jerk.

"You should be nicer to her, Rog," Jesse says, loading up on more Jell-O. "She's special, man."

Yeah. Maybe. I look over at Rhonda. She and her parents are paying their respects to Mrs. Montoya, and then they're gone.

I back away from Jesse, too angry to say anything else. Maybe I need to work on my attitude; it seems like I'm always pissed off about something. I'm probably not a whole lot of fun to be around. I step back and bump into somebody.

"Sorry," I say, turning around. It's Aunt Yolanda. "Oh, it's you!" I don't know why I said that, and I feel like a fool.

She smiles warmly—it's the first friendly smile that I've seen—and tosses back her long, black hair.

"Yeah, it's me, Roger."

I stand and stare at her. She looks good in her tight black sweater and long skirt. Discrete enough for a funeral but still great. She's looking at me, a faint smile tugging at her lips, and I realize she's waiting for me to say something.

"Sorry about Mr. Montoya," I mumble, reddening. I hate this blushing stuff; I wish I could control it so my butt or feet would glow red when I get embarrassed instead of my face. What a stupid system. You feel embarrassed, so your face glows to show the whole world and make you even more embarrassed.

Aunt Yolanda nods and shrugs. "Manny was a good brother. Just worked too hard." She's sipping something from a paper cup; it smells like bourbon. "C'mon. Let's go outside and talk."

I look around to see who she's talking to.

"Yeah, you," she says, smiling, as she heads outside. I stumble along after her.

The Montoyas have tidied up their cluttered back yard for the wake. Rusty tricycles and broken toys that normally litter the patchy grass are stacked neatly by the garage. Aunt Yolanda leads me to the rickety picnic bench, the only piece of patio furniture out here. She sits down and lights a cigarette. I stand, not sure what to she wants me to do.

"Sit down, I won't bite," she says, exhaling a smoke column and sipping her bourbon.

Sit down. Of course. You'd think I could've thought of that myself. I try to sit across from her, catch my foot on something invisible and crash-land on the bench with a thud. I'm such a spaz; I can trip over a blade of grass. Aunt Yolanda smiles.

"You known—" she starts, then stops. "I'm trying to speak more educated—*you've* known Jesse forever, huh?" She's trying to cover up the hard chick *vata* accent—it's like she wants to sound white. I can't imagine why she'd want to change the way she talks, unless she thinks it sounds uneducated. I've been around Mexicans so long that the way they talk sounds as normal as anybody else to me.

"Yeah, I've known him forever. Since I beat him up in first grade."

"That's right. You beat him up," she says, looking doubtfully at my sunken, scrawny chest and skinny arms.

"He wasn't as big as he is now," I say, acknowledging the obvious.

"He talk to God back then?"

Jesse and Jesus and Mary and miracles. The only time anybody wants to talk to me is when they want to know about Jesse; it's really beginning to annoy me, but at least Aunt Yolanda sounds like she doubts him, too.

"That came later," I say, hoping that's the end of the conversation.

"Think he's crazy?"

I look at her. She's gazing at me with eyes so dark and sharp and intense that I feel like I'm sitting here naked with my dick hanging out. She can see through me, inside me, wherever she wants. I don't know why she's bothering to ask me questions, because she already knows the answers.

"Jesse's...wrong."

She nods. "I think so too. His mama, though, I think she believes in him. Even Mando. I don't know about the other kids. Manny thought Jesse was going through some crazy kid thing that he'd grow out of it. But I think right before he died he was starting to get worried about him. And now that Manny's gone, I don't think nobody—anybody—can make him stop acting crazy. Except maybe you."

"I'm tired of worrying about Jesse. Everybody wants me to do something about Jesse, 'Jesse this' and 'Jesse that', hey, I'm all screwed up, too, I got run over and I've been a punching bag and I take shit all the time, but nobody seems to give a shit about me, everybody's worried about Jesse! He's a football star, he talks to Jesus, he's on his own." I've gotten so fired up I'm almost yelling at Yolanda. My breath comes in gulps and my face is hot and flushed. The boundaries between scars and skin suddenly ache, like they always do when I get excited.

Yolanda sits impassively. She snuffs out her cigarette and finishes her bourbon.

"I care about you, Roger."

"What?" I say. I sound like I'm retarded.

"You're okay for a white boy. You been—*you've* been a good friend to

Jesse, stood by him no matter what. I noticed, and I appreciate it. The whole family does. I'll pay you back one of these days, Roger. Promise." She smiles at me and the hairs on the back of my neck tingle, because unless I'm really mistaken I get the distinct impression she's talking about—no, couldn't be. But then she leans across the table and kisses me on the lips. A warm, soft, nice kiss that leaves me speechless.

"Someday," she says, and then she goes back inside the house. I sit alone at the rickety redwood picnic table.

I don't move for a long time.

We lost the first playoff game and just like that the football season was over. Coach Gutierrez said it was because they were stronger, smarter and tougher, which didn't leave us much to beat them with. Jesse played okay, but I think his dad dying might've bothered him. He didn't make his usual number of tackles, and their linemen and backs were able to block him. Coach Gutierrez didn't scream at him like he did at the other players, I guess out of sympathy.

With football season over, life has settled back into a routine, and I miss the after school structure of being team manager. Now I go to class, do what I have to do, and then hang out with Jesse and Patty on the afternoons and weekends.

Christmas is coming, and it's actually been cold lately. We even had frost on the lawn last night. I know the weather won't become anything really neat, like the snow you see on TV in beer commercials or on *A Charlie Brown Christmas*, but for here it's pretty cool. I'm even getting into the Christmas spirit.

I'm in my room, reading an article about Dick Butkus in the newest *Sports Illustrated* and listening to the Partridge Family singing *I Think I Love You* on my stereo. I'd never admit it to anybody, but I really like the Partridge Family.

Father Quinn sticks his head in my door. "Rog?"

I look up and I can immediately tell that something weird's going on. Father Quinn is easy to read.

"Jesse's here," he continues, "and he's brought somebody with him."

Great. Probably another loser he's conned into believing he's Jesus' best buddy. I wearily set the *Sports Illustrated* down and get up.

"It might surprise you," he warns.

"I'm used to surprises from Jesse."

I follow Father Quinn out into the living room. Jesse's there. So's Patty.

And so is Joe Fanucci. I haven't seen him for years, since the day he came to the door and apologized for running over me. He looks much older now, like somebody's grandfather, though he's probably Father Quinn's age; he's pale and his hair is thin and gray, and his once-muscular body is shrunken. He looks so bad I wonder if he's dying of cancer.

He glances up at me from his seat on the couch, and his eyes dart with guilt. He's so nervous and twitchy I expect him to jump up and run out of the house. I think Joe's afraid of me.

"Hey," I mumble, surprised that I'm able to say anything at all to him, considering how much I've grown to hate his guts since the accident.

His eyes quickly look away from mine. He stares at the carpet and whispers, "Hello, Rog."

Jesse grins like a big, brown, muscle-bound Cheshire Cat. "See, Joe! I told you he's filled with forgiveness."

I throw Jesse an annoyed look. His holy perkiness can grate, particularly when there's tension in the air. There is a long moment of silence while we all try to think of something to say.

Father Quinn is the first one to break. He can't stand a conversational void, so he slides into friendly priest chitchat.

"So, Joe, how've you been? I'd heard you moved away."

Joe squirms on the couch. I almost feel bad for the guy, because this is embarrassing and uncomfortable for him. Now he knows how I feel every day of my life with my scars and limp.

"Yeah. Moved to West Covina for awhile. But then I thought I might be able to get back together with Shirley, so I came back here. Didn't work out, though." Joe sighs and looks back at the carpet.

Nice going, Father Quinn. Remind him that his wife dumped him and didn't want him back. Ask him next if he's still drinking.

"Mmmm," Father Quinn says, looking concerned. He's going to probe and try to help, I can tell. "And have you been able to...work?" Translation: *Still a drunk?*

"Yeah. I'm working at the loading dock down at Pierce Manufacturing. Nothin' too great." He glances up at me, and our eyes meet. He nervously looks away; the patchy scars on my face are such a horrible a reminder of what he did that he can't look for more than a few seconds. His pained expression makes me more self-conscious than ever.

"That's great, Joe. Just great," Father Quinn says. More silence. Then, he plows on. "Have you...dealt with your issues, Joe?"

Joe shrugs and keeps his head down.

Patty chirps, "Tell them, Jesse!" She's so excited she can hardly contain herself. I have a cold feeling about this.

"Joe's come to me, Father Quinn," Jesse says, grinning proudly.

"Don't call me 'Father'," Father Quinn snaps. "What do you mean he's 'come to' you?"

"Joe's seen that I tell the truth. He wants to know Jesus and the Virgin Mary through me."

This is seriously weird. I just want to go back to my room and listen to the Partridge Family.

"You're going too far with this stuff, Jesse," Father Quinn says. "Joe's an...injured person. He needs professional help, not high school holy visions."

Jesse just smiles. "I saw Joe at the mall. He was sitting by the fountain, just watching the world go by. And I could tell he was sad, that he needed something out of life."

"That's right!" Patty adds. "I was there when it happened. Jesse saw Joe and he said, 'There's a soul in pain. I know this guy. I can help him'."

"So I went up to Joe and I reminded him what the Virgin tells me," says Jesse.

"Which is?" Father Quinn asks.

"That guilt over sin is a waste of time. There's no forgiveness in guilt. And that all he needed to do for salvation was follow me."

"For Christ's sake, Jesse, you're a high school freshman middle linebacker, not a prophet!" I've never heard Father Quinn cuss before.

Jesse smiles. "The Virgin always tells me that the holy men will be the hardest to convince."

"I'm an ex-holy man," Father Quinn grumbles.

Joe finally looks up from the carpet. "It's true what Jesse says, Father."

"I'm not a father anymore! I'm just a regular suburbia guy!"

Father Quinn's anger scares Joe back into staring at the carpet.

"If you spent a little time listening to me, Father Quinn, maybe you'd believe too," Jesse says, so sincere it makes me want to throw-up.

Father Quinn sits down on the Naugahyde Lazy Boy rocker. He looks pale. "I've listened to you for years, Jesse," he says, his voice quiet. "I've watched you claim your miracles and visions, I've seen your stigmata, I've prayed for guidance about how to deal with you, and I've never been able to figure out what to do. But I've decided now. You've gone too far with this, there are no such things as visions, there aren't miracles, and anything odd that's happened to you is the function of your own misguided mind. You need help, Jesse. You have a mental illness. And you *must* stop dragging other people into your hallucinations and your fantasies. You've got to stop it now. It's not cute anymore."

Wow. Somebody finally tells Jesse off. I'd like to hope that he'll listen to the words and think about things, that maybe he'll realize that he's off his rocker. I'd like to hope that—but, of course, I'd be wasting my time. Because Jesse is Jesse and Jesse is unreachable.

"It sounds like you've lost your faith, Father," Jesse says, sadly shaking his head. "It's too bad. I'll talk to the Virgin about you. Maybe she'll be able to help."

Father Quinn glares at him, but he says nothing more. He gets up, and the Naugahyde squeaks back into its original shape.

"Nice to see you again, Joe," Father Quinn says, and then he leaves the room.

I look at Jesse. He sits, smiling, content in the knowledge that he's snagged and converted Joe and pissed off Father Quinn, an old disbeliever. Patty stares at him with a gaze that borders on adoration. Joe glances up from the carpet, sees that I'm looking at him, then looks back down.

"You need to forgive Joe, Roger," Jesse says.

"For what?"

"You've held a grudge ever since he ran over you. The Virgin told me that if you don't forgive, you won't be saved, man."

"Yeah, okay, I forgive him," I say. I wish they'd leave.

"You have to mean it."

"Yeah, Roger, you have to mean it," Patty repeats after Jesse, like a well-trained parakeet.

"I said I forgive him, all right?!"

And now Joe looks up at me. This time he doesn't take his eyes from mine. "Please, Roger. You got to mean it. Ever since it happened, I...I...." He can't finish. The eyes go back to the carpet.

"What do you guys want from me?! Yeah, okay, I forgive you for messing me up, I forgive you for making me a limping geek, I forgive you for making my face look like fucking Frankenstein! Okay, is that good enough?!"

They look at me with sad, disappointed eyes. I feel like I've failed them, and a tidal wave of guilt hits me.

Jesse sighs and shakes his head. "You need to pray to the Virgin, Rog. I can't do everything for you, you got to do some of it on your own."

"Tell her to heal me, then I'll forgive everybody."

"Doesn't work that way, man. You know that."

Jesse stands, and Patty and Joe follow his lead. They've taken my place as Jesse's official followers. Good. I'm sick of always being the one to trot loyally behind him.

"Pray, Rog," Jesse says.

"Yeah, pray," Patty says.

"Please forgive me, Roger-Dodger," Joe says, and for just a split second his voice sounds like the old Joe who lived next door and leaned over the fence and traded insults with Dad. But as quickly as it appears it's gone, and he's draggy and defeated again. "You got to forgive me, you have to!"

No. I won't forgive him. Why should I? He ruined my life because he sucked up too many beers, it's not up to me to forgive him. I remember something I heard in a movie once that I thought was cool. So, just to be an asshole I say, "Jesus forgives. I don't."

Power. The feeling is great. Mastery over another person—it's a sensation I've seldom had. Now I know how terrifying guys like Danny Robledo feel when they lord it over weaklings like me. It's intoxicating, to think that my words can hit somebody hard, hit them where it really counts, make them flinch. I love it.

Until Joe begins to cry. Jesse and Patty put their arms around his shoulders, and they gently guide him out of the house. His weeping makes his whole body shake, and they all ignore me as they leave, as if I'm too repulsive to bother looking at.

I'm left standing alone. The sudden quiet feels heavy; if I listen carefully I can hear Father Quinn shuffling around in the kitchen, probably looking for a beer. He's been drinking a lot of beer lately, and he's starting to grow a gut. He'll look like Dad if he keeps it up.

I can't move. I'm glued to the carpet. The power that felt so good a few seconds ago now weighs me down so much that I feel like I'm being squashed. Joe asked me to forgive him and I kicked him in the face. *Nice going, Roger-Dodger.* He was sincere, all he wanted was to hear the words, "I forgive you" and he might've been able to get on with his life. But I wouldn't do it, I couldn't give him that much. How could I? *He* hurt me first. He ground my face into the asphalt, he wrecked me. *I'm* the one who's been hurt, I'm the one.

But no matter how much I tell myself that I'm right, I feel wrong.

I'm sitting in church with Father Quinn and Mom; we're staring at the Nativity scene by the altar. It's Christmas Eve midnight mass. Since all the once-a-year Catholics will straggle in and take up the seats, we're here forty-five minutes early, sitting in the dim light, while the organist plays background music of Christmas carols. This is the first time Father Quinn's been back to church since he married Mom, and everyone who's seen him has acted like he's infected with a killer disease. It doesn't seem to bother him that he's being shunned, but I can tell it bothers Mom a lot, and she sits squeezing Father Quinn's hand, trying to get strength from him.

The crib in the Nativity scene is empty, since Jesus hasn't officially shown up yet. I stare at the dusty straw scattered all over the altar, and at the plaster figurines, and the longer I look the more I realize I don't believe in any of it. The paint on Mary's blue veil is cracked and chipped, and the white flecks showing through makes it look like she has a bad case of dandruff.

The wise men hold their jars of frankincense and myrrh. The nuns told us what the stuff was for but I've forgotten. A little angel holding a banner that says something in Latin dangles above the manger on a piece of fishing line. I remember when the Knights of Columbus built the manger; Dad was the construction leader, and he spent an afternoon with his buddies cutting up two-by-fours and drinking beer. I was helping them, and I remember Dad getting crazy with the circular saw and laughing, "Cut it twice and it's still too short!" after he screwed up another piece of wood. He and his drunken, knucklehead buddies wasted as much wood as they used, and the manger they ended up with was lopsided and goofy-looking. I think that's why every year the altar society ladies who decorate for Christmas pile more straw on top of the manger—they're embarrassed by how half-assed it is. It's a little *too* humble, even for our humble Savior.

The Montoyas aren't here tonight; they usually go to mass on Christmas morning, although I'm not sure what's up with them this year. I haven't seen Jesse much since he brought Joe over a few weeks ago. We haven't talked much at school and he hasn't called me up to follow him around on his conversion missions at the mall. It was okay with me at first, but now, unbelievably, I'm feeling left out and forgotten. I don't understand myself. I've wanted to get out of his psycho "I've talked to the Virgin Mary and she wants to talk to you, too" business for a long time, but now that I'm no longer a part of it I'm jealous of the people who are.

It pisses me off that Patty and Joe Fanucci are his slaves. I must have some deep need to be led around like a moron. I'll bet it runs in the family. Mary Frances is off in a prison convent, being told when to breathe, and I seem to have the same weakness: "Tell me what to do, I'm too dumb to think for myself". I decide it's my parents' fault I'm like this. I wonder if Mom smoked or drank too much when she was pregnant with me? I'll have to ask her.

"I saw Jesse in the mall today," Mom said last week, pretending to be casual. She knew I was on the outs with Jesse and she was being nosy.

She'd been out shopping after her classes at the junior college; she's decided it's time to get her real estate license, just like Aunt Yolanda. For some reason, all these people seem to think that selling real estate is the secret of life. Who knows, it's probably as good as anything, although the appeal of showing people houses and hustling them to buy escapes me.

I was watching the local news when she came in, so I just grunted, hoping she wouldn't feel obligated to tell me more about her Jesse sighting.

She bustled around, taking off her coat and fussing with her purse. She cleared her throat, and I knew she was trying to decide whether she should continue, but Mom being Mom, she couldn't keep quiet. "I was a little surprised," she said.

I gave up trying to ignore her. "Why, Mom?"

"Well...Joe Fanucci was with him. I think they were trying to sell people something. I watched them, they kept going up to people in the mall, and Jesse would start talking, and he'd point to Joe, and there was some red-haired girl with them and she was talking and pointing, too. It looked to me like they were making people mad, Roger. Is he still doing that religious nonsense?"

She knew he was, so I don't know why she asked. But that's just Mom's way, she asks questions she already knows the answers to. Maybe it's her way of making conversation.

"Yeah, Mom. I hear he's been trying to convert people to the First United Church of Jesse Montoya."

"Oh dear. Why's Joe Fanucci with him?"

"You know why, I'm sure Father Quinn told you."

"His name is Steve," she said coldly.

I ignored her and continued. "Jesse convinced Joe that Mary really talks to him. And Joe's following Jesse around because he feels guilty about running over me and he wants somebody to forgive him. So I guess he figures that if Jesse really talks to Mary, and he sticks close to Jesse, then maybe Mary will tell Jesus to forgive him and he won't feel guilty anymore." It was the first time I'd said it out loud, and it surprised me how ridiculous it sounded. Joe was a pathetic loser, I decided.

Mom stood, looking bewildered. Then, her face cleared, all was forgotten, and she said, "Shall I whip up some sloppy Joes for dinner?"

I spent the rest of the evening trying to forget that my best friend had dumped me for a goofy red-haired girl and an alcoholic guilt fiend.

It's finally midnight and mass gets rolling. I'm tired and yawning and by the time the sermon starts I'm into a semi-awake dreamland.

I'm walking now, along a street that looks like mine but is different in that strange way that dreams change reality. I step off the curb and have a massive sleep twitch that wakes me up. I've kicked the pew in front of us, and Mom throws me a dirty look.

"Pay attention to the sermon," she whispers. Father Quinn looks over and smiles understandingly. Father Mora's giving a lousy sermon.

I try my best to listen and stay awake, but sleep soon returns. This time I'm on the sidelines of a football field, and some teams are playing, but they're not teams I know. I look at the defense to see if Jesse is playing middle linebacker, but it's not him. It's someone smaller. A play sweeps around to the sideline, and the small middle linebacker makes the tackle and rolls out of bounds at my feet. I look down at him, only his helmet is gone now, and his face, it's not a guy after all, it's Sister Mary Annunciata.

"Everything that happens to you is deserved, Roger. You're a sinner, you're going to hell!" she cackles like the witch in *The Wizard of Oz.* I back away from her and start running, only I run smack into a large man. I assume it's Coach Gutierrez, but when I look up, I'm looking into the half-paralyzed face of Monsignor O'Callahan. Snotty drool hangs from his chin, and he grimace-smiles at me with yellowed, cracked teeth.

"Going to hell!" he slurs, and then he starts laughing at me, and I turn to run away and Sister Mary Annunciata is there, and so's Joe Fanucci, and so's Jesse, and Patty, and Dad, and everybody's laughing and telling me I'm going to hell.

My eyes pop open and I'm back at midnight mass, the sermon is over and we're standing up to say the creed. I feel queasy, and for a brief, horrible moment I'm afraid I'm going to puke on the person in front of me. It passes, thank God, and I spend the rest of midnight mass sweaty and disturbed.

I can't get the picture of Sister Mary Annunciata and Monsignor O'Callahan out of my head.

I'm sitting in Mrs. Johnson's English I class listening to *Jesus Christ Superstar,* because Mrs. Johnson thinks it's a good example of English usage. I don't see the connection between a rock opera and high school English, but the music's okay, so I guess it could be worse. At least she's not making us diagram sentences.

Christmas vacation is over, and the daily grind is back to normal. I don't say much to Jesse, I try to avoid Rhonda Fairly, I don't have any other friends, so I spend most of my time by myself. At lunch I hide out in the school library, browsing through dog-eared copies of *Life* magazine or *Sports Illustrated.*

I see Jesse only in passing, while we're in the crowds of students trying to get to class, or by our lockers. It's not that we aren't speaking, Jesse's cordial, says "How'sitgoin'?" and gives me a head nod. It's just that our old friendship seems to have died. Patty is always hovering around him, although I've noticed at lunch when I sneak a glance at them that Jesse looks annoyed with her. I know him well enough to be able to read his face, and Patty gets the "you're bugging me" look more often than not.

But still, neither he nor I will make the first move at reconciliation. So we nod, head wave, and ignore each other. Ignoring somebody is a lot of work. It's stressful.

Rhonda Fairly is another story. Lately, for some reason, she's gone out of her way to be nice to me. She makes small talk when she sees me at lunch, and pretends that everything's okay and we're best buddies. For awhile I thought things might get interesting, because the rumor was that she and Bushman had broken up, but then I saw them holding hands during lunch, so I guess they patched up their problems. That makes seeing her and talking to her even harder. As long as Bushman's around, I can't see her as anything but a traitor.

I can't understand how they've stayed a couple so long. High school freshmen don't pair off and stay together; it isn't natural. The guys lucky enough to have girlfriends break up every two weeks and move on to somebody else. The majority of us don't have the luxury of worrying about breaking up with girls, so we stay on the sidelines and watch the players go through their changing partners. But Rhonda and Bushman are different. It almost seems...serious between them. But they're only fifteen, so how serious can it be?

Serious enough to bug me. Serious enough that I spend way too much time thinking about them. Serious enough to make me desperately want a girl of my own. But not just any girl. Rhonda. She's all I want, and as long as Bushman's velcroed to her, I don't have a chance.

The fucker.

I sit and listen to *Jesus Christ Superstar*, my mood foul and black. How much longer will Bushman ruin my life?

The phone rings five times before I wake up. The *riinnng* has burrowed its way into my dreams, and when I finally awaken I'm confused. I hear Father Quinn groggily answer the phone out in the hall, and a sudden sense of unease hits me. I'm instantly wide awake, and as I strain to listen to Father Quinn's muffled voice, my heart begins pounding. I look at my alarm clock: two-thirty. It has to be bad news.

Father Quinn stops talking, and his footsteps pad down the hall. He looks into my room, and now I'm really scared.

"Roger?" he whispers. "You awake?"

I hesitate for a moment, wondering if I should pretend to be asleep, but then I decide it will do no good. I might as well find out what's going on right now.

"Yeah?"

"That was Yolanda. Jesse's aunt?"

"Yeah?" Like I don't know who she is. Jeez.

"She...you need to get up. Something bad's happened."

I bolt upright in bed. "Jesse?!"

I can't see Father Quinn's face in the dim light, but I can tell things are bad. Mom comes up behind him, and puts her hand on his shoulder.

"Who was it, Steve?" she asks.

"We need to get dressed," he says. "We're going to the hospital. Jesse's been in an accident."

Jesse and I used to ride our bikes down to the hospital when we were kids and hang around the emergency entrance, hoping to see ambulances bring bloody people in. It seemed exciting and dangerous at the time, but now that I'm sitting in the ER waiting room at three in the morning waiting to hear about Jesse, the hospital has lost its appeal.

Jesse's family is gathered here with us, looking as sleepy and disheveled as we do. Aunt Yolanda, minus makeup and with pillow hair, still looks good. I mentally kick myself for looking at her instead of concentrating on worrying about Jesse.

Mrs. Montoya is pale and shaky. She hasn't even begun to get over Mr. Montoya's death, and now she has to deal with Jesse. Aunt Yolanda motions for me to come over.

"You know what happened?" she asks.

I shake my head.

"The priest didn't tell you?" I'm thrown for a moment who she's talking about until I realize she means Father Quinn.

"He said Jesse was in an accident."

She looks at Mom and Father Quinn; she shakes her head. "Priests," she mutters. She pulls me aside and sits me down in a plastic chair by the vending machines.

"Jesse was riding with that guy Joe, the one who ran over you. He was driving, and that red-haired girl was with them, too."

"Are they okay?"

"No. They're dead."

My head spins, I'm not sure if I'm going to stay conscious. I feel like I'm falling.

"What?" is all I can say.

"They was...they *were* at the mall, Jesse was doing his stupid preaching shit again, and they got kicked out by the security guys. So this Joe guy is giving Jesse and the girl a ride home, when he runs off the road into a telephone pole."

"Was...was he drunk?"

"Cops think so. They said the girl and Joe got killed instantly. Jesse shot through the windshield, they're operating on him. He was in here for five hours before they found out who he was and called us."

Joe Fanucci dead. And Patty. There's too much death around me. What if Jesse dies, too?

"Will he be okay?" I ask.

Aunt Yolanda shrugs. "I dunno, Roger." She stares off into the dark corner of the magazine-littered waiting room. I want to say or do something to make her feel better, but I'm so shocked myself that I can't move. She looks back at me, then leans over and hugs me tightly. I hug back; surprisingly, it doesn't seem awkward with her. I feel her begin to shake as she starts to cry, and I start to cry, too, and we stay together, hugging and crying, for a very long time.

The next thing I know it's morning and sunshine streams through the waiting room windows. I'm curled up across a couple of the plastic chairs. I sit up, stiff and sore, and look around. Jesse's family is still here, waiting, worried. Jesse's brother Mando smokes furiously, puffing cigarettes like they're the only things keeping him alive. He looks so angry and pissed off that if I were a doctor I'd be afraid to give him any bad news. Mom and Father Quinn sit nearby, and Mom smiles when she sees I'm awake. Aunt Yolanda stands by a window, watching a couple of crows flapping around outside.

I get up, stretch, and go over to Mom.

"Any news?"

"No, honey. Nothing yet. Jesse's still in surgery."

I look at Father Quinn. "How come you didn't tell me about Joe and Patty?"

Father Quinn sighs one of his priestly, weary sighs. "I wasn't sure you were ready to know. I'm sorry."

I wasn't ready to know? What's he talking about? I don't press it, but it makes me wonder what he's thinking sometimes.

We wait some more, I don't know how long because time has become strange—it doesn't seem to pass, but it does and you aren't aware of it—and finally a doctor comes out. He's dressed in green surgical scrubs, just like the guys you see on TV. He's old and he looks really tired.

He huddles with Jesse's family, and Mrs. Montoya listens intently, then begins to cry. Not good news, I suppose, and I prepare for the worst. The doctor talks to them a few minutes more, then leaves. Mrs. Montoya sits down on a plastic chair, her face twisted in pain. Her kids huddle around her, trying to comfort her; Mando hugs her and holds her hand. It's hard to believe that he can be so tender. Aunt Yolanda comes over to us. I don't want to hear what she has to say.

"He'll live," she says.

Mom, Father Quinn and I wait for what's coming next.

"But he probably won't be able to see," she adds, and now she begins to cry.

Mom hugs her, and Father Quinn puts a protective arm around my shoulder; I guess he thinks that'll make me feel better.

"He's blind?" I ask. Nobody bothers to answer.

"We have to pray for Jesse," Father Quinn says. "Our prayers can help him."

I pull away. "What for? If there was a God this wouldn't have happened in the first place!"

"Roger—" Father Quinn starts to speak.

"It's all bullshit, it's a lie, there isn't any God, there aren't any miracles, the only thing that happens is we get hurt and we die."

I'm speaking loudly, and Mrs. Montoya looks up at me and I feel bad for making a scene. I don't want her to feel worse than she already does, but Father Quinn's stupid nonsense about praying pisses me off. I shut up, move away from them, and plop down on a chair. I sniff back angry tears.

After awhile, Aunt Yolanda comes over to me.

"Not fair, is it?" she asks.

"It sucks."

"Guess you know better than anybody. That *cabron* Joe Fanucci hurt a lot of people. I'm glad he's dead, man," she says, lapsing into *vata.*

"Me too," I grumble, feeling a little guilty at first saying it, then deciding that he had it coming.

"You really believe what you said about God?" she asks.

"That there isn't one?"

"Yeah."

I shrug. "Doesn't seem like it to me. All you got to do is look around, praying doesn't help anything, bad stuff keeps on happening no matter what you do."

Aunt Yolanda nods. "Yeah, maybe you're right. The more I think about it... I wonder if Jesse will change his mind after this?"

"He hasn't been able to heal me," I say. "And I bet he won't be able to heal himself." Although as soon as I say it I remember that time in junior high when he fell off the basketball backboard and the cut on his forehead seemed to stop bleeding. But that was minor league, it wasn't blindness, and I'm not even sure anything really happened. I put it out of my mind. It was impossible. Probably one of those weird mind-over-matter things I've read about.

"*You'll* help him, though, won't you?" she asks.

"Sure."

"He's gonna need you."

I nod. I'll do what I need to do, because no matter what, Jesse Montoya is my best friend.

When Jesse finally comes home from the hospital, he reminds me of myself when *I* got run over by Joe Fanucci. I know how he feels—except for the blind part. He's stuck at home, being fussed over by his family, and he's getting sick of all the attention.

I've been going over every day after school, and we've resumed our friendship where it left off before Joe Fanucci showed up. Our easy understanding of each other has come back, and it feels good to be able to talk and laugh and just be pals again.

The crash broke Jesse's arm, and he got bad cuts and bruises all over. But the worst part was saved for his eyes. When Joe's car hit the telephone pole, it snapped the pole in half and blasted shattered wood fragments through the broken windshield. It was Jesse's bad luck that the pole-slivers peppered his face like little daggers, and shot into his eyes. They punched through the cornea, ripped up the jelly stuff inside, and lodged in the retinas. And when you mess up the retina, you're in big trouble. His eyes are still bandaged now, six weeks after the accident, and the doctors think he might be able to see light and dark and fuzzy shapes eventually—but that's about it.

The school district hired a tutor to keep Jesse up with our classwork. Jesse's not much of a student—he's always read a lot, but classes bore him.

"What's Miss Sandoval look like, man?" he asks me as we watch (actually, I watch; Jesse listens) a movie-of-the-week about a guy in the desert being chased by a tanker truck. Miss Sandoval is the tutor who's been trying to teach Jesse.

"She's a fox."

"Really? You know, man, I could tell by the way she talks. She got a good ass?"

I don't have the heart to tell him that Miss Sandoval is an overweight, acne-scarred student teacher with greasy hair.

"Great. Tight, perfectly shaped. Too bad you can't see her."

I shouldn't have said that, because the thought of not being able to leer at women makes him sad. I've got to be more careful about the sight-related stuff I say.

"What's happening now?" he asks, listening to the TV.

"The truck's still chasing Dennis Weaver."

"Is it getting closer?"

"Yeah. I think his car's starting to overheat."

"Shit."

It goes on like this, me translating the movie for his sightless eyes.

I wonder if this is how it's always going to be. I'm both flattered and annoyed that I have this power over Jesse. In the past, he's always been the strong one, he's always been the leader. Now that he's blind, will I get to be the boss?

He hasn't mentioned anything about Jesus or the Virgin Mary since the accident. Father Quinn's come to visit, and the new priest at church, Father Mora, has stopped by, but Jesse hasn't said a word about visions or miracles or religion at all. I was here when Father Mora came to talk to him, and Jesse was pleasant, but he didn't say or do anything to make you think he was anything more than a fifteen-year-old kid who'd been in an accident. I was relieved he didn't start in on "The Virgin says" game.

The movie ends when the tanker truck plunges over a cliff.

"So why'd the guy chase him, man?" Jesse asks.

"I dunno. Just because."

Jesse isn't satisfied. "He must've had a reason, you sure you didn't miss it?"

"I'm telling you, Jesse, the guy in the truck just chased Dennis Weaver all over the desert for no reason. Maybe he didn't like the car he was driving or something."

I get the feeling Jesse thinks I'm lying to him, or withholding vital information. This could be a problem if I end up having to be his eyes all the time. He's going to have to learn to trust me.

"Rhonda came by today," Jesse says.

"Yeah."

"She was nice, as usual."

"Yeah." I don't really care.

"She asked about you."

Now I'm interested. "Oh yeah?"

"She wanted to know the usual, why you don't talk to her, all that shit."

My heart starts thumping more than it should. I don't know why she has this effect on me. Jesse's head jerks up, his nose high, like he smells something.

"Hey, man. I can tell...I can feel it. You're all fired up about her. Fuckin' a, you're not a *joto* after all!"

"Shut up," I say, but I'm smiling. "You already got some weird blind sixth sense or something?"

"Maybe. Another fucking gift of the Lord." I can't tell if he's kidding or not.

"She ask...anything else?"

"Rhonda's just normal, man, she asks about people she knows. It doesn't mean she wants to get married or nothing."

Yeah. But when girls ask about me, especially Rhonda, I like the feeling.

We sit and wait for the movie credits to end. I don't know what Jesse's thinking about, but I've got Rhonda warmth inside. It's weird, I can go from almost hating her to wanting her in the span of a few minutes.

"I got a plan, Roger," Jesse says softly, bringing me out of the Rhonda warm zone. "You and me, we're gonna get better."

"You mean cured?"

"The Virgin told me if I showed my faith I'd be cured. And you would, too."

"Oh, man, not the Mary stuff again, Jesse. Can't you just forget about it? It's crazy!"

He sits serenely, as if he hasn't heard a word I said. The cuts on his face are healing to dull, pink scars, bumpy little slashes on his brown skin.

"Jesse?" I ask. "Jesse? Did you hear me? Forget about miracles, you're on your own now. You gotta figure out how to live with what happened to you. I can help you, I've been through it. But forget about the Virgin Mary. She's not gonna help you."

His head turns toward me. "You're wrong, Roger. She'll cure us."

I'm disgusted with him. He's completely gone into fantasyland now.

He grins at me as he says, "But we'll have to go see Her, first."

And even though I know better, I'd swear he can see right through those bandages and he's looking at me.

Chapter Thirteen

"Where is it?" Jesse asks.

"I'll get it for you," Father Quinn says.

"Where is it?" Jesse says again, insistently and with a threat in his voice. Father Quinn backs off.

"By your left foot."

The green wooden rental boat bounces on choppy swells; too much more and I might get seasick. Since we're on Iceberg Lake in the High Sierras and not the ocean, I don't know if it would be called seasickness. Maybe lake sickness.

Jesse just dropped his silver Rapala lure, the one that looks like a little minnow, and it floats in the mucky water sloshing around the bottom of the leaky boat. It worries me that there's so much water in the boat; Father Quinn assures us that it's okay, "These old wooden boats last forever. You couldn't sink it if you wanted to." I don't feel reassured, because I'm not sure Father Quinn's ever been fishing before, let alone in a leaky wooden boat.

Jesse flops his big brown hand around in the water, grabbing for the lure.

Father Quinn watches with concern. "Careful, Jesse, don't—"

"FUCK! *CABRON*!"

"—hook yourself."

"FUCK!!" Jesse tries to shake the lure from his index finger, but the vicious treble hook has him good.

"Hang on, man," I say, as he shakes his hand violently and lets loose with every Spanish cuss word I've ever heard. I grab the long-nose pliers from the tackle box. "Stop shaking your hand."

"Fuck, it hurts, man!"

"Yeah, so don't be a pussy. Here." I grab his wrist and inspect his finger. The front treble hook has gone all the way through the skin on the tip of his index finger. Blood oozes out through the puncture and dribbles down Jesse's arm.

"Oh dear," says Father Quinn. "We'd better go back and see if we can find an emergency room."

"Nah. I can fix it," I say. "I'll cut off the barb and we can push the hook back out." Father Quinn makes a face as if I just suggested we amputate the finger. "That okay with you, Jesse?"

"Just get the motherfucker out."

"I don't think that's a good idea, Roger. What if it gets infected?" Father Quinn asks.

"You worry too much, Father Quinn. Besides, the Virgin will heal him, won't she, Jesse?"

Jesse smiles through his pain grimace. "Fuck you, man. Get the thing outa my finger and I'll forgive you for your lack of faith, *puto*."

I have Father Quinn grab Jesse's finger and hold it while I snip off the hook's barbed end. Jesse squirms and wiggles a little, but at least he's not being a complete weenie about it. I push the hook back through the hole. By the time I've gotten it out, there's blood all over the place. I grab the dirty rag we've been using to wipe salmon egg goo and fish scales off our hands and wrap it around Jesse's finger.

"That's not sanitary," Father Quinn objects.

"It's okay. Neither is Jesse."

Jesse rubs his finger for awhile, then he tosses the rag down and sucks the little remaining blood from his finger.

"Taste good?" I ask.

"Tie the thing on for me, man," he asks. So I tie the Rapala onto his line, using the knot that Dad showed me how to tie a long time ago when he and I came up here.

We putt-putt along the shoreline, trolling, without any strikes. It's midday, and the fish have stopped biting. As we slap through the choppy water, I look up at the huge, towering mountains that surround the sparkling lake. Their bare, cracked peaks are still quilted with patchy snow, and it's hard to believe that in the summertime snow could be so nearby.

It's a warm day, and even with our shirts off and the wind blowing over us it's almost too hot. But it's a good heat, clear and mountain-crisp. There's not a hint of the ever-present smog that I'm used to at home, and it seems strange to be able to see miles into the distance without the brown, mucky shroud of L.A. smog.

We decide trolling isn't the way to go, so we anchor in a cove near a stream inlet to try our luck at still-fishing.

We drop Velveeta cheese and salmon egg-packed treble hooks over the side and let our reels unspool until the sticky, cheesy mess reaches bottom.

"The guy in the tackle shop said the browns were hitting these like crazy. I think he called them a California salad." Father Quinn giggles, impressed with his sudden ability to bullshit with grubby guys in tackle shops. I get the feeling that Father Quinn was always kind of a nerd. Even though he looks like a stud, and probably had girls climbing all over him when he was my age, I don't think he ever figured out how to behave around real people, the guys who smoke and swear and fish and say "pussy" and all that. When you decide you're going to be a priest when you're thirteen, like Father Quinn did, it separates you from the world. He's just now getting to learn how to be a real guy, and I think he's enjoying it.

Jesse lounges in the back of the boat, his Stevie Wonder wraparound sunglasses covering his almost-useless eyes, his muscular, hairless chest soaking up the rays. He has scars on his chest from the accident, but he's been lifting weights again, and he's starting to bulk up and look like the Jesse of old. In the bright, high altitude sunlight, his black hair glistens and almost looks blue.

"What you lookin' at, *joto*? Like me without my shirt on?" he asks, grinning.

It startles me to realize he saw me looking at him. Although he's almost blind, he can make out vague shapes and blurs, and sometimes he surprises me by what he *can* see. In the short time since he lost most of his sight, he's been able to figure out by sound and his remnant vision and maybe ESP most of what's going on around him. It's kind of creepy, sometimes. People think he's blind, and then he tells them what they're doing.

A couple of goofballs from another high school tried to fuck with him one day last week as we were wandering around in the mall. They were about ten yards away, in front of him, flipping him off, making faces, thinking he couldn't see them. It pissed me off but I didn't say anything, because I'd been trying to protect Jesse from some of the weirdness and nastiness around. As we passed by the guys, who were snickering and making the international jerk-off sign,

Jesse suddenly lunged at them, brought them both down to the concrete floor with a *thud*!, grabbed their heads in each of his meaty hands, and slammed them against each other.

Their heads *thwacked* like a pair of hollow coconuts, and Jesse leaned close to their glazed eyes and said, "You shouldn't make fun of handicapped people, motherfuckers."

He got up, left the two losers moaning on the floor, and we went on our way. He acted like nothing at all had happened.

"Good tackle, man," I said.

"Yeah. Probably would've gotten flagged for unnecessary roughness, though."

Jesse's adapted quickly to the changes in his life. Unlike me, he hasn't moped around or felt sorry for himself. He just seems to be able to deal with things. I wish I were more like him.

The boat rocks rhythmically and soon all three of us are dozing in the hot sun. I have a bad case of the nods; the harder I try to stay awake, the more my eyes want to close, and my head keeps dropping until my chin hits my chest and I pop back up again, only to repeat the same cycle a few minutes later.

Our trip to the Sierras has been great so far. It was Father Quinn's idea. He was browsing through an old family album, and he came across pictures of Dad and me on a trip up here when I was little.

"Hey, where is this?" he asked, looking at a picture of me holding a scrawny rainbow trout in front of the towering mountains. "It's beautiful."

I told him, and he decided then and there that he had to come up. "Just you and me, and maybe Jesse if you want. Just guys, you know? As long as your mom doesn't mind," he added quickly.

It sounded okay to me. Summer had been pretty routine so far—except for getting used to being Jesse's seeing eye Roger—and with Mom's blessing we were soon headed up Highway 395.

It seemed weird at first to be going on a vacation with Father Quinn and Jesse. I was used to Father Quinn being part of the family, but every so often when I looked at him I still saw a priest. And with a blinded and beat-up Jesse, I felt like I was in one of those strange, disjointed dreams, where things aren't quite normal.

We stopped at Lone Pine for breakfast, and over a gut-blaster of sausage and eggs and biscuits and gravy the vacation began to seem more right. Jesse ate like a pig, Father Quinn pretended not to notice that the weather-beaten waitress was flirting with him, and I watched them, smiling to myself, thinking that they were the two guys who, whether I liked it or not, would be tied to me forever.

We have three more days up here before we have to go home, and I already dread leaving. Descending back to the smog-covered lowlands is the last thing I want to do.

"Hey!" Jesse says.

I'm startled by his voice, and I realize I've been sleeping.

"You got a bite!"

I grab my rod and yank it to set the hook. Father Quinn coughs back into consciousness, and they watch as I wrestle with the rod.

"Man, it's huge!" I say, struggling to keep the rod tip up out of the water. "It's a monster!"

"Play it out, play it out!" Father Quinn shouts, parroting what he's heard other fisherman say when they've got a big one on.

I reel, but it keeps pulling line out faster, and I tighten the drag, but not too much because I don't want the line to snap, and now my heart's pounding, this is some fish, and my arms are getting tired.

"Is it still on?!" Jesse asks.

"Yeah, but I think he's getting tired!"

"Play it out, play it out!" Father Quinn screams again. Both Jesse and I look at him. He's so excited I think he's going to hyperventilate.

I reel and reel, but it keeps taking more line out, and pretty soon my arms are like rubber. I'm such a wimp. If it turns out to be a little 9-inch rainbow I'm going to be really embarrassed.

I glance over at Jesse; he's trying to watch with his feeble eyes, and I can tell he's excited. There's something about the unknown quantity of having a fish on the line, you don't know what kind it is or how big it is, but it's *there*, and it's up to you to bring it into the light. But my arms aren't going to last much longer, and I'm afraid I might lose it.

"Here!" I say to Jesse, handing the rod over to him. "I can't reel anymore. You land it!"

He doesn't need to be asked twice. He snatches the rod from me and begins to smoothly reel and pull, reel and pull, and soon we see a fish belly flash near the boat.

"There he is!" Father Quinn yells, grabbing the net. He almost falls out of the boat as he stands up to net it.

"You got him, Jesse, just ease him up to the boat!" I say.

Jesse coolly reels, and Father Quinn leans down, nets the fish, and pulls him up into the boat.

He drops the net and the flopping, exhausted fish into the water in the boat bottom. With its little remaining life, the fish splashes a couple of times with its big tail, then is still. Its gills flap weakly.

We're all gasping, excited by the big catch. Jesse leans close to the fish, squinting behind his sunglasses.

"How big is it?!"

Father Quinn untangles it from the net and the fish floats, uncovered, in the boat.

"Wow!" is all I can say.

"It's...it's the biggest brown I've ever seen!" Father Quinn says with reverence, like he's mentioning the name of Jesus. He acts as if he's a world-renowned expert on German Browns. It is huge, though, I have to admit. It's as big as some of the browns I've seen hanging on the walls of the tackle shops and restaurants up here.

"Can we get it mounted, Father Quinn?" I ask.

"Sure. If we can afford to. It's so...big!"

Jesse's leaning so close to the fish he's almost touching it with his nose. "Shit, man, I wonder if it's a record or something?"

As the three of us sit in the leaky, rocking boat, staring at a dead fish, surrounded by the most beautiful scenery imaginable, a wave of happiness and contentment washes over me. The *now* of being here with these two guys is perfect.

I've never felt better, and I don't want this moment to ever end.

We're sitting around a crackling campfire, eating potato chips and reliving our triumphant fishing day.

"Biggest German Brown in five years," Father Quinn says, shaking his head, as he drains another beer. He's had a six pack since we started the fire, and he's getting ready to crack another. I guess he figures that great events deserve to be saluted by beer.

When we got back to the marina, a big crowd gathered as the news of our catch quickly spread. Old Ned, the guy who owns the place, weighed the fish.

"Fifteen pounds, nine ounces," Old Ned said, squinting at the scale with watery blue eyes. "Sumbitch, he's a good-looking bastard." Old Ned ran a callused hand along the trout's side. He caressed it gently, like it was a tit or something. Guys and big fish have a special bond.

The fish had a huge gut, and his lower jaw curved up to a point. He looked like he was grinning. Rows of tiny, sharp teeth protruded from his jaw; he was a fierce and vicious presence in the lake, I realized, and I was almost sorry we'd caught him. He was designed to cruise silently, eating the weak and the young, the killer at the top of the food chain. Until we came along and caught him. I almost felt bad. But then I pictured how good he'd look mounted and hanging on the wall. I quickly got over my sympathy.

Jesse pokes at the campfire with a stick, and embers crackle and curl into the night sky. I lean back in my folding patio chair and stare up at the inky night. So many stars. I never notice stars at home. But then, at night I'm usually inside watching TV. Here, in the Sierras, night isn't something scary that you try to hide from; you want to be out in it, to savor the beauty, the clarity, the feeling.

"Hey!" I say, "that star's moving!"

Jesse looks up, although I don't know why because there's no chance he can see it. Father Quinn stares upward, and I wonder if he can see any better than Jesse with all the beer he's been chugging. But he can, because he sees what I see.

"It's not a star, Rog. It's a satellite."

I watch the white pinprick of light move slowly and evenly across the sky. It passes through the scoop of the Big Dipper and moves toward the horizon of mountain peaks.

"No way, man, you can't see those things," Jesse says.

"Yeah, you can, Jesse. They orbit fairly low, and they catch the sun and reflect it back. You can see them all the time if you look for 'em."

"Maybe *you* can see them," Jesse grumbles.

We sit silently for a while. The campground is fairly empty; there's a family a few spots over, but they're already asleep in their tent, and the only sound is the snapping of our fire and Father Quinn's occasional beer burps.

He opens the ice chest and takes out three cans. "You guys want a beer?" he asks.

This is interesting. At times like this I miss being able to make eye contact with Jesse. I never realized before how much of our communication was based on a glance or a raised eyebrow. Now, he sits, expressionless, his sunglasses looking ridiculous in the flickering firelight.

"Sure," Jesse says. This is no big thing for him. I know he's gotten drunk with his brothers before. Father Quinn tosses him a can. It bounces off Jesse's chest and thumps onto the dirt.

"Sorry," Father Quinn says, as I pick it up and hand it to Jesse. "I keep forgetting you're blind."

"Me too," Jesse grins. He pops open the beer, and it sprays him in the face.

We all laugh as Jesse wipes beer dribbles onto his sleeve.

"How 'bout you, Rog?" Father Quinn asks, holding a can out to me.

"Yeah, sure."

"Just don't tell your mom," he whispers, as if she might be lurking behind the trees somewhere.

Right, like I'll run and tattletale on him. This is heavy-duty guy stuff, sitting around a campfire, talking about fishing, and drinking beer. You don't go running home to Mommy and tell her what you've been doing. If she asks, you nod and remain noncommittal. It's the guy way.

I'm beginning to feel like a man.

I don't like the taste of the beer at first; it's too bitter. But as I drink more I get used to it, and by the time I'm into my second one I decide that it's good stuff.

Jesse drinks like a seasoned veteran, and I can't tell any difference in the way he's acting. But Father Quinn's had so much to drink that his speech is beginning to slur and he's giggling for no apparent reason.

"I really love your mother, you know, man?" he says to me. I don't know what to say, but I'd prefer that he keep his thoughts about Mom to himself.

"Great," I say. "Think there's any more fish out there as big as the one we got today?"

"Yeah, sure. But do you have any idea how much I love her?" he asks.

"How much?" says Jesse. I could kill him. Drunken talk about Mom isn't something I want to hear.

"So much," his voice trails off. He looks up into the sky. "You know, when I was a priest, I thought loving God was as intense...as it could get. Uh-uh. No way. Bullshit. Nothing can compare to loving a woman. Nothing."

"But don't you see, man, she *is* God!" Jesse says. "Right there, man, that's why God puts 'em here, to prove He exists!"

Jesse's excited by his lame philosophy, and I expect Father Quinn to just chuckle and humor him because he's being so obvious.

"You're right, Jesse, that's it, man!" Father Quinn says. I've never heard him say "man" so much before. He's regressing to be one of us.

"Aw, come on," I say, surprised at how heavy my tongue feels.

"No, man, that's why women are here, I know it!" Jesse says.

"He's right, Rog. Women are the only reason to live."

"Women? Or just my Mom?" I ask. Jeez, what if this guy dumps her for somebody else just because he's hot for females? It'd kill her.

"No, no, just your mom. She's *my* woman, the one who makes all the difference to me. But don't you see, Rog, we men, we need women. Men can't live without 'em."

"Unless they're *jotos*," Jesse adds.

"You like girls, I know you do, Rog. How about that Rhonda, she's cute."

"Rhonda's...nothing to me."

"He's pissed off 'cause she goes out with Bushman," says Jesse.

"Mmmm." Father Quinn studies his beer can. "There'll be others, I'm sure. How about you, Jesse? Got any hot prospects?"

"Too many, man. Don't know how to deal with all of them."

"Shit...." I say, and Jesse smiles. Father Quinn laughs, then suddenly looks serious.

"That girl in the accident, was she?—"

Jesse's smile vanishes. "Patty was just a believer, that's all. And God took her home early. She was lucky, you know? She didn't have to put up with doubt and shit. She believed, and they let her go to heaven." Jesse looks down at the ground. Even though he can't see, he still has the mannerisms of sight. "She was just a believer," he repeats in a quiet voice.

The beer has loosened everyone's tongues. Father Quinn looks hard at Jesse, then asks the question I know he's wanted to ask for a long time. "Do you still...have visions?"

"Not since the accident."

"Do you think—"

"I don't know," Jesse says. "It used to be easy, man. The Virgin or Jesus would show up every night when I dreamed, and sometimes they'd talk to me during the day or whenever they felt like it. Now, nothing."

"Why do you suppose they've stopped speaking to you?" Father Quinn asks. Even when he's drunk he can still slide easily into the priest/interrogator role. He was tough in confession; he'd always pump you and you'd end up confessing stuff you'd rather not.

"I must not be good enough," Jesse answers. "I dunno. I been thinking and praying a lot about it."

"Maybe it was all in your head to begin with, and the accident knocked the crazy shit out of you," I offer. Father Quinn throws me a dirty look. I don't know why my opinions always piss people off; they make pretty good sense to me.

Jesse smiles. "You'll believe one of these days, Roger."

That infuriating certainty has returned. His doubts are only momentary, that's what makes him so annoying. The rest of us wrestle with trying to figure out why life is the way it is, and Jesse Montoya just swears a couple of times and his doubt vanishes like smoke and he's back to being sure of everything again. I look at Father Quinn. He studies Jesse with a frown; I know he's as puzzled by Jesse as I am.

"So what's all this lead to?" Father Quinn asks.

He shrugs. "Dunno, man. They never told me. But I wanna talk to them again. I miss 'em."

"You can talk to them all you want, Jesse. It's called prayer."

"Me talking isn't the problem. I wanna hear back."

"That's faith. The rest of us have to be content to pray and hope they hear us."

Jesse grins. "They like me better, man."

I finish my beer, crumple it like a stud, and reach into the ice chest for another.

"Sure you haven't had enough there, tiger?" Father Quinn asks.

I take one, pull the poptop in defiance of Father Quinn, and guzzle. Unfortunately, in my quest to be cool most of the beer dribbles down my chin.

"See, what I'm thinkin'," Jesse says, unaware of my standing up for the right to drink beer, "is that when me and Roger go to get cured, they'll start talking to me again. Or at least the Blessed Virgin."

"Cured?" This is news to me.

"Yeah. We're gonna get cured. You and me, I'll see again, and you'll get rid of the scars and shit."

I look to Father Quinn. He sits, listening, interested. But he's no help.

"When's this gonna happen?" I ask.

"As soon as we go see Her."

"Where is She?"

"I think we have to go to France."

"Lourdes?" Father Quinn asks.

"Yeah, that's the place. Some girl had a vision there a long time ago, now people get cured and shit."

"I know the story," Father Quinn smiles. "Saint Bernadette, she was a little younger than you, she claimed the Virgin appeared to her."

"Yeah, and now you go there and drink the water and if you have enough faith you get better."

"It's not that easy, Jesse. Most sick people who go to Lourdes don't get cured, and the ones who do...well, some doubt the validity. There's plenty of people in the church who don't buy into the Marian stuff like Lourdes and Fatima."

"Whatever, man. We'll go, and we'll get cured. Huh, Rog?"

"To France?"

"Yeah, we'll work or something. Maybe your mom and Father Quinn can loan you the money."

I look at Father Quinn, and he just smiles and holds up his hands. "I don't know about that."

"We'll find a way to get there. The Virgin'll talk to me again if I go, I know she will, and she'll cure us. You want that, don't you, man?"

"How many beers have you had?"

"Not enough," Jesse says, holding out his hand.

Father Quinn gives him another. "Maybe I shouldn't be letting you guys drink, I think I'm corrupting you."

"Yeah, man, I might have to confess it," Jesse grins.

For some reason, maybe it's the beer, Father Quinn starts to laugh and he can't stop. He doubles over, laughing, trying to catch his breath.

Jesse's laughing too; I'm the only one who doesn't see anything to laugh about.

"I'm not going to France for some bullshit cure that isn't going to happen."

Jesse stops laughing. "Sure you are, man."

"Uh-uh. You can do what you want. Leave me out of it."

Jesse leans toward me, as if he can see me. The reflection of the campfire flickers on the surface of his wraparound sunglasses.

"It won't work if you don't have faith. Tell him, Father Quinn."

"Well...I'm probably not the best one to ask anymore."

"How come?"

"I'm not sure what I believe. Lourdes might be a bit of a stretch for me right now."

"Shit, man, am I the only guy with any fucking faith in God left?"

"Yeah, Jesse, 'fucking faith'. That's you."

"All right, guys," Father Quinn says. "Let's not argue. You believe what you believe. Let's forget about this stuff and just enjoy being here." He leans back in his chair and looks up at the sky. "Wonder if I can spot another satellite?"

Nobody says anything more. I glance over at Jesse. Even though it's dark, and he's almost blind and he's wearing sunglasses, I'd swear he's looking at me.

He holds up his beer can. And he smiles.

"Mary Frances is coming home!" Mom squeals. It's been a while since she's squealed.

Since she's started selling real estate, she's been less goofy. Being out in the real world seems to have made her realize you can't be goofy-mom and have any success. She's sold lots of houses, and listed a bunch more, and now the commissions are flowing in. Suddenly, we're more well off than we ever were when Dad was alive. Mom's making big money, which is a good thing, because the money Father Quinn makes being a counselor stinks. I think half the time he counsels people for free because he feels sorry for them. Father Quinn acts like he's still a priest sometimes; the only time I've heard him and Mom fight is over his unwillingness to charge people. She told him he was sweet and good and his heart was in the right place, but to knock it off and squeeze money out of his clients.

Mom's gotten tougher lately.

Until now. Until she hears that Mary Frances is coming home for a visit and bringing along a couple of friends.

"Isn't it wonderful, Roger?!"

"Yeah, great."

Mom's just gotten off the phone with Mary Frances and she's bouncing off the walls. Father Quinn and I are trying to read the paper. Father Quinn looks about as excited as I am.

"What friends is she bringing? I didn't think there were any other novices at the convent," he asks.

"She didn't say, just that it would be a surprise."

"Maybe she's going to get married or something." I give Father Quinn a sly smile.

"Don't kid about that, Roger. She's very devoted." Mom takes the nun stuff way too seriously. She would've died if she'd heard some of the nun jokes Father Quinn told us up in the Sierras while we were fishing. Apparently, some priests don't hold nuns in too high regard.

"When's she coming?" I ask, hoping I can weasel out of being here. It's not that I hate her or anything, I just don't understand her. She's like an alien; whenever she's around it's uncomfortable and weird. I know Father Quinn feels the same way, and if you could get Mom to be honest, I think she'd admit that Mary Frances gives her the creeps, too.

"Tomorrow night. We'll have a nice pot roast, it's her favorite." I don't have the heart to tell Mom that Mary Frances hates her pot roast. She always used to roll her eyes and make gagging motions whenever Mom made it.

Mom goes off into the kitchen, humming and happy. I look at Father

Quinn. He sighs and goes back to reading the paper. So do I.

When the doorbell rings Mom calls out, "Can you get that, Rog?"

"Sure."

Father Quinn's in the bathroom supposedly taking a crap. I think he's hiding out so I'm the one who gets stuck letting Mary Frances and her buddies in.

I limp over to the front door—my leg's been hurting more than usual lately. I open the door, already bored and resigned to a lousy evening.

As the door swings open and I look outside, my boredom vanishes and is replaced with disgust and fear. My throat slams shut, my stomach does a sickening flip, my knees get shaky and cold sweat pumps out of my pores.

Sister Mary Annunciata and Monsignor O'Callahan are on the front porch, grinning at me like a pair of evil hell-demons. Sister Mary Annunciata's yellow, ferret teeth are sharp and vicious. Monsignor O'Callahan sits in his wheelchair, drooling, making weird moan-gurgles.

"Hi, Roger!" Mary Frances steps in front of them and comes in the house, grinning. She's wearing her baby-nun costume and is far perkier than usual.

I'm speechless. I step out of the way as Sister Mary Annunciata pushes Monsignor O'Callahan's wheelchair into the house.

"Hello, Roger," she says, her voice slurring out each word with heavy sarcasm. Seeing her puts me back into first grade; I have the same sick, frightened feeling of being prey to a huge, cardboard-shrouded monster.

Most of the nuns I've seen lately have gotten rid of the black-widow look; some even dress like normal human beings. But not Sister Annunciata. She's wearing the same outfit she's always worn, and she looks even more medieval now that she's older and wrinklier. When I was in OLPS grammar school I thought for sure Sister Mary Annunciata was ninety years old. We even used to argue about it at recess. Now that I'm fifteen and I have some perspective on the world, I realize that she probably isn't all that old—maybe sixty-five or so. But, encased in her nun cocoon, with only her liver-spotted hands and saggy, jowly face exposed, she's agelessly aged. Like Satan.

Father Quinn comes out of the hall, folding the sports page he was reading in the toilet. He smiles at Mary Frances, but when he sees who's with her his face does a complete, horrified collapse.

"Oh!" he gasps, as if somebody punched him.

"Hello...Steven is it?" Sister Mary Annunciata says with undisguised contempt. "Are you enjoying the secular life?"

Father Quinn recovers enough to ignore her and look at Monsignor O'Callahan. "How are you, Monsignor?"

Monsignor O'Callahan groans and mumbles something unintelligible. The dead muscles on the one side of his face pull his eyelid down so that the fleshy red part that's usually hidden is exposed and raw. I can't look at him for more than a few seconds without feeling nauseated.

"Monsignor says he hopes almighty God forgives you," Sister Mary Annunciata grins.

"Where's Mom?" Mary Frances asks. She's standing in the living room, oblivious to the fact that she's brought home the last people Father Quinn and I would ever want to see.

"I'm right here, honey," Mom says, coming out of the kitchen wiping her hands. She stops in her tracks when she sees the hell-demons.

"Oh, Sister! And Monsignor! This is...a surprise."

No shit. I consider faking a seizure; I'd rather go to the hospital emergency room than spend time with these people.

"Told you you'd be surprised," says Mary Frances. Her pale, pasty skin, non-existent eyebrows and pinched, disapproving mouth are revolting. The convent has made her uglier.

"I...well, let's all sit down and visit," Mom says, then realizes that Monsignor O'Callahan is already sitting down. "I'm sorry, Monsignor, I meant, you know...."

Monsignor gurgles and throws his head back.

"Monsignor would like a glass of scotch," Sister Mary Annunciata announces. "No ice."

"I'll get it," Father Quinn says. "Anything for you, Sister?"

"Of course not."

Father Quinn nods and hurries into the rec room. I bet he'll take his time. Mary Frances sits on the couch next to Sister Mary Annunciata. Too close. Almost touching her. How can she sit next to that hideous thing? Mom and I sit across from them. I want to die.

"Well," Mom says. When she's nervous she says "Well" too much. "It's certainly nice to see you again, Sister. And you, Monsignor. You're looking better."

They let Mom's comment pass without response. Monsignor O'Callahan doesn't look better; he looks like he should've been buried years ago.

"Sister Mary Annunciata came back to the mother house a few months ago. And Monsignor's been living there, too," Mary Frances says, gazing lovingly at both of them.

"Really? Have you retired, Sister?" Mom asks.

"I'm a bride of Christ, a warrior for Him. Warriors don't retire."

"Oh."

"But Sister and Monsignor will be leaving the mother house soon. And I'll be going with them," Mary Frances says. She's got that "I've got a secret" grin that's always bugged me.

"You're being assigned somewhere else?" Mom asks, confused.

"No. I'm quitting."

"What?!"

Father Quinn wanders back in, looking like he wishes he were anywhere but here, and hands Monsignor O'Callahan his scotch. Monsignor holds it in his shaky good hand and tries to sip, but most of it dribbles out of the dead side of his lips. Sister Mary Annunciata takes the glass and roughly pours the scotch into his mouth. Monsignor makes a cooing, happy sound.

"Sister Mary Frances has decided to join the forces of light," Sister Mary Annunciata says, wiping Monsignor's chin.

Father Quinn sits on the couch with Mom and me. It's three against three, with the coffee table as the dividing line.

"I'm not clear on what you mean, Sister," says Father Quinn. "You're all moving to another convent? A different order?"

"We're starting our own!" Mary Frances says.

Over the years, we've gotten used to Mary Frances springing weird news on us, but this is the weirdest yet.

"I don't understand," Mom says.

"We don't care for the way the church has been perverted by liberal, humanistic dogma," says Sister Mary Annunciata. "Since Vatican II the decline has been precipitous. The Monsignor and I have decided that the Roman Catholic Church no longer stands for Christ's message. Therefore, we've decided there must be a movement to form a fundamental, conservative Catholic Church to fight back the heresies."

Father Quinn smiles. "A schism. Interesting. Will you be nailing your demands on a church door someplace?"

"Make fun at your peril, Mr. Quinn. Jesus doesn't forget, and neither do I."

An icy cold descends on the living room. The Catholic Church may be a bunch of garbage, but the thought of anybody quitting it to follow a psycho-nun, a drooling Monsignor, and my nutbar big sister is beyond belief. Nobody could be that stupid.

"And will you be pope?" Father Quinn asks Monsignor.

"*Glllr prorllled.*"

"If it's God's will, certainly," Sister Mary Annunciata translates.

Father Quinn's feeling frisky, I can tell. "And you, Sister. What will your role be in this reformed church?"

"That remains to be seen." She looks at me, her eyes beady and evil. "There are many souls to be saved."

Silence. Mary Frances grins stupidly. She loves doing this kind of outrageous stuff.

"Well, pot roast anyone?" We all look at Mom. She's a trooper. Smiling, the perfect hostess no matter that three maniacs are sitting in her living room talking about starting their own religion.

"Sounds great, hon," Father Quinn says, as he puts his arm around her and grins. He's doing his *Father Knows Best* imitation. All he needs is a cardigan sweater and a pipe.

Wonderful. Another forced dinner. I'm surprised I haven't starved to death over the years from all the rotten, tension-filled dinners I've had to suffer through—most of them Mary Frances's doing. We eat our stringy pot roast in silence; the only breaks are Monsignor O'Callahan's disgusting snorts and gurgles and Mom's, "Would anybody like some more?" questions.

I wolf down my dinner, hoping that if I eat fast it will speed everybody else up and things will end sooner. But since every bite of Monsignor O'Callahan's food has to be cut, chopped and pulverized before it's put in his mouth, dinner takes forever. He's like a huge, creepy baby.

I volunteer to clear the table, and as I'm taking away the dishes, Father Quinn asks Sister Mary Annunciata where they'll be living.

"The Monsignor has a house out in the Mojave Desert. It will be a perfect place to build our new faith."

"Isolation, eh? Maybe you all can spend forty days fasting and see what develops." Father Quinn is smirky; I wish he'd stop, because he's pissing Sister Mary Annunciata off, and that's not a good idea. I know from bitter experience.

"The Lord will smite the disbeliever," she says. *Smite.* That's the word Jesse said the Virgin Mary used when she nailed Monsignor O'Callahan. "Even the foulest sinner can be saved, if only he believes, Mr. Quinn."

Father Quinn leans across the table toward Sister Mary Annunciata. "You know, Sister, zealots have always annoyed me. Even when I was a priest, when some parishioner went overboard with the piety or condemnation of somebody they didn't agree with, I always tried to point out to them that just because they disagreed with someone, they didn't have the right to condemn. Toleration, that's what a true Christian needs."

"Nonsense. Christ's teachings are firm, they're clear. And those who don't follow them will pay with eternal damnation." Monsignor O'Callahan moans his agreement with Sister Mary Annunciata.

"It's good you're not a priest anymore, with attitudes like that," Mary Frances says.

"Please," Mom says, "let's drop this. Dessert anyone?"

"The whole of history is filled with people like you," Father Quinn continues, ignoring Mom. "'I'm right, you're wrong', that's caused more misery and suffering than anything else. Why can't you admit that people are different, try to help those who need help, forgive those who sin, and get on with living without judging everybody and calling them names?"

"You broke a solemn vow," says Sister Mary Annunciata. "You defied the will of Jesus Christ to marry...a...a *woman.* It's the evil ones like you who've defiled the Roman Catholic Church and made it a false religion."

Father Quinn leans back, shaking his head. "I wonder how many poor little children you ruined, Sister." He looks over to me suddenly. "What kind of nonsense did she teach you in first grade, Roger?"

I stand, frozen, in the kitchen doorway, holding dirty plates. They're all looking at me, waiting for an answer. I could kill Father Quinn. All I wanted was for this to end, for them to leave. Now he's dragged me into their stupid arguments. I say nothing.

"Well, speak up, Rog. Did she show you how to love Jesus?"

I look at Sister Mary Annunciata and Monsignor O'Callahan. Sister Mary Annunciata watches me, her beady eyes drilling me, her fake smile a sneer. Monsignor O'Callahan drools, his droopy hound face impossible to read. Mary Frances smiles too, and I notice that her smile is becoming like Sister Mary Annunciata's—mean and phony.

"Sister Mary Annunciata," I find myself saying, not aware that I've decided to speak, "is evil. She's the devil. She made me hate everything about religion, and I think she made me hate most people, too. If there is a hell, I hope she spends forever burning there." And then I turn and go into the kitchen.

I load the dishes into the dishwasher, amazed at what I've just said. But I have to admit, I feel great. Ever since Sister Mary Annunciata picked on me in first grade I've wanted to tell her off, but until tonight I never had the nerve. It feels *sooo* nice.

Nobody comes into the kitchen to yell at me as I expect, but I can hear heated discussion out in the living room. Pretty soon, the front door *slams*! and then the only sounds are Mom crying and Father Quinn trying to calm her down.

I decide it's probably time to go out and see how bad a mess I've made of things.

"It's okay, Sylvia, it's nothing we did, they're just nuts," Father Quinn is saying as I come back out. He and Mom sit on the couch; he's got his arm around her, and her body heaves with sobs.

"They're...*horrible*! They're making Mary Frances into some kind of holy monster!"

"Uh, sorry if I made things bad," I say, shuffling into the living room with my best "I've been bad" slouch.

"Don't worry about it, Rog. I pulled you into it. Those two are just so...sick. I've always despised them."

Mom looks up at me with red, teary eyes. "What did that nun do to you?"

"You remember, Mom. I told you and Dad, but you didn't believe me. She wanted to kill me." I tell her what happened in first grade, and the later troubles Jesse and I had with Sister Mary Annunciata. Mom listens, cries some more, and Father Quinn shakes his head and makes solicitous clucking noises at all the right times. It's nice, but I wish Mom would've listened to me back when all this stuff happened.

After a while, Mom calms down, Father Quinn calms down, but I'm still buzzing with excitement. I feel wonderful. Telling Sister Mary Annunciata off was the bravest thing I've ever done, and I'm proud of myself.

"Okay, man, here's the plan," Jesse says. We're at the mall, hanging around, wasting a lazy summer day.

"Plan for what?" I ask, feeling drowsy. We're sitting by the big fountain in the middle of the mall; I'm watching girls while Jesse bumbles around in his blind world, making plans for God-knows-what. My attraction to women gets stronger by the day; it seems like most of the time I'm thinking about sex or beating off or thinking about beating off. It's like I'm on fire all the time, and sitting at the mall watching girls is both pleasurable and painful. I'm not sure why I do it—maybe I'm an addict. The only problem is that girls aren't interested in me. If it wasn't for these stupid scars and my gimpy limp I'll bet I could get somebody. Fucking Joe Fanucci. I'm glad he's dead.

Jeez, what am I thinking? That's a go-straight-to-hell thought. I may not be real into the Catholic Church anymore, and I might not buy into Jesus and Mary and all the stuff about God, but I still believe in hell and the devil. It's much easier to believe in the bad things than the good things.

"The plan," Jesse continues, "is to make money."

"Yeah," I say, half listening. I find lately that I can make an occasional noise without really listening and he'll just babble away and I can dream about breasts. It's a talent I've developed that I'm rather proud of.

"My Uncle Luis, he's a contractor."

"Yeah."

"And he'll let us work for him. He's doin' the framing on a bunch of houses over off of Foothill, up by the miracle houses." Jesse calls the houses they built where we almost got burned up in the orange tree pile the miracle houses.

I'm watching a great-looking girl—I think she's going to be a senior this year—in a tight tie-dyed T-shirt and huge, flapping bellbottoms walk by. I'm trying to picture her naked, but Jesse's talking interferes with my fantasies.

"Work? What're you talking about?" I ask, reluctantly turning away from the girl to look at him. He's wearing his wraparound sunglasses. I've forgotten what his eyes look like.

"We gotta start making some money for next summer."

"What for?"

"So we can go to Lourdes and get cured."

"Shit, Jesse. Forget about it, we're both fucked up and we just have to live with it. That's life, man."

"Uncle Luis said we could start tomorrow. We gotta show up at six-thirty in the morning, and he said he'd pay us two bucks an hour! Two fuckin' bucks, man! You realize how much that is, *ese*?"

As usual, Jesse hasn't heard me. "We're not going to Lourdes. It's bullshit. And I'm not getting up at six-thirty in the morning during the summer to work for your uncle. No way."

"If we work full time until the end of the summer, I figure we can make almost a thousand bucks apiece by the time school starts! That's more than enough to get us to Lourdes next summer!"

"No. Besides, what kind of work could you and me do on a construction site that would be worth two bucks an hour?"

"Cleaning up shit. I can see enough to tell if there's shit on the ground like pieces of wood and stuff. Uncle Luis said he'd rather hire us than some dumb Mexicans." I don't understand how Jesse can say racist stuff like, "Dumb Mexicans." If I ever said anything like that he'd kill me.

"Go ahead, do what you want. But I'm not wasting my summer picking up junk around a bunch of new tract houses. Especially not to go to Lourdes."

Jesse's brown moon face breaks into a huge grin. "We're gonna go get cured, Roger...fuckin' A, good as new."

I start to argue, but then decide not to. There's no reason, because I already know the outcome.

Like it or not, tomorrow morning at six-thirty a.m., I'll be picking up shit at a construction site.

It's six-forty-five and I already hate this.

Uncle Luis is a pretty cool guy, but he's really busy and I get the feeling he's letting us work here because he feels sorry for Jesse.

"Take a wheelbarrow," he hurriedly told us when we started, "and go from house to house picking up the shit that don't need to be there. Take it over to the dumpster. Don't fuck around. And if you see any asshole inspectors or shit take off...you ain't legal to work here. Okay?"

Jesse and I nodded seriously and set off to work. Within a few minutes it was obvious that Jesse couldn't see well enough to be of much use, so now he's following me around and standing by while I heave junk into the wheelbarrow.

"I'll push it, man," he says as I quickly fill the wheelbarrow with debris. "Fuck, I can't see shit."

"Why's that a surprise? You're blind."

"How long we been doin' this?" Jesse asks.

I look at my diver's watch. I don't know why Mom gave me a diver's watch last Christmas—I don't even like to swim. "It's ten to seven."

"Shit!"

"What?"

"We almost made a dollar apiece!" Jesse says, proud and excited.

"Great." I'm already sweating. It's supposed to be over a hundred degrees today.

Jesse chatters for awhile about Lourdes and cures and how great it is we're earning money to get there, but pretty soon the heat gets to him and he quiets down. We soon have a system going: I fill the wheelbarrow, he pushes it, and then I guide him to the dumpster and we both throw the junk inside.

It's lunchtime now and my back is killing me. My hands are blistered and raw; splinters and metal shavings are embedded in my palms.

We're huddled with the other construction guys, eating lunch, in the only shady place in the whole tract—a half-roofed garage. The hot summer wind blows through the studs, but it isn't enough to cool us off.

I'm in a corner eating lunch with Jesse. Since we're just kids we're not included with the rest of the guys. They ignore us. The shirtless, huge-biceped construction workers are split into two groups: Mexicans and white guys. It seems strange to me that they can work together but when it comes time to eat they split up. But then, I guess it's kind of that way at school, too.

I eat the ham sandwich that Mom made for me. It's stale and hot, and I wonder if I'll get food poisoning from it. The construction guys toss their trash on the already filthy floor of the unfinished garage, and it pisses me off because Jesse and I will have to pick it up eventually, but I suppose they know that and that's why they throw their stuff on the ground. I'd be a pig too if I knew for sure that somebody else was going to pick up after me.

It seems weird that in a few months this neighborhood will be finished and new suburbia families will be moving in. The dad will be in this very garage, putting everything into an order that makes sense to him, while the mom will be inside, setting things up her way, and the kids will be out riding their bikes, exploring, getting used to their new home and town. These construction guys will move on to the next tract, and another hundred houses will sprout from an old orchard somewhere and the pattern will repeat. Strange. It seemed important when *I* moved in, when *I* was exploring, when *my* house was the new one. Now it just seems ordinary. And boring. More families move in, more kids, more pets, more suburbia. It grows and grows. What's the point?

We finish our lunches and go back to work. I didn't think it was possible, but the work is even worse now than it was this morning. There's something about stopping, eating lunch, and getting a little rest that makes going back to work impossible. I'm tired and hot and pissed off and I don't care what Uncle Luis is paying us.

"I'm gonna quit," I tell Jesse just before it's time to stop for the day. "I can't take this shit." I found an old pair of gloves after lunch, but it was too late to save my ravaged hands. The back of my neck is sunburned and raw, and I can tell that the edges along my scars are puffy and inflamed.

"Sixteen fuckin' bucks, man. We've already made sixteen bucks."

"Did you hear me? I'm quitting!"

"No you're not."

We're tossing junk into the dumpster; a rusty nail on a two-by-four scrap catches my forearm and leaves a nasty cut. Great, now I need to get a tetanus shot.

"How do you know I'm not? I just said I was."

"You want to be cured, man. You know you do."

"A cure won't do me any good if I die from this stupid job first!"

Jesse just smiles and tosses drywall chunks into the dumpster. I wipe the blood trickle off my arm, muttering to myself about how nasty this is, when I hear—

"Hey, is that Roger Donnelly?"

I turn and see Mr. Fairly, Rhonda's dad, striding toward us. He's wearing nice clothes and a hard hat; he's obviously not a construction guy.

"Hi, Mr. Fairly," I say. Jesse stops working and turns toward him. Jesse's hearing has gotten more sensitive; he can tell exactly where a sound is coming from and pretend to see. People who don't know he's almost blind are always fooled.

"Oh, Jesse isn't it?" Mr. Fairly asks. Jesse nods and smiles. "You boys doing a little work?"

Jesse and I hem and haw because we're not sure if we'll get in trouble by admitting that we're working for Uncle Luis under the table. Mr. Fairly laughs.

"Don't worry, I won't tell. Started working on construction sites when I was about your age myself. That's how I ended up going into civil engineering. I'm working on this tract. Just checking things out, seeing how it's going."

Jesse and I nod. Neither of us is all that skilled in talking to adults. Mr. Fairly looks around at the house skeletons rising up around us. "Gonna be a nice tract," he says. "Glad to see this land put to good use."

"Instead of groves?" Jesse asks.

"People can't live in orchards," Mr. Fairly says.

"They can't eat houses," says Jesse.

"Maybe not, Jesse. Touch,, son."

I look at Jesse to see if he knows what Mr. Fairly is talking about, but Jesse just smiles blandly. Mr. Fairly looks at me, suddenly interested.

"Haven't seen you for a long time, Roger. You should come by the house some time, I know Rhonda'd like to see you this summer."

"She would?"

"Of course. She said just the other day, 'I miss Roger Donnelly'."

"She did?"

"Sure did. I think you've hurt her feelings, son." Mr. Fairly's voice gets a little harder. I'm not sure if I should be scared or not. Mr. Fairly's one of those B.S.ing kind of guys who slams you hard on the back, acts like he's your all-time best friend, and then doesn't bother to acknowledge that you're alive the next time he sees you. I remember Dad grumbling after church one morning that "That Fairly guy's slicker 'n' snot. He oughta be sellin' insurance." Of course, Dad always complained about everybody, so who knows what the truth is.

"I didn't mean to," I finally stammer. "Hurt her feelings, I mean."

"Yeah. Well, women...girls, they get their noses out of joint real easy." Mr. Fairly sighs and stares off into the distance. "I'll never figure 'em out."

"What should I do?" I ask, baffled but curious.

"Drop by. Unannounced would be best. They like surprises. Talk to her. I just want my girl to be happy, and I think you might be the guy." He looks at his watch. "Gotta run, son. Nice talking to you."

Mr. Fairly turns and hurries off to do whatever it is a civil engineer does.

"Wow," I say, feeling a nice warm glow inside. Rhonda wants me to be nice to her, huh?

"He's fuckin' with you, man," Jesse says, tossing junk into the dumpster. "He wants something."

"How do you know?!"

"I know. Blind guys hear better. He was lying."

"Bullshit. He wouldn't lie about Rhonda. She's his daughter!"

Jesse stands up straight and stretches. He's taken his shirt off, and sweat pours down his hairless chest. He's getting strong again; the muscles are well defined and getting bigger. It makes me realize that my pasty, sunken chest needs to be forever concealed by clothes. No matter how hot I get, I'm never taking my shirt off in public.

"You gotta start listening when people talk, Roger. Don't hear what you want to hear, hear what they're saying."

"Yeah, right. Next time you talk to the Virgin, listen to what she's really saying, she's trying to tell you you're a psycho asshole!" I storm off, pleased that I've flattened Jesse with my savage wit, when I realize that he's blind and stranded unless I'm there to help him. Shit. I can't even tell him off and make a good exit. I go back. He's leaning against the dumpster, wiping sweat off his forehead.

"Quittin' time?" he asks.

"Yeah."

He reaches out, gently takes hold of my elbow, and together we head for home, sweaty, tired, and sixteen dollars richer after our first day of work. I don't say anything to him, but I'm not coming back tomorrow.

But I wimp out and keep coming back. In the two weeks we've been working now, I can feel that I'm actually getting stronger. I still hate the work, and it's been the hottest summer in years, so I've been miserable the whole time, but getting paid is kind of nice and I'm getting used to it.

I really *was* going to quit after the first day, but that night when I got home Mom and Father Quinn were so goofy and proud that I actually had a money-making job that I just couldn't bail. They would've been disappointed, and it pissed me off the next morning when I trudged off to work that I was so concerned about somebody else's opinion of me. Especially Father Quinn. Why did I care what he thought? He's not Dad, he's just an ex-priest who happened to marry Mom. For some reason, though, what he thinks is important to me, no matter how much I try to tell myself that it isn't. I hate that. I want to be able to go through life not worrying about what people think. I'm beginning to realize that, for me at least, that won't be possible.

So I kept on working, and after the first week, as my chewed-up hands began to harden and my sore muscles got stronger, I actually didn't mind the job quite so much.

What I did mind was listening to Jesse talk about going to Lourdes to get cured.

Every day, it's the same thing: "We're sixteen bucks closer to gettin' cured, man." The "sixteen buck" quote was the first thing out of his mouth when I saw him in the morning, and it was the last thing he said in the afternoon when we quit. At first I argued and told him the usual "No way am I going there with you, man," but pretty soon I gave up. There was no talking to Jesse about anything once he had set his mind to it.

As the money has started to accumulate, I'm beginning to think about what I'll use it for. It won't be long before I can drive, so it might go toward a car. A car. Freedom. Something for...dates.

Girls.

Rhonda.

I'm sitting in front of the phone, wondering if I should call her. In the two weeks since I saw her dad at the construction site, I haven't been able to get her off my mind. Should I drop by, like he said? Or should I call first, just to test the waters? Or should I be a pussy wee-wee and do nothing—which is usually what I do best. So far, pussy wee-wee has won out.

I don't know what I'm afraid of. It's not like she's some goddess I've never spoken to, like the cheerleaders who romp naked in my sexual fever dreams. They're the pinnacles of fuckability, the girls who are so far beyond losers like me that to even talk to them would require courage and self-confidence that I can't imagine. No, Rhonda's somebody who, while still a beat-off dream, is at least a little approachable, somebody I know and who, a long, long time ago kissed me.

Just remembering that makes my guts flutter. She kissed me. Sure, maybe it was a weird sympathy thing since Dad had died, and maybe she didn't mean anything by it, but it was still a kiss. And so far, it's the only one I've ever had from a female, excluding the gross ones from Mom and fat aunts and the strange one from Aunt Yolanda.

That's it. I'll call her. It's a balmy summer evening, and I've showered off the sweat and work grime. I feel good. I'm starting to tan (at least my face and arms are; I never take off my shirt), my muscles are weary but stronger, and I'm making money. What a stud. I pick up the phone, but the dial tone sounds threatening and I hang up.

Pussy wee-wee.

Be a man. Mr. Fairly said to drop by. Unannounced. Be a man. Do it.

"I'll be back later!" I call out as I leave. Mom says something, but I'm already out on the sidewalk and I can't tell what she said. I don't care. I'm going to Rhonda's house. Unannounced.

I walk through the neighborhoods between our houses. Riding a bike over to her house would be faggy, so walking is the only way. Getting a ride with Mom or Father Quinn...well, that'd be even faggier.

My legs carry me swiftly; I don't know if I'm imagining it, but since I've started working my limp seems less pronounced. Maybe I don't need any cure other than some butt-busting hard work. If only work would erase the scars and fix my torn-up ears.

I'm confident. I feel happy and alive. The sun has set into the summer smog, and the glow reassures me. This is where I've grown up, it's the place I belong, and even though some nasty things have happened to me, all in all, life's not too bad.

Especially since in a few minutes I'll be at Rhonda Fairly's house. Unannounced.

I turn the corner to her street. I'm almost to her house, and I'm strangely calm. It feels right to be here.

I come to her house and stand on the sidewalk; I gaze at her front door. Here goes.

I walk up, ring the doorbell, and wait. I'm still confident, but now nervousness wells up inside, because I realize I don't know what I'm going to say. I usually rehearse conversations ahead of time so I'll have a vague idea of what I need to say, but for some reason, this time it never occurred to me.

Shit. Now I'm scared. She'll come to the door, I'll stand here like a tongue-tied dope and stammer idiotic word fragments and she'll think I'm a complete fool.

The door opens. It's her dad. He's wearing a T-shirt and baggy Bermuda shorts; it looks like he was napping. His hair has that couch-matted look. I expect him to grin, welcome me with open arms, give me a hale-and-hearty "good to see you, come on in", but all he says is a weak little, "Oh."

"Hi, Mr. Fairly."

He blinks, as if he's trying to remember exactly who I am. Then I can see it dawn on him and he smiles. "Roger Donnelly! Sorry son, caught me napping, takes me awhile to get back to the planet. Come on in!"

This is the welcome I expected. I calm down. This is going to work. Tonight's going to be special.

"'Spose you're here to see Rhonda," he smiles with a grin that looks to me like it might contain a little bit of a dirty smirk. It seems strange coming from a father.

"Yessir. Is she here?"

"You bet, son. Rhonda! Somebody here to see you!"

"Is it Frank?" she calls out from her bedroom, and I immediately feel my heart plummet through the floor. Fucking Bushman. The way she said it sounded like she'd be excited if it was the asshole.

"Nope. Come see. It'll be a surprise," says Mr. Fairly, grinning.

My hope and good feeling vanished when Rhonda said the word "Frank". Now I'll need to fake it, try to be friendly and cool, and get the hell out of here as fast as I can. What was I thinking even coming here? Shit.

Rhonda comes into the living room, an expectant look on her irresistibly cute face. Damn, the older she gets the cuter she gets. I want to grab her and kiss her and never let go. When she sees me her expectant look vanishes for an instant, and I have the awful feeling that she's disappointed it's me.

But then a big grin appears and I feel relieved. "Roger!" she says, sounding genuinely friendly.

"Hi, Rhonda."

"Well, I'll leave you two kids alone. Nice to see you Rog." Mr. Fairly gives me a wink and a manly smack on the shoulder and goes into the family room. I hear him talking to Rhonda's mom, telling her I'm here, I assume.

"Wanna sit down?" Rhonda asks, gesturing to the couch.

"Sure."

We sit down a cushion-width apart. I'm not too nervous, but I'm not exactly at ease, either.

"You're tan," she says. "I've never seen you tan before. It looks good."

I feel myself blushing, but it's nice anyway. I tell her about the job.

"That's great," she says after I've finished. "Are you saving for a car or something?"

"Yeah. Sort of. But Jesse thinks we're going to use the money we make to go to Lourdes and get cured. He's crazy, as usual."

"I can see why he'd want to get cured. But why you? There's nothing wrong with you."

I'm flooded with the warmest, nicest sensation I've ever had. I look into her bright, clear eyes, her smile grabs me and I know I'll never be able to love anybody like I love Rhonda Fairly at this moment.

"Well...you know. The accident and stuff. I could use a cure."

She waves a dismissive hand. "What, a couple of scars, big deal. I mean, you get better looking all the time, I don't even notice the scars anymore. You shouldn't worry about them."

I shrug, trying to contain the excitement I feel at hearing her say I'm getting better looking. Jeez, I should've come over here a long time ago.

We talk about other things, I tell her about Mary Frances and the weirdness with Sister Mary Annunciata and Monsignor O'Callahan, she tells me about one of her brothers who got arrested for selling pot, and we talk and laugh and it feels like good old times.

Until she mentions Bushman.

"Frank's gonna try out for varsity this year," she says after we've been talking about Jesse and the football team. "He thinks he can skip JV and maybe even start. He's pretty good, you know? He scored like twelve touchdowns on the freshman team."

"Yeah, I heard." *Who cares about freshman football?* I want to say, *I was too busy on varsity*. A manager, maybe, but still, I was part of varsity.

"How come you don't like him?" she asks suddenly. "He's really nice."

"Not to me. Anyway, we've been through all this before, let's forget about it, okay?" I'm feeling pissed now. I wish Bushman would vaporize off the face of the planet.

We talk some more, but the mention of Bushman has poisoned what was a good time, and pretty soon Rhonda's giving me signals that it's time to leave. We've run out of things to talk about and she's saying, "You probably have to get up early tomorrow for work, huh?" She might as well tell me to get my ass out of her house. It's the same thing.

I make "gotta go" noises and we stand at her front door.

"I'm glad you came by, Roger," she says.

"Me too."

"Please don't ignore me like you have been. It hurts."

"Really?"

"Yeah, really. We're friends, we have been forever. I always want to be your friend."

"Anything else?" I blurt out. God, how could I say something so stupid? I want to melt into the carpet. I'm the biggest jerk in the history of the world. I might as well have asked her to go ahead and kick me.

Rhonda doesn't say anything for a long moment. She looks at me, and I can't read her expression.

"It's hard, Roger," she finally says, looking down at her feet. "I'm confused a lot."

"Me too," I say, forcing a smile. "Yeah, well, gotta go."

"I'm glad you came by," she says.

"You already said that."

She moves quickly toward me, so quickly that I almost flinch. She kisses me on the lips. "'Bye," she says, then she quickly goes back down the hall to her room, leaving me standing by the front door, utterly perplexed.

Mr. Fairly peeks out from the family room. He's got a strange little smile on his face, and I wonder if he's been watching us the whole time. "Take care, Rog. Don't be a stranger," he says, grinning.

I nod, confused and embarrassed, and leave. As I close the door behind me and walk to the sidewalk, I get the feeling that things aren't right here. But I don't dwell on it, because remembering the kiss Rhonda just gave me is much more pleasant than wondering about weird feelings. As it's always been with Rhonda, my encounter with her has left me more baffled than ever.

I'll never figure her out.

"What the fuck's wrong with you, man?" Jesse asks. We're dumping our ten-millionth load of drywall scraps into the dumpster. I haven't been in the mood to talk today, because after seeing Rhonda last night I didn't sleep well and now I'm tired and cranky and pissed off because I didn't stay and get her to kiss me some more. I'm deciding that everything boils down to sex. She gives me a nice, friendly little kiss, filled with warmth and affection, and all I want is more with tongue and nudity and the whole enchilada. I feel guilty thinking that, but I can't help it.

Guys are pigs.

"Nothin's wrong with me. I'm working," I snap, hoping he'll leave me alone. But that's not Jesse's way.

"Man, you act like you need pussy or something." He says "something" so it sounds like "some-theeng" and it annoys me. He's been sounding more Mexican lately.

"What would you know?"

"I been thinking," he says. "I gotta get some pretty soon, you know?"

"What?"

"Pussy, man."

"What would the Virgin say?"

Jesse stops throwing stuff in the dumpster and looks thoughtful. "Could be a problem. But I can't help it, that's the way God made me, you know? I wouldn't have the urge if they didn't want me to do it."

I guess that logic makes some sense, but I don't think a priest would agree. If impure thoughts are enough to put your ass in hell forever according to the church, what would actually doing *it* mean?

"Their rules don't make no sense," Jesse says, reading my mind. "I think they got it wrong. I wish the Virgin would talk to me so I could ask Her. She'd tell me the truth."

"Whatever," I say. My mind's back on Rhonda.

"What'd she do to you, man?"

"Huh?"

"Rhonda. That's why you're being so weird, isn't it? You go see her like her old man wanted you to?"

It pisses me off when he guesses what's going on, but now that he has there's no reason to lie. "Yeah."

"What happened?"

"Nothin'. We talked. It was okay."

"Then how come you're not acting like it's okay? You try and feel her up or something? She get pissed?" He's laughing at me.

"No. She...she kissed me."

"Yeah?" Jesse looks very interested now. And he's not laughing at me anymore.

"Yeah. It was her idea, too."

"Then what happened?"

"I left."

"That's it? You didn't make out or nothing?"

"It wasn't like that. It was...pure."

"'Pure'! What the fuck does that mean?"

"Well, you know, like nice. Not horny or anything."

"You didn't get a hard-on?"

"I didn't say that," I answer, feeling miserable. *Yeah, I wanted more, but what could I do?* "I think her old man was watching the whole time. You're right, something weird's going on with him."

"That dude wants something." Jesse finishes emptying the wheelbarrow and leans against the dumpster. It doesn't seem to bother him to stop and take long breaks; I'm afraid we'll get in trouble. "She still going around with Bushman?" he asks.

"Yeah. She told me that the fucker's going to try for varsity in the fall, too."

"Guess I'll have to hurt his *pinche* ass in practice."

"What?"

"In practice. He'll be trying to be a halfback or a flanker; I'll pop him a few times, he'll be back on JV before he knows what hit him."

"You're not playing football."

"Why wouldn't I?"

"'Cause you're blind!"

"So fucking what? I can see enough."

I look at him, standing there in his sunglasses, waiting for me to lead him around the construction site to pick up trash. There's no way that he can play football; middle linebackers who see only dim, blurry shapes don't start on football teams. But I don't say anything, because I can see he's angry.

We go back to work, Jesse stewing about being blind and realizing he probably isn't going to play football, me thinking and wondering and fantasizing about Rhonda Fairly. We work the rest of the day in near silence; this is the first time he hasn't mentioned Lourdes and cures.

But I'll bet that's exactly what he's thinking about.

Chapter Fourteen

I run along the edge of the tenth fairway at the Santa Luisa Country Club, hoping I'll catch the pass that's supposed to be thrown to me.

A zitty guy from school, a junior named Pandola, covers me, and I'm having a hard time getting away from him. Although a summer of working with Jesse at the construction site has strengthened me more than I thought possible, my legs still don't work as well as normal ones, and there's no way I can outrun or fake Pandola to get clear for the pass.

I hear shouts behind me, and I turn to see Kleinsmith—another zitty guy from school—scramble away from the onrushing defense and chuck the football as hard as he can in my direction.

Pandola turns, too, and he's already moving into position to intercept. I can't let that happen. Whenever we get a bunch of guys together to play football on the golf course, I usually get stuck being center or blocking or occasionally, when somebody's feeling generous, they hand off to me and I get a couple of yards before I'm tackled and smashed into the divoted turf. We play tackle, and even though somebody's always getting hurt, we look forward to our Friday afternoon pick-up football games. We've played all summer, and Jesse and I show up every week, exhausted by working full-time at the houses, but invigorated by the smell of the freshly cut grass and ready to play hard.

Jesse's the scariest guy out here, the only one who's actually played on the real football team. The guys who don't end up on his team grumble and bitch, because they know that sometime during the afternoon he'll probably hurt them. There's an unwritten rule that I'm always on his team, and I'm thankful for that. Getting tackled by Jesse is something I'd rather not experience.

He's a killer on defense, and I'm starting to think that maybe he *will* be able to play at school again. He seems to have a sixth sense where the ball is. He rips through token blocks and runs down whatever poor slob has the ball and squashes him. His lateral moves aren't what they were before the accident, but it's just a matter of time and reconditioning before he gets back to the way he was. The only difference is that now he can hardly see. Maybe that won't matter so much. Two-a-days start next Monday, and Jesse has vowed to win his old starting spot at middle linebacker. We'll see.

But right now, the football is falling toward Pandola and me, and we're bumping each other to get in position to catch it. He's winning.

Shit. He leaps in front of me at the last second, a move I can't possibly duplicate, and gracefully pulls the ball from the air. As he comes down I lock onto his waist, at least I'll make a good tackle, and as we crash down he loses hold of the ball and it goes bounding away. FUMBLE! I scramble toward it like a crab, scoop it up, and limp/run off toward the end zone—an imaginary line between a sprinkler head and a sand trap. Pandola's footsteps thud behind me, but he can't catch me, and by the time he tackles me I'm across the goal line. He slams me to the ground and grass burns my cheeks, but I don't care because I made a touchdown and I'm a stud. My teammates come running, everybody's yelling and happy.

"All right, fucking Donnelly!" Kleinsmith yells. I get pats on the back and hoots of congratulations.

"Nice going, Rog," Jesse says as he trots over. Somebody did a play-by-play for him; it's nice for me to be a hero for a change instead of him. Of course it is just a Friday afternoon football game on the tenth fairway, but at least it's something.

The game continues, and I'm quickly relegated back to my blocking duties; these guys have a short memory for heroes. As the light begins to fade into the late summer sky, I hear the sound of rumbling mufflers. A bunch of them. I know the sound, and I'm immediately worried.

Lowriders.

The game sputters to a stop as we all look out onto the street that runs alongside the tenth hole. Six Chevy Impala lowriders rumble to a stop. I hope they're friendlies—like Jessie's brother Mando and his buddies, but as their engines go silent and they begin to get out I know trouble's coming.

It's Danny Robledo and his pals.

Doors slam and a small army of pressed Pendletons heads across the fairway toward us. They're completely out of place, with their creased pants, slick hair, sunglasses and buttoned-at-the-neck Pendletons; the golf course is a place where checkered, lime green polyester pants pulled up to the nipples on fat old men is the official uniform.

Jesse comes up beside me. "Roger?" he asks quietly. I wonder how he knows it's me. Do I have a distinctive smell?

"Yeah?"

"Who is it?" he asks. He knows the sound of lowriders; what he can't tell is if it's friend or foe.

"Robledo."

"Fuck," Jesse mutters. He almost sounds scared; I've never heard that in his voice before.

"What's he want, man?" I ask.

"Me."

"Why?"

"I might've said some shit about him awhile back."

Now I'm getting scared. "Shit, what'd you do?"

"I was with my brother, we were cruising around, you know? And we saw—I mean my brother saw—Robledo cruising. Then fucking Robledo yelled some shit at us, and I yelled back. He won't fuck with my brother. But he'll fuck with me. Now."

"What'd you say to him?"

"*Cabron*, usual shit. The dude pisses me off. Kinda like the way Bushman pisses you off, you know? Just something about him. Fuck, I wish I could see worth shit."

Robledo strolls up to us, leading his crowd. Wisma is with them—the only white guy Robledo allows around. Wisma should change his name to Rodriguez or something.

"Hey, *pendejo*!" Robledo calls out. "What you doin' with these *pinche* white boys on a fucking *pinche* golf course, man? You a fucking *joto*?"

Jesse says something in Spanish and Robledo just laughs and shakes his head. "No way, man. You gotta pay for your shit, man."

Everybody backs away from Jesse and me. Kleinsmith takes his football and slowly backpedals down the fairway.

"Where you goin'?" Robledo yells.

Kleinsmith freezes. "Nowhere." He sounds like a little kid who's just gotten caught doing something nasty and the only thing he can do is deny it.

"Don't you wanna see your friend Montoya get his fuckin' *pinche* ass kicked, man?"

Robledo's friends laugh, and Robledo slowly takes off his sunglasses. His eyes never leave Jesse.

"You don't see so good no more, huh? Why don't you make a fucking miracle, man? Thought you could do that holy shit."

"I see okay," Jesse says. "I don't need no miracles, *ese*."

"You won't be no fuckin' football star no more. You'll just be with your *joto* white boy friends all the time. You're as fucked up as him, man." Robledo looks at me. *Shit*, I think, *please don't drag me into this.*

"Leave him out of it," says Jesse.

Robledo looks down at the ground, shaking his head with mock sadness. "Fuck. Fucking joto. Man, you need to stay away from white boys. You could be a vato loco if you wanted to, man, instead of a pussy coconut."

Oh-oh. Calling Jesse a coconut is the worst thing he could've said. Brown on the outside, white on the inside. You don't ever say that to any Mexican, especially one like Jesse. He may be blind, but he's tough, and when he gets pissed off there's going to be trouble.

I glance over at Jesse, and just as I move my head Jesse lunges at Robledo. Jesse's superior strength and football tackling skills nail Robledo before he knows what hit him, and they're on the grass, rolling around, beating on each other.

Jesse's attack sets off Robledo's friends, and they come charging at the rest of us.

We're dead.

Wisma makes a beeline for me, knocks me down, and pins me to the ground. I cover my face, waiting for the inevitable punches. None come. I meekly open my eyes, and Wisma is leaning toward my face.

"Pretend to hit me, *pendejo*, then run like fuck and get outa here."

"What?!"

"Do it, man!"

I look around, the *vatos* are kicking everybody else's asses. Jesse and Robledo punch each other, but it looks to me like Jesse's winning. I look back up at Wisma, decide to take him up on the offer, and pretend to punch him in the face—I miss by at least six inches—and he flies backward like Muhammad Ali hit him.

I scramble to my feet and run away, feeling guilty that Kleinsmith and Pandola are getting beat up, but hey, that's the way it goes.

I run as fast as I can, and the sound of the fight disappears behind me. Soon, I slow to a jog, then walk, as I wind through the spaghetti streets of suburbia back to my house.

I start to feel really bad that I left the guys behind. Will they think I'm a pussy? Doesn't matter, really, because most of them already do. I hope Jesse beat Robledo, but it's not like I could've done anything to help. Jesse can take care of himself.

I wonder about Wisma. He's saved my butt several times now, for no reason that I can see other than he's a cool guy. What I don't understand is why he hangs around with Robledo and the other hard guys. They're going to drag him into some major shit one of these days, and they'll leave his white ass hanging in the wind. He must realize that, but still he stays with them.

It's dark by the time I finally get home. Mom and Father Quinn are flaked out on the couch, watching *Bowling For Dollars*. Father Quinn is slowly turning into a dull suburbia guy. He's gaining weight, and his interest in social causes is starting to take a back seat to making sure the lawn is mowed and home repairs and maintenance are kept up. I think he's doing what he really wants to do now, and he's letting go of his past as an activist priest. He's even been talking about building a second story on they house, even though we don't need the space.

"I dunno, we could use it as an office or something," he said as he tried to sell Mom on the idea. She just looked at him like he was crazy—the same look she used to give Dad when he had looney ideas—and shook her head, smiling. He took that as a "yes" and started measuring and drawing sketches. He's been spending a lot of time up in the attic lately, thumping around, looking for headers and beams and making his big plans.

He reminds me of Dad.

"Good game?" Father Quinn asks, not looking away from the TV.

"Scored a touchdown on a fumble."

"Hey, great!" Father Quinn perks up. He likes it when on the rare occasion I do something guy-like. Then he and I can connect on a man level—we can bond over sports or girls.

"Yeah, it was pretty cool." I tell them how Pandola and I fought for the ball, and how I ended up with it and he squashed me in the end zone but it was too late. Father Quinn is impressed; Mom's not.

"You kids," she says, shaking her head in classic Mom-style, "are gonna get hurt. Do you have to play tackle? It's so dangerous, that's why they wear all the equipment in real games."

"Oh, Mom."

Father Quinn and I exchange glances. He understands. It's part of being a guy. Yeah, somebody gets hurt, but we all have fun doing it. It's a good hurt.

"I'm sure they're careful, Sylvia," Father Quinn says, but Mom doesn't buy it.

"Anyway," I add, "the game ended early. There was a rumble."

"Oh?"

"Yeah. Danny Robledo showed up with his gang. He was after Jesse."

Mom sits up. "Oh dear. You weren't involved, were you?"

"Well...I sort of punched a guy and got away."

Mom gasps. I feel guilty not telling the truth about Wisma letting me go, but when I see Father Quinn looking proudly at me I don't feel so bad. He's definitely getting to be more like Dad.

"Didn't hurt him too bad, did you, Rog?" he asks.

"Nah. Just enough to escape."

"My God, I don't know if I can take this. You're fighting with...Mexicans?!"

"Sure. But Jesse was on our side."

"But he's blind!" Mom says, horrified.

"He can still fight. Besides, he's not totally blind, he can see shapes and stuff. Enough to protect himself."

"Do you know what happened between him and Danny Robledo?" Father Quinn asks.

"Robledo doesn't like him. I don't know why. Just one of those things."

"I knew Danny's mother from when I was a priest. They had a tough life, I was afraid he'd turn out bad. He's got a couple of brothers in prison."

The phone rings and I answer it.

"Where the fuck did you go, man?" Jesse asks.

"I. popped Wisma and got away."

"*You* beat Wisma? Yeah, right."

"Believe what you want," I say, annoyed. "You okay?"

"Fuckin' Robledo. I had the fucker, then some golf course guy drove up in a cart and kicked us off. It's not over between us, man."

Jesse grumbles and sputters a while longer and I listen sympathetically. He finally finishes and I'm not sure what else to say, so I ask him, "How are you gonna take care of it?"

"Robledo?"

"Yeah."

"Either kill him or convert him."

"I don't think he's a good candidate for the First United Church of Jesse Montoya."

"Yeah. Shit, I wish the Virgin was still talking to me, She'd know what to do."

I sigh. The Virgin. He hasn't said much about her lately, but she's never far from his mind. We've worked all summer and he hasn't trolled in the mall for converts; I think he's lost interest since Joe and Patty died and he's not having Virgin Mary hallucinations anymore. Now all he cares about is going to Lourdes and getting cured. It's annoying, too, but I can understand selfishness better than I can evangelism.

"Was that Jesse?" Mom asks after I've hung up.

"Yeah. He's okay. They didn't get to finish. A golf course guy broke it up."

Mom looks at me with a strange expression, and then she bursts into tears.

Father Quinn and I look at each other helplessly. Neither of us is very good at dealing with Mom when she gets into a...woman mood.

"What's wrong, honey?" Father Quinn asks.

"It's just, Roger, he's growing up, and things are so dangerous...." and that's all she can say. She dissolves into tears and collapses against Father Quinn's chest. I figure he's got things under control so I go to my room.

School starts in a couple of weeks, and I'll be a sophomore. I'm actually looking forward to it, because recently I've started to feel different. It's like my mind works better now; maybe some of the nerves have grown together and the connections are starting to make sense.

I'm glad I've worked during the summer. I've made lots of money, I've gotten stronger, and I feel like there's a reason to be alive. I didn't know that spending eight hours a day in butt-melting heat picking up shit could be so healing.

I haven't had the nerve to go back to Rhonda's, but I'm going to pursue her once school starts. She's mine, I know that now. We belong together, and if I have to knock Bushman out of the way to have her, that's what I'll do.

Starting on the first day of school, September 6, 1971, my life will be dedicated to the pursuit and capture of Rhonda Fairly.

A blistering Santa Ana blows dusty heat as we line up outside the gym to pick up our class schedules. It seems like the first day of school is always hot and windy. Jesse's over in the M-Q line, trying hard to shuffle around and not look blind. The sad thing is, the harder he tries to be inconspicuous, the more he stands out. They've put me in most of his classes because Coach Gutierrez knew I'd look out for him.

"You're gonna help out, aren't you, Donnelly?" Coach asked at the first of the two-a-day practices before school started. He'd been working with Jesse on and off during the summer, seeing if he'd be able to play. Coach Gutierrez decided that a blind Jesse Montoya was still a better middle linebacker than anybody else who could see, so he wanted to make sure that Jesse's readjustment to school would be as painless as possible—and that football wouldn't be affected.

"Yeah, sure Coach, I can help out," I said, groaning inwardly at the thought of being Jesse's seeing eye Roger.

"I know you two are tight. That's good, friends are good, and Jesse needs your help. I've talked to Jesse and his Mom and the suits down at the office, and they all said that if it was okay with you, then we'd try it out, see how Jesse does in his classes with you helping. Don't mind, do you?"

What could I say? Coach Gutierrez looked down at me, his huge barrel chest threateningly close. If I said anything other than, "No problem, Coach Gutierrez" he could crush me with his gut and not leave a trace.

So I feebly said, "No problem, Coach Gutierrez," and everything was okay.

Tied to Jesse Montoya again. This time officially. I wonder if it will be like this the rest of my life.

I get my schedule and go find Jesse. He's standing forlornly off to the side as swarms of high school kids move around him. "Roger?" he says as I walk up.

"How do you do that?"

"What?"

"Know it's me. Do I smell?"

"It's the way you walk. I can hear you limp, man."

"Huh." That's reassuring. Just when I'm starting to feel better about my-self he tells me he can hear my limp. What flaws can people who see notice?

I look at his schedule. "Okay, we got all our classes together like Coach Gutierrez said we would. We got first period geometry with Mr. Sandoval."

He nods. Some giggling girls walk by and one says, "Hi, Jesse!" He smiles back in her direction.

"Who was it?" he asks after they're gone.

"I dunno. Some juniors and seniors, I think."

"Any good?"

"The one who said 'hi' was okay."

"What was she wearing?" he asks.

"Um...I dunno. Bellbottoms and a shirt, I guess."

"Tight?"

"Yeah."

"Big tits?"

"Yeah."

Jesse sighs. This is going to be tough. Jesse loves girls, he always has, and now he won't ever be able to see one clearly again. He'll have to imagine how they look, and I'll have to be his interpreter. It makes me realize that my scars and limp aren't so bad after all.

We go to geometry and I scout who's in the class. No sign of Rhonda. Shit. Mr. Sandoval's got a seating chart set up already with Jesse and me up front by his desk.

"This work out okay for you, Jesse?" he asks, ignoring me. Even blind, Jesse's the star. I feel like a servant.

"Roger's the one who has to do everything," says Jesse.

Sandoval looks at me with annoyance. He's an older guy with a flattop haircut. He looks like he'd be a football coach, but he isn't. He's just a nerdy teacher with a square head, which makes sense, I guess, since he teaches geometry.

"Sure, fine," I say. Sandoval nods.

A few more latecomers straggle in, and a girl named Lydia Balderama, who was in my algebra class last year, sits behind us. I don't think I've ever talked to her, but I have the impression she's nice.

"Hi, Roger. You get to be his babysitter?" she asks, gesturing toward Jesse. I'm surprised she knows my name, and I'm even more surprised she's popping off about Jesse. Jesse glares sharply in her direction.

"Who is that?" he demands.

"Lydia Balderama," she says.

"Do I know you?" Jesse asks.

"Not yet. How come a big jock like you needs Roger to lead him around?"

"What's your problem?" Jesse asks her.

"Don't have one."

Jeez, what's this girl doing? I try to referee and change the subject. "Have a good summer?" I ask her.

"Mr. Donnelly, if it's not too much trouble, do you think you could turn around and pay attention?" Mr. Sandoval asks. I feel myself turn red.

"Sure," I mumble. Lydia smiles at me, sweet and innocent, like we're best buddies. I can't figure out why Lydia's being so nasty to Jesse; I guess I was wrong about her being nice. This is going to be a long year if she decides that fucking with him is going to be her main source of entertainment.

I'm three minutes into being Jesse's guide through the school day and already I'm having big doubts about agreeing to do it. I get to be in the middle between him and whatever pops up, like sarcastic Lydias or killer Robledos.

Great.

Lunch. The great mixing. When everybody from the basics to the college preps to the honors dweebs gets thrown together in the cafeteria to eat bad food and glare at each other from the safety of their own little groups.

Since I'm both Jesse's guide and a sort-of football hanger-on, I'm allowed to sit with the football jocks, even though I'm hopelessly out of place. It's one thing to be team manager and toss balls and hand out Gatorade, but it's quite another to hang out with them as a semi-equal. I guess I shouldn't worry, though, because with the exception of Jesse, they all ignore me.

We make our way through the noisy cafeteria, our trays loaded with oatmeal-enhanced tacos, toward the jock table. Jesse follows behind me, not having any problem negotiating the narrow aisleways between the tables. I suppose he's listening for my limp-steps and is able to see enough dim, large shapes that he can tell where he's going. His talent at getting around improves every day.

As we sit down with the rowdy, pigging-out jocks, I see that Bushman is here. Rumor has it he'll get cut by the end of the week and go back down to JV, but in the meantime he's hanging out with the varsity guys and acting like he's King Crap.

We've avoided each other at practice, and he hasn't tried to pull any of his sneak attack stuff. He's been concentrating on making varsity, so his energies haven't been directed toward me. It's too bad, really, because now I feel like I might be able to stand up to him. And since I'm about to take his girlfriend away from him I'm bolder; I can't wait to see the look on his ugly freckled face when he finds out he's been ditched.

Assuming I can get Rhonda to ditch him. *Positive thoughts, Rog, you can do it.*

We sit and the good-natured nonsense flies between the guys. Every other word is "fuck" or, if it's Mexicans talking, "*puto*", "*cabron*", all the old standbys. I almost feel part of the team. Until Bushman gets up, walks behind me, and accidentally-on-purpose tips over his half-empty carton of fruit punch on my back.

"Sorry, man," he says, with his evil fucker smile.

Jesse got a little splash on his back, and he quickly stands and faces

Bushman. "You got somethin' on me, man," he says.

"Sorry," Bushman replies, this time sounding sincere.

Jesse leans in close to Bushman's face, and I expect punches to start flying. I can hardly wait. Jesse will kill him.

"Do you love Jesus?" Jesse asks.

"What?"

"Do you love Jesus?" Jesse repeats, urgently.

Bushman—and everybody else—is speechless. When Jesse stood up, looking pissed, everybody assumed Bushman was going to get his ass kicked. It was only right and fair. Not religious shit.

"I asked you a question, *pendejo*," Jesse growls.

"Yeah, sure, whatever man."

"Say it."

"What?"

"Say you love Jesus. And his Virgin Mother Mary."

Bushman looks around for help. A stupid smile creases his idiot face. "You're kidding, right?" he asks, hopeful now that Jesse's just playing with him.

"You don't love Jesus and his Virgin Mother?"

"Well...."

"God is great, asshole. And He don't like people who fuck with His little children."

Bushman looks for help from somebody. None is forthcoming. Jesse leans even closer; their noses almost touch.

"Make a choice, Bushman. Say you love Jesus and His Virgin Mother."

"But—"

Too slow. Jesse's big, meaty fist smashes Bushman's nose and Bushman goes down on the concrete floor, limp and out cold. Jesse sits back down and calmly resumes eating his lunch.

"I think you killed him," I say, looking down at Bushman.

"He shoulda said he loved Jesus. That's all it would've taken."

I look up and see Mr. Stanley, one of the math teachers who's stuck being a lunch monitor, heading our way. "I think you're gonna be in trouble, Jesse."

"Yeah. Probably."

He hurries to finish his oatmeal taco before he gets hauled off down to the vice-principal's office.

Bushman starts groaning and rubbing his bloody nose. Somehow, the fruit punch soaking into the back of my shirt doesn't bother me so much anymore.

Jesse got suspended for a couple of days, but Coach Gutierrez let him continue practicing anyway. Strangely, Bushman didn't get cut back to JV like everybody thought; Coach put him on varsity as a third-string tailback. Some of the guys think Coach kept him to use him as raw meat for practice.

Everybody on the team hates Bushman for fucking with Jesse; I wish I could say it was because Bushman fucked with me, but that's not the case. Anyway, watching Bushman get pasted three hours a day at practice by Jesse and the defense is very satisfying. Bushman won't even make eye contact with me anymore, and he doesn't sit at the jock table during lunch. I hate to admit it, but I almost admire the dickhead. He's taking abuse day after day, he knows he's a target, but still, he keeps at it. Maybe he's too stupid to know better.

It's the second week of school, and I've only run into Rhonda a few times. I've been charming and friendly—at least I think I have—giving her my best big smile and making clever small talk. She's been nice, smiling back and looking irresistible in her hot pants. Damn, she's cuter and cuter by the day. I haven't seen her with Bushman much, so that's a good sign, and I'm trying to work up the courage to ask her out on an honest-to-God date. Not being able to drive yet will be a problem, but I'm thinking maybe we can meet at the mall for a movie or something. Next time I see her I'm going to ask. Yep. That's it, pop the question, bag my Rhonda.

She *will* be mine.

I'm in my room doing some biology homework. It's late, about eleven, and I'm tired, but we've got a quiz tomorrow and I need to study. I like biology; learning about living things and how they work is fascinating. I've only been in the class a couple of weeks, and already I'm looking at things differently. I'm taking life less for granted; that any of this stuff works is pretty amazing. It almost intrudes on my "There's no such thing as God" philosophy. It's hard to imagine that life and all its complicated functions is accidental, although Mr. LoCarbano, our biology teacher, is big on evolution and random chance. But as I study and learn, I see that even my own pathetic body is an incredible machine.

I may need to rethink things; I'm not going back to being Catholic boy or anything, and I sure won't follow Jesse's weirdness, but it seems logical to me that somebody—or something—came up with all this stuff. I'm sitting here at my desk, breathing and thinking and in love with Rhonda Fairly. That can't be random. There has to be something behind it all.

Hmmm. I shrug and go back to studying diagrams of paramecium and cells. Maybe someday I'll figure out the secrets. Right now, I've got to study for the quiz tomorrow.

My mind wanders. I thumb through the well-worn biology textbook. Chapter after chapter.

Near the end.

Reproduction.

I scan the chapter, reading the dry descriptions of what happens after sex. Zygotes, cellular splits, hormones. It sounds so technical and boring, an amazing result from such a rough and weird beginning. Strange. You get horny, pop a chubby, have sex, leave sperm behind, and then, if everything works right, this automatic stuff kicks in and *bam*!, a new person comes squalling into the world in nine months.

Wow.

I smile to myself. The way I'm thinking I sound like one of the stoned dopers at school, the loaded fools who think everything is deep, who can study the backs of their hands for long minutes at a time and then say, "Wow, man. Heavy." Maybe I should be worried. I don't even get high, and I'm thinking like a doper. Is their loaded stupidity given off in the air, like the flu?

I reluctantly turn back to the chapter I'm supposed to be studying, but now that I've begun to think about sex I can't stop. That happens a lot. Pretty soon I'm staring at the pages, seeing the printing but not the words, thinking about sex and Rhonda Fairly.

Rhonda. She smiled at me today, said "Hi!" and stole my heart. I relive the two kisses we've shared, although the one after Dad's funeral doesn't really count because it was a sympathy kiss, but hey, I'll count it. A guy like me doesn't get many kisses. I try to recapture the feeling, the way my heart seemed to stop and pound at the same time, the way her lips felt, her smell, her smile.

Now I've done it. I'll never be able to go back to studying. I've gotten myself all worked up over Rhonda, and if things follow true to form I'll have a hard time getting to sleep.

I close the book, go through the pre-bed body maintenance routine, and soon I'm snug between the sheets, but still no more drowsy or relaxed than when I was trying to study. My Rhonda infection is severe tonight, so I decide to go ahead and go with it, and let my mind race with Rhonda thoughts.

I'm in the middle of a pleasant fantasy concerning rescuing Rhonda from some Robledo-like bad guys, with me as the hero/stud being showered by her kisses after I've kicked the bad guys' asses, when I hear a faint *taptaptap* at my window. At first I ignore it, but it happens again, and I wonder if it's raining out, but that's not possible, it was hot and clear today.

I reluctantly let go of my fantasy and listen. *Taptaptap.* Whatever it is, it's not going away; I sit up in bed and listen. *Tap* again, this time louder. I'm both scared and curious, so I get up and go over to the window. When I was a little kid I was scared of noises at night; I always thought vicious burglars were out there, just waiting for the chance to come in and kill me and steal my Wolfman models and my aquarium. I'm not that big of a chicken anymore, but still my heart is thumping and I'm scared. If it's something creepy, I've already made plans to run screaming down the hall to Mom and Father Quinn's room.

The noise is more insistent now. I stand at the window, with my hands on the curtains. Should I pull them open, or should I go get Father Quinn? It's a human-caused sound, that much is for sure. I hesitate, but my curiosity is stronger than my fear, and I slowly pull open the curtains.

It's a person, and when I see their silhouette against the streetlight and my eyes adjust and I see who it is, I wish I *had* run screaming to Father Quinn, because now my throat is frozen in horror and I can't move.

At my window is the pockmarked face of Freddie Montgomery.

I haven't seen Freddie since he went to prison for killing Mary Frances's boyfriend Ken. The last I heard he wasn't supposed to get out for another fifteen years, so the fact that he's tapping on my window late at night makes me think that maybe he's not supposed to be here.

"Open your window, Roger!" he whispers. He glances nervously over his shoulder. He's acting like an escaped prisoner. I'm tempted to yank the curtains closed and yell for Father Quinn. What if Freddie's got a gun? I've heard what happens to guys in prison; maybe he's here for revenge.

I'm about to go get Father Quinn when I look into Freddie's eyes. The minute I do, I can tell. He's not going to do anything bad. He's the saddest-looking guy I've ever seen. He's scared and for some reason he's decided to come to my window for help. I can't get the poor guy in more trouble.

I open the window, and he quickly climbs in my room. He's wearing jeans and a prison T-shirt. His zits have finally gone away, but now his face is cratered and rough. He's grown his hair long; it's parted in the middle and hangs to his shoulders like the Jesus pictures on holy cards. He's been lifting weights, too. He's bulked up and knobby with solid muscle. If I didn't remember him as a friendly goofball, I'd be scared to death.

He quickly closes the curtains and paces around my room. He stops and peers into my aquarium.

"Guppies?" he asks.

"Yeah. They've been breeding since I was in kindergarten. I don't know how many generations I've gone through."

Freddie nods seriously, as if this is important stuff.

"How you been?" I ask.

He looks over at me and smiles crookedly.

"Yeah, stupid question," I say, feeling like a dope.

Freddie sits on my bed, then bounces slightly, like the feeling of a real bed is a strange sensation. He runs his hands across the blanket and looks around my room.

"Big room," he says.

"I guess."

"I mean, compared to what I'm used to," he adds. "Felt good to be outside tonight." Freddie looks down, studying the carpet. "How's your mom?"

"Fine."

"Sorry about your dad."

I shrug. "It's been a long time. My Mom got remarried. Father Quinn quit being a priest to marry her. Did you hear?"

He looks up at me, frowning. "How would I hear?"

"I thought...well, maybe Mary Frances writes you or something."

"Nope. Got one letter from her after your dad died, then that was it." He sighs the longest, saddest sigh I've ever heard; it's so overdone I'd laugh if I could be sure he wouldn't kill me. "How is she?" he asks at the tail end of his monumental sigh.

"Well...." I tell him the whole story of her weirdness, including the latest stuff about Sister Mary Annunciata and Monsignor O'Callahan.

When I've finished all he can say is, "A nun?"

"Yeah. But a psycho one. I mean, even more psycho than the usual kind. She's kind of scary, Freddie."

"I've got to see her," he says as he stands up. He starts pacing around in my room again, and I'm afraid Mom and Father Quinn will hear him.

"You're not supposed to be out, are you?" I ask.

"I've got to see her," he repeats. "Where is she?"

"Somewhere out in the desert. We haven't heard from her since they came over for dinner, and that's been a few months ago. She hates us, man. She's crazy. You don't want to see her."

"Can you find out where she is?" he asks. "I've got to see her again."

"You broke out of prison to see Mary Frances?" I'm appalled. I'll never understand the power she has over Freddie. She's such a loser.

"I'll come back tomorrow night about this time. Can you find out by then where she is?"

"I'll try. If it's really important to you."

He comes over, his Jesus hair swinging against his shoulders, and pats me on the shoulder. "You're okay, Roger."

"Where'll you go?"

"I'll find someplace. The wash, an orchard maybe."

"There aren't many groves left. It's all houses now."

He shrugs and smiles, then hops out the window and runs off into the night.

I go back to bed, but I have a hard time sleeping.

I'm in geometry class this morning, wondering how I'm going to find out where Mary Frances is. We're working on some boring triangle problems, and Jesse is jousting with Lydia Balderama. She gives him shit every day, and he slowly seems to be getting used to her—I think he might even enjoy it. I've finally realized the reason she messes with him is because she likes him. It's pretty obvious, and I don't know why it took me so long to figure it out. My people observing skills aren't too hot.

Geometry is the only class we have with her, and she makes the most of the fifty-five minutes. When Mr. Sandoval isn't talking and lets us loose to work on problems, Lydia slides her desk up and joins us. The more I'm around her, the more I like her. She's not really pretty or anything, but she's cute in a boring sort of way. She's one of those girls who isn't into the *vata* hard chick Pendletons and eye makeup, but she's not a dull, pasty coconut either. She swears in Spanish and loves to give Jesse shit about his religious beliefs. "You seen Mary lately?" is her favorite question.

Jesse huffs and grumbles and makes weak attempts to sell her on his visions, but the effort is only half-hearted; it's been so long since he's had one of his Jesus and Mary hallucinations I'm not sure he even believes in it anymore. Anyway, Lydia's too smart, and he knows he'll never convert her—but he likes her enough that he doesn't mind taking her abuse.

We're working on the problems, going back and forth between geometry and Lydia's sarcasm, when a kid comes in carrying a pink office summons notice. Mr. Sandoval takes it, reads it, and looks over at me.

"Mr. Donnelly. Office."

I wander down find two cops waiting for me in the vice-principal's office.

I know what they want.

They go through the "Don't be afraid" speech, and then they ask if I've seen Freddie Montgomery. I lie convincingly and they ask a few more questions, but I can tell they're not interested in talking to me. I'm just a name on their list, and they're ready to head off to talk to everybody else who ever knew Freddie.

As they're leaving I ask, "Hey, do you guys know where my sister is?"

The older one, a bald guy with a big gut, looks at me, puzzled. "Yeah. We found her through her old convent."

"Can I have her address? I want to write her, and my parents don't know where she is."

"We're going to see your parents next, I'll let them have the address."

"Thanks."

"Sure. Remember, if you hear anything or see Montgomery, call us. He could be dangerous."

I nod, trying to look helpful and serious.

As soon as I get home, Mom is hugging me and borderline hysterical.

"Thank God you're okay, Roger!"

"Why?"

"Freddie!"

"Oh, that. Why wouldn't I be okay?"

"The police said he's dangerous! He might come looking for us!"

"Freddie's not mad at us, is he?" I ask, innocently.

"He's a murderer!" Mom's in an exclamation point mood, so I don't say anything else. "Stephen's driven out to Lancaster to see Mary Frances. The police have already warned her, but I want Stephen to bring her home."

"Lancaster?" The name is familiar. I remember now. It's a crappy town out in the desert that we've driven through on the way to the Sierras.

Mom hands me a piece of paper from the countertop. Mary Frances's address is scribbled on it. "The police found out where she is, apparently her mail is forwarded from the old convent."

"I don't think she'll come back home, do you?"

"My God, Freddie Montgomery is on the loose, he's probably going to try and find her, she'll come back, all right."

"What if Sister Mary Annunciata and Monsignor O'Callahan don't let her?" I ask.

Mom just shakes her head and goes into the rec room. I follow her out there to see what she's doing. She grabs a bottle of bourbon from the wet bar and pours a glass, then gulps it down, gagging.

"Uh, Mom? You think you should do that?"

She waves me off with annoyance and takes another gulp. I decide she's an adult and can do what she wants.

I leave her alone and watch the local news, but nothing about Freddie. I suppose that's not surprising, since our local channels are all L.A. stations, and L.A. is such a big place that to make the local news you've got to do something really bad.

Mom wanders in and plops down on the couch next to me. Her eyes are red from crying.

"What have I done to deserve all this, Roger?" she asks in a thick, slurred voice.

"Nothing bad has happened yet, Mom. I bet nothing bad *will* happen, either."

She leans back against the couch and closes her eyes. "I feel punk." Mom uses strange expressions sometimes; I guess that's the way people talked back when she was growing up.

"Maybe you shouldn't have any more to drink. Father Quinn will probably be back soon. With Mary Frances." I don't believe he'll pry her out of the crazy convent, but I don't tell Mom that.

She doesn't say anything more; she just lies back against the worn couch cushion with her eyes closed.

She tells me later to order a pizza, so I get a large pepperoni/sausage and when it comes I offer her some but she just shakes her head and stays glued to the couch, mumbling about Mary Frances and Freddie Montgomery.

Father Quinn finally shows up at about ten, and, of course, he's alone.

Mom jumps up at the sound of the car pulling into the driveway and runs outside.

"Where's Mary Frances? Why isn't she with you?"

He gets out of the car, weary and sagging. I feel bad for him; Mom's going to be impossible tonight.

"She wouldn't come with me," he says simply. "She trusts in the Lord." He says it as if he can't believe anything so ridiculous. It's hard to believe he was ever a priest.

"WHY DIDN'T YOU MAKE HER COME WITH YOU?!"

"Sylvia, please. I did my best. But the Monsignor and Sister Mary Annunciata have her so brainwashed she won't do anything without their approval. And they don't want her to leave."

Mom's eyebrows are moving furiously, she's sputtering with anger. Father Quinn takes her arm and leads her back into the house.

"Why didn't you just...take her?" Mom asks after Father Quinn sits her down on the couch and pours her another bourbon.

"She's an adult, Sylvia. And she's not afraid of Freddie Montgomery. There's no reason for her to be. The place they're living is very...safe." Father Quinn says "safe" with a strange inflection.

"What do you mean?" Mom asks. She's not so drunk that she can't tell he's hiding something.

"They...." Father Quinn pours himself a bourbon and takes a drink. "They have guns."

"What?!"

"They seem to think someone might attack them. I believe Sister Mary Annunciata said something about infidels."

"What's an infidel?" I ask.

"Non-believers." Father Quinn holds Mom's hands in his. "Mary Frances is gone for now, Sylvia. I think you need to realize that. She's not your daughter anymore. She belongs to them."

Mom starts crying again, but I'm glad Father Quinn told her. Mary Frances has caused her more misery over the years than anything else. It'd be better for everybody if we could all just forget about her.

"Guns?" Mom says in a whisper. "Is she safe?"

"I think so. They're paranoid, but I don't think she's in any danger. And if Freddie *is* looking for her, he'll be the one in danger, not Mary Frances."

I leave them on the couch and go to my room. I close the door and push my desk chair under the knob, just in case they want to come if Freddie shows up.

I wait, sitting in the dark. I think about Mary Frances and her gun-loving maniac religion. The thought of Sister Mary Annunciata being armed makes me queasy. If she'd been hiding a gun under her habit in first grade, I might be dead. How can religion make people so crazy? They all make a lot of noise about love and Jesus and forgiveness, but then they treat other non-believers like shit and act crazy. I've been surrounded all my life by religion, whether the standard Catholic stuff, the Jesse version, or Mary Frances's church of psychos. What little I know about history and wars makes me realize that a lot of the trouble in the world has been caused by people's religions. I just don't get it. Religion doesn't seem to be doing any good. All I see is hypocrisy, lies, and nastiness. There can't be a god; nobody good could dream up something as awful as human beings. Now the devil, he's much easier to believe in. You see his shit every day. You don't see much of God.

It's almost midnight and I'm starting to nod off when I hear the faint *tap* at my window. I quickly open it, and Freddie climbs into my room. He smells, and his clothes are muddy and torn.

"Where you been?" I ask.

"Hiding out in the wash. Anybody looking for me?"

"Oh yeah." I tell him about the cops sniffing around. He nods, only remotely interested, as if I'm telling him about somebody else's problems.

"Did you find out where Mary Frances is?" he asks anxiously. That's all he cares about.

I hand him the address scribbled on a piece of notebook paper. "Father Quinn went out there today to try and bring her home. Mom's afraid you're going to try and hurt her."

Freddie smiles and shakes his head. That long hair swings at his shoulders. I can't get used to it; he'll always be flattop Freddie to me.

"I'm not gonna hurt her. I love her."

"Why?"

"Just do. Always have. You'll understand someday, Rog. You'll fall in love with somebody, and no matter what you do, no matter how hard you try, you won't be able to make it go away. It's like a virus or something. Every day, every night I've been in prison, not an hour has gone by where I haven't thought about Mary Frances. I can't live without her."

"If they catch you they'll lock you up for good, won't they?"

"Probably. But I don't care. If I can see Mary Frances just once more before I die, then I'll die happy. I won't go back to prison," he adds, his voice hard. He's suddenly an intimidating escaped convict, and I'm scared. But just as quickly he softens back to his gooey, Mary Frances lovesick Freddie self.

"Be careful, Freddie. Father Quinn said they have guns."

"Who has guns?"

"Mary Frances and her crazy friends. I don't think you need to worry about Mary Frances or the Monsignor, but look out for Sister Mary Annunciata. She's psycho."

He nods seriously. "Thanks, Rog. I'll never forget your helping me."

"It's okay," I shrug. "Be careful, man."

Freddie flashes a confident smile, then climbs out the window and runs off into the darkness.

I sit up for a long time, thinking about Freddie and Mary Frances and love. I don't understand how he can love her so much, but it's pretty cool what he said. The more I think about it, I do know what he means about love; that's how I feel about Rhonda.

I'd do anything for her.

The next day I leave Jesse with the jocks at lunch and go looking for Rhonda. She usually has lunch with some of her friends, or sometimes Bushman, but today, the day I want to corner her and make my move, she's nowhere to be seen.

Bushman is with his stupid buddies from the JV team; he thinks that since he's on varsity he's a big stud, and the morons on JV seem to agree with him. They hang around him like he's some kind of hero. He must not tell them that he's nothing more than a living tackling dummy.

I find one of Rhonda's friends and ask her where Rhonda is.

"Outside, I think. She's sad today."

"How come?"

"She broke up with Frank."

This is too good to be true! My job just got that much easier. I'm the happy medicine she needs. I go looking for her. She's not hanging out in the grassy quad, or by the basketball courts. I wonder if she's gone home, or is in some classroom; then I spot a small figure way out on the football practice field sitting by the chain link fence. It's so far away I can't tell if the figure is her, so I go investigate.

As I get closer I see her long hair, and I recognize the way she's sitting. It surprises me I know her so well that I can tell by her posture it's her; all those years of sneaked glances have permanently burned every detail of her into my brain.

She's looking down at a spiral notebook, scribbling furiously. I assume she's working on an assignment, because as I walk toward her she doesn't look up. That's how Rhonda is: when she's studying or concentrating on something, she's obliviously single-minded.

"Hi," I say softly, trying not to startle her.

She jumps anyway as she looks up. Her eyes are red from crying. "Oh! Hi, Roger." She sniffs and closes the spiral notebook.

"Are you okay?"

She shrugs. Seeing her this way kills me. My chest tightens and my own eyes feel wet. "Can I sit here with you?" I ask.

"Sure."

We sit in silence for a few moments. Birds flit among the orange trees in the orchard on the other side of the fence. The familiar tart odor of hot, dusty orange leaves and freshly cut field grass is soothing. The sun warms us; the chain link we're leaning against is hot through my shirt.

"Frank broke up with me," she says.

"Oh. Sorry," I say, trying to sound sincere but secretly thrilled inside.

"He's going out with Tammy Moore now," she says. Tammy Moore's a JV cheerleader. Rumor has it she's a slut. Perfect match for Bushman.

"I'm really sorry, Rhonda. I'm sorry you feel bad." It's lame, but I don't know what else to say.

"It hurts. I really like Frank."

We sit in silence. A warm gust sweeps over us, and the smell of the orange trees is even stronger than before.

"What were you writing?" I ask.

"Poems. I write poems when I'm sad."

Uh-oh. Poetry is such a girl thing to do. The only time I've read poems is in English classes when I've been forced to. The language bugs me; poets never say what they mean, they hide everything behind flowery words and weird punctuation. But even though I hate poetry, I'd make an exception to take a look at Rhonda's if she offered. I'd like to know what she's thinking.

I decide to be daring. Sometimes you've got to take a chance and maybe it'll pay off. I put my arm around her shoulder, and to my astonishment she leans against me and puts her head on my shoulder.

"I'm glad you've always been my friend, Roger."

I'm so filled with warmth toward her that my throat is slammed shut. My head spins and I'm afraid I might pass out as I smell her hair and feel her against me. I squeeze her tighter and she responds. This feels like the most natural thing in the world.

"I know sometimes you haven't liked me much," she continues. "I mean, about Frank and everything. But at least you've stuck with me all this time. I appreciate that."

"Well, it's because...I really like you," I mumble. *Really like you*, shit, I sound like a dork.

"I like you, too," she says, smiling. She snuggles against me. This feels so nice. And it's not even sexual or anything. No hard-ons or dirty thoughts to spoil the romance. At least, not yet.

"I was wondering, since you and Bushman have broken up, if maybe you'd...want to hang around with me." Wow, I'm getting really brave. That came out without me realizing I'd said it.

Rhonda pulls away and looks me in the eye. "Well...." she says, and until the small smile appears I have the horrible feeling she's going to tell me to get lost. "Okay."

"Really?"

"Yes." She gives me the nicest smile. It's the same smile she snagged me with back in grammar school.

"Wow."

I sit, staring at her, realizing that something great has just happened. I've been dreaming about this moment for years, and now that it's here I don't have the faintest idea what to do. Rhonda playfully arches her eyebrows at me as if she's waiting for the punch line to a joke.

"Uh, I'm not sure what to do next," I say, feeling myself turn red. "Do we shake hands or something?"

Rhonda laughs, leans toward me, and we kiss.

My head is swimming, her lips feel so nice, and she leans in and we kiss long and hard, and if I died right now I wouldn't care.

"For Christ's sake, Montoya, just because you're blind doesn't mean you don't HIT!" Coach Gutierrez is right in Jesse's facemask, screaming at his odd, milky gray eyes. The only time I see Jesse's eyes anymore are during football practice, and I can understand why he refuses to be seen without his sunglasses.

The accident scarred his eyes, and eye scars aren't pretty. It might help in a game, though. Jesse has always been scary-looking in a football uniform. With his dead, vampire eyes he's even more frightening.

"Sorry, Coach. Didn't see him," Jesse mumbles.

"Come off it, Montoya! You pussy tackled him after you found him, you don't need eyes to tackle! Show me a little more desire, or you're gonna be sittin' on the bench!"

Coach stomps away, and the scrimmage resumes. The next play, Jesse sniffs out the ball carrier and crushes him. It's Bushman, and Jesse hits him so hard that Bushman doesn't get up right away. It's Bushman's bad luck that he was Jesse's victim after being chewed out.

Bushman. I smile at the thought that I now possess Rhonda. As Bushman struggles to stand, his bleary eyes scan the field like he's looking for a friend. He glances at me, and his eyes widen for a moment, then they roll back in his head and he flops on the grass, out cold.

"Hell," mutters Coach Gutierrez as he trots over to Bushman. "Wish this kid was tougher." He waves me over, and I run out with the first aid box. Coach Gutierrez cracks an ammonia inhalant and waves it under Bushman's nose.

Nothing. I've never seen that before.

Coach cracks another and practically shoves it up Bushman's left nostril. Still nothing.

The assistant coaches and the trainer huddle around Bushman, and now they start to look worried.

"Bushman?" Coach Gutierrez asks. "Bushman, wake up!" But Bushman doesn't move. Coach Gutierrez looks closely at him. "Oh shit, he's not breathing!"

They carefully pull Bushman's helmet off, and Coach Gutierrez starts artificial respiration. The team gathers around, silently watching. I hate Bushman, but this is scary.

A warm gust blows across the field, thick with the scent of orange blossoms. It's strange, because the oranges don't usually bloom this time of year, but the blossom perfume is the strongest I've ever smelled.

The air feels weird, mild and soothing, in contrast to what's happening. With the blossom smell I almost feel sleepy.

I watch Coach Gutierrez try to make Bushman breathe; it's a dream, blurred and disjointed, but it snaps into clarity as Jesse steps up, pulls Coach Gutierrez away from Bushman, and kneels next to him.

"Whataya doing, Montoya!?" Coach shouts, but Jesse doesn't hear him.

He's in the miracle zone.

It's been so long that I've almost forgotten what it's like. The look of peace and detachment is upon him, and I can tell he's transported into his fantasy world of Jesus and Mary and miracles.

Jesse leans over Bushman, who still isn't breathing, and touches his chest. He throws his head back to the sky, closes his eyes, and his lips move in silent prayer.

Coach Gutierrez makes a move toward him, then stops. It's as if even Coach can tell that something beyond him is happening and he shouldn't interfere.

I stare, at once repelled and fascinated, wanting to step forward and tell them that Jesse can't help Bushman, that they better call an ambulance, that Jesse's nuts and his delusions are dangerous, that if they want Bushman to be okay they better get Jesse away from him. But I don't move. I can't. I don't know why. I don't want Bushman to die, which surprises me. He's tormented me since eighth grade, I've wished him dead a million times, but now, when he might actually croak, I want him to be okay.

But not enough to do anything.

The orange blossom smell is so strong now that its cloying sweetness is almost nauseous; the way we all stand, slouching, watching Jesse pray over

Bushman, it's like the odor has us stoned into dull inaction.

I try to move my head in Coach Gutierrez's direction, but my body won't follow my brain's command.

Oh shit, I think, *Bushman's going to die, and it'll be Jesse's fault, and nobody can do anything about it.*

My mind races ahead in ridiculous fantasy. Will I go to Bushman's funeral? I'll have to, I suppose. Rhonda will want to go, and since we're a couple now I have to be with her through thick and thin. It'll be hard, but for Rhonda, I'll do it. I hope it's not an open casket, though. I don't like looking at dead people. When Uncle George died he had an open casket, and as we filed by I noticed that his nose hair was sticking out in the same gross way it did when he was alive. It surprised me that the funeral guys didn't trim it.

I don't want to have to look at Bushman's dead freckles, but since Rhonda will be weeping inconsolably—he was her old boyfriend, after all—I'll go with her. I won't look in the casket, though. I'll concentrate on comforting her. That's my job now.

I'm shocked out of my fantasy by Bushman's gasping choke of returning life. Jesse is standing over him now, and the smell of the orange blossoms suddenly disappears. Bushman is coughing and gagging, and color returns to his face.

I hear sound again, guys talking, Coach Gutierrez and the other coaches yelling orders, and from the silent, orange-scented peace chaos has emerged.

Jesse turns and walks away from Bushman, who now is yammering that he feels okay and that practice can continue. The coaches order him not to move, and in the noise and disorder of the moment, Jesse comes to me. How he knows where I am I still haven't figured out.

"I cured him," he says.

"Maybe he would've been all right anyway," I say.

"Bullshit, *ese*. And you know it, too."

"Yeah, right man. The Virgin come by?"

Jesse looks troubled. "No. Not like the old days. I could feel her presence, but she wasn't...there, you know?"

"No. I don't know. You're lucky Bushman came to, man. If he croaked and they decided it was your fault you woulda been in a lot of trouble."

"Still no faith, Roger? What's it gonna take to make you believe?"

"We're not fuckin' third graders anymore, Jesse. You can't keep doing this shit. You're gonna hurt people."

"I cured Bushman. He was on his way to dying until I laid my hands on him and channeled the Lord's power."

He's so full of shit that I can't control my anger. "Then channel the Lord's power to fix your own eyes, asshole!"

"It don't work that way. We've already talked about this before. That's why we have to go to Lourdes."

I give up. I don't know why I bother.

We wait until the ambulance shows up. They load the protesting Bushman on a gurney and roll him off the field. As he rolls by, he looks at Jesse. Confusion clouds his face, then he smiles. "Thanks, man," is all he says.

Strange. He was out cold when Jesse was praying his miracle mumbo-jumbo. How would he know to thank him for anything? Jesse merely nods graciously, and Bushman gets rolled to the waiting ambulance.

Coach Gutierrez makes the team run wind sprints the rest of practice. He avoids Jesse. I think he's afraid of him.

On the way home, I decide to go by the counseling center where Father Quinn works. I'm troubled by what happened at practice today, and maybe Father Quinn can help out. He's as skeptical about Jesse as I am, and he's a good person to talk to when I need to be reassured that Jesse's a whacko.

I wait in the grubby reception area, thumbing through sticky, five-year old *Newsweeks*, while Father Quinn finishes talking to a Mexican lady and her little kids. Father Quinn has been working more nights at the center lately, and I'm starting to wonder if something's wrong between him and Mom. They don't fight, but they're not as lovey-dovey as they used to be. Mom's immersed in her real estate business, Father Quinn's busy trying to help people, and their lives don't seem to connect much anymore. Even when Father Quinn's at home, he's always puttering around on some home improvement project or planning how to trim the shrubs so they're perfectly square. He's got this mania about geometric plants. As I grow up and watch the people around me, I'm realizing that nobody seems to be able to stay happy and content very long. That worries me. I hope things will be different for Rhonda and me. I'm already making plans to spend my life with her—although we have yet to go out on a real date. But it never hurts to plan ahead.

Father Quinn finally finishes with the Mexican lady, and I go into his cluttered, grimy little office.

"Hi, Rog!" He's all smiles. I like that about Father Quinn: he always seems happy to see me.

"Hi. Got some time?"

"Sure. I've don't have another client for awhile. Your mom know where you are?"

"She's working tonight, too."

"Oh yeah," says Father Quinn, sounding a little sad.

"Jesse did another miracle today. At least he thinks he did."

"Oh dear."

I tell Father Quinn what happened. He sits, listening seriously, resting his chin on a little steeple of his fingers.

"It's wrong, Father Quinn," I tell him after I've finally finished.

"Sometimes you just can't do anything about a situation, Roger," he says. "I run into that all the time. I want to help somebody, but I can only do so much. Life is like that. Sometimes you have to sit back and watch, no matter how much it bothers you. You want to do something, you desperately want to do something, but you can't. I think that's the position you're in with Jesse."

"I don't want to be around him if he's gonna keep doing this stuff."

"That's your choice. But you guys have been best friends forever, you think you can walk away from him?"

"I dunno," I say, feeling like a traitor.

"Talk to him. Communication is always the best choice."

I give Father Quinn a long look. "You know what it's like trying to talk to him. He won't listen to anything. He's sure he's right."

"A true believer," Father Quinn says, nodding. "They're tough."

We talk for awhile more, but he doesn't offer any real help. His next client shows up, so I leave and head for home, unsatisfied and no closer to figuring out what to do about Jesse than when I arrived.

Father Quinn tried to help, but when it comes to Jesse he's as much in the dark as I am.

When I get home, there's a strange car parked in the driveway. It's a new Chevy Vega, and at first I'm alarmed because I think it's the cops looking for Freddie, but the more I think about it, the less likely it seems that cops would drive a Vega.

I go inside, listening carefully. I hear Mom's voice out in the living room, and then a guy speaking to her. Their voices are low, and punctuated by occasional laughs. Must be a friend, or maybe somebody from her work.

For some reason, I go to the doorway to the living room and stop. I'm not usually a snoop, but tonight I feel like eavesdropping.

I peek into the living room. Rhonda Fairly's dad is sitting on the couch with Mom. They both have drinks in hand, and they're acting very friendly.

"They're cute kids," Mr. Fairly's saying. "Glad they finally seem to be getting together. Didn't care for that Bushman kid. But then, I've never met anybody with red hair I've liked."

Mom laughs too loudly. I recognize it; it's her drunk laugh. Why is he here?

"Well, I know Roger's had a crush on Rhonda for a long time." She's using her flirty, pretend-whisper voice. Two things piss me off: that she's talking about me, and that she's acting so weird around Rhonda's dad.

"Ah, young love." Mr. Fairly holds up his glass in a toast. They clink glasses.

I decide I'd better wander in before anything else happens.

"Hi," I mumble in my best annoyed teenager voice.

"Oh, hi, honey," Mom answers, setting her glass down on the coffee table and sliding a little farther away from Mr. Fairly. "You know Rhonda's dad, don't you?"

"Sure. Hi."

"Good to see you Rog," he says, with a big crocodile grin. "Just dropped by to say hello to your mom, tell her the news."

"What news?" I ask.

"'Bout you and Rhonda," he says with a wink.

"Why didn't you say anything Roger?" Mom asks.

I shrug. "Nothin' to say."

"Well, I think it's pretty big news if you and Rhonda are dating," Mom says, sounding annoyed. "I'd like to have heard it from you."

Mr. Fairly stage whispers to Mom. "You know how us guys are, Sylvia. We keep our secrets." Mr. Fairly grins at me with sharp, yellow teeth. I like this guy less and less. "Isn't that right, Rog?"

"I guess."

"Have you asked her out yet, honey?" Mom asks.

"Mom! We'll see what happens, okay? You'll be the first to know."

"Guess I should be going," says Mr. Fairly. He sets his drink down and stands up. "Hope we'll be seeing more of you, Sylvia. And Steve, too, of course. Maybe we can have you all over, fire up the barbecue."

"I'd like that," Mom says, still in her irritating flirty voice. I wish she'd stop.

Mr. Fairly says his good-byes and heads off.

"You stinker," Mom says after he's gone. She pinches me and giggles. I can smell the booze on her breath. "Rhonda's a little doll! When were you planning on telling me?"

"It's not like we're getting married or something."

"And she's Catholic...that's so important."

"Important for what?"

"The future. You know."

"How come you were drinking with Mr. Fairly?" I ask, hoping to change the subject back to her.

"Why, being sociable. Friendly. I've known Bob Fairly for years."

"Uh-huh."

"And he's excited that you and Rhonda—"

"Why's he care?" I interrupt.

"Because she's his daughter. And he wants her to be with a nice boy. A nice boy like you."

"I don't see why he has to come over here to drink with you to tell you that I might go out with his daughter."

"Roger! What are you saying?"

"I just don't see—"

Mom's eyes tear up, and she flops down on the couch and grabs her sweating highball glass. "Sometimes I need to feel...special." She sniffles and snorts back tears. Shit, what am I getting into?

"Hey, I'm sorry, I didn't mean to make you cry." I hate tears; I feel useless and dopey when somebody's crying. They're in the middle of some horrible, life-changing catastrophe and all I can do is stand around with my hands in my pockets and mumble.

"You don't understand, Roger. You're too young. But with all that's happened to me, I need to be reminded that I'm still...attractive."

"Isn't that what Father Quinn's for?"

Mom just sighs and finishes her drink.

Father Quinn comes walking in a few minutes later, looking glum and guilty. He silently goes to the couch and hugs Mom; I don't know if he had some kind of ESP thing, but he seems to know that Mom needed him to come home.

I leave them hugging each other on the couch.

Rhonda's dad is going to be a problem.

*   *   *

THANK YOU.

That's all the note says. It's printed in block letters on lined notebook paper. When I got home from school and football practice today, an envelope was sitting on the kitchen counter.

Mom was busy making spaghetti; in the last few days she's made sure to be home every night, as has Father Quinn. They seemed to realize that working all the time was messing stuff up between them, so they're trying to fix things. Good. As much as I'm madly in love with Rhonda Fairly, her dad gives me the creeps, and I don't want him sniffing around Mom anymore.

"Got a letter, Rog," Mom said as she stirred the Ragu. "No return address," she added.

I picked up the envelope and studied it. Postmarked *Palmdale, CA.* I had a feeling I knew what it was, and I tried to slip it into my pocket unopened, but Mom was way too nosy to let that pass.

"Aren't you gonna see who it's from?" she asked, her innocent smile hiding not-so-innocent intentions. It was the same smile she gave me when she asked, "Do you ever look at girlie magazines?" when I knew for sure she'd found my stash of Playboys hidden in the closet.

I didn't bother to argue, I ripped open the envelope and took out the sheet of paper. "It just says 'Thank you'."

"Who's it from?"

"Dunno."

"That's odd."

"Yeah. Weird."

I went to my room, and she stayed in the kitchen, stirring her Ragu, suspicious but not able to do any more about it.

I studied the paper for a long time. It had to be from Freddie

Montgomery. The childlike block printing, the Palmdale postmark—Palmdale's right next door to Lancaster, where Mary Frances is—and the simple audacity of sending it had to be Freddie's doing. He must've seen Mary Frances; maybe they let him stay with them. She's all holied-up now, so I can't imagine anything romantic between them, but I suppose I'll never know. Mary Frances won't communicate with us, and Freddie can't, so for the time being it's a mystery.

But I do feel kind of cool that I played a little part in it. I'm a dull guy, I never do anything daring or dangerous, and helping Freddie was as close as I've ever come to being truly wild. I toss the paper in the trash and hope Mom will forget about it.

I want to call Rhonda. We've been hanging out together at school during lunch, taking long walks along the perimeter of the football practice field. The past few days have been the sweetest days of my life. Time with Rhonda is beyond wonderful. It's delicious.

We haven't really talked about anything important, we've just chattered and gotten to know each other better. She's told me lots of stuff about Bushman, stuff that almost makes him sound human. He must be schizo. According to Rhonda, Bushman was always polite and nice to her. Even when they broke up, he was cool about it, telling her that he was just looking for a little more "space", whatever that means. His loss is my gain.

We've even held hands as we walk. Mine get sweaty and clammy, although she's too nice to say anything about it. Hers are always warm and dry; comfortable, a lot like her. Every second I'm around her, I'm falling deeper in love.

It's great.

I go into the hall and dial her number. I'm not sure what I'm going to say, but I just want to hear her voice. I might even tell her about Freddie Montgomery.

"'Lo?" It's her dad. I resist the urge to hang up; the sound of his oily voice irritates me.

"Hi, Mr. Fairly, it's Roger Donnelly. Is Rhonda there?"

"Hey, Rog, how are you? How's your mom?"

"Fine," I say, trying to sound icy, but I don't think he catches it. I haven't mastered the adult art of passing messages along by the tone of my voice.

"So, looking for Rhonda, huh?" he says. I'll bet he's smirking.

"Yeah. Is she there?"

"Sure. By the way, how's your mom? Wait, already asked you, didn't I?" He laughs loudly.

"Like I said, she's fine, Mr. Fairly." I think that maybe he's drunk.

"Good, good. Tell her I'll drop by some time. Got some real estate to talk with her."

I wait and say nothing more. I'm beginning to regret calling. Talk real estate with her, yeah, right. How can somebody as nice as Rhonda come from a guy like this?

He slams the phone down on something hard, and I hear him yelling for Rhonda.

"Hello?" she says in her high, sweet voice. Wow. My heart thumps.

"Hi. It's me. Roger, I mean."

She laughs. "I know your voice, Roger."

"Oh." I feel stupid. I haven't been around her enough to feel at ease yet.

We talk about nothing, and before I know it we've been on the phone for half an hour. Time with Rhonda loses meaning. It's just now.

"Let's go out Friday night after the football game," I blurt. Must've been a subconscious thing. A real date was the reason I called.

"Okay. Pizza or something?" she asks, sounding excited, which makes me feel even better.

"Sure. We'll figure something out."

She doesn't reply. I hear noise in the background, voices that I can't make out.

Rhonda gets back on the phone. "Sorry, Roger. I have to go now. Frank's here."

Bushman. Motherfucker.

He hasn't been back at school since Jesse killed and resurrected him. The rumor was he was recuperating from a concussion, and the doctors didn't want him to come back just yet. Fine with me. My sympathy for him vanished as soon as I found out he wasn't hurt badly. Now he's popped back into my life to irritate me.

Shit.

"Okay," I say, trying to sound cheerful. "See you tomorrow."

"'Bye," Rhonda says, but already I can tell her attention is aimed at Bushman and I'm no longer on her mind.

The phone clicks as she hangs up, and I stand in the hall for a very long time, staring at the phone.

"Hey, man," Bushman says.

I'm putting the stuff away after practice, tossing the ball bags into the equipment room, when I hear Bushman's voice behind me. The team is stomping into the locker room, sweaty and beat, and I assume he's talking to somebody else.

So I ignore him.

"Donnelly?" he says. It's Bushman's first day back at school and football practice since Jesse squashed him, and he tip-toed through practice today, obviously gun-shy, but Coach Gutierrez didn't get on his butt. How could he? The guy almost died last time. I suppose Coach will cut him some slack for a little while.

I turn and face Bushman. I'm filled with dread. Not that I'm as afraid of him as I used to be—I don't think he'll try to kill me, and even if he did, I can sort of fight back—but he irritates and annoys me, and I'd rather not have to admit that he exists.

I don't say anything. We stand, facing each other, him in his stinky practice jersey, holding his helmet, me in my usual geek-wear Levi's and paisley, flesh-colored shirt. Mom buys my shirts; I'm going to have to make her stop.

I wait. Bushman looks unsure of what to do next.

This is the first time I've really been close and looked at his face. He's getting older; his face is longer, losing the baby fat, and scraggly red whiskers sprout from his cheeks and chin. Man, he's ugly. How could Rhonda stand this guy?

"I, uh...." He looks down at the floor. "I'm sorry." He seems to shrink, like he's becoming a little kid before my eyes.

"Sorry for what?" I ask.

"For fucking with you. I jumped you at the football game last year."

"I figured."

"Yeah. So I'm sorry for all that stuff."

I don't know what to say. Of all the things Bushman could've said to me, I never expected this.

"I'm sorry," he says again, fishing for a response.

"Fuck you, Bushman," is the only thing I can think of.

"I'm sorry. And I forgive you," he says.

"Forgive me for what?"

"For being angry at me. I understand, man."

He turns and clatters off in his cleats toward his locker. The asshole forgives me? I can't believe it.

I'm riding home with Jesse and his brother Mando a little later. "Did Bushman talk to you?" Jesse asks.

"Yeah."

"And?"

"I told him to get fucked."

Jesse's brother looks in the rearview mirror and smiles. He'd never admit it, but I think he doesn't hate me. Since I've been Jesse's seeing-eye dog, Mando has actually been friendly—or at least as friendly as a *vato* lowrider can be to a white boy.

"Did he say he was sorry?" Jesse asks.

"How do you know what he asked?" I ask, a cold, sinking throb in my gut.

"We talked. He came by my house last night."

"Fucking *pendejo*," Mando mutters, shaking his head.

"Shut up, man! You gotta learn about forgiveness too, *ese*."

"Hey, Jesse," I say, "if you wanna be Bushman's butt buddy, go right ahead. But don't be dragging me into it. The dude's a motherfucker, always has been, always will be."

Jesse's brother nods. "Right on, *ese*." I don't know why he's my ally, but it feels good to have a truly frightening hard guy agreeing with you.

"You're both wrong, man," Jesse says with his infuriating piety. "Bushman repented. He saw the light while he was dead."

"He wasn't dead!"

"He was. And through the powers of the Virgin I brought him back. He appreciates it, man. He knows. And now he wants to make up for any bad he's done in his life. And that includes fucking with you, Roger."

Mando turns up the radio. *Cisco Kid* is playing; the perfect lowrider song. He thumps the rhythm on the tiny chain steering wheel. If we're lucky, maybe he'll bounce the air shocks at the next stoplight.

We ride the rest of the way home without speaking; the only sound is the radio: "*Cisco Kid, was a friend of miiine.*"

The morning fog has burned off, and now, at lunchtime, it's become a mild September day. I like the way the air feels on days like this. It's not too hot, and if it's smoggy you can't tell because there's leftover haze in the air from the fog. The sun is pleasant and relaxing. Days like this make me glad that I live here, although there's not enough of them to cancel out the hot, smoggy hell days. I guess it beats blizzards, though.

Maybe part of the reason this day feels so good is that I'm sitting out by the chain link fence next with Rhonda.

Rhonda. Every morning I wake up excited and edgy, electrified by the knowledge that today I'll see her, hold her hand, maybe even kiss her. I'm so far in love I can't imagine being without her. I had no idea this would be so strong. The long years of crushes on cute girls or vague longings were no preparation for the smash-you-in-the-face power of being head-over-heels in love. I'm losing weight, and Mom asked the other day if I was feeling okay.

"You look thin, honey."

Father Quinn was washing the dishes and he looked back over his shoulder, smirking. "I think Rog has the Rhonda flu."

They had a good laugh at my expense, but he was right. Being in love is like a disease. All the dopey romance movies and love songs know what they're talking about. Love's the weirdest thing.

It's also the nicest feeling I can imagine.

We're having lunch, chattering about anything and everything, when I decide to ask the question that's been bugging me for the last few days.

"What did Bush...Frank want the other night?" I try to keep my voice light and mildly disinterested, but I don't do a very good job. My throat pinches and my voice squeaks.

Rhonda looks sad. "It was weird."

"Why?"

"He wanted to apologize. I don't know what he felt guilty about; he didn't say. He just kept saying over and over how sorry he was for everything."

"Huh." Too bad Jesse didn't crush the jerk a few years earlier. It would've saved me a lot of aggravation.

"I think when he got hurt at football practice it really scared him."

"He apologized to me, too," I say, and then I'm immediately sorry I brought it up.

"Really? For what?"

She knows the story. "Just...some things."

"He's so nice," Rhonda says, and I feel a hot stab of jealousy in my throat. I try to make it go away, but the sound of her saying good things about Bushman is too much to bear.

"Yeah. Nice."

Rhonda smiles and grabs my hand. "Well, I hope you were friendly to him. Whatever happened between you before, he wants it to be over now. I'm glad you're so understanding."

I guess now's not the time to tell her that I told Bushman to get fucked.

We talk some more about non-Bushman things, and we kiss lightly a couple of times. Life is good.

Then, we hear sirens. Coming toward the school. An ambulance and a police car roar up to the cafeteria, and Rhonda and me, being nosy high school kids, wander back over to see what's up.

A huge crowd is gathered outside the cafeteria, and in the hubbub it's impossible to see what's happening. Some teachers try to get the crowd to disperse, but to no avail.

Rumors are flying, and I overhear the names of Danny Robledo and Jesse.

"Oh shit," I say to Rhonda. "I think Jesse's involved in this!"

The ambulance guys roll a gurney out of the cafeteria. Danny Robledo is strapped to it. His normally dark skin is a sickly gray-brown cast, and his jaw is grotesquely distorted and swollen.

Like he got punched by somebody incredibly strong.

Then I see Jesse being escorted out by the vice-principal and a couple of cops. They pass nearby, and somehow Jesse senses I'm here.

"Hey Rog! Come with me!"

I leave Rhonda and follow Jesse and the cops to the vice-principal's office.

This shit just never ends.

Chapter Fifteen

Danny Robledo was in the hospital for almost a month.

Jesse's punch busted his jaw, and they had to wire it shut and fix the shattered bones around his eye socket.

I've heard a lot of different stories about what happened, and Jesse won't talk about it, so this is the best version I've been able to come up with:

While I was outside that day, talking to Rhonda and being dreamy in love, Robledo was getting ready to duke it out with Jesse.

Since the rumble on the golf course last summer, Robledo and his pals had kept their distance from Jesse. I'd see them at lunch sometimes, throwing nasty glares across the cafetéria at Jesse, who was blindly oblivious, but they never made any moves to kick his ass. I think even Robledo was afraid of messing with Jesse when the rest of the football team was around.

The day that they fought Robledo was prowling the cafeteria, looking for trouble. On the days he was feeling aggressive—which was most of them—

he'd wander around, smacking into poor, innocent slobs, looking for a fight.

Jesse was standing in line waiting to scoop up a couple of soggy burgers when Robledo decided the time was right to fuck with him. I guess he figured it was safe since the rest of the football team was already at their table, pigging out on the calories they'd need for that afternoon's practice.

Robledo walked up behind Jesse, threw a forearm shiver into Jesse's back, and knocked him down. He cussed him out in Spanish and everybody around them scattered because they knew what was coming next.

Jesse slowly got to his feet, didn't even look angry, and stood before Robledo. Robledo, as always, was dressed perfectly in *vato* lowrider regalia: creased Pendleton buttoned at the neck, pressed Levi's, and slicked-back hair.

They said stuff to each other in Spanish, Jesse took off his sunglasses and set them down on the counter, and the fight was about to start.

Except that Robledo whipped out a switchblade. Jesse heard the snap of the blade, and did a Kung fu-style kick, somehow seeing the knife with his dim eyes. It flew out of Robledo's hand and clattered harmlessly back in the cafeteria kitchen.

People who saw the next move say it was incredible. Jesse made such a quick lunge that he was a blur, and his fist hit Robledo's face so fast nobody really saw it happen. The next thing everybody knew, Robledo was lying on the red tile floor, his jaw shattered, in a growing pool of blood. Jesse squatted down next to him.

Jesse slipped his sunglasses back on, put his hand on Robledo's deformed cheek, and said: "The Virgin probably won't heal you this time. But I want you to know, I forgive you, *ese*. And when you're better, we'll be a team for the Virgin, man. This is the first of the sacrifices you'll have to make. Probably be bigger ones ahead, too."

Robledo gurgled bloody teeth onto the floor and passed out.

Some people claimed that after Jesse hit Robledo, they saw a gun tucked in Robledo's belt. I don't know if I believe it, but if it's true, then Robledo's even scarier and more dangerous than I thought. Even the toughest of the *vato locos* don't bring guns to school; they stick with switchblades and pieces of chain. Jesse's lucky Robledo came at him with a just a switchblade.

The high school did their usual huffing and puffing, threatening to expel Jesse, but in the end, knowing Robledo was involved, they decided it was a case of self defense and let Jesse off with two weeks' suspension. And they kicked him off the football team.

That was the worst part. Jesse was devastated, and so was the rest of the team—including Coach Gutierrez. For some reason, Coach thought it was my fault Jesse and Robledo got into a fight.

"You were supposed to look out for him, Donnelly!" Coach yelled at me when he first found out Jesse was off the team.

"I wasn't there when it happened, Coach."

"It was your job to be there!"

I thought Coach Gutierrez was being unfair, but I also realized how upset he was about Jesse. Jesse was his personal project, even before the accident. Coach saw Jesse as a young version of himself, and now that Jesse had fallen from the track that Coach had set, he was pissed off, and I was the most convenient person to blame.

So I took his abuse in silence, and he eventually cooled off, and a couple of weeks later he apologized.

With Jesse off the team, being manager wasn't as interesting anymore. I hadn't realized how much I kept an eye on him when we were out there. Sitting on the sidelines watching practice and hauling balls and first aid kits around was boring now.

And then there's Bushman.

He's become a born-again fag. Every day at practice, and during school when he can trap me, he begs me to forgive him and tells me he wants to be my friend.

The first time it happened I was in the bathroom during lunch. Since I knew Jesse and other guys on the football team, I was one of the few wimpy white boys who could go into the bathroom to pee and not worry about getting the shit kicked out of me. It's not that the smokers and hard guys liked me, they just ignored me—which was okay. At least I could pee unmolested. There are a lot of exploding bladders of unlucky wusses at lunchtime.

Anyway, I was leaning toward the urinal, taking care of business, when I noticed somebody step up to the urinal next to mine. There was a line of urinals along the wall, and it's bad form to step up next to somebody when there's other empty ones further away. I didn't look over, because that would've been a breach of guy etiquette too, so I finished, buttoned up my Levi's, and as I turned to leave locked eyes with Bushman. He was peeing happily, with a big dopey grin on his face.

"Hey, Rog."

I nodded and flushed.

"How you doin', man?" he asked.

"Okay." I wanted to get out of there as fast as I could. The smokers and assorted bathroom scum were taking notice of Bushman and me and I didn't like the feeling.

"Can I talk to you?" he asked, zipping up.

I shrugged and we hurriedly left the bathroom. Bushman tagged after me across the quad.

"I feel really bad about the stuff I did to you. I'm really sorry I was so mean. I don't know why I'm like that, you know?"

"Yeah. Well, whatever."

"I know you came to my house a long time ago. After that time you tried to kill me in junior high. My mom told me."

His mom. I'd almost forgotten. The really ugly lady who was a drunk. If I remembered correctly, she didn't like him all that much, either.

"Yeah. I guess I did."

"Did you come to apologize?" he asked. There was an eagerness in his voice that was annoying. If puppies could talk they'd sound like him.

"I don't remember."

"I think you did, man. You're a good person. I see that now. I'd like to be more like you, Roger."

I stopped walking. I was completely appalled by this guy. It was easier to understand him when he was a bullying pig; I didn't know how to react to the new, pussied-out Bushman.

"What do you want?" I asked.

"Your forgiveness."

I just shook my head and walked away. He didn't follow.

After that, he'd pull the same thing whenever he had the chance. After practice, as the other guys on the team would line up for water or peel off their sweat-soaked jerseys, Bushman would tag along with me, chattering inanely and always making sure he asked me to forgive him.

I never did.

Jesse moped around for awhile after he got kicked off the team, but he soon shook off the depression and dived back into the Virgin. For the last year or so his heavy-duty preaching, come-join-me-and-Mary business had been muted. After Joe Fanucci and Patty died, I thought that maybe he'd finally outgrown his religious weirdness. He was hot for Lourdes, and he occasionally lapsed back into old weird habits, but I really thought the worst was past. He seemed to be slowly sliding into normalcy.

But after the Bushman cure and the Robledo attack, Jesse jumped back into the First Church of Jesse Montoya with a vengeance. He decided that since he was off the football team he'd put his energy back into Jesus and the Virgin.

Lydia Balderama started spending more time with him, going to his house to study, and taking over my role as Jesse's eyes. It was okay with me. I was more interested in hanging out with Rhonda, and since Jesse was back into the religious stuff, I was glad to let Lydia deal with him.

"Doesn't he bug you with the Virgin stuff?" I asked her one day in geometry when Jesse was home with a cold.

"Nah. I don't take him seriously."

"Doesn't that piss him off?"

"Nothing pisses him off. Especially me," she said, giving me a smile and a knowing look.

I'm getting the feeling that they might be serious about each other. Lydia's funny and sharp, and she doesn't buy into Jesse's bullshit, which seems fine with him. He's willing to overlook her lack of belief because, well, she's cute. And smart. That matters.

My inaugural date with Rhonda went way better than I could've expected. After the football game—which we lost—Rhonda and me hitched a ride with some of her older friends to the Pizza Palace. We laughed and talked and had a great time. By the end of the evening, I felt closer to her than I thought possible, completely at ease and calm, my usual self-consciousness erased. I didn't once think about my scars or my ugly ears; I usually find a way to keep my hands near my face, so I can cover the red, angry scar edges, but on that night I forgot about it. All I cared about was being with Rhonda. It was wonderful to be with a beautiful girl, one I'd been in love with for as long as I could remember, and know she liked me.

Life was good.

We've gone out a few more times since, to the mall for movies and hot dogs at Orange Julius. I'm really beginning to wish I was sixteen, so I could buy a car and take her out the right way. In less than a year I'll be there, and then my life will really take off.

If I work for Jesse's uncle again this summer, I'll have enough saved to buy something really hot—maybe a GTO or a Mustang. Rhonda and me, cruising in my Mustang. Wow.

We had our first really serious make-out session the other night. I'd gone over to her house to study, which we actually did for awhile. Her sleazy dad hovered around at first, grinning like a reptile, but then he finally wandered off to bed with the already sleeping Mrs. Fairly—she goes to bed really early for some reason, maybe to get away from her disgusting husband—so Rhonda and I were as alone as we ever get. We started with nice, friendly little kisses, and pretty soon we were hot and heavy. I lived dangerously and tried to hold her boob, but she pushed my hand away—in a gentle way. Maybe next time.

By the time I left that night I was so hot and bothered that when I got home I went straight into the bathroom and beat off. I didn't bother to turn on the water or pretend to be brushing my teeth. Father Quinn even knocked on the door and asked, "You okay, Rog?"

"Yeah!" I said, trying to sound normal, but it's hard to have a conversation when you're flogging yourself.

I slept fitfully that night, my dreams filled with disjointed sex. Rhonda was there, and even Aunt Yolanda put in an appearance. When I woke up I was surprised at how pleasant the thought of Aunt Yolanda had been. I'd seen her occasionally at Jesse's house; she lived there on and off with her kids. Jesse said that she was having trouble finding the right guy to live with, and her real estate income was sporadic, so sometimes she'd have to move in with them for awhile. But it didn't seem to bother Jesse's family much when some cousin or uncle or aunt would come and stay. Since Mr. Montoya died, Mrs. Montoya had gotten even nicer and welcomed anybody who wanted to live with them. She still gave me big fleshy hugs whenever she saw me, and sometimes she seemed more like my mom than Mom did.

Aunt Yolanda never pulled any of her sleazy come-on stuff with me anymore; I guess she figured that since I was older it was time to treat me with more respect. She was also busy being respectable now, selling real estate and all, and she was big into brown power and *La Raza.* When I saw her she was distant but friendly, and she never mentioned things she did in the past. It was okay with me; that stuff was embarrassing to think about now—although some of the sex things, like the time she danced so close, could still bring on a pleasant memory hard-on.

Aunt Yolanda is a kid memory, as much as grammar school or climbing around orange trees. She's filed away in my past, and though I still see her, the Aunt Yolanda of now isn't anything like the old Aunt Yolanda. She's changed; she acts different, she looks different. The big hair is gone; she parts it in the middle and wears it long and straight. And she dresses nicer, not cheap and sleazy anymore—Levi's and Indian-looking vests, with lots of beads and turquoise jewelry. She's still a great-looking woman, but I've outgrown her. That sounds stupid for a fifteen-year-old, zitty nerd to say, but it's true.

So now when I see her at Jesse's, it's a friendly "How's it goin'?" and nothing more. I'm surprised that she'd show up in a sex dream, but not altogether unhappy about it.

The homecoming dance is in two weeks, and Rhonda and I have our plans set. I never thought I'd be excited about a dance, but then, I've never had a girlfriend before. That changes your outlook on everything.

The theme is *Knights in White Satin*, the cool Moody Blues song, and I'm expecting a night of romance and total Rhonda Fairly enchantment. I'm acting like a geek, but I don't care. I want to be with her more than anything in the world.

Rhonda and I are sitting out in our customary lunchtime spot by the chain link fence, talking and laughing and making plans for the dance, when I see someone running across the field toward us. I don't pay much attention at first, but as the person gets closer I see the telltale outline of a fresh Pendleton and slicked-back hair. Uh-oh. A *vato* is headed our way.

"Who's that?" Rhonda asks.

"I dunno," I say, getting worried. This is unusual *vato* behavior. They don't usually move very fast. As he gets closer, I see who it is. Wisma.

He staggers up, gasping. He's run a long way.

"Hey, Donnelly, man!" He bends over, hands on his knees, trying to catch his breath.

"Hey," I say, exchanging a glance with Rhonda.

"Hi!" she says, cute and perky as always.

Wisma looks up; sweat runs down his face. I've never seen much of an expression on his face before, but now he looks scared.

"It's...Montoya, man," he says, gasping.

My guts turn cold. Another Jesse catastrophe. This is getting old.

"What? Is he okay?"

"Robled..." Wisma hawks up a loogie and spits on the grass. Rhonda's smile fades. She's a girl about gross guy stuff like spitting loogies.

"Shit," I say. "Did Robledo come after Jesse?" I expect the worst. I thought Robledo was still in the hospital.

Wisma shakes his head violently. He's scaring me.

"What is it?" Rhonda asks. "Is Jesse okay?"

"Yeah...it's Robledo."

"What, did Jesse go get Robledo in the hospital or something?" I ask.

"Worse, man."

"Will you tell us?" Rhonda asks.

"You gotta help me, man. I helped you out before," Wisma says to me. The guy's pleading—this is really scary.

"What?"

"I think Montoya converted Robledo to some bullshit *pendejo* religion, man."

Rhonda and I both start to laugh. Wisma looks at us like we're crazy.

"I was in the fucking hospital, man, and Montoya was there, and he was fucking holding Robledo's hand like a fucking *joto*, man. They were praying and shit!"

Wisma says this with a look of such disgust that he might as well be saying that Robledo was wearing pink tights and playing with a Barbie doll.

"Jesse does that sometimes," I say.

"But it's *Robledo*, man!"

Apparently a hard-ass Robledo is Wisma's God, and if he can't believe in Robledo, who *can* he believe in?

"I don't know what to do," I say. "Maybe Robledo will go back to being a psycho lowrider when he gets out of the hospital."

"Man, I fucking hope so," Wisma says. "Will you talk to Montoya, man? Tell him to leave Robledo alone."

"Jesse's hard to stop."

Wisma's crushed. I feel bad for the guy, because he's been so cool to me in the past, and I wish I could help him. But if Robledo wants to pray with Jesse, there isn't much I can do about it. "I'll talk to him, man," I say, and Wisma brightens a little.

"Thanks." He turns and walks off across the field, his usual cocky white-boy *vato* strut beaten down to a Roger Donnelly-like shuffle.

"Robledo praying with Jesse?" Rhonda says. "What next?"

"Who knows..."

Jesse is in geometry the next morning, and Lydia is fighting with him about something. They do that a lot. Even though they seem to be crazy about each other, one of them will say something that pisses the other off, and they'll argue or throw the silent treatment around until somebody gives. I've noticed that it's usually Jesse who gives in first.

I interrupt their sniping. "How's Robledo?" I ask.

Jesse looks over at me; at least I think he's looking. Those sunglasses. "Okay, I guess."

"I hear you been visiting him in the hospital."

Lydia glares at him. "You let yourself get near that ugly little vato loco? He tried to kill you!" She's gotten very protective of Jesse lately. She's really taken over my role.

Jesse shrugs. "He's decided to make a change in his life."

"To what?" Lydia asks. "From a psychotic killer lowrider to an altar boy?"

"Sort of. He wants me to help him find the Virgin. He's an okay guy, you know. Just had a hard life."

Lydia is about to explode she's so mad. I smile. It's fun to stir up trouble.

Class starts, and we have to shut up, but I can hardly wait to see what Lydia does to Jesse afterwards.

When I see them again at lunch, they're all lovey-dovey. Shit. That's the problem, Lydia can be furious, but then Jesse caves in and sweet talks her and everything blows over. It's disappointing. Nobody ever seems to be able to make Jesse squirm. I don't know why I'm so anxious to see him in a bind, maybe it's because since first grade he's always been calm and cool and I've been a whiny, hysterical fag. He's my best friend, but I still sometimes wish he'd fuck up. Nothing gets him down, not blindness, not anything. It's annoying to a mere mortal like me.

Rhonda and I sit with them at lunch, and no mention is made of Robledo. Until I bring it up.

"So? What's with Robledo?"

Jesse shrugs. "He'll be okay. They got his jaw put back together. I'm glad. I felt kind of bad about it, you know?"

"He's the one who went after you," Lydia reminds him.

"'Blessed are the peacemakers'," Jesse says.

"How'd you manage to convince him to be religious?" Rhonda asks.

"Just my natural charm," he says, shooting her his big, toothy, Indian chief grin. When he turns it on, he really is irresistible. It pisses me off.

"It won't last. Robledo's too much of a psycho. What if he's bullshitting you right now, just trying to soften you up so you let your guard down so he can stab you or something?" I ask, feeling and sounding grumpy.

Jesse shakes his head sadly, so disappointed in me. "Roger, Roger...what's it going to take to get you to have faith."

"He's right," Lydia says, "Robledo's crazy."

Jesse sighs. We're all so tedious for him. "You don't understand. People change."

As if on cue, the ultimate changer, Bushman, sits down next to me. "Hi!" he chirps. I get the crawly feeling on the back of my neck, like a thousand fleas marching in formation. Bushman bugs me more now than he ever has.

Rhonda smiles and chatters warmly with him. I feel the jealousy rising as I watch her smile, and, it seems to me, flirt with the asshole. Seeing Rhonda be nice to him dredges up all my insecurities, and I instantly go from being Roger Donnelly, semi-stud with an impossibly cute girlfriend, to Roger the limping, scarface geek. Maybe that's why I despise Bushman so much—he has the power to instantly make me hate myself.

Jesse and Lydia are yammering in Spanish, laughing and obviously in love. Rhonda and Bushman talk across me like I'm not even there. I feel like the biggest dope in the world.

Bushman and Rhonda finally run out of things to talk about, and Bushman looks at me. I'm eating an oatmeal burger, and I'm right in the midst of biting off a huge chunk and a limp pickle slice hangs over my lip when Bushman asks: "Have you thought about it, Roger?"

I slurp the pickle into my mouth, and I notice the look of distaste on Rhonda's face as she watches me eat like a pig. But hey, it's not my fault, they went from ignoring me to suddenly wanting to talk. You should at least warn somebody who's trying to eat an oatmeal burger.

I swallow the chunk whole, and the lumpy mass glugs down my throat. I'm afraid I might choke, but it finally splats into my stomach like a brick.

"Well?" Bushman asks.

Jesse and Lydia have stopped talking, and everybody's looking at me. Waiting.

I decide to play dumb. "Have I thought about what?" I ask innocently.

"Forgiving me." He says it without the slightest self-consciousness.

I hate him, I hate him, I hate him. He gazes at me like he's in love with me, his dopey eyes framed by red everywhere—eyebrows, eyelashes, hair, freckles. My burger churns in my stomach. How could Rhonda have ever kissed this guy? It occurs to me that the lips I've kissed have kissed his. Jesus, I've kissed Bushman second-hand! It's gross enough to make me want to floss.

They're all waiting for me to say something. I look at them, watching me expectantly. Jesse has his wise, Buddha smile.

I panic. "I'm gonna get a cookie, anybody else want one?" I don't wait for an answer, I just scurry away like a cockroach and leave them, sitting at the table, watching me flee.

I'm a cowardly piece of shit, but one thing's for sure: I'm never going to forgive that asshole.

The homecoming dance is two days away now, and I'm so excited I can hardly sleep. I lie awake, my stomach fluttery, and think about Rhonda. I don't know why a stupid dance has me so fired up—after all, I've already gone out with her and we've kissed a whole bunch. But there's something permanent, something important about going to a major high school dance with her. It's as if we'll be making a public statement, that people who don't already know we're going out will now have no choice but to acknowledge that Roger Donnelly and Rhonda Fairly are a couple. And all those people who've ignored me, or treated me like shit (which isn't many; I think I'm more invisible than anything else), will have to pay attention now. They'll have to respect me, and my scars and my gimpy walk won't matter anymore.

Because I have Rhonda Fairly.

Football practice ran long tonight; Coach Gutierrez was convinced that most of the team was being lazy, so he punished them with wind sprints and made them run the perimeter of the practice field five times. Guys were puking and even the ones in the best of shape looked like they were ready to die. I have a feeling everybody will try harder at practice next time.

Darkness is dimming the smoggy mountains, and by the time I make the turn and walk up my street, the streetlights have flickered on. Since Jesse got kicked off the team, I don't have a consistent ride home anymore, so most of the time I have to walk back, unless Mom's out and about or Father Quinn gets off work in time to get me. But I don't mind walking. It gives me time to think, and lately, with Rhonda on my mind every hour of the day, awake and asleep, it's one more chance to fantasize about her.

As I get close to home, I see that Mr. Fairly's Vega is parked in front of our house. Shit. Father Quinn isn't home yet, so the slimeball's alone with Mom. I'm not sure whether I should charge in to protect Mom's virtue, or if I should just hang around outside and wait for him to leave. I'm in a delicate situation. I'm madly in love with his daughter, so I don't want to piss him off, but I don't want Mom doing anything stupid, either. Her mood seems better now than it was the night she said Mr. Fairly made her feel special. Father Quinn has been more solicitous, and she's seemed happy. As far as I know she hasn't seen Mr. Fairly since then.

I trust Mom, but I don't trust Mr. Fairly, so I decide to go in the house and see what's going on. I need to look out for Mom; she's always been nice to me, and now that I'm slowly turning into a man, I need to get over worrying about what I want and look out for her.

The second I open the door I regret it. I hear Mom crying big, noisy, snot-filled sobs, and Mr. Fairly cooing to her in his oiliest voice, "C'mon, Sylvia. Be a sport about this."

They look up as I enter the living room. Mom turns away and wipes tears from her cheeks, and Mr. Fairly breaks into the biggest, fakest grin I've ever seen. They're sitting on opposite ends of the couch; Mom is squashed against the armrest like she wants to blend into the upholstery.

"Hiya, Rog!" Mr. Fairly says.

"Hi. You okay, Mom?"

Mom makes a croaking sound that I take to be a "yes".

"Looking forward to the big dance?" Mr. Fairly asks, as if we can have a normal conversation with my Mom weeping on the couch.

"What's going on, here?" I ask, trying to sound in control.

Mr. Fairly gets up. He looks down at Mom, who's still busy wiping tears and snot on her sleeve. His tone turns instantly cold and hard. "You're sure, Sylvia?"

Mom nods. "Just go. Please!"

Mr. Fairly shakes his head and brushes past me. "You're Mom doesn't know what she's missing, Rog," he says. His expression is cold, hard and scary. Fear shoots through me.

He slams the door on his way out, and I go over to the couch and sit next to Mom. I'm not sure what to say, so I hug her. I guess it's the right thing to do, because she hugs back hard and cries but I think it helps.

"What'd he do to you, Mom?" I ask, not really wanting to know.

"Oh...." she sniffs and the crying slows a bit. "I don't know if I should tell you, it's grown-up stuff."

I wonder how old I'll have to be before I qualify as a grown-up. In her eyes, probably never.

"I wish you'd tell me," I say.

Mom sighs heavily. "He wanted...to have an affair with me."

Jesus. I'm sorry I asked. This is way out of my league. Is that how it works, you go over to somebody's house and ask them if they want to cheat on their husband? Is it that bloodless? It reminds me of the guys who go door to door selling vacuum cleaners.

"The guy's a jerk," I say.

"I don't want this to affect you and Rhonda."

"It won't. She's not like him."

"Don't tell her!" Mom says, suddenly horrified.

"I won't say anything to anybody. Are you gonna tell Father Quinn?"

"I don't know. I think so. He should know. He already knows what Bob Fairly's like."

Mom pulls away from me, her tears now stopped. She even manages a smile.

"Are you and Father Quinn okay now?" I ask.

"Better." Mom stands up. "Want some dinner? Steve should be home soon."

"I'm glad I got here before he did. What would've happened if he caught Mr. Fairly here?"

Mom grins. "He probably would've made him say three *Our Fathers* and three *Hail Marys*." We both laugh. I'm glad I was able to make Mom feel better.

But as I switch on the TV and watch the local news, and as I listen to Mom bang around out in the kitchen, I can't get the cold, scary look Mr. Fairly gave me out of my mind.

I hope I'm wrong, but I've got a bad feeling he might try to get even.

Two hours.

Two hours until I go pick up Rhonda for the homecoming dance. The game was last night, and we kicked Santa Clarita's ass, 45-21, so everybody's in a great mood.

Tonight, the dance. I'm in the bathroom, combing my hair over and over, inspecting my face (not too many zits; that's the beauty of scars, zits can't poke through), and doing my general inventory.

My hair's gotten longer, and I'm parting it in the middle. Father Quinn says I'm starting to look like a water buffalo, but I think he's just envious because his forehead has moved back to the middle of his head.

Mom's been acting like a geek, all giggly and stupid because it's my first dance. It's embarrassing, but at least it's better to be going with a real girlfriend than sitting at home pretending it doesn't matter but inside it's ripping you up that you're such a loser.

I know *that* feeling.

We're going with one of Rhonda's friends and her boyfriend. Thank God I didn't have to get Mom or Father Quinn to drive us—that would've been humiliating beyond all imagining.

My problem now is that I'm ready to go, but they won't be picking me up for another two hours. I'm already hot in my wide tie and brown polyester suit. Mom took me down to Sears and we got what I thought was the coolest-looking suit they had. I just didn't realize it would be so hot.

I bought a pair of brown buckle boots; my feet are getting bigger by the day, but with the bell-bottom pants, my humongous feet are hidden a little. I'm no movie star, but I think I look as good as possible. For me.

When I go into the kitchen, Mom and Father Quinn start applauding. Father Quinn laughs and Mom starts to cry.

"Yeah, yeah, all right, real funny," I say, feeling myself redden.

"Looking good, Roger. A true stud," Father Quinn laughs. It's strange to hear him use words like "stud".

"You look so...grown-up," Mom sniffs. She has the irresistible Mom urge to hug me, which she does, and then she brushes imaginary hair out of my eyes. "You need a hair cut."

"No I don't. I'm growing it longer," I say, just to get a rise out of her.

She clucks and shakes her head, then hugs me again. "You and Rhonda should have a wonderful time. I remember the first dance I went to," she says, and then she launches into a long, boring story that I've heard a million times about the time she went to the prom with a guy named Skip.

Father Quinn listens politely. I know he's heard her stories a million times too, but he's always patient and polite. All those years of sitting in confessionals and listening to people confess to swearing and beating off has given him the talent to be a good listener. Either that or he's paying no attention but he's good at looking like he cares.

Time drags as I wait. One hour. Forty-five minutes. Drag, drag, drag. The tie digs into my neck. I'm starting to get nervous, and I don't know why. It's not like Rhonda's a stranger or anything. Maybe it's because I can't dance. I know I'll look like a dope, but nobody cares, and Rhonda's too nice to say anything mean, but I'm still a little apprehensive. Too much of my life has been spent looking stupid; I'd hate to make a fool out of myself because my dancing is faggy. Of course, I can always use the crippled excuse. Sure, if it comes up, if I catch somebody snickering at my lack of rhythm or making fun of me, I'll just limp up to them, give them my best steely glare, and say, "I don't know what you're laughing at, asshole. I think I dance pretty good for somebody who got run over by a truck. You got a problem with that?" In my fantasy world, whoever was fucking with me backs down, apologizes, and I'm a swashbuckling stud.

If only real life could be like my fantasies.

It's six-thirty. They should be here any minute. I jump up and look out the window every time I hear a car, but it's not them.

Mom and Father Quinn are watching the news, giggling at my nervousness.

Time passes. They're late. Shit, let's go, I'm ready.

Six-forty-five. Seven.

"Maybe you should call Rhonda, honey," Mom says. "I hate to betray my sex, but you know women. We're always late."

"Amen," says Father Quinn.

They laugh an annoying married couples' laugh, thinking they're helping but all they're doing is pissing me off. I say nothing. Where the hell is Rhonda?

I wait another ten minutes, then I dial Rhonda's number. No answer. Okay, that's a good sign, they must be on their way.

Time passes. My cheap suit gets hotter. I feel like I'm wrapped in Saran Wrap. Father Quinn wanders off to the spare room to do some work, and Mom is out in the kitchen poring over the multiple listing book. She can spend hours looking at tiny, blurry, black-and-white pictures of houses for sale. She says she likes to keep up on what's on the market.

She showed a house the other day that was one of Aunt Yolanda's listings; she hadn't studied the listing in the book and took a client to look at the house. She said it was the most hideous place she'd ever seen. The owners were pigs, and they had a bunch of little kids who left a grimy booger line on every wall. "If I'd only studied the multiple listing book," she sighed. I don't know if the book lists booger lines or not, but Mom apparently decided that more studying was in order to avoid embarrassing situations.

But none of that matters now as I sit in the living room, waiting for Rhonda to show up. What the hell's going on? This isn't like Rhonda. She's polite, and if there was a problem or a delay she'd call. *If she could.*

Maybe that's it. Maybe her friend's car broke down, maybe they're changing a tire someplace. Sure, that's got to be it. Makes perfect sense.

Or they got in an accident! Shit, now I'm worried and scared. What if something terrible has happened? What if people are hurt, what if something's happened to Rhonda?

I hurriedly look up the phone number of Lisa, Rhonda's friend who was supposed to take us to the dance. I call her house, and her mom answers. I ask if Lisa's there, her mom says no, she's at the dance. Hmmm. If there's been an accident, she hasn't heard about it yet.

"When did she leave?" I ask.

"About an hour ago," she says. "Who is this?"

"Uh, Roger Donnelly. They were supposed to pick me up."

Her mom doesn't know what's going on, but now I've got her worried. I hang up, feeling guilty, but I want to know where the hell they are!

"Did you get hold of anyone, honey?" Mom asks.

"Uh-uh."

"Strange. Want me to give you a ride over to Rhonda's?"

"There's no answer. They must be on their way. I'll wait outside."

I don't want to talk to anybody, I'm too nervous and worried. I stand out in the driveway, looking up at the stars, waiting for Rhonda to show up. I am suddenly lonely and afraid.

I realize how much I'm in love with Rhonda. Being with her has taken me out of myself, made me see that another person can be the most important part of your life. It's good and bad, because along with the wonder and greatness of being in love is the fear that it might be taken away, that something bad can happen and snatch away the thing that's changed your life. If something has happened to Rhonda I'll die. Just die.

I'm walking down the street before I realize that I'm walking, and soon I'm trotting, then running, toward Rhonda's house. I don't know why, I've already called and nobody's home, but I'm so worried and crazy that I have to do something, and running to Rhonda's house is the only thing I can do.

I'm gasping and sweaty, my carefully combed hair flies in the breeze, my vinyl suit sticks to me like chewed gum, but I've got to find Rhonda. I've got to see that she's okay, I've got to tell her I love her, hug her, kiss her, I've got to see my Rhonda, see that she's okay, and I don't care if my new suit is sweaty and my hair is messed up.

I need to see that she's all right.

As I turn the corner onto her street, my gaspy, panicky breath can't get enough oxygen into my lungs, and I realize that I'm being stupid. I stop running, stand on the sidewalk among the tidy tract houses and try to catch my breath. Jesus, what am I doing? Rhonda's late picking me up and I imagine horrible accidents and get hysterical. I'm such a fag. She's probably at my house right now, wondering where the hell I am. And here I am, standing on the sidewalk a few houses down the street from her house, sweaty and gaspy and a fool. Now what?

I walk slowly toward her house. The lights are on, and her dad's Vega is parked in the driveway. I wonder why nobody answered when I called? Maybe he just got home. I'm not sure if I should go to the door asking where Rhonda is, because then they'll be worried, too. And the thought of having to talk to Mr. Fairly is gross, but it's too important that I find out about Rhonda, so I go to the door and ring the bell.

Nothing. No sound from inside. I ring again. I hop from foot to foot like I have to pee, but it's just nerves and fear. Never in my wildest dreams did

I think that this dance would cause such emotional commotion. How come everything has to be so difficult?

I ring the bell again, and this time I hear the sound of somebody coming to the door. The door opens a crack, and Mrs. Fairly peers out.

I almost never see Mrs. Fairly. Whenever I come over, it always seems like she's just gone to bed or isn't feeling well. As she fearfully looks out at me, I realize why. Her baggy, red-rimmed eyes, messy hair, and the smell—she's a drunk. She reminds me of the way Bushman's mom looked.

Rhonda's never mentioned a word about it.

"Hello, Roger," Mrs. Fairly says. She rolls the "r" in Roger with a slurry sound.

"Hi. Is Rhonda here?"

Mrs. Fairly looks confused. "Rhonda?"

"Your daughter," I say, then immediately regret being a smart-ass. She can't help it if she's a fucked-up drunk.

"I...she's at a dance, I think." Mrs. Fairly rubs her puffy eyes. "It's late."

I'm about to respond when Mr. Fairly's big, meaty hand takes hold of Mrs. Fairly's bony shoulder and pulls her from the door. "I'll handle this, dear," he says, his voice filled with fake concern.

Mrs. Fairly smiles vacantly and nods, then walks away. I'm face to face with Mr. Fairly, and his phony smile evaporates. He looks at me with that look I've seen before and know so well—the "you're a little crippled weasel" disgusted look.

"What can I do for you, Roger?"

"Is Rhonda here?"

"No."

"Where—"

"I think you'd better go home, Roger." He starts to close the door, but I put my foot in it. It seems like a good idea until I realize how strong he is and my foot is getting squashed. My spiffy new boot is scuffed, and it feels like the door edge is cutting the leather. Mr. Fairly finally opens the door, shaking his head.

"Maybe you should be a salesman, Roger. You're a pushy little shit."

Oh-oh. He's pissed. Well, I don't care. I just want Rhonda.

"Rhonda was supposed to come by my house with her friend Lisa and pick me up for the dance. Do you know where she is?"

"She's at the dance." He says it with a cruel smile. I feel my stomach go hollow.

"How come..."

"She decided not to go with you."

If he had stabbed me in the gut I wouldn't have been more shocked. "What?"

Mr. Fairly grins at me now. He's having fun. "How's your mom?" he asks.

"Okay," I whisper, feeling dizzy. My gimpy leg is aching and it feels like it won't support me. "But why didn't Rhonda call me?"

"I always liked your mom. Helluva nice gal. Too bad, really."

"What's too bad?"

"That the families won't be seeing each other any more. Would've liked to had a barbecue, gotten together, all that. Even would've liked to have gotten friendly with your stepdad the priest. Don't know him all that well, though."

I regain enough control to begin to understand what's happening. "You tried to get my mom to sleep with you."

Mr. Fairly smirks at me like I'm an idiot. "She tell you that? These women," he sighs, shaking his head. "Amazing what fantasies they have."

"What did you tell Rhonda?"

"My daughter decided you weren't her type," he says. "And I agree with her. I mean, look at you, son. Rhonda's a beautiful girl. She can do better than a scarred up little cripple like you. No offense."

I raise my fist to hit him, but he's so much bigger and stronger than me that all he does is grab my fist and push me back like I'm a baby.

"Go home," he says, and he shuts the door in my loser face.

I stand, staring at the door, shaking with anger and impotence. *Mother-fucker*! Wait a minute, she went—

"WHO'S SHE WITH? WHO'D SHE GO TO THE FUCKING DANCE WITH?!" I pound on the door, screaming and yelling, but he doesn't answer. The lights inside go out, and I'm alone on the front porch, shouting at a dark door.

I start running. I don't know where, I just run, I don't notice that I'm tired, I don't notice that my lungs are exploding, I don't notice that my bad leg is so sore and weak it will hardly move, I just run—

She dumped me, she let her asshole old man talk shit about me and she dumped me. I can't fucking believe it, she's so nice, she's so smart, how could she let him convince her to dump me?

I run through neighborhoods I've never been in before, and backyard dogs bark as I pass by, I hear doors open, people talk, cars drive by, but I don't stop, I run, trapped in my sweaty new Sears suit, my new boots rubbing blisters onto my heels, gasping, running nowhere—

And then I'm at school. I stagger into the parking lot by the gym. It's filled with cars, and I hear the sounds of the dance inside, music and fun, the sounds of things I should be part of, not standing out in the parking lot sweating like a pathetic pig.

I move slowly toward the gym's front entrance; light and music pour out the doors and spill onto the concrete outside, a brew of noise and color, of breezy good times. A couple of couples stand in the shadows out front, sneaking cigarettes or pot, I can't tell which. A chaperone, the crabby typing teacher, Mr. Haskins, peers outside occasionally, keeping an eye out that nothing too bad is happening.

I move toward the doors, irresistibly drawn but dreading what I'll find. I try to catch my breath; it comes in huge, gasping gulps, it feels like I'll never get enough oxygen inside my lungs, and my bad leg hurts so much it's almost useless. But I stagger on, closer, past the furtive smokers, and I come to the door, hesitate, and then go inside the noisy gym.

Homecoming banners hang from the raised basketball backboards. Dancing couples cover the hardwood floor. It's almost unrecognizable as the gym. I watch as they dance, some close, some apart, all having fun.

Couples. I should be out there with Rhonda.

The music—right now *Love the One You're With*—blares through big speakers. Mr. Haskins looks curiously at me; I can only imagine how bad I look. I brush past him and scan the crowd, looking for Rhonda.

I see lots of people I know, but nobody notices me. They're too busy doing what they're doing to pay attention to sweaty Roger Donnelly in his new Sears suit. It's a good thing so many people are crammed in here and the light is low; even I blend in.

I know Jesse and Lydia won't be here; Jesse hates this kind of stuff, and Lydia will do whatever Jesse wants, so tonight they're over at her house—I think Jesse's trying to convert her parents.

I push through people, bumping, not caring that I'm rude or that nasty glances are thrown my way. I move through them, my head swiveling back and forth, I've got to find her, I've got to talk to her, and then I see it—

Red hair.

Bushman.

Dancing with Rhonda. She's smiling, happy, acting like she's having a good time, like he's the guy she'd planned to go with all along. Like I never existed.

I stop dead. I can't move. I stop breathing. Suddenly I'm not angry; I'm sad. Betrayed. It's the worst feeling I've ever had in my life.

The music stops, and as it does Rhonda glances my way. Her smile disappears, and then Bushman turns, and when he sees me his smile gets bigger.

"Hi, Roger!" he says, so absurdly upbeat and stupid that I'm mad again. "How you doin'?"

I can't say anything. I'm paralyzed. The asshole knows I was supposed to be with Rhonda, how can he be so perky? Rhonda, at least, looks guilty. She touches Bushman's arm, he turns and she whispers something to him. His smile disappears and he says, "Oh," and then he walks away into the crowd without looking back at me.

Another song starts, *Tighter*, and it's slow so most people dance close, and I stand, ten feet away from Rhonda, we gaze at one another across the dance floor, people dance between us, but I can't move, I want to die.

And Rhonda slowly, very slowly, moves toward me.

"Let's go outside," she says, taking hold of my arm and gently pulling me toward the door.

She looks so beautiful tonight. She's wearing a long, tight, shiny dress, and her long hair is curled. She's so fucking irresistible, and she should be with me.

We go out the door, past Mr. Haskins, who eyes us warily—I don't know what he thinks we're going to do, Rhonda's a straight-A goody good and I'm a limping geek—but we ignore him and go outside into the shadows beside the gym. During the day the sides of the gym are handball courts, and we're standing in the middle of one that just yesterday I was playing on. Now it's a dark, frightening spot, a place where I'm about to get my romantic ass kicked. I just know it.

"Didn't my Dad call you?" she asks. I can see her wide eyes clearly in the darkness, and I catch an occasional waft of her perfume. Carnations. The smell reminds me of the funerals I used to serve when I was an altar boy. They always had carnations all over the place.

"He didn't call me. Nobody did. I sat around and waited for you to show up, then I went to your house."

"And did he tell you then?"

"Tell me what?"

"He...said I couldn't see you anymore."

"Why?"

Tears leak out of Rhonda's eyes. "He said, no, he just told me I couldn't see you anymore. He said if I did he'd ground me for the rest of my life. And I wanted to go to this dance more than anything, so—"

"I thought you wanted to go with *me*! I thought that was the important part!"

"It was," she says, and I catch a whiny, annoying tone in her voice I haven't noticed before. "But, it's the homecoming dance, Roger, and I really wanted to go."

"With fucking Bushman?!"

"He *was* my boyfriend before," she says. "And since the accident at football practice he's changed, and I've been talking to him, and he's so nice..." She sputters to silence; it must sound lame to her, too.

"So I'm dumped without a word? I thought we...I thought stuff was good between us!"

"It was, I guess. But Frank—"

"Fuck Bushman! How could you do this to me?!"

Rhonda sniffs back her tears, but now she's looking at me like I'm the one who's out of line.

"Please stop cussing at me."

"Why shouldn't I fucking cuss? I thought you were nice, Rhonda, and sweet. But this is mean, it's nasty, it's wrong!"

"I'm sorry," she says. She's starting to sound angry. "I'm really sorry. But my Dad—"

"You know why your dad doesn't want you to see me? You know the real reason?"

"No."

"He wanted to sleep with my Mom, he was over at our house trying to get in her pants, and I fucking caught the sleazy asshole—"

"No! Stop it!"

"—And he was begging my Mom to cheat on Father Quinn."

"No!" She's shaking her head, covering her ears, crying again.

"Your dad's scummy, Rhonda. I don't know what's going on in your house, but your dad's a liar, and he's bad, and it's not fair for him to make you ditch me."

She's crying hard now, and I don't know if it's because she knows what I'm saying is true or she thinks I'm crazy or a little of both.

Mr. Haskins hears the noise, and he comes out to investigate. "What's going on out here?" he says in his best authority voice.

"Nothing. A little argument," I say.

"Well knock it off. If you can't get along, either come back inside or go home."

"Okay," I say, really wanting to say "Okay, asshole".

I reach out to hold Rhonda, but she pulls away. "My Dad is right about you. He's always said you were weird, especially since the truck ran over you. He said your Mom was weird too, to steal Father Quinn from the church."

"Hey, that's bullshit! Father Quinn would've quit whether my mom asked him to or not. And so what? At least he had enough guts to admit that he loved her and he did something about it. He didn't ditch her because he was afraid of what people might think." I don't think she catches my sarcasm. She just shakes her head and wipes away her tears.

"I'm sorry, Roger, I really am. But there's nothing I can do. And I don't appreciate you saying those terrible lies about my Dad."

"Does your mom drink?" I ask, knowing the answer and wanting to stab her a little. I thought that asking her would make me feel better, that by knowing a dirty little secret about her family some power would come back to my side, but the sad, crestfallen look on her face only makes me feel worse.

"Fuck you," she whispers. Rhonda doesn't usually cuss, so this hits me like a bullet. She brushes past me, and I get one last delicious whiff of her perfume, and a stray stand of her hair touches my face.

And then I'm alone. The other couples have gone back inside, and I'm by myself in the inky darkness. The music from inside the gym is muted, and I can hear the bass *thump* against the wall. It's strange; hundreds of people are a few feet away, dancing, laughing, having fun, but I feel like I'm on top of a mountain, completely alone, with no hope of ever seeing another human being again. And right now, I don't care if I ever do. It seems that all people do is hurt you, deceive you, lie to you. Fuck them. Fuck them all.

I lean against the wall, hands in my pockets, feeling like a fool. My polyester Sears suit itches; I guess it's not designed to sweat in. I close my eyes and try to stop thinking, try to clear my mind, try to melt into the wall. I hear footsteps. Someone's coming out of the gym. I don't bother to open my eyes, it's probably somebody coming outside to smoke, but the footsteps come my way, and I think, *Shit, it's probably Mr. Haskins, he's gonna kick me out*, and just as I open my eyes, expecting to see the faint outline of his bald head in the darkness, I hear the voice that goes with the footsteps.

"Hey, Roger."

Bushman. Fucker. He's the cause of all my problems. He's humiliated me, beaten me up, taken my girlfriend, everything rotten that's happened to me in the last few years, Bushman's been there. *Fucker.*

"Are you okay, man?" he asks. I'm glad it's dark, I can't see his ugly-ass freckles.

"Having fun with Rhonda?"

"Yeah. Sure," he says, and I'm all the more pissed off. He's too stupid to lie.

"You can have her," I say. "I just hope that someday she stomps on you the way she stomped on me."

"I'm sorry about that, man. I didn't know. Her old man's kinda weird sometimes. But I wouldn't have come with her if I knew she didn't tell you. She told me you guys broke up."

"She lied."

"Sorry. Wanna pray together?"

"What?" My mind's cloudy, I'm only hearing part of what he says. "Pray? What the fuck are you talking about?"

"Jesse told me that prayer in bad times helps. I mean, I never even thought about praying until after, you know, the accident."

I can't take this, Bushman giving me prayer lectures. It's too much, I've been dumped, humiliated, and he's involved, whether he meant it or not, I hate his ass, always will, and he's the one who has to pay.

"Get the fuck outa here, Bushman."

"C'mon, try, Roger." He bows his head. "'Oh most heavenly Father, please give Roger strength to help him—"

I kick Bushman in the balls. His prayer ends in a gaspy "Mmmmphhh!" as he falls to the concrete. I start to walk away, leaving him moaning and writhing, when the anger hits me. It's the white hot, blinding, uncontrollable rage I had way back when I beat up Jesse. I don't think, I just feel, and I kick Bushman and it feels good, *smack*, his head, his side, his head again, *hey, these new boots are pretty good*, I kick him, over and over, it feels so good, something wet spatters my face, is it raining? No, it's blood. Bushman's blood.

And then hurting him suddenly stops feeling good. I come back from the white place, where anger and pain blend together into blind, vicious pleasure, back to the world, back to the dark beside the gym, and I look down at the dim shape of Bushman. He lies still, and it's hard to tell in the dark, but I think blood stains his shirt. I wipe the spatters off my face. Shit, what if I've killed him?

I kneel next to him and roll him over so his freckles face the night sky. "Bushman?" No response. I lean closer and listen. He's breathing, at least.

Now what to do? Go get help? Run inside and get Mr. Haskins, have him call an ambulance, admit that I'm a psycho who tried to kill Bushman, face up to what I've done and live with it? That would be the right thing to do. And all my life I've usually tried to do the right thing. I even start to move toward the gym doors, but then Bushman stirs and groans and I freeze. He's making noise, he's probably not going to die, I must've just stunned him when I was in the white kill zone. Now that I hear him, I get angry again. Hey, let Rhonda take care of him, let her nurse his fucking red-haired ass back to health. He had it coming. They betrayed me, Rhonda did to me what I just did to Bushman—except she did it without laying a hand on me.

No, I'm not going to help him. He's fine, probably better than I was after he jumped me that night of the football game. *It's payback, asshole, how's it feel? I've been down on the ground, too, I've had the shit kicked out of me, too, and you did it. Fun, huh?*

I feel myself sliding back into the scary white anger place, I feel the urge to go attack him all over again, but this time, I use every ounce of willpower I possess, I hold it back, I won't let it take over this time, he's starting to mumble and sit up, so I run over to him, deliver one—just one—last kick with my new boot to the side of his head, I tell myself this is the last time I'll ever do something like this, he "Mmmmphhs!" and crumples back onto the ground, and I run off into the night, exhilarated, horrified, angry, disgusted.

Most of all disgusted.

I hate myself.

I don't know what time it is when I knock on Jesse's door. I don't remember coming over here, I just suddenly realize that I'm standing at the front door to his house and I want to talk to him. No matter what happens to me, it seems like I always want to go back to Jesse; he's the one person I can talk to. Maybe he can make me feel better, if he'll stay away from the "pray to the Virgin" stuff.

I knock again, and I start to wonder how late it is. I don't want to wake everybody up. I'm not sure who's living here at the moment; a big brother or two, some little brothers, maybe a cousin or in-law. At Jesse's house you never know.

I decide that maybe it's not the best idea to be here, and I turn to leave, when the door opens and the porch light clicks on.

"That you, Roger?" asks Aunt Yolanda.

I turn and face her. She's standing in the doorway, bathed in the odd yellow light of the front porch bug light.

"Oh. Hi. Sorry, did I wake you up or something?" I say, surprised at how calm I am talking to her. Aunt Yolanda's been in and out of my life forever, and I'm not afraid of her anymore.

"Nah. Doing some work."

"Looking at the house books?" I ask, pointing at the multiple listing book she's holding.

"Yeah," she says, throwing me a big grin. "Your mom probably does the same thing all the time, huh?"

"I guess real estate's like a religion or something."

Aunt Yolanda smiles. She looks nice tonight. She's wearing a baggy "Brown Power" T-shirt and old sweat pants. Her long, black hair hangs straight far beyond her shoulders, and she's started wearing rimless glasses. She's almost unrecognizable as the over-made-up hard chick I remember from when I was a kid.

Aunt Yolanda's really pretty now; she's older, and she's better. Looking at her, I think that maybe older women are the way to go. I like the way they look lived in, and it seems like maybe they've got their lives figured out better than the girls my age—specifically Rhonda Fairly. It's academic, I guess; I'm fifteen now, and I have a good idea that as far as women are concerned, I'll never have any control. They're like a case of the flu—it just hits you, and you have to deal with it.

"Nice suit," she says, and I can't tell if she's making fun of me or not.

That's always been the way with Aunt Yolanda; she says things with a friendly smirk. "You been playing football in it?" she asks. She's lost most of her *vata* way of speaking, although just now when she said "You" it came out as "Chew". It must be hard to change your speech; I could never sound any different than I do now.

I look down and see that my stiffly creased polyester pants are crinkly and spotted with Bushman's blood. I ripped my tie off and threw it somewhere when I was running around town, and my boots are scuffed and blood-spattered. I look and feel terrible. The marathon running has left me feeling near death all of a sudden.

"I think I'm sick," I say. "Is Jesse here?"

"No. He's out someplace with Lydia. What's wrong with you?"

"I..." Weariness slams me, and my knees buckle. The next thing I know I'm lying on the porch, looking up into the yellow bug light. Aunt Yolanda's concerned face looks down on me.

"Shit, Roger, what's wrong with you, man?!" She sounds Mexican again; it must come out during times of stress.

"I...ran a lot tonight. Tired, I guess."

She helps me back to my feet; my rubber legs barely support me. She leads me into the house, holding my arm, and I wobble to the couch and flop down.

"Jesus, you're shaking," she says as she gently strokes my forehead. "You don't feel like you've got a fever."

"I don't have a fever. I know what's wrong."

"I'll get you some water," she says, and she hurries off into the kitchen. I look around. I've been in this living room a million times; it feels like home. Toys litter the carpet, as always. A new generation of Montoya kids is passing through, leaving it in its perpetual state of disarray. There probably will always be little Montoyas here.

Aunt Yolanda comes back in carrying a glass of water. I take a sip to be polite, then I realize that I'm parched and thirsty. I drain the glass.

"Better?" she asks.

"Yeah. Thanks. Is Mrs. Montoya here? I don't want to wake her up," I say. I've just noticed the wall clock says one-thirty.

"She's asleep. Everybody's asleep or out having fun. Except you and me," she says, that teasing sound in her voice again.

"I thought I'd be having fun tonight, too," I say. "Didn't turn out that way."

"You got girl problems, Roger?" That smirk is still in her voice.

"I feel pretty bad, you know. It's nothing to make fun of, Yo—" I stop. I've never called her anything before.

"You can call me Yolanda. We've known each other for a long time."

"Yolanda." To say her name to her face feels strange. This whole thing feels strange now. Lying on the couch, alone with Aunt Yolanda, having a conversation with her—it's too weird. I'm suddenly aware of all the times I used to beat off while fantasizing about her. I haven't lately, but I still feel stupid and guilty now that I'm here talking to her.

I look into her eyes, and I can't make myself look away. She seems to sense my discomfort, so she looks away and then takes the water glass and sets it over on the top of the TV.

"Feeling better?" she asks.

"Yeah." Maybe I should talk to her. "You're right. It is a girl."

"I know. Whenever a guy's upset, that's usually why. We love to make your lives miserable. It's what we do best. Want some more water?"

"No, thanks." I sit up. My head's still pounding, but my lungs feel like they're starting to work again. I don't think my legs will carry me anywhere for awhile, though.

"So what'd this girl do to you, Roger?"

"She dumped me."

"Mmmm. White girl?"

"Yeah."

"That's your mistake. You should've gone for a beautiful brown girl, Rog. Not a nasty little white girl. Brown's the way to go. Like maybe a young version of me."

"You're not old." I don't know why that came out so quickly, but I'm glad I said it, because she smiles and tilts her head in a way that looks good.

Really good.

"Oooh, broken heart but you still know how to flatter. No wonder I always liked you."

She's teasing me again, and I feel stupid. She sits next to me on the couch; closer than I would've sat. I read someplace that everybody has a personal comfort zone, that we feel uncomfortable if somebody invades our space without permission. She's invaded my space—our arms are touching—but I don't mind. Not at all, actually.

"So. Tell me what your little white girl did to you." She's looking at me, her face close to mine, almost leaning against me. I see my reflection in her glasses. Maybe it's just because of the curvature of the lenses, but I look like shit. I hope it's an optical thing, but I have a bad feeling that I really *do* look that bad.

"Well?" she asks.

So I tell her. Everything. I go all the way back to grade school, Dad's funeral and that first kiss, Bushman kicking my ass and me kicking his.

I talk for an hour. She listens, nods, occasionally asks a question, but most of all she's just there, listening to me tell my pathetic little tale of being in love with Rhonda. As I get to the end of the story, I realize something about Rhonda: she's weak and she's shallow. I was head-over-heels in love, but she wasn't, and when she had to make a choice, instead of treating me right, instead of being decent and kind, she tossed me away like a snot-filled Kleenex and went back to the new, improved, holy-fucking-Bushman. Bitch.

By the time I finish I'm completely spent. I must look like the guys on the team look after they've survived a tough practice and half an hour of wind sprints.

"You think you've had a tough time, huh, Roger?"

I shrug. "Yeah. I guess."

"Maybe you have. Gettin' run over was probably no fun. But this girl treating you like this, that's just life. It feels bad when it happens, but you'll get over it."

"I probably shouldn't have tried to kill Bushman, though. That might've been the wrong thing to do." Talking about what I did to him made me feel guilty. That and the dried blood on my pants.

"Forget about it. The *cabron* had it coming."

I'm liking Aunt Yolanda more and more. She reaches over and takes my hand. It startles me, and I jump. "What're you afraid of, Roger?" she laughs.

"Nothing." I pull my hand back and glance at the clock. "Shit! It's almost three, I've gotta call home, my mom's probably going crazy."

"Tell her you're staying here tonight. It's so late and all."

There's a strange sound in her voice. But I guess it makes sense. I've stayed over here plenty of times before. I call Mom, and she's berserk at first that I haven't called sooner, but I finally get her to calm down, and she's glad I'm staying here. By the time I get off the phone, Aunt Yolanda's lying on the couch, watching me with a sly, sleepy smile.

"All these women in your life makin' you feel bad, cheating little white girlfriends, worried moms..."

"Where's Jesse?" I ask, realizing he should be back by now.

"He won't be back tonight. He and Lydia stay out together a lot lately."

"They do?"

"I thought he was your best friend. Don't you know what's going on?"

"I guess not."

"I know how it works. He'll probably be a daddy soon. *Pendejo* won't listen to me, though."

Wow. Jesse's having sex with Lydia and he hasn't told me? This is huge, this is the news of a lifetime, what we've been talking about and dreaming about forever, and he's doing it and I didn't know? I feel betrayed.

"I'm tired." Aunt Yolanda gets up and turns off the light. "C'mon."

I follow her into the hall, expecting her to point me into Jesse's room. I figure she'll say, "He's not here, just use his bed." But she doesn't. She stops in the hallway, and I almost crash into her. She holds her finger up to her lips, makes a "Ssshhh" sound, then takes my hand and leads me into—her bedroom.

She silently closes the door, then turns to face me. My heart starts to pound, but I don't know what I'm afraid of, she's not going to do anything.

She pulls off her T-shirt. She's not wearing anything underneath, and her large, brown breasts are close enough to touch. Shit, the wet dream of a lifetime, only this time it's real. I stand like a dope, staring at her tits. I can't not look at them. They're better than any fantasy I've had, or any Playboy foldout I've flogged to. I'm light-headed, and I realize I've stopped breathing. I gasp, and look up at Aunt Yolanda. I expect her to be smiling—or smirking—at me, but she's not. She's watching me closely, her lips tight, with a strange expression I can't read.

"You like?" she asks quietly.

Do I like? What, is she nuts?! Like—love, want, *ohmygod I gotta touch those*— I look back down. "Yeah," I mumble, my voice thick and heavy.

She moves toward me and takes my hand. She slowly puts my hand on her breast. "Go ahead, do what you want," she whispers. I stand there, my palm over the front of her breast, and I don't know what to do. Should I squeeze it? Rub it? Do nothing?

It's soft, so soft, and warm, and I feel her nipple harden under my touch. I give it a mild squeeze, and Aunt Yolanda's eyes widen slightly and her lips part. A hard-on sprouts in my polyester pants, and I'm starting to like this so much I grab her other breast with my other hand. She smiles.

"You *do* like, don't you?"

"They're beautiful." Stupid thing to say, but it's true.

"Go ahead, do whatever you want..." She stands close to me, and she closes her eyes. I can't believe it, but she seems to be enjoying it. A beautiful woman is letting me squeeze her tits and she's enjoying it!

I've died and gone to heaven.

"Kiss them," she orders, and I eagerly obey. God, it's better than I can believe. I'm starting to go crazy, I kiss and lick them, gently bite the long, brown nipples, Aunt Yolanda moans softly, I bury my head between them—

And then Aunt Yolanda grabs my hands, pulls them to her butt, and slides them inside her sweat pants. I get bold, and I push her sweat pants down, then her panties, and she doesn't object, now she's naked against me, I'm rubbing her ass, it's so smooth and nice, and I look down and see the black hair between her legs and I'm just about out of my mind—

Then she steps back, steps out of the sweatpants, she stands, naked in front of me, she looks down at the telltale bulge in my Sears polyester pants, and she reaches over and unbuckles my belt.

"Not all women are bad, Roger," she says, smiling. "I'll make you forget about that little *puta.* She don't know what she's missing."

As Aunt Yolanda pulls down my pants, I close my eyes and try to forget about Rhonda. About how much she hurt and betrayed me.

Slowly, as Aunt Yolanda works on me, I *do* forget Rhonda, and the only thing I can think of is how good this feels and how I hope it never stops.

Chapter Sixteen

The 747 bounces on sharp turbulence and thumps my head against the headrest. I feel like I've been stuffed inside this roaring thing for a year. I've only flown a few times before, and they were short trips from L.A. to San Francisco with my parents; this twelve hour marathon from L.A. to London is sheer torture.

Jesse snores in the seat next to me, his mouth hanging open, a drool cord dangling onto his T-shirt. The ever-present sunglasses have slid down his nose, and the hard white scars around his eyes stand out against his brown skin.

We're in the very last row of the giant plane, right in front of the toilets. Every few minutes annoying kids or fat people totter down the aisle, desperate to pee, and seem to always lose their balance right when they get to my seat. They tip, bang against me, grab my seat to stay upright, and then don't bother to say, "Excuse me." Besides that, it's noisy, hot, cramped and the dinner they served us stunk.

I hate flying.

It's dark out now, and I assume we're somewhere over the Atlantic. We've still got a few hours before we get to London, and most of the passengers seem to be asleep. I don't know how they do it. When the stewardesses turned down the cabin lights and tried to fool everybody into sleeping, I figured, *yeah, right*, as if three hundred people can pretend it's really bedtime while stuffed into a noisy aluminum tube. But it seems that many can, and as I look around I see that I'm one of the few losers who's awake.

Every time I look over at Jesse and see how peaceful and comfortable he looks, curled up and cozy against the window with the tiny airline pillow and thin blanket, I get annoyed. As usual, what's hard for me is easy for Jesse.

I stare out the window, past Jesse's drooling face, into the darkness beyond. It's scary, to be here, not knowing where we are, bouncing through the night, headed for something I really don't want to do. But here I am, it's July 1972, and I'm on my way to Europe with Jesse.

Lourdes, actually.

Last summer at this time, when we were working at the housing tract and Jesse yammered his bullshit about saving the money to go to Lourdes to be cured, I'd blown him off and paid little attention. There's no way, I'd thought, that I was going to use the money I saved for a car to fly to Europe for something stupid like this.

And yet, a year later, I'm sitting on a Pan Am 747, heading for a bogus religious place with a deluded messiah looking for a cure.

Last fall, after the homecoming dance from hell, I'd settled into a dull routine of school, home, and occasionally hanging out with Jesse. Rhonda—when I saw her—refused to acknowledge my existence, and Bushman just plain avoided me. If he saw me walking down the hall, he'd turn and scurry away. He didn't even ask me to forgive him anymore. I don't know if he ever told anybody what I'd done to him, but I think Rhonda knew. The few times we made eye contact she looked at me as if she hated me. Strange. She's the empty one, she's the one who squashed my heart, but *I'm* the bad guy in her mind. I'm still amazed that she could've dropped me the way she did; I'll never forget it.

The only bright spot during that time was what happened with Aunt Yolanda the night of the dance. Wow. I still beat off to it. I'd hoped that she might invite me back, that maybe what happened that night wasn't a flukey one shot deal. That would've been fine with me.

But no. I started hanging around Jesse's house a lot more, almost as much as when we were kids, but Aunt Yolanda was merely pleasant and distant, and she never mentioned what we'd done that night. After a few weeks, I realized that she'd only done what she did out of pity. What I've heard guys call a "sympathy fuck." It was nice of her, I guess. But when I saw that it wasn't going to happen again, there wasn't a whole lot left in my life to look forward to.

So school and life went on. I finished out the season being team manager—we didn't get into the playoffs, mostly because our defense sucked. If Jesse hadn't been kicked off the team, a lot of people thought we would've had a good chance. Instead, we went 4-5 and ended the season in disinterest.

Once football was over there wasn't much for me to do. Jesse and Lydia were like Siamese twins; every time I dropped by his house to see if Aunt Yolanda was interested in doing anything for me, Lydia was there. I started to feel like I was getting in the way. They were cool about me hanging around, and Jesse always seemed happy to see me, but I could tell that they wanted to be alone together—and that Roger was a friendly pest.

But the biggest surprise happened during Christmas vacation. It was the down time between Christmas and New Years, when the fun part of vacation is over and you're starting to dread going back to school, that I knew Jesse's life was growing apart from mine, and that I'd never understand him.

I wandered over on an unusually cold afternoon. It had snowed up on the mountains the night before, and we had an alpine-looking backdrop to our normally hot, smoggy town. As I walked down the street to Jesse's house—I'd gone over hoping to sniff around Aunt Yolanda again (I was starting to feel like a male dog who's always butt-sniffing)—I saw a couple of lowriders parked in front. Not that unusual, considering all the people who came and went from the Montoya house, but these lowriders I recognized. The blue Impala with *Baby I'm For Real* stenciled on the back window was Danny Robledo's. I'd heard he was out of the hospital, but he hadn't put in an appearance at school before vacation.

I was tempted to turn around and leave, because I had a feeling it might be weird or dangerous, but my curiosity got the better of me, so I went ahead and rang the doorbell.

Jesse's brother Mando opened the door. He looked like he just woke up, his long hair was matted and his eyes red-rimmed. He just gave me a silent head nod and walked away. I'll never figure the guy out. Sometimes he seemed human, others he was just a nameless hard-guy. He might've been stoned most of the time, I'm not sure.

So I went inside, hoping Aunt Yolanda was around, but she must've been out working. In the living room I found Jesse, Robledo, Lydia, and a bunch of Robledo's lowrider *vato locos*. Wisma was there too, looking confused and ill at ease. Jesse was sitting on the couch, and all the *vatos*, their Pendletons creased to perfection, were sitting on the floor at Jesse's feet.

Robledo's jaw was wired shut. His lips parted in an unnatural grimace, and his cheeks were still swollen, like somebody recovering from the mumps.

Robledo watched Jesse, his black eyes boring into Jesse's sunglasses with an intensity that was scary. I wondered if he was going to try to kill Jesse. But then I listened to what Jesse was saying.

"...And the Virgin, if you pray to Her, ask Her for shit, She'll help you out, man...." And then Jesse seamlessly lapsed into Spanish, talked for awhile, popped back into English, and went on like that, going back and forth between languages for no apparent reason, for the next half hour.

These were the hard-ass *vatos*, the scariest guys at school, gathered around listening to Jesse preach, and they acted like they were paying attention.

I couldn't believe it.

"That you, Roger?" Jesse asked when he reached the end of his mostly incoherent sermon. At least it seemed incoherent to me.

"Yeah."

Robledo looked over at me, and my guts flopped. The guy had the most intimidating stare in the world. He reminded me of boxers at weigh-in, where they try to stare each other down. I immediately looked away.

"Roger's not a believer," Jesse said. "Yet."

"How come you don't believe, *ese*?" one of the lowriders asked. All eyes turned to me. I looked to Lydia for help, but she just smiled.

"Sometimes it's hard to believe in shit, even if you're right there being part of it, huh, Roger?" Jesse said. "See, you guys, you didn't believe in what I was sayin' at first, you even fucked with me, then when Danny saw, you all saw, too. Roger, he never had to try to believe, it was part of him, but he don't want to see that. He's turned his back on it, man."

Robledo jumped up and came at me. I knew I was a dead man, I flinched and backed away, but he just kept on coming. He got right into my face and thumped my chest with his finger.

"Youshouldfuckin'listentohim, *cabron*!" he hissed through his wired-shut teeth. "Don'tbeno*pendejo*!"

"Don't waste your time, Danny," Jesse grinned. He was in his superior Buddha mode, and it pissed me off. "Roger won't believe until he has proof.

Like that dude in the bible...wouldn't believe Jesus was around until he could stick his finger in the spear hole."

"Thomas," Lydia said. "That's why they say somebody's a doubting Thomas."

"Help me out, Lydia," I said, panicked. "You don't believe that Jesse's got a direct line to God, either."

Lydia shrugged. "Maybe. He's pretty convincing though. If you really listen to him."

Shit. Another ally lost. Robledo stood in front of me, breathing heavily, trying to stare me into belief.

"I'll get Roger to believe in me," Jesse said. "He just needs his proof. That's why we're going to get him cured this summer. In Lourdes."

"I'm not going with you!" I said. Shit, all I wanted was to see if Aunt Yolanda was around, all I wanted was another sympathy fuck. I didn't realize I'd get sucked into one of Jesse's warped theological sessions.

But he was right. In the end I did give in about going to Lourdes, and I'm still not sure why. Maybe because, deep down, even though I don't believe in God or miracles, I'm still *hoping* for a miracle. I want the scars to go away, I want to walk and run like everybody else, I want to look normal again. I'm not a monster, but I'm different enough that it bugs me, and I've hated every minute of being different. So yeah, Jesse conned me, and I spent seven hundred bucks to fly to Europe with him to look for a miracle that I'm pretty sure won't happen.

Jesse came over to my house with Lydia one night last spring. Mom had invited them for dinner, because she'd never met Lydia, and she wanted to check her out.

"Jesse's been Roger's best friend since grammar school," she told Father Quinn. "I feel like I'm his second mother. And I haven't even met this girl he's been dating for so long."

"Then let's have a barbecue!" Father Quinn said. He had become such a happy suburbia guy that it was hard to remember he was ever a priest. He lived for barbecues and yard work. He was Dad reincarnated.

Jesse and Lydia showed up, and things quickly seemed weird. It was like they were friends of Mom and Father Quinn, not me. They visited and chatted easily, and I found myself envious at their easy social calm. When I was around most adults I clammed up. I figured they weren't interested in anything I had to say—and they usually weren't—and somehow, talking to adults struck me as unnatural. They were the people in charge, the ones who ruled my life, always telling me what to do and when to do it, so having a pleasant conversation with one of them seemed like consorting with the enemy.

But here were Jesse and Lydia, friendly as could be, sipping Cokes while Mom and Father Quinn nursed their cocktails, and I sat off to the side, silent and sulky.

It was then, while I sat there, semi-pouting, that I realized what an asshole I was. I tried to imagine how I looked to other people. Not just scarred and gimpy, but whiny, a pouter. I wondered how I got this way. I think I was a pretty normal little kid, at least until Joe Fanucci ran over me. That was the big change. After that, once I'd become different than everybody else, I changed. I decided that I'd have to work on it, I'd have to force myself to be more social, friendlier, less of a jerk. Nobody likes a jerk.

"Lydia's pregnant," I heard Jesse say, and that snapped me back into the present. Father Quinn was in mid-sip of scotch, and he started to cough and gag.

"Excuse me?" Mom said. She kept her smile glued on, like she always did when something unmentionable was mentioned. She made me proud.

"Yep. I'm gonna be a dad," Jesse said proudly, putting his arm around

Lydia. Lydia smiled, but it was hard to tell if it was genuine or forced.

"Well, have you talked to anyone about it?" Father Quinn asked, always the counselor.

"Nope. You're the first ones we've told. We're pretty happy, you know?" Jesse looked over at me. I smiled and shrugged, even though I knew he couldn't see it. But he smiled back in that odd way of his, like he'd heard my lips move over my teeth. A blind guy who saw things. It unnerved me every time.

"What will you do?" Mom asked. "Adoption?"

"I'm going to keep it," Lydia said softly.

"You're only fifteen, it could start your life off in the wrong direction," Father Quinn said. "I've seen it happen lots of times, young girls having babies, and they end up poor and unhappy. It's not a good situation for anybody."

"It won't be that way with us," Jesse said with a touch of defiance. "We're different."

"Kids always think that, honey," Mom said. "And they're usually wrong. Especially you, Jesse, how can you help support this baby? I mean, since you're blind."

"I won't be for long," Jesse said. "I'll be seeing 20/20 by the end of summer."

"How?" Father Quinn asked.

"Me and Roger are going to Lourdes. The Virgin will cure both of us."

Mom and Father Quinn just looked at each other. I felt like I was falling into a spinning blade, about to be chopped into tiny little pieces. Dragged along with Jesse Montoya again.

"I'm not going anywhere," I mumbled, but nobody seemed to hear me.

Mom and Father Quinn were upset about Jesse and Lydia's baby, and they spent the next few weeks worrying about it. Father Quinn went over and talked to Jesse's mom, and though she was upset, she had the attitude that *hey, it happened, they'll have to deal with it.* That made good sense to me. Father Quinn, being an old priest and counselor, wanted to stick his nose into everybody's business and fix everything. Sometimes you just had to let things happen. Mrs. Montoya understood that; she'd seen lots of life, good and bad, but she never let it get her down. She always seemed upbeat and happy, no matter what stupid things somebody in her family did. She never judged anybody; she just welcomed them, hugged them, fed them lots of great food, and loved them unconditionally.

With Jesse and Lydia so tight and preparing to be mom and dad, I didn't see them much the rest of the school year. I gave up going over to his house hoping that Aunt Yolanda might have mercy on my horny soul. She was pleasant and polite, but it was obvious nothing would ever happen. So I spent a lot of time alone, long afternoons at home reading books or watching the tube, not really doing a whole lot of anything. I'd spend hours out in the back yard, letting the warm afternoon breeze bathe me in smoggy bliss, and sometimes I'd smoke pot that I'd started buying from the dopers at school.

I can't say I really enjoyed getting stoned, but it was something to do. The serious dopers devoted their lives to the pursuit of great highs, and it seemed like a waste of time to me. They floated around, with their long, greasy hair and tie-dyed shirts, patched bellbottoms, saggy butts, communicating in incoherent grunts and mumbles about great the Columbian shit they scored or trading brightly colored pills like marbles.

I wasn't interested in that. When I smoked, I was always alone, and always bored. I'd get a buzz and sit outside, close my eyes and listen to birds and bugs and distant traffic. Sometimes I'd think about Rhonda, and with the pot haze I could daydream without the anger I usually had when she came to mind. I'd picture us together again, I'd remember those lunchtimes sitting out by the fence, the smell of orange blossoms, we'd laugh and kiss and hold hands, and I'd ache with the memory. I'd go light another joint to soothe the pain, and it would soothe it a little bit, but the daydream would always leave me sad no matter how much I smoked. I don't know why, but I kept doing it, kept thinking about Rhonda, kept torturing myself with memories. I tried to tell myself it was stupid, just juvenile nonsense, I was only fifteen, we wouldn't have stayed together anyway, but no matter how much I tried to convince myself it was no big deal, I couldn't make the pain and humiliation go away.

I was outside one Friday afternoon, stoned and basking in the warm springtime sun, when Jesse and Lydia came by. I wasn't in the mood to talk; I'd gotten used to my afternoon stoned alone time, and I was annoyed they'd disrupted it. I was even more irritated when Jesse started talking.

"We gotta go get our tickets, man," he said.

"No."

"You want to be cured, don't you?"

"It's all bullshit, there's no cures. There's not even a God, you *pendejo*." It felt good to call him a *pendejo*; I never would have said it if I weren't stoned.

But it rolled right off him. "We can get there for seven hundred bucks. L.A. to London, London to Paris, then a train down to Lourdes. Seven hundred bucks to be cured. That and a little faith...not a bad deal, Rog."

I looked at Lydia. "Tell him he's fucking crazy, would you?"

"What if he isn't?" she said. I'd forgotten; she was on his side now.

"No. Go get healed if you want. Count me out. It's bullshit." I was sounding kind of one-note, but at least I was being firm for a change.

"You wanna be a crippled loser the rest of your life?" Jesse asked.

I thought that was unnecessarily harsh, even through my pot haze. "Fuck you," I mumbled.

"Maybe you guys could go down to Guadalupe. The Virgin appeared there, too, and it's closer," Lydia said, trying to be helpful.

"Not the same," Jesse said. "Lourdes is the place for cures."

"I don't care where you go," I said, closing my eyes and trying to ignore them. I wanted to get back into that calm, warm, lazy place; stoned in the sun. "See you," I said, assuming that would make them leave.

Jesse didn't take the hint. He moved closer to me, and he leaned between my face and the sun. I had no choice but to open my eyes. His face was inches from mine. His mouth was twitching strangely, and his expression was pained. Afraid. I'd never seen that before. And then, to top it off, a tear rolled out from underneath his sunglasses and trickled down his cheek.

"I fuckin' need you to go, man," he whispered. "I can't take this blind shit no more."

I was stunned. I thought he'd taken everything in stride. The fucker had been lying all this time. He was as scared and screwed up about life as I was. I should have found it comforting, I guess, but I didn't. It was just another example that proved to me that everybody's faking it, that you can't believe anything. *Thanks, Jesse, you just made me even more cynical.*

"Can't Lydia go with you?" I asked, trying to be gentle. I had enough class to realize now wasn't the time to go after him.

"She can't afford it. Besides, you're part of the deal, you know? The Virgin always included you, man, you were around when I talked to Her. There's no cure without you, and I don't think She'll talk to me again unless you're there."

"Jesse—"

"Please. It's the last favor I ever ask, man. But have some *cajones* and try...what if *you* get cured, too? Seven hundred bucks...seems worth it to me."

I stared at my reflection in his sunglasses. My scars looked thick and angry, and my eyes were red. I had the vacant look of a stupid doper. Shit, what was I becoming?

"When do you want to go?" I asked.

"I was thinking July."

"Fine. Okay."

The momentary fear and uncertainty on his face disappeared, and he grinned broadly. Got his way again.

Mom and Father Quinn were reluctant at first; they thought I was too young to be running around Europe with Jesse—by July I'd be 16—and they were afraid I'd get my hopes up about a cure.

"I'm only doing this for Jesse," I told them. "I don't believe in miracles."

"Well, honey," Mom said, forever the true believer, "miracles do happen sometimes. It's just that you can't count on them to happen when you want them."

I looked at Father Quinn, and he said nothing. But he smiled and I knew he was with me. As time had passed I think he'd become more and more of a disbeliever in anything religious.

In the end, they reluctantly agreed to let me go, and so, early on this foggy July morning, we drove down to LAX.

I was excited in spite of myself. To walk through the international terminal and know I was going overseas! It was pretty cool. I pulled my passport out of my crispy new Levi's pocket and touched the dark green cover; it reassured me, made me feel special and grown-up, to see the seal of the U.S. on the cover, and open it up and see a goofy black-and-white picture of me inside. My own passport. What a man. I slipped it back into my pocket as we walked up to the Pan Am counter.

Mom looked ready to cry, as usual. Anything new or strange, or anything that reminded her that her kids were growing up, made her cry. Since we'd lost contact with Mary Frances at the nut-convent, I was Mom's only maternal target. She may have cried occasionally at the thought of Mary Frances deserting us, but she'd done a good job of redirecting all her Mom energy at me.

Father Quinn chattered all the way to the airport, reminiscing about the time he went to Rome when he was in the seminary. His stories were boring—how exciting can a seminarian's vacation be?—but we listened politely. Jesse sat quietly with me in the back seat, pretending to stare out the window through his blind eyes. His unusual silence didn't surprise me. He hadn't said much in the weeks leading up to the trip, retreating into a strange, holy silence, but he and Lydia had a noisy, gooey farewell this morning at his house, and I overheard him tell her he was excited, and that in a week he'd be *seeing* her. He said "seeing" with such force that it startled everyone, and Lydia started to cry. Her belly was swelling with their kid—I was still trying to get used to *that* idea—and I hoped crying wouldn't make something bad happen. She whispered, "Take care of him" to me as we got in the car, and I smiled and reassured her that I would.

I wasn't sure what I'd do when he wasn't cured—because I was sure he wouldn't be—but I'd worry about that when it happened. This was his idea, and if his dreams didn't turn out, it was his own fault. He was a big boy now, and he had to learn to deal with disappointments. I think I had him beat in that regard. I'd had a lot of disappointments in my sixteen years; I was getting talented at living with them.

We got all checked in, then set off to the gate. We passed through a long, underground tunnel, then rode an escalator up to the departure gates. The giant Pan Am 747 loomed outside. As soon as Mom saw it she began to cry.

"Jeez, Mom, it's just a plane," I said, embarrassed that people in the waiting area were staring at her.

"You're so young...." she sniffled, and Father Quinn hugged her. She dribbled and sniffed for the rest of the time we waited, and I was glad when we finally boarded to get away from her. The way she was acting, it seemed like she was sure the plane would crash into the ocean or something.

Now, sitting here, waiting for the sun to rise, I wonder what I'm getting into. I'm excited to be on my own, going on a long trip without the long shadow of parents lurking over me, but I also have a vague feeling of dread. Like a dream that's going along okay, but then the lights go out and a hand reaches out and grabs your shoulder and pulls you down, and all you can do is scream and hope you wake up before you hit the bottom.

I guess that's more than a vague fear; I wish I knew what I'm afraid of. A cure? Or a lack of a cure? I know nothing will happen for me, since I don't have faith. But I wonder about Jesse. What will he do when his Virgin hallucinations don't pan out? If Jesse loses his faith, I'm afraid he could crash hard, and I don't know if I could catch him.

I look out the plane's window, past Jesse's snoring head. A rim of orange light glows on the horizon, and I can see land far off over the shimmering ocean. The sunrise cleanses me, makes me feel safe again. Sculpted clouds glow orange as the sun quickly rises, and the sudden, blinding light warms me. Jesse senses it, too, and begins to stir, coughing and gurgling back into consciousness.

With the new morning I feel happy, and I don't know why.

"We almost there?" Jesse asks, his voice thick with sleep.

"Yeah. It's morning, man."

He leans against the window for a moment, and the plane thumps on a wave of turbulence. "Sun. It's warm," Jesse says. "I'll see Her soon."

"Who?"

"The Virgin, man," he says with a dreamy smile.

And as he says that, all the good morning warmth drains out of me, and I feel cold and cramped, bumping over the Atlantic ocean, on the way to a place I know is a lie.

We change planes in London, catch a quick flight to Paris, then get on a train headed for Lourdes. My body, unused to the stresses of travel, is exhausted and constipated. I'm not one of those lucky people who can sleep anywhere, especially in something that's moving. I envy people like Jesse who can instantly drift off in a bouncing plane, or an airport terminal, or any non-bed kind of place. For some reason I have to stay awake, see what's going on, no matter that my exhaustion is turning my brain to mud, I still have to keep an eye on things. I think it's because I don't trust anybody or anything; if I stay awake, watching, nothing bad can be done to me. Weird, but that's the way I am.

By the time we get to Lourdes, after a long, clackety-clack train ride through the nighttime French countryside (somehow we've lost another day during travel; I'm not quite sure how), I'm so miserably tired that I don't care what happens to me.

"I can feel *Her*," Jesse says as we get off the train. I'm lugging my duffel bag and trying to guide Jesse so that he doesn't tumble off the train. I'm so tired I can barely make my legs do what my brain orders.

"Who?" I ask.

"The Virgin."

"Right."

Jesse gets off the train with no trouble; I'm the one who trips and falls on his stupid, klutzy face.

"You okay?" Jesse asks.

Luckily I fell on my duffel bag. "Yeah, fine." I get up, embarrassed, as people around me jabber in a dozen languages. As I'm getting up, I realize that many of the people on the train are messed up. Some are on crutches, some are skinny and cancerous looking, others have scars, injuries, weird rashes, you name it.

All of the sick ones look worse than me, and I feel guilty. I complain and moan about how unfair things are, but I'm surrounded by people who are sicker or more injured than I am, and they all seem happy and excited. I decide it's because they're like Jesse: they believe. Morons. They'll be getting back on this train in a few days, still sick or disfigured. We'll see how happy they are then.

We leave the train station and walk through the town, following the directions we were given, toward our hostel. It's early morning, and low gray clouds hang over the valley. Cool, misty air bathes my face.

"What's it like, man?" Jesse asks. "It smells good here."

I look around. Low, forested hills surround the town, and the *Gave de Pau* winds through the small valley. We walk along the river, and I look at the buildings of the town. It's clean and pretty, and unlike anything I've ever seen in Southern California. It's...old. That's the difference. You can feel the centuries of habitation, and especially the last hundred years of faithful sick people coming here looking for miracles.

We pass by narrow streets, cluttered with stores selling Lourdes memorabilia: Virgin Mary water bottles to store your miracle water; plastic Virgin statues surrounded by blinking lights; Bernadette biographies in every language you can imagine. It's early now, and none of the stores are open yet, and the streets are mostly deserted, but I can imagine how it must be once all the faithful crowd into these same narrow streets, headed down to the grotto to see the Virgin and get their miracle.

"What's it like, Roger? You awake, man?" Jesse asks again.

"It's...hard to explain. It's really pretty. Kind of like something you'd see in a movie or something." That's it. Lourdes is like a big pretend movie set. "I don't think they have smog here," I add, and Jesse laughs.

Dotting the hills are larger hotels, much newer than the rest of the town. I guess they cater to the richer pilgrims—or just plain tourists who drop by the town to see what it's all about. I get a strange feeling here, of the combination and collision of the spiritual and business. I found a book in the library about Lourdes, and Jesse insisted I read it to him before we came. The guy who wrote it had the same feeling, that the souvenir stores selling plastic glow-in-the-dark Virgin Marys and all the other cheesy junk profane the mystical holiness of what supposedly happened here.

Maybe. But the so-called miracle of Bernadette's visions and the holy springwater and miracles and all the rest are pretty cheesy on their own, if you ask me. And the people who make a living selling all this crap aren't forcing anybody to buy it. They're providing a service.

We finally find our hostel, tucked away on a small side alleyway. Window boxes filled with cascading red geraniums greet us, and the small, whitewashed building, stuck between a souvenir shop and a cafe, is pretty and inviting. I like the way everything is different here than what I'm used to at home.

We go inside. The lobby is a bare, white room, with only two things hanging on the walls: a large iron crucifix and an overly holy and somewhat creepy watercolor of a hovering Mary floating above Bernadette in the grotto. The picture is weird and off-putting; it looks like something out of a Star Trek episode. I expect to see Captain Kirk and Spock lurking behind the rocks, their phasers set on stun.

I ring the bell at the counter.

"Hope it's not too early," I say to Jesse. I'd feel bad if our arrival makes somebody get out of bed. Bed. The thought of the word reminds me that I'm just about ready to die. All I want to do is sleep.

I'm about to ring the bell again, when a girl comes out to the desk. She's tall and thin, with pale, almost translucent skin. She's wearing kind of a funny-looking blue jumper thing and a strange white hat. At first I think she might be a nurse, but then I realize: she's a baby nun.

She's about our age, and plain looking. Until she smiles. Her sharp, pale features are transformed by the simple act of a smile. When she smiles, she's beautiful.

She says something in French. Such a strange language; it sounds like people have a cleft palate when they speak it.

"We don't speak French," I say, slowly and too loud, like she's deaf. "Do you speak English? Or Spanish?"

She laughs again. "Which would you prefer?" she says in perfect English.

"*Espanol*," Jesse says, and she rattles off a response so fast I can't catch a word of it.

"You have a weird accent," Jesse says when she's finished.

"No, you do!" she says, and she laughs again. We've got to keep her smiling; it's wonderful.

"How many languages do you speak?" I ask.

"Only four. English, French, Spanish and German. I can get by in Italian and Dutch, too."

"Wow. What are you?"

She looks at me, puzzled. "A girl?" she says.

"No, no, I mean like French, English, whatever."

"Spanish and Polish. I grew up in a convent, this is where I learned to speak so many languages." Her English is almost perfect, but she speaks with an odd cadence, probably the result of having so many different words for the same things floating around in her brain.

"You are staying here?" she asks.

"Yeah." I give her the reservation confirmation slip and she gives us the key to our room.

"Follow me," she says, still smiling that great smile. "You are here to ask Our Lady for cures?" she asks as we climb the squeaky stairway to the third floor.

"Cures? You think there's something wrong with us?" Jesse asks, grinning, as I lead his blind ass up the stairs.

She stops and blushes, irresistibly cute. "Oh, I'm sorry, I thought—"

"It's okay. Jesse's just messing with you," I say, and she looks blankly at me. I realize she doesn't understand what "messing" means. "He's teasing you."

Her smile reappears, relieved that she hasn't hurt our feelings.

She opens the door to our room and leads us in. It's bare, except for a big crucifix on the wall, a couple of beds, and a rickety desk. I hear the roar of plumbing down the hall.

"The WC is at the end of the hall," she says. "Dinner is downstairs at seven."

"What's a WC?" I ask.

She looks down, a small blush staining her cheeks. "Toilet?"

"Oh, yeah, sure. Thanks," I say.

She nods and goes out the door. "I hope the Virgin helps you. I'll pray for you."

"What's your name?" Jesse asks.

"Maria." She closes the door, and the room is now sterile and cold without her smile.

"Figures," Jesse says. "Probably Maria Teresa name-a-saint...just like a Mexican."

"She's cute, man," I say, wishing she'd come back. "Except she's gonna be a nun."

"You can make her change her mind. You're a stud," Jesse laughs as he feels his way to one of the beds and lies down on it. "I gotta sleep." And within a few minutes he's snoring softly.

I take off my shoes and lie down. The bed is hard and lumpy. I stare up at the cracked ceiling, then glance over at the window. The red geraniums outside are the only colorful things I can see.

I want desperately to doze off, but I'm so exhausted that I'm too tired to sleep. All I can do is lie here, staring at the ceiling, listening to Jesse's gurgles and snores. He slept the whole way here, I can't imagine that he'd be tired now.

My mind wanders, and I begin to wonder what I'm doing here. This is nuts. Yeah, okay, so it's nuts. I'm only sixteen, when you're sixteen you do crazy things. I decide I'll just try to enjoy it, like a trip to a museum I'm not interested in, but I'll make the effort, and observe the goings-on with the detachment of a hardened newspaper reporter or professional skeptic.

Maria the baby nun makes things more interesting, too.

After a long while I finally drift off to sleep thinking of her smile.

I awaken with a start. *The smell, the air, the feel—where am I?*

A momentary wave of panic floods through me, I'm disoriented and dizzy, I lurch up in bed. I see the red geraniums outside the window, and I remember. Lourdes. Miracles. Cute baby nuns.

I run my hands through my hair; it's wet and nappy. I must've drooled and slept in a spit puddle. My head is cloudy, and I have that awful groggy sensation I get when I take a nap in the afternoon. I don't see how people can enjoy naps; I always feel afterwards like I've been slammed with a two-by-four and run over by a truck.

Bad choice of words. I know what it really feels like to be run over by a truck. This is unpleasant, but nothing like that.

Jesse's kneeling by his bed, deep in prayer. I haven't seen him do this in a long time, and I wonder if he's in one of his self-induced miracle chatting-with-the-Virgin psycho sessions.

"You're awake finally," he says, and I'm relieved he's just doing run-of-the-mill praying.

"Yeah. I was tired, man. Mary beam down yet?"

"Fuck you, Roger. And no. She hasn't talked to me yet. But She will. I can tell. She's nearby."

I roll my eyes, but the effect is lost if the person you're eye-rolling is blind.

"I'm hungry," I say, and my stomach growls on cue.

"This isn't going to work if you don't cooperate, man," Jesse says, still kneeling with his hands folded in prayer.

"I'm here, isn't that enough? You didn't tell me there was other stuff."

"There aren't miracles without faith."

"You've got plenty of faith. You got extra. You got mine."

Jesse bows his head, like he's saying the name of Jesus. The nuns back in grammar school taught us to always bow our heads when we said the name of Jesus. I stopped doing it a long time ago, but I've noticed that sometimes, even when I'm cussing and a "Jesus" pops out, my head involuntarily nods.

"'Amen'," he murmurs, and he gets up and sits on the bed. "It won't work if you don't help," he says, sounding miserable.

"I can only do what I can do, Jesse. I can't believe in stuff that's bullshit. I'm here, okay? That's as good as it gets."

He nods, which surprises me. He seems resigned, which also surprises me. He's dreamt about coming here for such a long time, and now that he's here he seems depressed and unsure. I guess maybe even *his* faith has limits.

After we clean up we go downstairs for dinner. The hostel dining room is large and sterile, just long tables with simple place settings surrounded by rickety folding chairs. This place reeks of Catholic. It reminds me of the parish hall at Our Lady of Perpetual Sorrows. Almost all the seats are taken, and Jesse and I end up in the far corner, surrounded by people who all seem to know each other and are speaking in a language I can't identify.

There's a mixture of young and old here, pious ladies, wrinkled and saggy but faith-filled—I know the type, I've seen them at church mumbling over their rosaries—and younger people, some our age. One whole table is filled with a group of chattering high school girls. They're talking and laughing loudly in Spanish, and I can tell Jesse's trying to eavesdrop, but it's hard with the people near us yammering noisily in their mystery language.

"I wonder if there's any Americans here?" I say to Jesse. "Everybody looks foreign to me."

"*We're* the foreigners, dumbshit," he says.

Several old nuns circulate, leaving steaming pots of what looks like stew on the tables, along with plates with hard rolls. I ladle the stew in my bowl and give it a try. It's wonderful, rich and tasty, unlike anything I've ever had before—a whole lot better than the cans of stew with the giant fingerprint on top that Mom opens at home.

I'm disappointed that Maria isn't here, but then I see her come out of the kitchen with water pitchers, and as soon as she sees us that big smile appears.

"Hello," she says. "You're room is fine?"

"Great. We slept all day."

She looks like she'd like to stay and talk, but a stern, grumpy old nun gives her a look and she smiles apologetically and glides away.

"Man, she's cute," I say to Jesse, but he's slurping up stew and not listening.

We pig out on the food, ignored by everybody else in the place. We're about to head back up to our room when the Spanish girls bring out a guitar and start singing.

They're laughing and giggly, and the songs are unfamiliar to me, but several of them have really pretty voices, and the effect is nice and enjoyable.

"They sing good," Jesse smiles, leaning back in his chair and contentedly rubbing his gut.

Everybody watches the Spanish girls, some clap and sing along—though it's hard to tell if they really recognize the song. Even the nuns who run the hostel watch, smiling, enjoying the impromptu show.

A couple of the girls are really great looking, too, and I lean over to Jesse and whisper, "Too bad you can't see this, Jesse."

Jesse frowns, and I realize how frustrating it must be for him not to see. I feel bad I brought it up.

They start dancing now, and everybody is clapping and having a good time. The nuns bring out bottles of wine—they must save it for special occasions—and pretty soon we're all feeling even better. The Spanish girls start doing flamenco dances, stomping the floor, clapping, and in my wine-hazy mind I'm picturing sex with them. Amazing how the male mind works. A fun, unexpected, spontaneous good time, and I can't just enjoy it, I've got to spice it up with sex fantasies. God, we're disgusting.

Maria the Baby Nun sits down next to me, looks around to make sure none of the boss nuns are watching, and takes a sip of my wine.

"You are having fun?" she asks with that great smile.

"Yeah!"

She's having a good time, too, and seeing her sneak wine and laugh I realize she's just a goofball kid like the rest of us. She has to be adult and holy when the bigshots are watching, but she's a fifteen-year-old girl, and when you're fifteen you've got to have some fun once in a while.

The music gets louder, the dancing and clapping, the room heats up, the wine goes down easy, one of the Spanish girls spots me and comes over, grabs my arm, pulls me to them, tries to teach me flamenco, I look like a clown but I don't care, I'm stomping the floor, I look over and see Maria watching and laughing, leaning over to tell Jesse what's happening, he's laughing too, and the night goes on and I love it, I'm having more fun than I can remember, it's like the homecoming dance I was cheated out of going to, and the night goes on with music, dancing, wine, and the smiles of Maria, the Baby Nun.

My head throbs this morning, it's payback for the fun last night. Jesse is awake and perky, and it annoys me. He drank as much as I did last night, but it didn't seem to bother him. More proof that I'm a weenie.

"Hurry up, man, we gotta eat and then go down to the grotto!" Jesse says, finishing buttoning his shirt.

"Can the water cure my fuckin' head?" I ask, groaning at the thought of listening to Jesse be devout all day.

"Hey, this is serious, quit bein' disrespectful."

I sit up, my feet hit the cold floor. My head's going to explode.

I take a shower and it helps a little, but I still feel like I've got a bad case of the flu.

We go downstairs. The dining room is quiet and deserted this morning; we're the last ones to eat. There's fruit and rolls out, and some juice and coffee. That's it. I don't know what I was expecting, maybe some boxes of Cap'n Crunch.

"What's the plan?" I ask after I've choked down some coffee. I don't like coffee, but I'm hoping it'll help me feel better. I'm starting to think it wasn't such a good idea, though, because now I feel like I'm going to puke.

"We'll go down to the grotto, we'll go inside the basilica, pray for awhile, then we'll go to the waters."

"Great." Maybe I can sleep in the church while he's praying.

"You gotta concentrate, man. The Virgin won't talk to me unless you concentrate."

I don't get the connection, but I say, "Yeah, sure," and bite off a chunk of a hard roll. Maria is nowhere to be seen this morning; the only person around is a wrinkly nun, and she's throwing us irritated glares. We're probably cutting into her free time, and she's giving me the creeps staring at me.

"Let's go," I say, grabbing an apple.

In a few minutes, we're on our way down to the grotto. Jesse is silent, and I can tell he's concentrating on listening to the sounds and feeling the air for some sign of his old, estranged buddy, the Virgin Mary.

We walk down the *Boulevard de la Grotte*, the main road to the grotto and churches and the area called the *Domaine Religieuse.* It's a circus. Each side of the street is lined with memento shops, bright yellow Kodak signs flapping in the morning breeze, plastic Mary statues, bottles for holy grotto water, knick-knacks, tacky religious junk of every description.

The street is packed with wall-to-wall people, chattering in dozens of different languages, browsing the shops, dodging cars and tooting taxis and the strange blue rickshaw-like covered wheelchairs containing sick people. Kids, looking like little white-shirted donkeys, pull the wheelchair/wagons; I assume they're paid by somebody to lug the sick people down to the grotto. I feel hemmed in and suddenly nervous, like I've got some kind of crowd phobia that's going to make me start screaming.

"This don't feel right," Jesse says as I lead him through the throng. People keep bumping into us, and nobody says "excuse me". You'd think they could tell Jesse is blind, that they'd be a little more polite, but they don't seem to give a shit. These people are here for the cures, they think they're good and virtuous and holy, but they can't be bothered to be polite to a blind Mexican. Everybody's so wrapped up in what they're here for that they can't see anyone else's affliction.

As we walk past the curio shops and through the crowd, I begin to notice how many ill and crippled people are here. It makes sense, of course, there isn't any other reason to visit Lourdes, but as I look around at the limping, sickly bodies, shopping for plastic Mary trash with grim glee, I can't help but be repulsed.

"I don't know about this, Jesse," I say, and I describe what's going on around us.

"It'll be better down at the grotto," he says, trying to convince himself that this isn't a huge mistake. "She'll be down there. I know She will."

There's a drastic change as we enter the *Domaine Religieuse*, the collection of churches, the grotto itself, and other religious buildings. The tacky shops are gone, and the area by the river is beautiful and park-like. The Gothic spires of the basilica soar into the sky, and the air here seems cleaner, less polluted by the nasty commercial scent of easy pilgrim cash.

A sign in many different languages warns about pickpockets, but even that invasion of reality doesn't detract from how pretty it is here by the river. The crowds are more spread out, some in the basilicas—which are really three different churches stacked on top of each other—some by the grotto, others in the buildings where the springs are piped to large baths, still others just strolling around the grounds and enjoying the scene.

"Okay, this is more like it," I tell Jesse. "It's kind of like a big park, and the church is over there." I point him in the direction of the basilica, and he squints up into the sky.

"Yeah. I see the steeple," he says. To him, "seeing" is a faint, dim outline, but I guess it's better than nothing.

"You wanna go in the church?" I ask.

"Yeah. I think She's here."

I lead him up one of the two huge stone ramps that lead to the uppermost church, the Basilica of the Immaculate Conception. The view from up here is beautiful: the river, rolling, forested hills, brilliant blue sky set off by an occasional puffy cloud. A refreshing breeze blows over us, and I decide I like it. A lot. I've never been to the Pacific Northwest, but this is what I imagine Oregon and Washington must feel like. The feeling here reinforces what I've always thought: that the heat, smog, and boring sameness of Southern California sucks.

Jesse inhales deeply, and he seems to relax. We go inside the church. It's ornate and huge, with lots of statues, stained glass windows depicting the visions of Bernadette Soubirous, and soaring stone ceilings. I know it's not that old, but it seems medieval, and being inside makes me feel like there's a connection with long-dead people, people who believed and left their mark in stone and glass. It's almost enough to make me want to believe in God and the Catholic Church again—almost, but not quite.

People kneel, praying silently. I hear the mumbles of a few saying the rosary, and the clicking of beads against the wooden pews. Jesse feels for a pew, slides in, and kneels down. His head drops immediately down into prayer, and I'm left to sit next to him, people-watching, admiring the cool architecture of the church.

Minutes pass, and I soon become bored. You can only look at the inside of a church for so long, especially if you're not praying and you don't believe in anything. Time grinds by, and soon we've been there an hour and I'm going nuts.

"Jesse!" I whisper, but he doesn't move. He's been frozen in his holy making-contact-with-the-Virgin position the entire time. I'm not even sure he's still breathing.

I lean back in the pew and sigh loudly, hoping he'll hear it and get the message. But he doesn't react, so I sigh again, louder. Still nothing. I don't think he's in the miracle zone, though. I've seen him slide in that enough to know the body language, and this isn't it. I have a feeling he's completely aware of what's going on, but he's trying to force himself into a trance.

"Hey, look, the Virgin's hovering over the altar!" I say, and Jesse snaps up to attention.

"What?!"

"Oh, my mistake. It was just somebody taking a picture with a flash bulb."

I'm almost afraid, because maybe it was just a little mean to fuck with him, and I'm half-expecting him to punch me, but instead he begins to laugh.

"Let's get outa here, nothing's gonna happen."

I guess he still does have a sense of humor.

We go back outside and walk along the river, down toward the grotto. It's paved and walled here, so it's hard to picture what it looked like when Bernadette had her supposed visions. We come to a long line of people, and I can see they're waiting to file through the grotto which is far ahead. It's like the line at

Disneyland for the Matterhorn.

"Maybe She'll be there," Jesse says. The little kid yearning in his voice is sad.

"Yeah, maybe," is all I can say. I feel bad for him.

The line slowly moves, and I see a couple of old women I recognize from the hostel. Last night they were laughing and singing, drinking wine and enjoying the happy youth of the Spanish girls. Now, they're pale and grim, shuffling toward a place they think has miracles, mumbling prayers and reverently wishing for help for whatever ails them.

I think the real miracle was last night at the hostel, where everybody forgot their problems and just lived for the moment. I have a feeling there'll be no miracles for the old ladies today.

The line creeps closer, and I give Jesse a running commentary of what it looks like and how it feels.

"Okay, there's a big overhang of gray rock, and it's all covered with bushes and stuff, and there's an altar right outside the grotto—"

"What's the grotto look like?" he asks, very intense.

"Like a cave." We get closer, and I can see inside. "It's not even a cave, really, it just goes inside the hill a little bit. It's all paved with marble, and there's like a little pool inside."

"The spring!"

"Yeah, I guess." I look above me. "Hey, this is cool, there's a wire hanging up above us, and there's a bunch of crutches hanging off of it!"

"Cures!" Jesse says reverently. "There were pictures of the crutches in that book you read, remember?"

"Yeah." I gaze up at the old, sooty crutches. A bank of candles flickers beneath them. It's pretty impressive to see them hanging there, but I can't really believe in it. I'd have to see the people who were cured—before, and after. And I notice there's no fake legs or arms or glass eyes up there. Cures are only limited to stuff you can't really see, I guess.

We come to the grotto. A couple of priests are saying mass on the altar outside, and a big crowd stands in front. Except for the priests, who are droning through the mass in some language that sounds sort of like Spanish but isn't—Italian, maybe?—it is eerily silent, considering all the people hanging around.

We file behind the altar, into the grotto. A statue of the Virgin is up in a niche in the rocks, and the spring itself is covered with Plexiglas and lit from below. It looks fake and goofy. The rock inside is worn smooth, I assume from the thousands of holy fingers that have touched it over the years. Sick people on gurneys, their heads rolling from side to side, some coughing and gagging, are let in at the head of the line to pay their respects to the shallow little cave. It's strange, an otherwise ordinary place, a divot in a rock mountainside, now built up and developed into a shrine, and all these people silently filing through believe in it with all their hearts and souls. Old women dab away tears, and even some men look moved. The sick people are the saddest. The ones who are aware are so...expectant. It's like they expect thunder and lightning and boom!—insta-cure. I look over to Jesse. He's got that look, too.

"We're inside now," I whisper, and I explain how the bubbling little spring is covered with plastic. Jesse reaches out and reverently touches the surrounding stone. I find myself hoping he'll start screaming, *"I can see!"* but, of course, nothing happens. The moving snake of pilgrims pushes us through, and we're back outside again. After you go through the grotto, you end up at a bank of faucets where dozens of taps dispense the holy grotto water for all who believe.

"Anything?" I ask.

"I...thought I felt Her, man. She's close."

"You want some of the water?" I ask.

"Yeah."

I go over to a tap, then I realize we didn't bring a bottle or container. "We'll have to come back later," I tell him. A French cop "ssshhs" me. I guess the spigots are holy, too. It seems strange that a cop would be patrolling miracle faucets. France must not have separation of church and state.

"I'll just...." Jesse moves next to me. He leans over and lets the water run over his big brown hands. He jumps, as if it's hot or electric, then moves them under the water again. "Take off my sunglasses, man." I do as he asks. He cups his hands and lets them fill with water.

I watch, feeling a sudden, weird intensity. Jesse drops to his knees, his lips moving in prayer, and he raises his dripping hands up, the water sloshing out of them, and then he splashes his eyes with the water, and I feel a jolt go through me, *shit, it is a miracle, he's gonna get cured!*

And his head drops down, and I think he's in the miracle zone, maybe he's really hearing the Virgin, he rubs his eyes like they itch, and then he looks up at me, and I think he can see me, his eyes blink and flutter, and—

"It didn't work," he says.

"You can't see?"

"No different, man." His voice is thick with disappointment.

"Shit," I say, and the cop "ssshhh's" me again.

"But I *feel* better," says Jesse, putting on a brave front. "Maybe if I pray more. And you try harder."

"Yeah, okay, I'll try harder," I say. Maybe I'm not as much of a non-believer as I thought. For a minute there I was almost convinced that he was cured. This place is like Fantasyland. The longer you're around, the more you believe in make-believe.

Jesse squats dejectedly, wiping the not-so-holy water off his dripping face. I watch other people—mostly older—reverently fill their plastic jugs and bottles with the water. I wonder if it has an expiration date. If you take it home and don't use it will it go bad and become devil water? Some of these people don't look sick, are they taking the water home so they can leave it in the medicine cabinet, next to the Maalox and the Vaseline, ready in case of sickness or injury?

I'm ready to move on, maybe go get some lunch in town, but Jesse stays in his unhappy squat, rubbing his eyes, so I don't bug him. This is his trip, I have to remember, it's important and meaningful for him, and I'm his pal, so I need to stand back and let him do whatever it is he needs to do.

As I wait, I watch people come and go, and lapse into my not-unusual state of awake/daydream. I seem to have this talent—I can be awake and sort of aware, enough that I don't look strange, but while I'm in this state I can let my mind wander a million miles away and lose track of what's happening under my nose. Sometimes it worries me, because now that I'm driving I'm afraid I'll fade out and run a red light or something.

So right now, by the gushing spigots of holy water, I'm daydreaming about Maria the Baby Nun. And for once in my life, I'm thinking about a cute girl and it's pure. I haven't pictured her naked or anything; I must have respect for the habit after all. What I'm fantasizing about is her smile.

When we go home in a few days, and I say good-bye, never to see her again, I know her smile will stick in my memory forever. Shit, the power they have, do women know it? I can't imagine any guy having the control that an average female has over us. Look at Rhonda; I was madly in love with her for years, then she turned weird, and I'll never get over it. In twenty years I doubt if she'll even remember my name. And Maria the Baby Nun; in a month my face will be a faint blur in her memory, if that. But I'll still be dreaming about her smile.

Women have it easy.

Noise and disorder bring me out of my thoughts. I look up, toward the far end of the holy water spigots. Bunches of people are grouped around somebody in a wheelchair, and a rising rumble of voices disturbs the reverent silence. The cop rushes down there to make them be quiet.

"What's that?" says Jesse, looking up.

"I dunno. There's somebody in a wheelchair, maybe they died or something."

"Let's go see."

We walk toward the commotion, and other people hurry past us, headed toward it. It's like a fight during lunchtime at school, when the word gets out and everybody wants to see what's up.

As we get closer the excited chatter of voices gets louder, and I try to make out words I understand, but nobody's speaking English. One of the dancing Spanish girls from last night runs past us, and I hear her saying over and over, "*Milagro*!"

"What's that mean, Jesse?" I ask.

"Miracle," he whispers.

As we get closer I'm not sure if I'm excited or just plain scared. There's something spooky about it here, the faith so strong that people lose their senses, and the hanging fog of mysticism over everything. Whoever and whatever is in that wheelchair is the end result of too much belief, too much faith, too much blind enthusiasm for holy nonsense.

The throng of people around the wheelchair gets bigger by the second, and when we get there we can't see into the crowd to see what's going on.

"What? Somebody cured, man?" asks Jesse.

"I can't see. We need to get closer."

That's all the encouragement Jesse needs. He drops his shoulder and uses his middle linebacker strength to punch a hole through the crowd. These old and infirm pilgrims don't stand a chance. We cut through them like butter.

I follow Jesse through the yelling crowd, and as we near the center I finally hear somebody speaking English.

"Praise be to Jesus and His most holy Virgin Mother!" an old woman's voice shouts. I freeze. *I know that voice.* Jesse recognizes it, too, and stops moving. He spins toward me.

"Fuck! Is that?!—"

"*'Hail Mary, full of grace, the Lord is with Thee. Blessed art Thou amongst women, and blessed is the fruit of Thy womb, Jesus. Holy Mary, Mother of God, pray for us sinners, now and at the hour of our death. Amen'!*" The crowd goes completely silent as the woman shrieks another *Hail Mary.*

Jesse and I stand, gaping, shocked, it can't be true—

It's Sister Mary Annunciata.

Monsignor O'Callahan stands next to his wheelchair. He's not drooling anymore, and although his right side still looks a little droopy, he's obviously light years better than he was before.

"What's *she* doin' here, man?!" Jesse asks me.

"Monsignor O'Callahan, he's here, too...he's standing up." A violent chill shoots through me, electric cold in my spine. "This is weird, man, the Monsignor's—"

"He's cured!" Jesse gasps. "Fuckin' a, he's cured, *cabron*!" Jesse's voice cracks; he sounds like he's going to cry.

I can't believe this, I'm in a nightmare, Monsignor O'Callahan looks bewildered, like he's just awakened from a coma and can't remember what happened to him so long ago. Sister Mary Annunciata keeps shouting *Hail Marys*, and the crowd begins to recite prayers in their own languages.

I'm seized by a dreadful fascination, I can't turn and leave, I move toward them, and I pull Jesse along with me.

Sister Mary Annunciata looks my way, and she's as shocked to see me as I am to see her, because she immediately stops praying.

"Sinners!" she hisses. "Go away! There's no hope for you here."

Monsignor O'Callahan looks at us with bleary, wet eyes. His face is dripping; Sister Mary Annunciata must've splashed him with holy grotto water right before his...cure. Cure. I can't believe it. How could somebody like Sister Mary Annunciata, somebody mean and evil, help out with a cure? It doesn't make any sense, this has to be a mistake. Maybe Monsignor O'Callahan healed himself because he bought into this stuff. No decent God could help these two and leave Jesse blind, it's not fair. It's just plain wrong and mean.

Monsignor takes a wavering step toward us. His mouth moves, and at first only a croaking grunt comes out. He raises his arm and points at Jesse, and he step/staggers toward him, he reminds me of the way Frankenstein walked in the old movies.

"You are wrong, sinners...."

The crowd watches, fascinated and silent. They're looking at Jesse and me and as soon as Monsignor said "sinners" a murmur rolls through the crowd, somebody must understand a little English, because now I hear somebody say "*Diablo*"—devil—and I know we're in trouble.

"Let's get outa here, Jesse," I say, feeling the eyes of the people bore in on us.

"How come the Virgin cured you?!" Jesse asks, ignoring me. He moves toward Monsignor and Sister Mary Annunciata. "Your faith is wrong!"

"'*Hail Mary, full of grace*—" shouts Sister Mary Annunciata. She takes Monsignor O'Callahan's arm, and he begins to pray with her, quietly, in his slurry voice.

"It's not fair!" Jesse shouts back at them, and I try to pull him away.

"—Blessed art Thou amongst women'—"

Jesse sputters Spanish cuss words, and someone shoves him, chattering in an ugly language, and we've got to get out of here or they're going to kick our asses, so I yank Jesse away and we run through the crowd, somebody throws a punch—

"—Pray for us sinners, now and at the hour of our deaths, Amen'."

"It's not fucking fair!" Jesse shouts at the crowd, at Sister Mary Annunciata, at Monsignor O'Callahan, and, I suppose, at the Virgin. But nobody's listening to him, they've lost interest in us, they're watching Sister Mary Annunciata and praying along, some drop to their knees and bow their heads in reverent prayer.

I drag Jesse away; we finally stop underneath a stone archway in the basilica's ramp. I'm gasping and scared, I've never been in the middle of a mob before, never had those looks of hate and contempt aimed at me. Jesse collapses against the stone wall, tears running down his cheeks.

"This is fucking bullshit, man, how could She cure him? He's bad, he's everything She used to tell me was wrong with religion, I thought She made him have the fucking stroke to punish his *pinche* ass!"

"Did you know they'd be here?" I ask. It occurs to me that this is all too convenient, too tidy. "I mean, what are the chances we'd just happen to be here at the same time as them?" This pisses me off; what the hell is Jesse up to?

"It wasn't no fuckin' coincidence. It's a faith test or something. They set us up, man."

"Who?"

"Jesus and the Virgin."

I don't believe him, but I don't press it. He's too upset; now isn't the time to accuse him of dragging us over here to face down Sister Mary Annunciata and Monsignor O'Callahan. I don't know why he'd want to do something like that, but then, I don't know why Jesse does a lot of things. I decide to be a good guy and try to make him feel better.

"Maybe you got this all wrong, Jesse."

"What do you mean?"

"Maybe...I dunno, maybe Monsignor O'Callahan isn't really cured, maybe he just, you know, willed himself to be better. Like a self cure."

Jesse wipes the tears from his cheeks and hawks up a big loogie. "Yeah. Maybe."

"Father Quinn thinks lots of stuff happens because people want it to happen. Most miracles, you know? He always thought anything you did was from...inside you."

"Father Quinn doesn't believe. He's thinks I'm crazy."

"Yeah. But he still likes you okay."

That gets a smile from Jesse. "Monsignor O'Callahan didn't look perfect did he? Like he was totally cured?"

"He looked like shit. He was standing up, and he mumbled, that's all." I don't say that even *I'm* wondering if he got cured. Guys with strokes don't usually stand up and start talking again. But I don't say that to Jesse. "That had to be it, Jesse. It was psycho—whatever that word is. Psycho-asthmatic. Like the times your hands and feet have bled." He gives me a sharp look. Now why did I say that?

"It's stigmata. A gift of the Spirit."

"Okay, bad example. But Monsignor O'Callahan, I don't think the Virgin did anything for him." It seems weird to be talking about the Virgin like I believe in Her.

Jesse leans against the rock, disconsolate and whipped. I don't know if he's convinced there was a Monsignor O'Callahan cure, but one thing's for sure: no miracle for Jesse Montoya.

"Why won't the Virgin talk to me anymore, man? I've done everything I thought She wanted. And then She kicks my ass and makes me watch Monsignor O'Callahan get cured. That's nasty."

"I dunno, Jesse. This stuff's beyond me. Forget about it, just go on with your life. You sit around waiting for visions you're gonna waste a lot of time and stay pissed off forever."

"I thought She'd cure me...."

"I know." I feel like I should hug him or something, but that seems faggy, so instead I take his arm and lead him away. "Let's get outa here."

We walk slowly out of the *Domaine Religieuse*, back up into the town and past the cheesy souvenir shops, bucking the tide of believers on their way down to the grotto. It no longer seems quaint or pretty, just mean and jumbled. I want to get out of here as soon as possible, back to my hot and smoggy hometown, a place that's real, a place I know and understand.

Seeing Sister Mary Annunciata and Monsignor O'Callahan here has sickened me. She's been an evil part of my life for almost as long as I can remember; I'll never escape her. If Jesse somehow knew they'd be here and arranged it so we'd be here too, then he's crazier than I thought. I don't know what to think. I can't believe in a Jesus and Mary holy set-up, I can't believe it's a coincidence, but I can't *really* believe that Jesse knew. So how'd this happen?

I don't pray much anymore, but now, as we walk back up to the hostel, I'm praying. I'm praying that Sister Mary Annunciata dies, I'm praying that I get the chance to piss on her grave. I decide there's no way it could be a coincidence that she and Monsignor were here at the same time as us; maybe we were set up by the devil. Where the hell is God? How come we always get our asses kicked by bad stuff? Getting Jesse's hopes up for a cure, just to stomp on him by curing Monsignor O'Callahan and ignoring him, that's cruel.

Maybe Jesse needs to start praying to the devil; he's the only one who seems to make things happen.

Tonight at dinner we're shunned. The word has spread that somehow we were involved with the forces of darkness at Monsignor's cure, and everybody avoids us like we're glowing red refugees from hell. The giggly Spanish girls tonight eat silently and quickly leave, and the grim nuns won't leave a water pitcher at our table.

There's no sign of Maria the Baby Nun.

"How come it's so quiet?" Jesse asks.

"They're afraid of us."

"Oh. This is bullshit, man."

A pinch-faced old lady glares at me from across the dining room. She looks like she wants to kill me.

"I'm thirsty," Jesse says.

"They won't bring us water. I'll go find some."

I get up and go through the swinging doors into the kitchen. Maria the Baby Nun busily washes dishes at the sink.

"Hi."

She looks up, startled. "Hello." She looks back down and scrubs her dirty plates. Great, she thinks I'm evil, too.

"Could I get some water?" I ask, trying to sound light and non-threatening.

She quickly fills a pitcher and hands it to me. "You...had an interesting day?" she asks.

"You could call it that," I say. "We're probably going to leave early.

Things didn't work out."

"I'm sorry." She looks down.

"Don't believe everything you hear."

"You knew the man who was cured?"

"Yeah. Only we can't understand why he would be cured and Jesse wouldn't. It isn't right."

"You shouldn't try to understand God. He works in His own way."

"Yeah, well his way sucks."

She frowns, like she doesn't understand what "sucks" means, which is just as well.

"You don't believe, do you?" she asks.

"I don't think so. It's hard for me."

"I'll pray for you," she says, giving me a tentative smile.

"Thanks." *Please smile some more*, I think. *It's so nice.*

We stand awkwardly. I'd like to say something cool and nice, but no words come to me. She keeps smiling, which feels good, and I realize I've over-stayed. It's time to go. I'll probably never see her again.

"Well. See you," I say. When I get nervous, like I am now, I feel bigger, like I've grown to giant goober size. I become aware of my hands and feet, and my body feels out of proportion. It's extreme self-awareness. I hate it.

"Good-bye," says Maria the Baby Nun. That smile. It kills me. "Try to love God. He loves you."

I take the water pitcher and leave. She's so cute, so nice, so sincere. I'm madly in love with a girl I'll never see again.

Life sure is fun.

Jesse and I finish eating. By the time we're done, everybody else has left. They all ate hurriedly and skittered away, afraid that our evilness would get their faith dirty.

We head back up to our room, and as I'm leading Jesse up the stairs, he suddenly stops.

"Let's go down to the grotto," he says.

"What for?"

"One more try, man."

"Jesse—"

"C'mon." He tugs me back down the stairs. He's unbelievable. He's like a compulsive gambler, *just one more pull on the slot machine, he thinks, I know the jack-pot's coming up next.*

We hurry down the darkened streets, back to the *Domaine Religieuse.* The nightly candlelight procession is in progress; thousands of pilgrims singing *Ave Maria,* their flickering candles like a big glowing snake slithering along the river and up the ramps to the basilica.

Jesse wants to go back to the grotto, so we push through the procession and go down to the river. Only a few people are at the grotto, which is dimly lit and creepy. The flickering bank of candles beneath the hanging crutches bathe them in yellow light, and they seem to hover above the ground, looking for cripples to attach themselves to.

"Okay, Jesse, we're here."

He nods silently and drops to his knees in front of the altar. His head drops into prayer, and I stand, impatiently waiting for him to finish. I just want to get the hell out of here. I'm afraid Sister Mary Annunciata and Monsignor O'Callahan will pop out from behind a rock, like Jack-in-the-box demons rising up from hell.

We stay here for a long time. Jesse prays, at least I assume he's praying. He kneels absolutely still, the only sign of life is an occasional breath. It seems like he's sleeping.

I walk over to the stone wall above the river and watch the black water move by. It's a clear night, and a sliver of moon reflects on the slick surface, breaking into tiny white shatters that seem to skitter, like those weird bugs that run on the water and get gobbled up by hungry trout.

I stare at the river; my mind goes into neutral and I don't know how long I stand here. When I finally snap out of it I realize I don't hear the sound of the *Ave Maria*-singing pilgrims anymore, and the air is colder. The moon has moved behind the mountains, and I'm shivering.

"Hey man, you okay?" I hear Jesse say. I turn, startled. He's standing behind me.

"Yeah. Sure. You done?"

"Let's get the fuck outa here."

I guess his prayers weren't answered. The Virgin blew him off. Maybe this will be the final blow for his faith. Maybe he'll be more like me now.

We hurry back up to the hostel, through the now-deserted streets. It's after midnight, and most of the faithful are curled away in their rented beds, dreaming of Mary and Bernadette and holy cures. I wonder how many people leave here pissed off and disgusted like us.

Jesse doesn't say much the rest of the time we're here. We wait at the railway station to catch the early train to Paris, and we ride back up in silence. The countryside is pretty, until we get to the outskirts of the city, but I'm beyond really noticing or caring. By the time we're on the 747 and flying home, even I'm tired enough to sleep.

As the huge plane bounces among the clouds, I dream of demons and nuns and monsignors, of drowning in holy grottos and being rescued by smiling

Baby Nuns named Maria.

I don't dream of cures.

Or miracles.

Chapter Seventeen

Armando Jesus Montoya was born on August 15, 1972, the feast day of the Assumption of the Blessed Virgin Mary.

Catholics are the only ones, I think, who believe that Mary got zapped straight to heaven without dying first. The logic is that since she was the mother of God, she shouldn't have to suffer through the messy business of old age, or getting cancer, or having a heart attack like the rest of us. I guess it makes sense; if you believe in all the rest of the religious stuff, you'll buy into that, too. I'm not sure why the Protestants don't believe in the assumption; maybe they've got a problem with blowing up Mary's importance.

I was at the hospital with Jesse while Lydia gave birth. Most of Jesse's family was there: his mom, his big brother Mando, some assorted cousins and Aunt Yolanda. Aunt Yolanda was more excited than anybody else. She paced around the waiting room, smoking, nervous and worried.

Jesse, though, was calm. He sat on a hard plastic chair, hiding behind his sunglasses, thinking about God knows what.

"You should be in there *halping* Lydia," Aunt Yolanda said, sounding more Mexican than ever. When she was agitated and around the family, her carefully learned honky accent veered back into *vata*-land.

"She didn't want me in there. She'll be fine."

Aunt Yolanda shook her head disgustedly. I think she wanted Jesse to be better and different from the men in her life; so far, though, he was living up to the guy rules—especially Mexican guys—about babies: enthusiastic interest in the conception part, and lessening interest in everything afterwards. If it's a boy, there are sports to get interested in later. But that's a long way after the wrinkled prune/alien is born, after diapers and crying and weirdness that guys don't want to understand.

"*Pendejo*," she muttered. Jesse just smiled and waited.

Mom showed up, giggly and excited. She chattered with Mrs. Montoya, hugged everybody in sight, and embarrassed me as usual. Mom has the unique ability in everything she does to humiliate me. Jesse calls it the Sylvia cringe factor. Usually only a word or two from her will leave me shaking my head in embarrassment, silently begging her to go away. It's not that I don't love her—it's just that I wish she wasn't such a dork. But I guess that's the way moms are.

We waited forever, until the obstetrician finally came out and told Jesse everything was fine and he was the father of an eight-pound boy. There was lots of hugging, and most of the women cried. I even saw Jesse's big brother Mando wipe a tear away, but luckily he didn't know I saw him. If he had, he probably would've killed me.

Aunt Yolanda cried the hardest. She was in a hugging frenzy, and when she hugged me it fired me up, even though I knew it was just a new baby celebration hug. Sixteen-year-old testosterone is a hard thing to control.

Lydia brought little Mando home to her parents' house. They weren't thrilled that she'd had a baby, but her family was close and loving, so they supported her as best they could. She spent a lot of time with the Montoyas, too, because Aunt Yolanda and Mrs. Montoya insisted that they help take care of Mando. Aunt Yolanda took days off work just so she could stay home, coo at Mando, and change his diapers and bathe his little brown body.

He was a cute little guy, all flabby cheeks and squirmy limbs. His hair was already thick and jet black. And when he cried the whole world knew about it; the kid had a set of lungs. There was no doubt: when Mando Montoya wanted something, he demanded it, and you had to deliver. I wondered if he'd end up being an aggressive ass-kicker when he got older.

I hung around Jesse's house on the days when Mando was there. I'd never been around a baby before, and I thought it was kind of cool to hold him and let him grab my fingers with his strong, pudgy hands. The diaper business was kind of gross, but the women fought over the chance to change him, so I never got stuck with that duty. Jesse's brother Mando spent a lot of time holding his namesake too. It was funny to see a terrifying guy like Mando holding a baby in his tattooed arms, tickling and giggling like a goofball.

One day, while I was watching TV with Jesse and holding Mando, I saw Aunt Yolanda watching me from the hallway. She had a strange smile on her face, one of those knowing, aren't-you-cute looks that reminded me of Mom. Mando was asleep in my arms, breathing deeply, content and happy. I liked holding him, but I would never admit it. People might think I was a fag.

"What?" I said to Aunt Yolanda, who was still smiling at me. She was wearing a United Farm Workers T-shirt. Every time I saw her she was wearing a different Chicano-themed T-shirt.

She just shook her head and said, "You're too much, Roger." I don't know what that was supposed to mean, but afterwards, every time I was there I felt self-conscious if I got anywhere near little Mando.

Jesse took fatherhood with his usual calm. He played with Mando, did all the good dad stuff, but he also seemed distant. He and Lydia had talked about moving in together, but they didn't have any money—and neither of them wanted to quit school—so it remained talk, and Mando ended up being raised by a dozen people in a huge extended loving family—which seemed like a pretty good way to do things, I thought.

School is about to start again, and I can't believe I'll actually be a junior. I'm getting seriously old. Mom and Father Quinn have started bugging me about SAT tests and colleges, but I can't bring myself to worry about that stuff. It seems too distant, too unreal for me to be thinking about it yet. I guess what bothers me is that I'd have to admit that I'm soon going to be an adult, and I'll have to learn to be on my own. As annoying as it is to be a kid and have your life ruled by parents, it's probably better and easier than being in charge of yourself. Seeing Jesse and Lydia having to suddenly grow up with a baby has made me stop and think; I'm not sure it's something I want to do.

But I've got no choice. Mom and Father Quinn have made it clear that if I don't go to college, I go to work, but either way I'm out of the house.

"It's nothing personal, Roger," said Father Quinn. "It's just that your mother and I feel that eighteen is adult, and it's time for you to be out there. We'll help you with money for college, if that's what you decide to do." Mom sat next to him on the couch as he told me, looking sad and miserable. I think it was Father Quinn's idea for me to hit the road as soon as possible, and Mom was just going along with him. I was pissed at first, but as I thought about it, I could understand why he thought I should leave. Mom had smothered me with attention ever since I got run over, and it wasn't healthy for either of us. If Dad were still alive, he'd probably have told me the same thing.

Besides, maybe Mom and Father Quinn wanted the house to themselves; that way they could run around naked or do whatever weird stuff they wanted to do.

But any decisions were a ways off, and I decided to not think about it.

Denying reality was a skill I was serious about developing.

It's the Saturday before school starts, and I'm hanging around Jesse's house. Lydia and little Mando are here, and Aunt Yolanda and Mrs. Montoya are clucking around like they always do. I wonder what it'll be like for him when the novelty wears off and he's just another little kid underfoot. I hope he's enjoying all the attention.

We're watching college football, and Keith Jackson's voice screams out of the TV. Jesse is yawning and bored, though. Mando spent the night here last night, and he had a stomachache or something and screamed all night long. Not that Jesse did any of the parenting or soothing—his mom and Aunt Yolanda did—but the crying kept him awake and now he's pissed off.

Lydia's holding Mando, leaning against Jesse's shoulder. It's a picture of domestic (the unmarried and not living together variety) bliss. She's changed since Mando was born; she's quieter now, and she doesn't have the same spark or hell-raising look in her eye anymore. When we got back from the nightmare trip to Lourdes, Lydia was the one who took it the hardest. She'd bought into Jesse's positive "the Virgin will cure me" business, and when we shuffled off the 747 back in smoggy L.A., defeated and whipped, the hope in Lydia's eyes flared out and vanished the minute she saw that Jesse was still blind and I was still limping and scarred.

Jesse refused to talk to anybody about the trip, so it was up to me to tell everybody what happened. Lydia cried, Mrs. Montoya shook her head sadly, and Father Quinn was furious.

"O'Callahan?" he shouted as we drove home from the airport. "This proves the whole thing's a sad, pathetic sham...no God would cure somebody like O'Callahan."

"He looked sort of cured to me," I said. I'd thought about it a lot on the plane ride home. *Something* strange happened there.

"Sham. Purely psychological, pathological, something...but no miracle," Father Quinn said, forceful and annoyed. Mom just kept looking into the back seat at me with red, wet eyes. She wasn't saying anything, but I knew she was thinking, *Thank God my little boy's back safe and sound!*

"Yeah, maybe," I had said, watching the smog settle over the mountains. I didn't know what to think about anything anymore.

"You gonna manage the team this year?" Aunt Yolanda asks. She plops down on the saggy couch next to me. Keith Jackson is yelling *"Fumble!"* and Mando is crying.

Being so close to Aunt Yolanda is arousing, but she acts unconcerned. It's amazing to me that she's never once acknowledged what happened that night; not a day has gone by where I haven't thought about it—or beat off to it.

"I dunno," I answer, moving away from her. She leans into the void and touches my shoulder with hers. I'm pinned between Aunt Yolanda and Lydia and Mando.

Sweat pops on my forehead. It's nice these guys treat me like part of the family, but togetherness is sometimes too much.

"How come you're not sure," Aunt Yolanda asks. I look over at her. Her hair is big today, and she looks good in her ever-present T-shirt. I glance down at her tits. Man, I can't believe I've actually kissed those things....

She watches the football game through glasses perched on the end of her nose, and I can't tell if she's asking because she's interested or if she's just talking to be talking. I've noticed people do that sometimes, especially to me. They ask questions but then don't listen to my answers.

"I'm just not sure if I want to do it this year, that's all."

"You gonna play, *mijo*?" she asks Jesse. She's been nice to him since we got back from Lourdes. I've never heard her call him anything but *pendejo* before.

"No."

Mando starts screaming. Lydia gets up and takes him to the kitchen. Jesse sits, annoyed, arms folded. I'm silent, feeling self-conscious and foolish squished next to Aunt Yolanda. She looks over at us and then gets up.

"Man, bunch of losers." She leaves us alone with the TV.

Jesse and I sit, watching the game. There's a strange feeling in the room.

"We need to go see them," Jesse says.

"Who?"

"Monsignor O'Callahan."

"Ah, fuck Jesse, forget about it."

"I was talking to Danny and the guys about it."

"Robledo? What for?" Jesse still has Robledo and the rest of the lowriders following him around. They read the bible together and Jesse preaches at them. It's the only religious thing Jesse does anymore, and I think it's more of a social thing for him than anything else. I don't think he believes in much now that the Virgin let him down, but he feels obligated to Robledo. Besides, Robledo's such a red-hot believer that if Jesse cut him loose he'd probably kill somebody.

"Danny thinks we should go see them. Maybe O'Callahan can, I dunno, get me in touch with the Virgin."

"What, you think he takes messages for her or something? It's nuts, Jesse, forget about it. They're all a bunch of psychos, including my sister. You don't wanna go there."

"I think Danny's right," says Jesse, ignoring my protests—as usual. "You got to confront stuff in life, you know? Maybe if we go talk to them we can understand why."

"The only thing you'll understand if you go there is that they're nuts. You think Sister Mary Annunciata can help you? Or wants to help you? And Monsignor O'Callahan, even if he had some kind of cure, that dude's mean and nasty. Father Quinn thinks the cure was probably just some mind over matter deal."

"Father Quinn has no faith."

"And neither do you," I say. Jesse says nothing for a moment, and we listen to the football game.

"Yes I do," he finally says, so softly I can barely hear him. "I believe the Virgin still loves me. She loves all of us. This is just a test."

What can I say? He refuses to face reality. "You'll be sorry if you go out there to see them. There's no answers for you with those people."

Jesse says nothing more; he stays hidden behind his sunglasses, alone with his fantasies of miracle cures and the Virgin who loves him unconditionally. When Lydia comes back with Mando, now quieted with a bottle plugged into his mouth, Jesse makes no acknowledgement of them. Idiot. He's off in religious loony-land when he should be here, in his living room, with his girlfriend and his son.

They're what are important in his life now. I don't know why he doesn't see that.

Jesse decided not to play football this year, even though Coach Gutierrez begged him to. Coach tried to get me to talk Jesse into it, but there was no way to get him interested. He was busy after school working for his uncle on some new tract houses, and he needed to funnel whatever money he made to Lydia and Mando. He had no time for foolishness like football.

Things are very different at school now. We're juniors, so we feel like grizzled veterans compared to the little spaz freshmen and sophomores. Lydia is Jesse's guide through part of the day, and the school district hired some student teacher to help Jesse the rest of the time, so I'm cut out. It's okay with me; Jesse's been weird lately, and I need to worry about getting decent grades, so it's for the best.

I see Rhonda from time to time, but we don't have any classes together. She goes out of her way not to look at me; maybe she feels guilty. Good. I hope she feels guilty the rest of her life for what she did. I'll never forget the way I felt that night, running like a dope through her neighborhood, being laughed at by her dad and dumped by her.

The only thing that bothers me a little is what I did to Bushman. But he's still alive and well and annoying—although he won't get anywhere near me. He's big into born-again stuff now, having split off from Jesse and joined up with some bible-thumping Baptist church. He and his few nerdy holy buddies spend their lunches having bible study and praying out in the field, down the fence from the dopers toking their latest Maui Wowee and across the field from the lowriders plotting their latest rumble.

And me. I go to school, study, get by. Nothing much going on in my life. I get the occasional crush on a girl, but I don't act on it. I don't trust them anymore, plus I figure if I did try to get one she'd just reject me. Lately, as I've gotten taller and older, I've noticed that my scars don't seem to be stretching to cover my growing bones. They look taut and bright white, like they're ready to rip apart and reveal muscle and gristle underneath. They hurt, too, all itchy and achy. I can't imagine any girl wanting to get near me. I feel like a monster.

So I spend a lot of my time alone. Jesse's busy with Lydia, I don't have a girlfriend, and I'm not in the mood to bother trying to get new friends. It's just easier to be by myself.

I'm eating lunch alone when Wisma comes up and sits down next to me. He's still a wannabe *vato*, with the Pendletons and slicked back hair. He's stuck with Robledo and the other born-again lowriders, but I know he's never bought into any of it. I think he hangs around, hoping Robledo will come to his senses and they can go back to being an ass-kicking gang of badass lowriders.

"Hey, man," he says. He unwraps a greasy cheeseburger and scarfs it down.

"Hey."

The thing about Wisma is that he never makes eye contact with you. It's like he's talking to the table.

"You comin'?"

"What?"

"To see the priest who got cured. We're all goin' out there Saturday."

"Shit."

"The dude really get a miracle? You saw it."

"I dunno what really happened. But you guys shouldn't go there."

"Montoya and Robledo want to. Montoya said your sister lives there, she's a nun or something."

"She's crazy like Sister Mary Annunciata and Monsignor O'Callahan. It's trouble if you go."

Wisma shrugs. "We're leavin' Saturday at around nine. Be at Montoya's if you wanna go."

"You don't believe any of this stuff, do you?" I ask.

"No. It's bullshit."

"Then how come you hang around with these guys?"

Wisma sighs and looks up at me. I've never noticed before, but his eyes are brilliant blue, and when he looks at you he seems shy, not a hard-ass at all. That must be why he doesn't look at people; it gives him away.

"Nobody else to hang with," he says. It makes sense; with Robledo Wisma has fought with every other gang of lowriders around. None of them are going to let him join up; white boy *vatos* aren't in high demand.

"Can you talk Robledo out of this?" I ask. I'm afraid and agitated suddenly. I have a feeling this might turn out bad, and it's avoidable.

"You ever try to talk Montoya out of doin' something?" he asks. "Robledo's even worse, man. The fucker decides to do something, he does it, and if you try and stop him he kicks your ass."

"I'm not getting near the place; there's no reason to go there. Jesse won't get any miracles, it'll only piss everybody off. If you're smart you won't go either."

Wisma crumples his cheeseburger wrapper and expertly tosses it into a trash can across the cafeteria. Good shot.

"I don't got no choice," he says, getting up. "And neither do you, man." He walks away, leaving me alone with my stomach churning indigestible wads of lunch.

I feel like I'm going to be sick, but I know one thing for sure: I'm not going with them on Saturday.

It's Saturday morning, eight forty-five, and Robledo and everybody else is already here.

I'm such a fucking idiot, I can't believe I'm doing this. Last night I went to bed, positive that I'd sleep late, shuffle out of bed around ten, read the paper, eat some Froot Loops, maybe study a little and work on an English paper that's due next week, catch some rays out in the back yard, help Father Quinn change the oil in the car—just basic Saturday stuff. Going out to the First Church of the Holy Fruitcakes wasn't on the agenda.

But then I couldn't fall asleep. As hard as I tried, I couldn't make myself think about anything else. I tried everything, including dredging up the Aunt Yolanda sex memories. Nothing. I couldn't even get a hard-on. My mind kept going back to the trip to the desert, to miracles, to fear. I couldn't sleep because I was afraid. It made no sense to me, that I'd want to go along with these guys if I was afraid. Being the pussy that I am, you'd think I'd have found a reason *not* to go, a way to avoid what I thought would be unpleasant at best, and maybe something a lot uglier.

But I couldn't. Maybe it's natural nosiness, the fear of missing out on something, even if it's something you don't want to see. Whatever the reason, it's Saturday morning and I'm at Jesse's house, ready to go out to the desert with them to see my nutty sister and the two people who've always scared the crap out of me: Sister Mary Annunciata and Monsignor O'Callahan.

I have a feeling Freddie Montgomery is there too, but he doesn't bother me. I know he's an okay guy, even if he loves Mary Frances. Nobody's perfect.

Five Impala lowriders sit at the curb, painted and polished to perfection. These guys take good care of their cars. I knock on the front door, dreading what I'm doing but unable to stop. Mrs. Montoya opens it, and gives me one of her big warm squishy hugs.

"You're going with Jesse and the boys?" she asks, a big grin creasing her jowly face.

"Yeah. Thought I'd go along."

She hugs me again and tousles my hair. I don't know why she's always hugging me, but I like it. It's good to have a spare mom.

Robledo and the lowriders mill around in the living room, impatient to get going. Jesse sits on the couch, oblivious, alone behind his sunglasses. Maybe he's praying, maybe he's daydreaming, or maybe he's having doubts about going. Whatever, he's just sitting there.

"Roger? That you?" he asks, looking up. As always, he can sense my presence.

"Yeah."

"You gonna come with us?"

"I guess."

His face brightens, and he jumps up. "Let's go!"

Robledo leads him out, and the rest of us follow. Robledo acts like he's Jesse's bodyguard. He wears mirrored wrap-around sunglasses all the time now, too. I guess he wants to be like Jesse.

I ride in Wisma's Impala; it only seems right that the two white guys be in the same car. Wisma's car is lower than low; I wonder if he thinks that by being the lowest lowrider he'll be more Mexican. He's got *Tears of a Clown* written on the back window in that angular graffiti writing, and the black tuck-and-roll upholstery is the best I've ever seen. Everything that can be chromed, is; it's an Impala that's a rolling work of art.

"How'd you afford to fix this up so good?" I ask.

"Stole shit. Sold pot. The usual."

Oh. I guess I don't really want to know how lowriders operate. It occurs to me that there might be arrest warrants out for Wisma. Great, I'm riding with him, I'll get dragged to jail and spend the rest of my life in San Quentin with *vato locos*.

We caravan along the freeway, Robledo's car at the lead. I'm squished in the back seat of *Tears of a Clown* with Ernie Ochoa and Joey Nava, two of the scariest guys who hang around Robledo. Neither acknowledges that I exist; they glumly stare out the windows, alone with their terrifying lowrider thoughts. It amazes me that these guys stick with Robledo now that he's a born-again religious freak. I can't believe they've all had religious conversions; I think they may be more like Wisma: they're afraid of Robledo, and they're hoping he'll go back to being the scary felon that he was in the good old days.

We cruise up Highway 14 toward Palmdale. Every mile we drive, the hotter it gets. The one thing Wisma's Impala isn't equipped with is air conditioning. The windows are open, and hot desert air blasts in, mixing the odors of our sweaty bodies into a nauseatingly gamy stench that for some reason won't leave the car. Wisma turns up the stereo, and the throbbing rhythms of Curtis Mayfield pound through my head.

As the mountains get drier and scrubby cactus sprouts alongside the road, I get more apprehensive. I don't want to see Mary Frances and the rest of them; I wish I hadn't decided to come along. What the hell could Jesse be thinking? Is he going to beg Monsignor O'Callahan to help him get a cure? Will they pray together? Will he try to convert them to the follow him? He knows them, he must realize they hate him. I don't understand what this trip will achieve besides stress and irritation for everybody involved. Maybe we'll be lucky and they won't be there.

Our slow-moving caravan of lowriders comes over the crest of the hill leading into Palmdale. The Mojave Desert sprawls in front of us, its flat desolation broken by occasional dead hills and craggy mountain stubs. When I've come over this hill before, I've been headed up to the Sierras and funtime fishing; those times it was a pleasant sight, the desert's dry monotony reassuring me that it led to snowy mountains and happy vacations. Now, knowing where we're going, it's depressing and hot, a forbidding place that's nothing but trouble.

We get off the freeway and drive along a rural road, past ramshackle trailers and scruffy ranches. The few people out in the miserable heat warily watch us pass; they don't see many lowriders out here. I expect to be shot at, or pulled over by big-bellied sheriffs at any moment.

We wind through desolate hills and scattered Joshua trees. The heat blasts us, and I can see that Ochoa and Nava are hot and pissed off. Wisma drives, his elbow resting on the door, his slicked back hair not moving at all in the blast-furnace wind.

"Fuck this shit," he mumbles. "We almost there, Donnelly?"

"I dunno. I've never been here."

"Fuck...."

I'm not sure how Jesse knows where we're going, but he and Robledo in the lead lowrider seem to be sure of where they're headed.

We drive further into the desert, past any noticeable habitation, up into a dry box canyon. The sheer sides appear suddenly, and before I know it we're in a miserable hot shade that's even worse than the beating sun. The crumbling canyon walls look like they could slide down and bury us at any moment.

Robledo turns off the main road onto a bumpy gravel road, and within minutes the beautiful lowriders are covered with red dust.

"Man, my fuckin' paint!" Wisma moans. "If I get a fuckin' chip...." The words hang in the boiling air. What, he's gonna kick Robledo's ass if his car gets hurt? I don't think so.

We bounce along the rutted road, bottoming out on the worst bumps. Chopped Impalas aren't made for off-road driving. Wisma mutters curses to himself, and Ochoa and Nava are starting to look pale and sick. Come to think of it, I'm feeling queasy too, but I don't think it's because of the ride.

We come to a rickety wooden gate covered with *private property* and *keep out* signs. Off to the side is a sandblasted, sun-bleached wooden sign: *Joshua Ranch.*

Joshua....

Something tugs at my brain. A memory. *Watch out for Joshua.* Shit, the catechism class, when Sister Mary Annunciata came in, Jesse told her: *Watch out for Joshua.*

The blasting heat isn't a problem anymore. I'm shivering.

"Fuck, get us out of here, Wisma! Now!"

"Whataya talkin' about, man?"

"Just do it! Turn around!" My heart crashes against my chest, I'm panicking, but all Wisma does is look at me with annoyance.

"Just be cool, man," he says. "We're here, we gotta see it through."

One of Robledo's buddies gets out of the lead car, unlatches the gate, and we drive on.

My dread mounts; I can't catch my breath.

We roll further into the reaches of the canyon, and as we round a bend on the gravel road a ratty old house looms before us.

It looks like a ramshackle farmhouse, but there could never have been a farm around here. Maybe it was part of a cattle ranch, or maybe religious nuts have *always* lived here. Who knows?

We crunch to a stop in the gravel, and slowly get out of the lowriders, stretching and sore from the long, hot ride. I'm used to seeing these guys at school, or cruising around town. They look ridiculously out of place here, stuck in the middle of nowhere, standing around their dirty lowriders, dressed up in their *vato* costumes and mirrored wraparounds.

It's quiet. A few far-off birds chirp, a slight hot breeze through the desert brush, that's it. No sounds of people, and no signs of life inside.

"You sure this is it, man?" Robledo asks Jesse. Stupid question. How would Jesse know, he's fucking blind!

"Yeah," Jesse says softly. "We're here."

I lean against Wisma's car, trying to calm down and catch my breath. Wisma throws me a glare. "Don't touch the fucking car!"

"Sorry, man." I stand, take a deep breath. I feel a little bit better until the memory: *Watch out for Joshua.* I panic all over again.

"Let's go," Jesse says to Robledo. Robledo leads him to the sagging front door. We follow along behind them like a bunch of ducklings. Jesse, ten greased-back lowriders, and me. If I lived here I'd call the cops right now.

I haven't seen or talked to Mary Frances for a long time, and I don't know what I'll say to her if I see her. It's like I used to have a sister, but she died, and now I'm an only child. Mom and Father Quinn don't talk about her much anymore, although every so often I can tell Mom's been crying and thinking about her.

Robledo and Jesse stand at the door. Robledo knocks hard, and peeling paint flies off and flutters to the ground.

"Hey!" Robledo calls out, demanding the appearance of someone. Robledo's the kind of guy who could say "Hey!" to the sky and make clouds part and the sun shine.

"I gotta talk to you, Monsignor!" Jesse says. His voice is shaky and nervous.

Nothing for a moment, and Robledo raises his hand to knock again when the door flies open. Sister Mary Annunciata, dressed in her best black habit, fills the doorway, oversized and intimidating. Even Robledo takes a step back.

"Sister—" Jesse says, knowing somehow it's her.

"You are *trespassing*!" she roars. "Get out before the almighty Lord smites you to *hell*!" Smite. There's that word again.

"Sister, I need to talk to Monsignor O'Callahan, I have to know if the Virgin—"

Monsignor O'Callahan pushes past Sister Mary Annunciata and comes outside. His skin is gray, and he shuffles oddly, like the left side of his body is just along for the ride but doesn't contribute anything. His mouth pumps as he slowly tries to form words.

"The...Virgin Mother loves her children...but not you, you're sinner, repent, pray...." Monsignor O'Callahan looks worse now than he did at Lourdes. Other than the fact the he's not in a wheelchair, there's not any improvement.

"I *have* been praying!" says Jesse. "I've been praying forever, but She won't talk to me anymore!"

"That dude don't look cured to me, man," whispers Wisma. "He looks like shit."

I nod, thinking Father Quinn was probably right. What happened at Lourdes was self-induced psyche stuff, and it's already worn off. There weren't any miracles.

"All of you are *evil*!" Sister Mary Annunciata snarls. "You are *Satan's children*!"

The white-hot anger shoots through me like electricity. It's back, and I'm scared because it only shows up when something bad's going to happen, when I'm going to do something I shouldn't do—

Watch out for Joshua.

I'm sick of Sister Mary Annunciata, I've taken her shit forever, and I'm not willing to listen to her anymore.

"You're a psycho, Sister. You always have been, you always will be, so do us all a favor: treat Jesse with some respect and keep YOUR FUCKING MOUTH SHUT!"

She lurches backwards like I've hit her. Damn, it feels good. She's not a monster at all. She's just a bully, and when you face them down you can kick their asses. You've just got to have the courage.

I stand, smug and smirking. The white-hot anger flows through me, I've got the power, Sister Mary Annunciata can't do anything to me anymore, and now I'm glad we came here.

Jesse turns toward me, aghast at what I've said. Monsignor O'Callahan sputters gargling stroke-talk, and the rest of the lowriders are watching all of us, unsure what to do. Even Robledo looks at me with what I imagine is newly found respect.

When the steel pipe smashes against the side of my head, I'm more surprised than anyone. The rest of them saw it coming, and right before I smelled my blood and stars glittered before my eyes, I saw Robledo make a move toward me, but it was way too late for him to help.

Watch out for Joshua.

I open my eyes and am staring into the sky. Wispy cirrus clouds wheel above me, and as my vision clears I see faces. Robledo, the other lowriders, and Mary Frances gaze down at me. Mary Frances is holding a bloody pipe.

"Get up, Roger," she says, swinging the pipe threateningly. Robledo and the lowriders back away from her. It's the first time I've ever seen Robledo look scared. "You shouldn't have said that to Sister Mary Annunciata," she continues. "You're evil."

I sit up, my head's pounding and I'm dizzy and weak. The white-hot anger disappeared when Mary Frances smacked me. Now I'm back to being pussy-boy Roger again.

"Shit, Mary Frances, what're you doin'? You coulda killed me!"

"Apologize to Sister Mary Annunciata for your foul words," Mary Frances says. I try to focus on her. She's wearing a black habit like Sister Mary Annunciata's, one of those stylish-for-the-fifteenth century covers-every-square-inch with cloth and cardboard numbers that even the most religious nuns don't wear anymore.

Sister Mary Annunciata stands behind Mary Frances, grinning madly at me. Her beady eyes scrunch to flabby slits when she smiles, and her teeth are stubbier and grosser than I remember. They're soft and cheesy and rotten.

"Apologize," Mary Frances threatens again, waving the pipe.

"I'm sorry, okay?! Shit, I'm your brother, Mary Frances, what's wrong with you?"

"You're a sinner, Roger. You're not my brother. You're filled with the evil of Satan."

I don't bother to argue. I get up on wobbly legs and almost fall over. Wisma grabs my arm and props me up.

"You okay, Rog?" Jesse asks.

"Yeah, fine," I say, wiping a smear of blood off the side of my face. Mary Frances split open one of my scars, and it won't stop bleeding.

Jesse's crestfallen; this isn't exactly what he'd envisioned. Monsignor O'Callahan leans, tilted to one side, looking at me and smiling with an ugly half-smile, half-frown; his face is divided into two opposing sections. He's utterly creepy.

"Please, Monsignor," pleads Jesse. "Help me to be cured, help me to see the Virgin."

Monsignor's mouth moves, silently at first, then the words come out in slurred spurts. "Stop your blasphemy, the Virgin will...smite you...."

"Hey, *pendejo*, this is bullshit, man!" Robledo blurts out. Patience isn't one of his gifts. "Can you help Montoya out or not, man? If not we'll get the fuck outa here."

"*Repent* your evil ways, sinner!" Sister Mary Annunciata says.

"I'm gettin' sick of you, bitch," Robledo says, and then turns back to Monsignor. "And you too, *pinche* priest."

Nobody says or does anything for a long moment, until Mary Frances starts to come at Robledo with the pipe.

Robledo sees her coming, and he backs away, and I think he's just going to sidestep her, but then he pulls a pistol out from under the Pendleton, *oh shit, he's got a gun!*

"Fuck you, *puta*!" he shouts, and then screaming and yelling starts from every direction. Mary Frances swings the pipe at him, Sister Mary Annunciata screams threats, Monsignor O'Callahan shuffles into the fight, the lowriders move in on Mary Frances, but she keeps swinging the pipe, Wisma dives in and lets go of me and I drop to my knees, and Jesse stands amid the confusion, doesn't know what's going on, impotent to do anything about the trouble he's started, and then—

A loud *CRACK*! Time slows down, I don't recognize the sound, don't know what it was until I see:

Robledo's head explode in a spray of bloody mush. He's dead before he hits the ground. A spatter of wet brains and bone splinters sting my cheek.

He flops to the ground, and a blood pool grows around his newly soft and distorted face. The bullet blew out the bones and architecture of his head, and now his face is wavy, like an image printed on wrinkled cloth.

Silence. I try to stand, but I'm still too dizzy from Mary Frances's pipe and the sight of Robledo's body. The lowriders back away, too stunned to speak, looking around for the shooter.

Mary Frances is shaking uncontrollably, and she drops the pipe and backs away. Sister Mary Annunciata grabs her and hugs her roughly, enveloping her in her huge habit. But the hug isn't friendly or comforting; it's as if she's latched on to Mary Frances and won't let anybody take her away.

"Robledo?" Jesse says weakly. He wipes blood and bits of gray matter off his face. His sunglasses are covered with Robledo's brain. "What happened?! Roger? Somebody tell me what's going on!"

"Somebody shot him...." I say, surprised that I can talk at all. My voice quivers and my throat wants to slam shut.

"Get out! *GET OUT!*" screams Sister Mary Annunciata.

Monsignor O'Callahan lurches over and vomits, and the queasy unreality of the sickening violence leaves a couple of the lowriders puking too.

"The Virgin can't let this happen, we've gotta pray for Her to help us...." Jesse says, dropping to his knees. He bows his head, his lips move, and everybody looks at him like he's nuts. Wisma grabs his arm and pulls him to his feet.

"Listen to me, *ese*, we gotta fuckin' get outa here, there's somebody fuckin' crazy shootin', let's go!"

"*NO*! We've gotta pray to the Virgin!"

Wisma drags Jesse toward the car, and the rest of us follow. I stand, my head reeling, and move away from Robledo and toward the waiting lowriders. I stumble over something and look down. It's Robledo's gun. When he got shot it must've flown from his hand. I don't know why, but I lean over and pick it up. It seems like the right thing to do.

"DROP IT, ROGER!"

I spin toward the voice. Freddie Montgomery moves from behind the house. He's pointing a rifle at me as he takes small little steps in my direction.

"You heard me, Roger," he says, this time quieter and friendlier—at least as friendly as you can be while you've got a gun aimed at their heart.

"Freddie! Hey man, I—"

"Drop the gun."

"'*Hail Mary, full of grace, the Lord is with thee'!*" Jesse starts yelling. He pulls away from Wisma's grasp and heads back in my direction.

"'Blessed art Thou amongst women—" Sister Mary Annunciata answers.

"'*And blessed is the fruit of Thy womb, Jesus'!*" Mary Frances prays quietly with them. Monsignor O'Callahan has quit puking and he mumbles the prayer too. I can't believe it. There's a dead guy on the ground, Freddie might shoot me, and they're having a fucking group rosary?!

Freddie moves toward me, but for some reason I can't make myself drop Robledo's gun.

"You shouldn't have shot Robledo, Freddie," I say.

"He was going to hurt Mary Frances. I couldn't let that happen."

"Self defense!" Sister Mary Annunciata says between words of the prayer.

"You used to be okay, Freddie. These people have made you bad." He continues to move toward me. He's shaved his head, and the acne pits seem deeper than before. He's grubby and dirty and his eyes look crazy. "How come you stay here?" I ask.

"Beats prison. And I love Mary Frances."

I look over at her. Sister Mary Annunciata still holds her tightly, and they're saying *Hail Marys*. Monsignor kneels in the dirt and he prays. I look over at Jesse. He's also down on his knees praying. Wisma and the lowriders watch, unsure what to do next. They're definitely *not* praying—at least not out loud.

I look at Robledo. Flies already buzz around him. This isn't right. Robledo was a mean, scary asshole, but he didn't deserve to get his head blown apart. He was just reacting to a situation in the way he thought he should. Robledo wasn't big on the subtleties of talk. But he didn't deserve to die.

I look back at Freddie. He raises the gun to his shoulder. He seems serious about shooting me, which surprises me. You'd think he'd cut me some slack since I helped him find Mary Frances and stay out of prison. You just never know about people.

"Last warning, Rog," he says.

I look over at the unholy trinity of Sister Mary Annunciata, Mary Frances, and Monsignor O'Callahan. They're mumbling *Hail Marys.* Mary Frances is crying, so at least she has some humanity left. Monsignor O'Callahan prays along, but he sways like he's about to fall over. He looks terrible. I think what's happened is beyond even his religious mania. Maybe he realizes that his "cure" didn't stick, and he's holed up out in the desert with crazies, and now he's involved in a killing. Only Sister Mary Annunciata still looks crazy...like a true believer.

"Shoot the evil little minion of Satan if he doesn't obey!" Sister Mary Annunciata shouts at Freddie. Mary Frances squirms and cries but can't get out of Sister Mary Annunciata's grasp. I'm glad she's willing to stand up for me.

"Shoot him, Freddie, he's evil," shouts Mary Frances.

I guess she's not on my side after all.

And now, suddenly, I can't understand the noise.

Everybody's yelling, shouting *Hail Marys*, waving their arms, but I don't know what's happening. The lowriders and Wisma scream at me, Jesse's yelling something I can't understand, Freddie's trigger finger is twitching, Monsignor O'Callahan stands up, shouting slurred words, maybe prayers, maybe warnings—who knows?—Sister Mary Annunciata screams, Mary Frances screams, *what are they all saying?*

I really should drop the gun, walk away, wait for the cops to come, wait for everything to be sorted out, but I can't. I don't want to. I don't care if things get sorted out. All the years, all the times of taking shit from everybody, or being ignored, or being used...fuck 'em all. The white-hot anger builds in me, I can feel it rising up—

And Sister Mary Annunciata, the ugly black cow from hell, she's crazy, she's yelling for Freddie to *shoot me* for Christ's sake, she's stolen my sister and made *her* nuts, she's filled with hate and insanity and religious psychosis, somebody really needs to do something about her.

Maybe I should.

It'd make perfect sense, actually. I'm the one she's bedeviled all this time, I'm the one she hates, yeah, it's my problem to take care of.

The screams and shouts recede to a distant droning buzz, like bees working in flowers, and I turn toward Sister Mary Annunciata and aim the gun at her. I wonder if I can get a shot off before Freddie kills me. I'm not scared, really, just curious. My reflexes feel good, but for all I know the bullet is headed my way already and there's no way I can get a shot off before I splatter into death. I don't care, though.

Watch out for Joshua.

I squeeze the trigger, but before anything happens I'm slammed from the side and knocked to the ground. I assume it's the bullet from Freddie's rifle ripping into my body, and I suppose a white-hot stab of pain will follow, and then my life will drain into the desert dirt with my blood and I'll be no more—

But I feel no pain, and I realize that I've been knocked over by somebody, not a bullet. I open my eyes and see that Jesse is lying on top of me. He must've jumped at me when he saw...but he can't see, so how could?—

"Get back in the house, hurry up, back inside!" yells Freddie. I wiggle out from underneath Jesse enough to see that Freddie's herding the three holy psychos into the house. Mary Frances is yelling and pointing at me, but I can't tell what she's saying. So is Sister Mary Annunciata. I've never seen her look so angry. She doesn't like it when you point a gun at her.

The gun. Where is it? I crawl out from underneath Jesse and look in the dirt for the gun. If I find it, I can still get off a shot at Sister Mary Annunciata before they get into the house. But I don't see it anywhere. I look back at Jesse. He's trying to get up, but he's having trouble. I can't tell why.

"How come you hit me?" I ask.

His brain-spattered sunglasses are crooked on his head. His face looks weird; something's wrong.

"The Virgin...told...me to save you...." He smiles.

"The Virgin's talking to you again?"

"The Virgin...has plans...for you. She told me...." He's holding his hand to his side, and he suddenly starts coughing and pulls his hand away. It's covered with blood, and more blood spurts from his side.

"Shit, what happened?!"

"I think...Freddie shot me instead of you...." He keels over onto the dirt. Wisma and the lowriders surround us, I go to Jesse, cradle his big head, pull off his sunglasses. The scars on his eyes don't look so bad. Is it my imagination?

If I didn't know better, I'd say he's looking at me.

He smiles.

Freddie and the others are back inside the house, and now that I see Robledo's gun is beneath Jesse's arm it's too late to use it. I had my chance to finish Sister Mary Annunciata but Jesse stopped me. And he saved my life.

"You'll be okay, you'll be okay!" I say, desperately hoping the spurting blood from the bullet wound will stop. "Ask the Virgin to fix it, man!"

He smiles. "Too late, Roger. No more miracles...."

"Go get some help!" I yell at Wisma and the others. A couple of the low-riders run to their car and roar off.

Jesse twitches and gasps, and a bloody gurgle comes from deep in his chest and dribbles out his mouth.

"You'll be okay!" I say, hugging him tightly.

His body begins to shake, then convulse, horrible wet noises come from his chest, I hug him tighter—

"Don't die...." I whisper. And for the first time in ages I start to pray. But it's too late. He focuses on me one last time, a smile on his face, and then his eyes roll back in his head and the wet breaths give up to a last rattling chatter and he's still.

It's like he could see.

CRACK,CRACK,CRACK,CRACK! Gunshots from inside the house, I expect a bullet to slam into me, the remaining lowriders dive for the ground, but we realize the bullets aren't for us. They're staying inside the house.

One last *blam* and then everything is quiet again. I hold Jesse, his head pressed against my chest, I try to will him back to life but it won't happen, and the prayers that I was saying fade away. I hear only the wind and distant birds.

I look at Jesse. His face is calm and the smile still there. I wonder if he really could see me. It seemed like he could. Maybe he finally got his miracle.

I whisper: *"'Hail Mary, full of grace, the Lord is with Thee. Blessed art Thou amongst women, and blessed is the fruit of Thy womb, Jesus. Holy Mary, Mother of God, pray for us sinners, now and at the hour of our death. Amen.'"*

I sit in the dirt, cradling Jesse, and say *Hail Marys* until the police finally arrive.

The Virgin never answers me.

Epilogue

1994

Epilogue

They say the smog is better now than when I was a kid, but I'm not sure I believe it. Maybe your throat burns less than in the past, but it seems to me that the mountains are shrouded by smog—which is the criteria I use—just as much as they used to be.

I'm sitting in clotted traffic in the Sepulveda Pass. It's August, and the day is broiling hot; a gooey inversion layer traps us under its lid, and as we crawl up the pass from West L.A., our collective cars and trucks pump even more crap into the air. I wonder how it can ever clear. And when it does, where does this stuff go? I know it blows out to where I grew up, but after that, then what? Does it go up into the atmosphere and out into space? Does it drop back to the ground and become dust out in the desert? Nobody ever says anything about that. Maybe it all gets breathed, and everybody who lives here has shit-filled lungs that look like smokers' lungs, black and sticky and inefficient. The thought makes me queasy, but then, so do a lot of things about life.

As soon as I get moving again—I assume the traffic will clear when I get past the Ventura Freeway interchange—the air conditioner in my brand new, needlessly four-wheel-drive Explorer will work better and I won't be so sticky and hot. But I wonder if maybe the reason I'm so uncomfortable is because of nerves.

I'm on my way to pick up Mando. He called me last night, and in his quiet, precise voice said, "I'm ready to go now." I knew immediately what he meant. He wanted to see *where* his dad was killed.

In the twenty-plus years since Jesse died, I've often wondered when Mando would ask about what happened, when he'd want to see where it happened to try and make sense of it all.

After Jesse was buried and life settled back into its dull routine, I'd go visit Lydia and Mando whenever I could. Lydia wasn't able to deal with Jesse being gone; she stayed sad and withdrawn. Mando, though, never seemed to notice or care that he didn't have a father.

As Mando got older, he never asked about what happened to his dad. Lydia would try to tell him, but he'd always just shake his head and run off to play with his friends. I used to get the feeling he already knew what had happened, although I don't know who would've told him. From the beginning, Mando was always a little bit different.

He walked and talked way early, he was reading when he was four, and he could unnerve even the most formidable adult with his dark, penetrating gaze. Mando was a blend of Jesse and Lydia, superficially resembling both but very different in his temperament.

He was a strong, good-looking kid, and from the start women of all ages paid him lots of attention. Aunt Yolanda doted on him, and whenever Lydia couldn't take care of him—which was often as the years passed and her life fell apart—Aunt Yolanda would step in and keep him for long stretches of time.

Lydia's parents were willing to let Mando stay with the Montoyas; I think they never warmed up to Mando because of the way they felt about Jesse. They blamed him for ruining Lydia's life, and Mando was a daily reminder they could never escape. They were good people, always supportive and willing to try and help, but Mando was a grandson to them in name but not feeling.

Lydia finished high school, and she gave college a shot. She had vague ideas about being a lawyer someday, or maybe a social worker—she never settled on anything in particular. She spent a couple of semesters in junior college, but she slowly sunk into a drug-fueled despair and dropped out. Her parents let her live at home with Mando, who by then was in preschool, and she spent her days stoned and eating, and pretty soon she ballooned into a sullen, fat doper. It was heartbreaking to see somebody who'd once been so quick and clever become slow and disinterested in everything. Mando spent more and more time at the Montoya's house, and Mrs. Montoya or Aunt Yolanda did the mom chores that Lydia was unwilling and unable to do.

Lydia took off in 1978, and nobody ever saw her again. She left a rambling letter behind, begging everybody to forgive her but saying she couldn't handle things anymore and she was real sorry but she couldn't be a mom to Mando. Aunt Yolanda offered to adopt Mando, and Lydia's parents didn't object, so he became a permanent member of the huge, ever-changing Montoya household, and life went on.

Mando went to Our Lady of Perpetual Sorrows grammar school and passed through uneventfully. Most of the nuns had died out or retired, and baby nuns weren't coming up to fill the ranks, so the teachers now were low-paid, well-meaning kids right out of college who were willing to teach for peanuts until they could get a real job at a public school.

Mando did well and never had to contend with psycho nuns or heavy-duty religious indoctrination; even though it was still a Catholic school, the lay teachers were more interested in teaching than saving little souls. He was lucky; I wish it had been like that when Jesse and I were there.

I pass the Ventura Freeway interchange, and the traffic thins, and before I know it I'm on the 210 heading east. The air conditioner blasts cold air again, and I'm less nervous now that I'm moving. In an hour I'll be at the Montoyas' house. It'll be good to see everybody. In the last few years I've only been out there once, for Mrs. Montoya's funeral.

She had a heart attack and died in her sleep, a smile still on her face. If there is a heaven she's the one person who should be there.

Going back to the old home town feels strange; the cliche about the place you grew up seeming smaller when you return is true. But it's not just smaller; there's something creepy about it now. The orchards are long gone, replaced with housing tracts and shopping centers and strip malls, and there's a suburbia orderliness that's both attractive and off-putting. When there were still a few groves around, the place had a feeling of reality, that even though we lived in orderly little tracts there were still places nearby where possums skittered through trees and little boys could play and build forts and pretend they were a million miles away. Now everything is concrete and planned and sterile.

But home had soured for me long before. As soon as Jesse and the others died, home wasn't home anymore, and getting out was all that mattered to me.

There was so much death during the fall of 1972....

As I cradled Jesse's head and he died in my arms that hot day, the gunshots we heard from inside the house were Freddie Montgomery shooting Sister Mary Annunciata, Monsignor O'Callahan, Mary Frances, and himself.

He killed them all with one shot each to the head, then he stuck the rifle barrel in his mouth and blew the top of his own head off. The sickening horror of what happened there was too much for any of us to deal with, and in the following years we were all affected by it—none as bad as Lydia, but the shadow was over all our lives.

Mom had a nervous breakdown and spent years in and out of hospitals and treatment centers, first to cope with the shock of Mary Frances's murder, then to kick the tranquilizer habit she'd acquired during the earlier treatment.

Father Quinn lost his zest for suburbia life, and he began dabbling in Eastern religions and weird mystical nonsense. He came to believe that Jesse was some kind of prophet and that he missed his chance for redemption because he didn't listen to him. His guilt and Mom's twitchiness made them grow apart, and they finally split up in the mid-eighties. Father Quinn sold all his worldly possessions and set off to find truth.

I got a postcard from him a couple of years ago saying he was living at a Buddhist monastery in Kansas (I didn't know there *were* Buddhists in Kansas) doing odd jobs and searching for the true meaning of life. Whatever. I always liked Father Quinn, but now that I'm older I see that he's spent most of his life lost. I doubt he'll ever find the meaning he's looking for.

Once he and Mom divorced, Mom seemed to come out of her years' long depression. She sold the house and moved to a tiny apartment in West L.A., and she got a job in an escrow company. She even began to date again, and I was astonished when she started hanging out with much younger guys. Through my sons' eyes I couldn't see that she was still attractive, but these guys seemed to like her.

Jesse's big brother Mando went crazy for awhile after Jesse died; he hooked up with some older lowrider buddies, and they fought and raised hell all over the place. He got arrested a few times, spent some quality time in county jail, and then he slowly straightened out his life. He got a job as a truck driver, moved in with an old girlfriend, and started having babies. Now he's middle-aged, still scary-looking, with a slew of kids and a still pristine '65 Impala lowrider. I'll bet he's put $50,000 into the thing over the years.

Aunt Yolanda kept on in the real estate business, and she eventually got a broker's license and opened her own office. She never got married again, or even lived with anybody. She once told me that her men days were over, that all men were sickening pigs and she'd had enough. Then she leaned over, patted my knee, and laughed, "You excluded, Roger." I still think of the time we had sex; I'd love to have had another chance with her. But it was one of those one-shot deals. It's too bad, because as she's aged she's gotten better as far as I'm concerned.

When Mrs. Montoya died, I thought the family might fall apart, but Aunt Yolanda stayed in their old house, and from what I hear the usual riot of aunts and uncles and cousins and kids and god-knows-who pass through and fill the Montoya house with noise and rowdy love.

Wisma and the lowriders were lost and alone after the killings. Without their leader, they were kind of pathetic. Slowly, though, Wisma took charge, and he became the leader of the gang. It was a first: a honky wannabe Mexican in charge of a lowrider gang. Wisma had done the impossible: he'd replaced Danny Robledo.

Bushman stayed holy, and he even came up to me shortly after the killings, oozing concern and forgiveness. "Sorry about your loss, Roger. Maybe if you came to Jesus you could find peace."

I was so wiped out after what had happened that all I could do was nod. I didn't have the energy to want to kick his holy ass. He looked at me, his blazing freckles and big red hair a reminder of what I used to hate, only now I couldn't hate him. I didn't care. "I forgive you," he whispered as he slithered off into the school lunchtime crowd. Other than that time, though, he never spoke to me again.

And Rhonda Fairly. She did the right thing, of course. Rhonda always did the right thing. She was at Jesse's and Mary Frances's funerals, she said all the soothing words, sent sympathy and mass cards, hugged me and Mom and everybody who needed to be hugged, and then she waltzed back out of my life. I'd see her at school, and she'd be affable enough, but there was always a certain reserve—I think it was guilt. She and Bushman continued to date, and by the time we graduated from high school everybody assumed that someday they'd get married.

They went off to UC Santa Barbara, got degrees in useless things, dull jobs in dull businesses, and eventually did get married. Within a few years they were divorced.

"I heard he hit her," Mom told me. She kept in touch with old friends from church, and the jungle drums were always beating when there was nasty gossip to spread.

"Guess he's not so holy after all," I said.

"Maybe you should call her," Mom said casually. It bothered her that there was no woman in my life. I just smiled, kissed her on the forehead, and ignored her. That's the best way to deal with Mom.

And then there's me. Twenty-two years since Jesse died, all that time has passed, and sometimes I don't think I've grown up at all.

I finished high school, a sullen loner befriended only by Wisma and the lowriders, with mediocre grades and a cloudy head. I smoked a lot of dope during those times, but I wasn't in with the social dopers. I got stoned by myself and spent lonely days in a pot haze. I needed to be numb, and it was the best I could do. I tried praying, too, but that didn't work, and after awhile I completely gave up on God. I was convinced there was no God, had never been one, that everything existed by chance or accident, and that how my life unfolded was my choice and fate's choice but certainly not God's.

I went to JC and lived at home. Mom and Father Quinn forgot about kicking me out when I turned eighteen; with all that had happened, I think Mom would've been happy if I lived at home forever.

I sat back and watched Mom and Father Quinn's marriage go belly up; there wasn't a thing I could do to help. In 1976, among all the bicentennial hoopla and bullshit, I had a choice to make. I had a useless AA degree and nowhere to go. I'd worked odd jobs, construction for Jesse's uncle, some zit-producing fast food stuff, but now I was an adult, I needed to leave the house and go out on my own, and I didn't have a clue what to do next. Then, as had happened many times before, Wisma came to the rescue.

By the time Wisma graduated from high school—one of the few lowriders who did—he'd become a whole lot whiter. He went to JC and stumbled into a computer programming class, the kind where in those days you had to make punch cards to program, and he found his niche. He hooked up with some other guys in the class who were complete and utter nerds—guys he would've killed in high school—and they spent every spare minute playing on the clunky computers. He went from being leader of a lowrider pack to leader of computer geeks. They went en masse to UCLA and started designing computer games in their spare time. They were even starting to make some money; it had advanced beyond the nerd/hobby phase. I guess that seeing people get shot made Wisma realize that being a hard-ass *vato* wasn't the career path he wanted to take. Nerds don't usually kill.

Wisma was still looking out for me, and while I didn't share he and his new friends' computer mania, I hung around them for want of anything better to do. I tagged along when they went down to UCLA, and while they were going to school I worked crappy jobs in West L.A. and stayed in the ramshackle house they rented in Palms.

As they started selling games and getting free-lance programming jobs, I became their shit-work gofer. I ran all over L.A., dropping things off, picking stuff up, doing whatever they needed. As their business grew, Wisma started to cut me in on the money they were making, and as time wore on I became an important part of their team. I discovered I could come up with good ideas, that I had a natural business sense that complemented their computer geek talents and Wisma's man-in-charge abilities.

By the time they all quit school—none of them needed to bother graduating, they were making too much money—Wisma had given me the title of executive vice-president and a salary to boot. We were still a bunch of long-haired, Levi and T-shirt clowns who had no business running a business, but we prospered in spite of ourselves. The nerds kept busy designing software for advanced games, and soon we had another group writing stuff for businesses. I was along for the ride, and by the early eighties I was more self-assured and confident than I would have ever imagined.

Except where women were involved.

I dated occasionally, usually women who worked for us, but nothing much ever came of any of them. I had sex once in a while—I think they were sympathy fucks, or maybe "fuck your way up the ladder" types. I never fell in love with anybody. I didn't think I could anymore, and even if I did, I could never get over the idea that my scars and gimpiness were repulsive and no woman would ever really want me.

I worked and worked. I didn't have a life outside of work, so I worked more. Wisma tried to get me to throttle back, but I didn't want to. If I wasn't working it just reminded me how lonely I was.

So the years went by, the company grew, I made good money and became a suit-dweeb executive guy, and my life basically sucked.

I felt lost. After Jesse died nothing seemed right. I figured at the time that I'd get over it, that shock and grief just had to wear off, but they never did. I always felt unstuck and disconnected, like life swirled around me but I wasn't a part of it. I tried going back to church a few times, but it was just noise and empty ritual. There was no hope there. And I tried therapists, but they only relieved me of money and nothing else. I found myself thinking seriously about New Age stuff, crystals and past lives and all the wacky Shirley Maclaine stuff, but then I'd investigate further and laugh at myself for even considering such nonsensical bullshit.

When Father Quinn went Buddhist I gave that a look, but it seemed too austere. I sampled religions like people sample wines, and I spat them all out. Nothing fit. Nothing was right; when you looked closely they were all riddled with holes, and I didn't have enough faith to fill in the spaces. The Unitarians had an unusual outlook: believe in anything or nothing, it doesn't matter. But at least they still sang Christmas carols. Maybe that was enough for some people, but not for me.

So I went along, feeling empty, not knowing what to do. Twenty years after he was gone I still missed Jesse, I missed his crazed beliefs, I missed his energy and simple faith. He may have been nuts, but he was filled with life. I wasn't. I was a walking dead guy with a lot of money and nothing inside.

I'm amazed to find myself living in the mid-nineties, far removed from my youth and heading into deep middle age. I wonder what people think now when they meet me. Sometimes, when I'm traveling on business and have to do the schmooze "Howareyounicetomeetyou" I can tell that people are looking at me strangely, wondering about those scars. They're asking themselves, "Wonder what happened? Kind of gross-looking. How'd this guy get to be a bigshot looking like that?" My scars have gotten thicker and harder with age. I've been to plastic surgeons, and they've sanded and blasted and grafted but it hasn't really helped. And my gimpy legs have gotten gimpier with age. I'm always aware of how I look and I know I probably shouldn't be, that your inner being is what matters, but I can't help it. My experience has been that people *do* judge you by how you look, that what's inside is secondary to the outside. The world is a superficial place; that's just the way it is.

When I told Wisma (I still think of him by his last name; it's one of those high school things that's stuck) I was going out to Palmdale with Mando, he paled and looked disturbed. Since he'd become rich and powerful, his natural confidence had gotten even stronger, and it wasn't often that he was thrown off-balance. That was the thing I admired most about Wisma: no matter what, he was always in control.

He'd married a gorgeous model named Trina ten years ago, and they've had a slew of kids. He's got a big house in Hawaii, and they spend part of the year there, and part of the year at another place in Tahoe. He wanders down to L.A. occasionally to do business, which he always does decisively, but his mind now is more on enjoying his beautiful wife and his kids and his rich life. I envy him.

"Why're you going out there?" he asked when I told him about the trip.

"Mando wants to see where it happened."

"You shouldn't go. It's a bad place. It's...bad karma," he said. I smiled. It's still funny to me to hear him talk like a yuppie white boy. He's lost all traces of his *vato* accent, and it's hard sometimes to remember that he was ever a low-rider hard-guy.

"Mando needs to see it. I'm surprised it's taken him this long."

"He can drive, why do you need to go?" Wisma asked. I was touched by Wisma's concern. I've never understood why he's looked out for me all these years. I guess inside he's just a nice guy.

"I think he's looking for...a guide. I was there, I saw it happen, he wants to understand."

Wisma shook his head. "You shouldn't go, Roger. You should tell Mando to forget about it and get on with his life."

We went back and forth for awhile, but he finally gave up when he saw that I was serious about going. I felt I owed it to Mando. And Jesse's memory.

"Don't let it upset things, man," he said, slipping for a moment into his old *vato* talk. Then he *hugged* me—I don't think Wisma had ever touched me before—and he left my office. It was all very weird, but I suppose it was understandable. The killings had been the pivotal moment of our lives, the thing that hooked us together, and even though we never mentioned it, the unspoken memory was strong and indelible.

I speed along the freeway toward my hometown; a rising nostalgia clenches my insides. Whenever I come out here, the same feeling hits me as I pass familiar offramps and the mountains looming beyond the freeway move into the perspective I remember from youth. Memories hit me, both good and bad. The strange and exciting times of my childhood with Jesse, fragments of a lost, dreamlike past: riding bikes, goofing off during long summers, the accident, miracles, Rhonda....

It's blisteringly hot; I dread getting out of my climate-controlled Explorer. As I've gotten older, heat bothers me more and more. I can't believe that I used to live and play in this sweltering shit. At least the smog's not too bad today; I can see the mountains' familiar outlines and that's soothing.

As I pull up to the Montoya's house I see that nothing much has changed. It's the usual riot of cars, kids, and happy, noisy disarray. The neighborhood's gotten more rundown over the years, or maybe it just looks that way to my rich man's eyes. I park and am immediately surrounded by kids looking at my Explorer and me. White guys are rare here, and I'm an exotic visitor. I get out and my ears are assaulted by the annoying *thump* and *"Yo, 'ho bitch!"* of rap music blaring inside the house.

The kids chatter at me, and I assume some of them are Montoyas, but I'm not in the mood to be friendly, so I just move through them and go to the door. Before I have a chance to knock, Aunt Yolanda opens up.

"Hiya," she says, smiling. She's gotten a little fatter over the years, and her hair has gone mostly gray. The glasses are bifocals and they magnify deep wrinkles in the corners of her eyes, but in spite of everything age has thrown at her she still looks good. My heart quickens at her smile and the memory of the night of the homecoming dance.

"How you doing, Yolanda?" I ask.

"You know," she shrugs. "The usual. Still a rich boy?"

"They haven't figured out yet that I don't know what I'm doing."

She leads me inside. It's as it's always been: cluttered and messy. It's comfortable; I feel like I've come home.

Mando is sprawled on the couch reading a book. As he sits up I can see that it's a bible.

"Hey, Rog," he says with a casual head wave. We shake hands, and I'm surprised, as always, at how big and strong he is. My hand tingles from his grip. He's grown into a strong, handsome guy. I can only imagine the women who've crawled all over him. It's not fair.

The rap music shakes the walls; it's coming from one of the back bedrooms. "Turn that shit off!" Aunt Yolanda yells, and in a minute somebody turns it down. A little.

"*Pendejos*," she mutters. "You wanna take some of these kids with you, Roger? They're making me crazy."

Mando gives her a big hug and a kiss on the forehead. "You talk tough like a big bad bitch, but you don't mean it, Yolanda. You love us."

Aunt Yolanda wiggles free of his grasp and gives him a playful punch in the stomach. He just laughs at her.

"Let's go, Rog," he says, and he heads out the door.

He's wearing ultra-baggy, gang-banger shorts, a huge T-shirt and untied Nike high-tops, but in spite of the oversized clothes I can still see how muscular he is. Even in Jesse's good-shape days, when he was lifting and working out constantly, he wasn't as buff as Mando.

"He thinks he's a real stud," Aunt Yolanda says, watching him leave.

"I think maybe he is," I say.

"Let's go!" Mando yells from outside.

"Take care of him," Aunt Yolanda says, her voice suddenly filled with concern. "He's big and strong but I don't know how big and strong he is inside."

"We'll be okay," I say, not really knowing if it's true. I stand awkwardly, looking at Aunt Yolanda. I've never known how to act around her.

Mando solves the problem by laying on the Explorer's horn. "Gotta go," I tell her, and she grabs my arm and stops me.

"Take care of him," she says again. She kisses me softly on the lips and the years melt away.

I go outside, weak-kneed, and get in the Explorer. Mando slips on a pair of ultra-hip sunglasses and throws me a grin. "What's up with you and Yolanda?"

"Nothing."

"You almost act like you did her once, man."

I start the engine and say nothing, but I feel myself turning red. Mando laughs at me.

We drive toward Palmdale. There's enough smog in the sky so that the late afternoon sun is filtered in that dull, lifeless way that baked-out Southern California summer days have. I'm always amazed when I travel to other parts of the country, places that have real weather, by the difference in the light. A brilliant autumn afternoon without pollution, a crisp bite in the air—I see and feel those things and I realize what I missed by growing up in California.

We drive down the 210 toward Highway 14; I remember riding in Wisma's lowrider on this road, toward Jesse's death. The thought makes me give an involuntary little gasp.

"Never been back out there, huh?" Mando asks, reading my mind.

"No."

"I never really wanted to go, either," he says. "But then the dreams started."

"What kind of dreams?"

He looks out the window at the passing brown hills. "Smoggy today," is all he says.

We drive in silence for a while longer, and I begin to get a bad feeling....

"Jesse used have dreams. He imagined that he was talking to the Virgin. Anybody tell you that?"

"Yeah. Yolanda did. You believe him?"

"No. Jesse was...." I can't bring myself to say the word to Jesse's son.

"Crazy?"

"Maybe. Misled. Confused."

"You thought he was crazy. Don't feel bad, everybody did. Yolanda wanted him locked up for awhile, when he was doin' all his preaching in the mall."

"I wish she had. He might still be alive."

"Nah. They wanted him to die. He had to."

"Who?"

Mando looks at me and grins. "You know more about it than me, Roger."

I have no idea what he's talking about, but he's giving me the creeps. Mando has a way of looking inside you, a perceptive sixth sense that Jesse had, too. When I'm around him, I realize how simple-minded I am about others. I've never been able to read people—even obvious ones.

"How come you never got married?" he asks.

"I never came across the right woman."

"What about Rhonda?"

The freeway seems to waver; I wonder if we're having an earthquake. "How do you know about her?" I ask weakly.

"Yolanda told me, I think. You ever talk to her?"

"No. She...was a long time ago. It was just a stupid high school thing."

"Sometimes the early stuff is real."

I look at him, annoyed. "What're you, a fucking philosopher?"

He laughs. "Sound like my old man, huh? I hear he used to piss you off, too."

"Runs in the family."

"You still think about her a lot," he says. It's not a question, it's a statement.

"Yeah."

"Should look her up. Shit changes with time. You might be able to hook up with her again."

The freeway is definitely wavering. I blink and it clears. I realize now why it looks funny: there are tears in my eyes.

"You don't know what you're talking about," I say, trying to sound tough but blowing it because my voice cracks.

"You know what the thing about women is?" he asks. "It's that we think they're perfect. I mean, a regular guy, if he's not a fag or an asshole, he thinks women are so different, so much better, that he can't believe it when one does something shitty or stupid. We figure we're always the fuck-ups, we're the ones who have the bad thoughts, who betray and cheat—and most of the time it's true, guys are the problem. But women, they mess up too. It's just that they're not usually as mean as we are."

"That's not news, Mando. Anybody who's been on the planet awhile has that figured out."

"I don't think you do, Rog. You been pissed off and fucked up over twenty years by what she did to you way back when. Get over it, find her, see what's up."

"It's not that easy."

"So you find her, you're looking at her face-to-face, what do you say?"

"Mando—"

"What do you say, *pendejo*?" he says, his voice suddenly hard.

I look over at him. His face is serious, and I'm glad he's wearing sunglasses because his eyes would drill a hole in me.

"I'd ask her why she did it."

"You already know why. She was a pinhead and she let her old man talk her into it."

"You know an awful lot about this," I say, getting more annoyed. "Is there anything Yolanda *didn't* tell you about me?"

"She didn't tell me you did her, but I figured that out on my own. So, anyway, what do you say to Rhonda, man?"

"I dunno. How about: 'How you doin', screwed up anybody else's life lately?'"

"Nice. Guaranteed to get you laid."

"Honesty works. Then I'd say, 'Sorry you ended up with that idiot Bushman; I wish you'd listened to me, I was right about him the whole time.'"

"Okay. Bitter but okay."

I'm getting into this now. "Then I'd tell her, 'You shoulda stuck with me.

We could've had something special, we could've gotten married and had a bunch of rugrats—if that's what you wanted—and we could've had a good life.'" This strange monologue has me feeling sad and emotional, but I don't stop. I don't want to stop. "'I always loved you, even after what you did to me. That hasn't changed....'" I can't think of anything else to add, and I'm starting to feel self-conscious. Mando smiles oddly. I think he's pleased that he bullied me into acting stupid.

He's got enough class not to push it further. "I'm thirsty," he says, "let's get a Coke, man."

I pull off the freeway onto Foothill Boulevard in La Crescenta. The smog shrouds the mountains here, a crud curtain filtering the summer sun. God, I hate Southern California. I decide I need to move, maybe I'll go to Hawaii like Wisma, or build a place up in Tahoe. I've got enough money; I don't know why I haven't done it sooner.

I turn into a McDonald's and park near the plastic playland. Screaming kids frolic in Ronald McDonald's cathedral of the burger. I hate their food, but as a business guy I admire their marketing. Pure genius.

I'm about to turn off the engine when Mando reaches over and touches my hand.

"Not here," he says quietly. He seems to be concentrating deeply, like he's praying. I think his eyes are closed.

"Why not?"

A strange hesitation. "Their...Coke's shitty. Watered down. Find a...Burger King."

"Mando, what the hell difference—"

"Find a Burger King," he says, and there's a definite threat in his voice. He's gotten weird and intimidating as he's aged, and as I drive out of the parking lot and back onto Foothill, I find myself wondering if he's on some kind of drugs. Meth maybe? I've heard that can make you mean. I'll have to ask Aunt Yolanda if she knows what's up with him, because he's not acting normal.

I drive a couple of blocks and spot the Burger King sign. I park, and this time he doesn't object when I turn off the engine. "Okay?" I ask.

"Yeah. Let's go."

"I'll wait."

"*Let's go,*" he says, leaving no doubt that I'm going in with him. I shrug and get out into the hot, smoggy murk. Maybe he's broke and he wants me to buy.

We get to the front door and he opens it for me. He smiles. "After you, man." That weird smile again. What's going on with him? Must be drugs.

A blast of grease-scented air-conditioned wind hits me as I go inside, and I get an immediate fast food headache. There's something about that smell and the frenetic workers that always gets to me when I go in a fast food place. I glance to my right, toward the hard plastic chairs and tables. A few customers scarf up burgers and fries.

My head is pounding; what's wrong with me, do I have a brain tumor or something? For some reason my eyes lock on a lone woman eating her lunch. I see only her profile, but I can't force myself to look away; she dips a fry into a ketchup puddle and raises it to her mouth.

And with that movement everything changes. I don't smell the greasy air, the headache vanishes, I don't hear noise, the other people in the restaurant seem to disappear, and my vision becomes ultra-clear, like the way a hawk spots a mouse from a thousand feet up. I'm in a zone of complete concentration and complete shock. I don't know if Mando is still behind me, but for now it doesn't matter.

Because the only thing I see, the only thing that exists, is that woman dipping french fries in ketchup.

It's Rhonda.

I stand, watching her eat. Dipping fries. What do I do? It occurs to me that Mando somehow knew where she'd be, he steered us here, I have that same creepy feeling I used to get when Jesse went to the miracle zone. These Montoyas are something different, something scary, but right now I can't do anything about it, I can't even move, I don't know what to do.

Rhonda solves the problem by looking over at me. Her french fry stops in mid-flight and a ketchup blob splats on the table.

"Oh God...." she whispers. "Roger?"

A smile tugs at the edges of my mouth, and I study her. Age has treated her well. Her hair is short now, and lighter, and from what I can tell she's still trim. As the shock fades from her face and is replaced by a smile, the old Rhonda returns. She's cute and irresistible and I'm a kid again. I've looked at her pictures a million times in our high school yearbooks, and I've painted idealized memory portraits in my mind, but seeing her again, twenty-two years later, I see that my memories and the grainy pictures haven't done her justice. She's beautiful, and it hits me hard to think what might've been.

"What's wrong with you, man?" Mando asks, and the sounds of the restaurant fade back in. I smell the grease again, too.

I turn to him. "How did you know?" I whisper.

"Know what?" He acts so innocent I almost believe him.

"That...she'd be here?"

"Who?"

"Rhonda!"

He looks over at her, and a smile creases his big, flat, brown face. "No shit?! That's Rhonda?"

She's standing up, and I start to move toward her. Mando tags along.

"Hi...." I stammer, and nothing else comes out.

Rhonda moves toward us, and I think she's just going to smile and say hello, but then she lunges at me and hugs me tight. She's wearing shorts and a thin blouse, and I notice that her legs still look good. She clings to me, her head buried in my shoulder, and I slowly raise my arms and hug her back. She's pressed against me and it feels so good.

We stand, hugging, for a long time. I don't want to stop, but she eventually pulls away. Her eyes are filled with tears, and she roughly wipes them.

"God, I don't know what's wrong with me, I'll cry over anything...." She looks over at Mando, and she frowns for a moment, then realization hits her. "You're Jesse's son!"

"Yeah. I'm Mando." He grins his lady-killer smile and holds out his hand to shake hers, but she hugs him instead.

"I knew your dad," she says. "We all went to school together."

"Mando knows," I say, throwing him a look. "Mando knows a lot of things."

She disentangles from him and looks back at me. She's beautiful. So I say so. "You're beautiful, Rhonda."

God, what did I say that for? *Once a doofus, always a doofus.* She laughs, but I notice she's also blushing.

"Thanks...you look good, too," she says. *Yeah right, like my scars are things of beauty.* We stand, an awkward silence building. "I hear you're rich!" she blurts, then she's immediately embarrassed. "God, that was stupid." We laugh and the tension is gone.

We join her at her table and start talking. I bring her up to date on me, mostly work stuff about the company and Wisma—stuff she probably already knows—and then she tells us a short version of her life the last twenty years, although I notice she leaves out any mention of Bushman.

She's bounced around, working mid-level personnel manager kind of stuff at companies all over L.A., nothing too exciting. She went back to school for awhile—she thought she might be a lawyer (why does everybody want to be a lawyer?)—but in the end that didn't work out, so she settled back into the drudge work that most people learn to live with.

"It's a living," she sighs when she finishes. I've noticed a lot of people who get sucked into doing things they don't want to do end up tired and bored but unable to escape. It's too bad. I'm lucky that I got into something that's fun—and lucrative. I could retire tomorrow and live happily ever after if I wanted to. But I don't tell Rhonda; it'd make her feel bad.

Rhonda hesitates, then asks what I'm sure she already knows. "You married, Roger? Kids or anything?"

I tell her no, "never found the right woman." It's my usual answer when that question comes up. I know some people think I'm gay—or an amoebae-like non-sexual being—because I'm not married. The nineties aren't as open-minded about us unmarried folks as some would like to think.

"As far as kids," I continue, "this ugly sucker is about as close as I got." I tap Mando's arm, and he smiles good-naturedly. "How about you?" I ask, also knowing the answer.

"I suppose you knew I married Frank." I nod. "It didn't work out," she says with a sigh. "I'm like you; haven't found the right person."

That awkward feeling is back. Mando breaks it quickly.

"Man, you two are depressing. Wanna know about me?" he asks Rhonda.

"Everything," she grins.

"I'm young, strong, smart, good-looking—"

"Humble," I add.

"Lots of women, good times, you name it," he continues. "Being Mando Montoya is as good as it fuckin' gets. I'm not beat-up and worn out like you two."

"You will be," I mutter.

"Lemme have a couple bucks, Rog. Still gotta get a Coke, man."

I give him the money and he goes to the counter. I look at Rhonda. Alone with her. It's been so long.

"He's cute," she says. "Like Jesse."

"Yeah. In a lot of ways."

"He's not...religious, is he?"

"You mean nuts?"

"Devout."

"No. I don't think so." But after what's happened this afternoon I'm not so sure. "We're going out to where Jesse died. He wants to see the place."

There is a long silence as Rhonda looks at Mando. She looks back at me, and now she's sad. "I blew it, Roger." I'm not sure what she's talking about, so I don't say anything. "I messed up my life."

Mine too! I want to say, but I just nod silently.

"I thought I had everything figured out, I thought everything would be easy. Boy, was I wrong."

"I learned that a little earlier," I say. I'm starting to feel more confident, so I tell her: "You helped teach me."

Rhonda looks down at the plastic tabletop. She reddens and her eyes fill with tears. She looks up at me.

"I'm so sorry, Roger," she whispers. "I don't have any excuse for what I did. Other than being a stupid kid."

I shrug. "That's the way it goes. I'm over it."

"I don't think you are. Guys don't get over things like that easily."

Mando plops down, slurping his Coke. "You ready to go, Rog?"

"Not too watery, is it?" I ask.

He grins. "Just right, man. Sure glad we came to BK instead of Mickey D's." He looks at Rhonda. "Wanna come with us?"

"I can't...things to do, you know."

"Okay." He gets up, drains the Coke, and tosses it in the trash. "Nice to meet you. Let's go." He heads out the door.

"Doesn't waste time, does he?" says Rhonda.

"Mando's focused." We sit silently for a moment, looking at one another. The ache inside me grows; she's beautiful and grown up now and I still want her.

"I'd...like to see you again, Roger."

"Me too." I whip out a business card and hand it to her. "I give these out to all the women I meet. The only problem is, they never call."

She laughs. "I will." She writes her number down on a napkin and gives it to me. Our hands touch and we both freeze. It's like a too-intimate gesture we're not ready for yet. "Well," she says, "I hope the trip out there isn't too painful for you."

"I don't think so. It's for Mando, anyway. He needs to see it, so I'll humor him."

I stand, and so does she. I'm not sure what to do next. A handshake seems dorky, a hug a little too much. But she decides for me, and we hug. Tightly. Damn, it feels nice. She finally pulls away, and then gives me a gentle kiss on the lips.

"Call me," she whispers.

I pull her to me and give her a long, hard kiss. She's startled, then we both respond, and I'm in heaven.

It's a lot easier to forgive than I thought.

"Weird how we ran into your old girlfriend, huh?" Mando says as I pull the Explorer onto Highway 14. We drive under the spider web of overpasses, the ones that always crumble in earthquakes.

"How'd you know she'd be there?" I ask. "You been spying on her or something?"

Mando yawns. "You ever pray, Rog?"

"No."

"How come?"

"There's nobody listening."

"That's what I used to think, too. But then I started having these dreams—"

"Lemme guess: Jesus and Mary tell you what a great guy you are?"

"Hey, man, I can't help it if I'm fuckin' wonderful."

"Did Yolanda and the rest of the family tell you about your dad? About his dreams and his supposed miracles and all that?"

"Yeah, sure. I always thought it was bullshit, though. I thought he sounded like he was fucked up on drugs and shit."

"He wasn't a doper."

"Yeah. Whatever. But I never believed in that shit. Until They started talking to me."

"Jesus and Mary?"

"Yeah. Mary, mostly."

Here we go again. The old Jesse creepy sensation crawls through my guts. "What do they tell you, Mando?"

"Lots of stuff. That I've got a job to do for them."

"Being?"

"My dad used to go out and try to preach to people, didn't he? In the mall and stuff."

"Yeah."

"He had the right idea, he just didn't know enough to really change anybody. To convince them to follow him. I mean, if you're gonna preach and convert people, you've gotta reach lots of 'em to make a difference."

"The world's full of idiot bible-thumpers, Mando. They come to the door, they're all over the TV, they're in politics. There's way too much religion already, that's why there's so much hate and killing. It's the old 'I'm right, you're wrong' bullshit. Be religious, go to whatever church you want, but just leave everybody else alone. It's not worth it."

"So what I'm thinking," he continues, ignoring me, "is that maybe, just maybe, you can help reach people. Mary said you play a big part, you're the key. Maybe that computer shit you do."

"Forget it. The net's the last place to get messages out, it's just noise and shouting and nerds."

"Whatever, man. Anyway, you'll figure something out to help me."

"Fuck, Mando, I don't want to hear this! It's Jesse all over again. I don't want to get involved. I've already done my time with a hallucinating religious nutbar, and I had to watch him get splattered for his trouble! I'm not doing it again!"

Mando looks at the passing dry, scrubby scenery. "Man, it's hot out here. Must be tough for stuff to survive."

"Did you hear what I said?" His selective hearing pisses me off.

"Did you ever forgive that dude who ran over you?"

"What?"

"You should. You need to do that before anything else, man. That's what Mary says. 'Roger's gotta forgive before he can be saved.' That's what She said."

I'm too angry to speak. I don't know if I can keep driving. Something churns inside me—anger, fear, I don't know what, but I feel disconnected and.... Dread. That's the feeling—black, endless dread. He's dragging me someplace I can't escape.

"You forgave that chick Rhonda. Look how easy it was. Five minutes before you saw her, you were trash talkin' all this shit, how you'd tell her off, then when you see her you get all pussied out and sweet. End up hugging and kissing. They're right, Roger, forgiveness is the way to go. Do it for that *maricon* drunk who ran over you and everything'll work out. You'll be saved."

"Saved from what?" I manage to say.

"Yourself, man."

We drive in silence for a few minutes. Canyon Country and its condo-covered hills come into view. Sometimes it seems like every square inch of Southern California is occupied.

"I don't want to forgive the asshole," I say, surprising myself by speaking. "He ruined my life."

"How?"

"Look at me!"

"You got a few scars, big fuckin' deal. Lotta homeboys been fucked up in fights look a lot worse than you, and they don't cry about it."

"You don't understand."

"Hey, I understand. I understand you're a whiny white boy who wants to fuckin' pout the rest of his life instead of doing something decent."

I'm about to cuss him out, but I realize it'll do no good. He's as pig-headed as Jesse was. We drive on in silence.

The Explorer cruises smoothly on the freeway, and the crispy-cold air blowing out of the vents gives lie to the burnt-out, baked terrain. I just want to get there, show Mando the place, and get the hell out. Seeing him, being badgered by him, reminds me of Jesse. I'm sick of Montoyas. After this, that's it. I'm cutting them out of my life. I don't care what happens to him; I'm sick of this. I've had a twenty-two year respite since Jesse died, and I don't need his kid to drag me back into religious nut land.

"What would it take?" he asks.

"For what?"

"To make you forgive. What kind of proof you want?"

"Drop it, Mando."

"Shit, you hooked up with Rhonda again, seems like that might start you believing. Guess not, though. So what's it gonna take?"

He's dredging up all the old feelings I hate. "Tell them to cure me," I say. "Then I'll believe. All of Jesse's little tricks and miracles, us bumping in to Rhonda—I don't know how the hell you did that—but none of it convinces me of anything. There's too much bad that's happened in my life to make me believe there's anything or anybody out there watching over us. So prove it to me, Mando. Tell the good old Virgin Mary I need proof. Because, I'll tell you what, the only thing I believe in is me."

"You ever see *The Wizard of Oz*?"

"Yeah, of course."

"You know at the end, where the witch tells her that she always had the power to go home, all she had to do was want it really bad?"

"Yeah."

"Same thing with you, man. All you gotta do is want it, ask for it, you'll get it."

"So click the heels of my sparkly red pumps together three times and I'm cured, huh?"

"Fuck yeah, man. That's it."

"Okay. I really, really believe. So how come I'm not cured?"

"Because you're lying. You have to mean it."

"I don't know how to mean it."

Mando sits, quietly pondering. He takes off his sunglasses and studies me. "Pull over, Roger."

"Why?"

"Just do it!"

I ease the Explorer over to the shoulder. I glance down to make sure my cell phone is in its cubbyhole. Not that I don't trust him, but you never know when you might need to call 911.

He bows his head like he's going to pray. *Christ, he's loonier than Jesse was.* This is a mistake, what the hell am I doing with this guy? His head jerks up and it startles me so much that I lurch back and smack my head on the door.

He grins at me. "Okay, man." His eyes are wide, and he bores in on me with such concentration that it scares the crap out of me. I start to reach for the cell phone, he's too intense, crazy intense, and I look back up at his eyes....

He reaches toward me, *oh shit, is he going to strangle me?* I'm really scared now, his hand touches my forehead, pain explodes, *oh God, he's killed me—*

And then everything goes black.

When I awaken I'm in the passenger seat of the Explorer. The windows are rolled down, and hot, dry air blows over me. I sit up, trying to clear my head, and look outside.

Where are we? It looks familiar, but I'm not sure what happened.... Mando, shit, that's right, where?—

My eyes focus and I see him kneeling a few yards away. He's rubbing his hands in the dirt, picking up handfuls and throwing it into the air; dusty clouds float on the breeze.

I stagger out of the Explorer and look around. It's so familiar, I've been here but I can't remember when. Broken concrete and a half-burned pile of wood scraps are nearby, and as my brain clears I realize where we are: this is where Jesse died. The house that Mary Frances and the others lived in has long since been demolished.

"How...did we get here?" I ask. My voice is thick and gummy.

Mando stops tossing dirt and turns toward me. "I drove. I been here lots of times."

"I thought you wanted me to show it to you?"

He grins. "I lied. This trip wasn't for me, man. It was for you."

The hot wind funnels through the box canyon; a small dust devil kicks up beside Mando. Being here, seeing the place again, I feel the ghosts of Jesse and my sister, the loss, I'm confused, something feels different.

And suddenly I'm not afraid anymore. Mando grins at me.

"Believe, Roger. They love you, They always have. And now, if you'll let 'em help you, you'll be okay. Give in, asshole, admit you believe."

"What'd you do...to me back there?"

"I mighta done something to your sorry white ass you won't believe. Last chance, they ain't gonna give you more proof."

Proof. I can't believe in anything without proof.

"What're you talking about?"

"How's your fucked up leg feel?"

Oh shit. My legs feel...different. Normal? Can't be.

"Go look in the mirror, asshole," he grins. "But before you do, think about what you gotta do to repay the gift, man. You gotta forgive that dude."

"Joe Fanucci?"

He just smiles and goes back to praying.

My mind's still foggy. Rhonda pops into my memory, the kiss we shared at the Burger King. She's back in my life and it feels so good. Somehow a good thing happened—God, Mando, whatever, somebody made it happen. I'm relaxed now, maybe even content for the first time in...forever.

I'm complete. Rhonda's back, things are falling into place, where they should've been years ago. And Joe Fanucci, okay, yeah, *It's okay now, Joe, I'm sorry I treated you so bad*—

And as soon as I think the words, *I forgive you,* my body goes limp. It's like I've been drugged, the way Demerol makes you feel when it hits your brain.

Mando hoots wildly. "It's about fuckin' time!"

A jolt slams me, like being hit by lightning, and the drowsy drugged-out feeling blasts to hyper-awareness. I can see the air, smell the colors, taste the sky—

"What happened?" I ask.

Mando stands and comes over to me. "Your life's different now. Shit, took you long enough, man. You coulda done this with my dad."

Something *has* changed. I'm rejuvenated, refreshed, unafraid. And I don't feel the nagging distrust and dislike that's lurked inside me for so long. I think I might be able to like people again.

"Did...you cure me?" I whisper, feeling silly asking but starting to wonder.

He just grins. I flex my legs. The ever-present ache that's been there ever since Joe Fanucci ran over me seems to be gone. *Joe. Poor Joe.* He was a fucked-up mess and I treated him bad. The anger and hate I've felt toward him has dissolved into pity.

But the cure, *a cure!,* that's what I'm thinking about now. I reach up to touch my face; Mando grabs my hand before I get the chance.

"What's the big hurry, Rog?" he grins. "Don't got enough faith to believe? Gotta see right away?"

I smile back at him. "Never hurts to check."

"Would it matter?" he asks. "Whether or not the scars are there, aren't you different now then you were before? The miracle ain't about some patchy-ass scars or getting back together with an old girlfriend. It's about faith, about believing in something besides yourself."

"Okay, sure." I try to reach up and touch my face, but his grips stays firm.

"Fuck, you're a slow learner, man." He shakes his head, but the smile stays on. He's messing with me and enjoying it.

"I'm stuck with you like I was stuck with Jesse, aren't I?" I ask.

"Till the day you die, *pendejo.*"

I guess I can live with that; it's not really a surprise. From the day I met

Jesse I knew deep down inside that my life would be different. Forever.

But now, *shit*, I want to see if I'm *really* cured. "Lemme look!" I whine. Mando laughs and shakes his head. He lets go of my hand.

I decide I don't want to touch, I want to see. So I go over to the Explorer, grab the rearview mirror on the passenger side, and pull it toward me.

I have a new strength and assurance, a childlike vigor. I imagine that my face feels different, like the patchy scars have blended away to soft, smooth skin. But I'm still not sure if I can believe. I can't make the doubts go away.

Until I see.

It's hard to throw off the years, years of certainty that miracles don't happen. Years of being convinced that everything's a lie. There's no God and Jesse was a good guy who was a psycho. Monsignor O'Callahan and Sister Mary Annunciata were crazy, too, and O'Callahan wasn't cured at Lourdes, it was just hysteria, all that's happened in my life—including my fresh new faith—is just fate and accident and a lie.

Still....

I *do* feel different. And as I look over at Mando's grinning face I realize he's right, I am different, even if I'm not cured.

I believe again.

I move the rearview mirror, my shoulder comes into view. I gently pull it toward me to see for myself. Mando's chuckling softly, amused by my shaky, fledgling faith. I hesitate.

"Go for it, Roger. Take a look, man. The power, dude. It's amazing shit."

I swallow hard, afraid and excited by what I'll see. I pull the mirror toward me.

My reflection slides into view, and in a brief second I'll know for sure—

If there's such a thing as miracles....

www.ingramcontent.com/pod-product-compliance
Lightning Source LLC
LaVergne TN
LVHW041051080826
845145LV00007B/1534